Jessica Sorensen lives in Wyoming with her husband and three children. She is the author of numerous romance novels and her first new adult novels, *The Secret of Ella and Micha* and *The Coincidence of Callie and Kayden*, were both *New York Times* and kindle bestsellers.

Keep in contact with Jessica:

jessicasorensensblog.blogspot.co.uk
Facebook/Jessica Sorensen
@jessFallenStar

The author that everyone is talking about . . .

'What **a beautiful love story**, couldn't put it down. This is a fairy tale love story full of passion, lust and emotions. Love it and would highly recommend it'
Amazon Review

'**Captivating. A brilliant book**. I couldn't put it down once I picked it up!'
Amazon Review

'I absolutely adored and loved this book . . . I could not put this book down. Wonderfully written about the innocence and heartache of love in a sharp and concise style . . . [A] **powerful and captivating read** that had me hooked throughout'
handwrittengirl.com

'The **sultry, tense atmosphere** is supported by interesting characters . . . I loved their chemistry and I was championing them from the start'
solittletimeforbooks.co.uk

'What an **emotional roller coaster** of a book!'
Amazon Review

'I loved this book – an **absolute page turner**. Not at all what I expected – didn't want it to end!'
Amazon Review

The Coincidence of Callie & Kayden

JESSICA SORENSEN

sphere

SPHERE

First published as an ebook in 2012
This paperback edition published in 2013 by Sphere

A CIP catalogue record for this book
is available from the British Library.

ISBN 978-0-7515-5260-7

Printed and bound in Great Britain by Clays Ltd, St Ives plc

Papers used by Sphere are from well-managed forests
and other responsible sources.

MIX
Paper from
responsible sources
FSC® C104740
www.fsc.org

Sphere
An imprint of
Little, Brown Book Group
100 Victoria Embankment
London EC4Y 0DY

An Hachette UK Company
www.hachette.co.uk

www.littlebrown.co.uk

For everyone who wasn't saved.

Prologue

Callie

Life is full of luck, like getting dealt a good hand, or simply by being in the right place at the right time. Some people get luck handed to them, a second chance, a save. It can happen heroically, or by a simple coincidence, but there are those who don't get luck on a shiny platter, who end up in the wrong place at the wrong time, who don't get saved.

"Callie, are you listening to me?" my mom asks as she parks the car in the driveway.

I don't answer, watching the leaves twirl in the wind across the yard, the hood of the car, wherever the breeze forces them to go. They have no control over their path in life. I have a desire to jump out, grab them all, and clutch them in my hand, but that would mean getting out of the car.

"What is wrong with you tonight?" my mom snaps as she checks her phone messages. "Just go in and get your brother."

I tear my gaze off the leaves and focus on her. "Please don't make me do this, Mom." My sweaty hand grips the metal door handle and a massive lump lodges in my throat. "Can't you just go in and get him?"

"I have no desire to go into a party with a bunch of high school kids and I'm really not in the mood to chat it up with Maci right now, so she can brag about Kayden getting a scholarship," my mother replies, motioning her manicured hand at me to get a move on. "Now go get your brother and tell him he needs to come home."

My shoulders hunch as I push the door open and hike up the gravel driveway toward the two-story mansion with green shutters and a steep roof. "Two more days, two more days," I chant under my breath with my hands clenched into fists as I squeeze between the vehicles. "Only two more days and I'll be in college and none of this will matter."

The lights through the windows illuminate against the gray sky and a "Congratulations" banner hangs above the entrance to the porch, decorated with balloons. The Owenses always like to put on a show, for any reason they can think of: birthdays, holidays, graduations. They seem like the perfect family but I don't believe in perfection.

This party is to celebrate their youngest son Kayden's graduation and his football scholarship to the University of Wyoming. I have nothing against the Owenses. My family has dinner over at their house occasionally and they attend barbecues at our place. I just don't like parties, nor have I been welcomed at one, at least since sixth grade.

When I approach the wraparound porch, Daisy McMillian waltzes out with a glass in her hand. Her curly blond hair shines in the porch light as her eyes aim at me and a malicious grin curls at her lips.

I dodge to the right of the stairs and swerve around the side of the house before she can insult me. The sun is lowering below the lines of the mountains that encase the town and stars sparkle across the sky like dragonflies. It's hard to see once the lights of the front porch fade away and my shoe catches something sharp. I fall down and my palms split open against the gravel. Injuries on the outside are easy to endure and I get up without hesitation.

I dust the pebbles from my hands, wincing from the burn of the scratches as I round the corner into the backyard.

"I don't give a shit what the hell you were trying to do," a male voice cuts through the darkness. "You're such a fuckup. A fucking disappointment."

I halt by the edge of the grass. Near the back fence is a brick pool house where two figures stand below a dim light. One is taller, with his head hanging low and his broad shoulders are stooped. The shorter one has a beer gut, a bald spot on the back of his head, and is standing in the other's face with his fists out in front of him. Squinting through the dark, I make out that the shorter one is Mr. Owens and the taller one is Kayden Owens. The situation is surprising since Kayden is very confident at school and has never been much of a target for violence.

"I'm sorry," Kayden mutters with a tremor in his voice as he hugs his hand against his chest. "It was an accident, sir. I won't do it again."

I glance at the open back door where the lights are on, the music is loud, and people are dancing, shouting, laughing. Glasses clink together and I can feel the sexual tension bottled in the room from all the way out here. These are the kinds of places I avoid at all cost, because I can't breathe very well in them. I move up to the bottom step tentatively, hoping to disappear into the crowd unnoticed, find my brother, and get the hell out of here.

"Don't fucking tell me it was an accident!" The voice rises, blazing with incomprehensible rage. There's a loud bang and then a crack, like bones splitting into pieces. Instinctively I whirl around just in time to see Mr. Owens smash his fist into Kayden's face. The crack makes my gut churn. He hits him again and again, not stopping even when Kayden crumples to the ground. "Liars get punished Kayden."

I wait for Kayden to get back up, but he stays unmoving, not even bothering to cover his face with his arms. His father kicks him in the stomach, in the face, his movements harder, showing no sign of an approaching end.

I react without thinking, a desire to save him burning so fiercely it washes all doubts from my mind. I run across the

4

grass and through the leaves blowing in the air without a plan other than to interrupt. When I reach them, I'm shaking and verging toward shock as it becomes clear the situation is larger than my mind originally grasped.

Mr. Owens's knuckles are gashed and blood drips onto the cement in front of the pool house. Kayden is on the ground, his cheekbone cut open like a crack in the bark of a tree. His eye is swollen shut, his lip is ruptured, and there is blood all over his face.

Their eyes move to me and I quickly point over my shoulder with a very unsteady finger. "There was someone looking for you in the kitchen," I say to Mr. Owens, thankful that for once my voice maintains steadiness. "They needed help with something...I can't remember what though."

His sharp gaze pierces into me and I cower back at the anger and powerlessness in his eyes, like his rage controls him. "Who the hell are you?"

"Callie Lawrence," I say quietly, noting the smell of liquor on his breath.

His gaze travels from my worn shoes to the heavy black jacket with buckles, and finally lands on my hair that barely brushes my chin. I look like a homeless person, but that's the point. I want to be unnoticed. "Oh, yeah, you're Coach Lawrence's daughter. I didn't recognize you in the dark." He glances down at the blood on his knuckles and then looks back at me. "Listen, Callie, I didn't mean for this to happen. It was an accident."

I don't do well under pressure so I stand motionless, listening to my heart knock inside my chest. "Okay."

"I need to go clean up," he mutters. His gaze bores into me for a brief moment before he stomps across the grass toward the back door with his injured hand clasped beside him.

I focus back on Kayden, releasing a breath trapped in my chest. "Are you okay?"

He cups his hand over his eye, stares at his shoes, and keeps his other hand against his chest, seeming vulnerable, weak, and perplexed. For a second, I picture myself on the ground with bruises and cuts that can only be seen from the inside.

"I'm fine." His voice is harsh, so I turn toward the house, ready to bolt.

"Why did you do that?" he calls out through the darkness.

I stop on the line of the grass and turn to meet his eyes. "I did what anyone else would have done."

The eyebrow above his good eye dips down. "No, you didn't."

Kayden and I have gone to school together since we were in kindergarten. Sadly this is the longest conversation we've had since about sixth grade when I was deemed the class weirdo. In the middle of the year, I showed up to school with my hair chopped off and wearing clothes that nearly swallowed me. After that, I lost all my friends. Even when our families have dinner together, Kayden pretends like he doesn't know me.

"You did what almost no one would have done." Lowering

his hand from his eye, he staggers to his feet and towers over me as he straightens his legs. He is the kind of guy girls have an infatuation for, including me back when I saw guys as something else other than a threat. His brown hair flips at his ears and neck, his usually perfect smile is a bloody mess, and only one of his emerald eyes is visible. "I don't understand why you did it."

I scratch at my forehead, my nervous habit when someone is really seeing me. "Well, I couldn't just walk away. I'd never be able to forgive myself if I did."

The light from the house emphasizes the severity of his wounds and there is blood splattered all over his shirt. "You can't tell anyone about this, okay? He's been drinking...and going through some stuff. He's not himself tonight."

I bite at my lip, unsure if I believe him. "Maybe you should tell someone...like your mom."

He stares at me like I'm a small, incompetent child. "There's nothing to tell."

I eye his puffy face, his normally perfect features now distorted. "All right, if that's what you want."

"It's what I want," he says dismissively and I start to walk away. "Hey Callie, it's Callie, right? Will you do me a favor?"

I peer over my shoulder. "Sure. What?"

"In the downstairs bathroom there's a first-aid kit, and in the freezer there's an icepack. Would you go grab them for me? I don't want to go in until I've cleaned up."

I'm desperate to leave, but the pleading in his tone overpowers me. "Yes, I can do that." I leave him near the pool house to go inside, and the very crowded atmosphere makes it hard to breathe. Tucking in my elbows and hoping no one will touch me, I weave through the people.

Maci Owens, Kayden's mother, is chatting with some of the other moms at the table and waves her hand at me, her gold and silver bangle bracelets jingling together. "Oh Callie, is your mom here, hun?" Her speech is slurred and there is an empty bottle of wine in front of her.

"She's out in the car," I call out over the music as someone bumps into my shoulder and my muscles stiffen. "She was on the phone with my dad and sent me in to find my brother. Have you seen him?"

"Sorry, hun, I haven't." She motions her hand around with flourish. "There are just so many people here."

I give her a small wave. "Okay, well, I'm going to go look for him." As I walk away, I wonder if she's seen her husband and if she'll question the cut on his hand.

In the living room, my brother Jackson is sitting on the sofa, talking to his best friend, Caleb Miller. I freeze near the threshold, just out of their sight. They keep laughing and talking, drinking their beers, like nothing matters. I despise my brother for laughing, for being here, for making it so I have to go tell him Mom is waiting out in the car.

I start toward him, but I can't get my feet to move. I know I need to get it over with, but there are people making out in the corners and dancing in the middle of the room and it's making me uncomfortable. *I can't breathe. I can't breathe. Move feet, move.*

Someone runs into me and it nearly knocks me to the floor.

"Sorry," a deep voice apologizes.

I catch myself on the doorframe and it breaks my trance. I hurry down the hall without bothering to see who ran into me. I need to get out of this place and breathe again.

After I collect the first-aid kit from the bottom cupboard and the icepack from the freezer, I take the long way out of the house, going through the side door unnoticed. Kayden's not outside anymore, but the interior light of the pool house filters from the windows.

Hesitantly, I push open the door and poke my head into the dimly lit room. "Hello."

Kayden walks out from the back room without a shirt on and a towel pressed up to his face, which is bright red and lumpy. "Hey, did you get the stuff?"

I slip into the room and shut the door behind me. I hold out the first-aid kit and the icepack, with my head turned toward the door to avoid looking at him. His bare chest, and the way his jeans ride low on his hips smothers me with uneasiness.

"I don't bite, Callie." His tone is neutral as he takes the kit and the pack. "You don't have to stare at the wall."

I compel my eyes to look at him and it's hard not to stare at

9

the scars that crisscross along his stomach and chest. The vertical lines that run down his forearms are the most disturbing, thick and jagged as if someone took a razor to his skin. I wish I could run my fingers along them and remove the pain and memories that are attached to them.

He quickly lowers the towel to cover himself up and confusion gleams from his good eye as we stare at one another. My heart throbs inside my chest as a moment passes, like a snap of a finger, yet it seems to go on forever.

He blinks and presses the pack to his inflamed eye while balancing the kit on the edge of the pool table. His fingers quiver as he pulls his hand back and each knuckle is scraped raw. "Can you get the gauze out of that for me? My hand's a little sore."

As my fingers fumble to lift the latch, my fingernail catches in the crack, and it peels back. Blood pools out as I open the lid to retrieve the gauze. "You might need stitches on that cut below the eye. It looks bad."

He dabs the cut with the towel, wincing from the pain. "It'll be fine. I just need to clean it up and get it covered."

The steaming hot water runs down my body, scorching my skin with red marks and blisters. I just want to feel clean again. I take the damp towel from him, careful not to let our fingers touch, and lean forward to examine the lesion, which is so deep the muscle and tissue is showing.

"You really need stitches." I suck the blood off my thumb. "Or you're going to have a scar."

The corners of his lips tug up into a sad smile. "I can handle scars, especially ones that are on the outside."

I understand his meaning from the depths of my heart. "I really think you should have your mom take you to the doctor and then you can tell her what happened."

He starts to unwind a small section of gauze, but he accidentally drops it onto the floor. "That'll never happen and even if it did, it wouldn't matter. None of this does."

With unsteady fingers, I gather up the gauze and unravel it around my hand. Tearing the end, I grab the tape out of the kit. Then squeezing every last terrified thought from my mind, I reach toward his cheek. He remains very still, hugging his sore hand against his chest as I place the gauze over the wound. His eyes stay on me, his brows knit, and he barely breathes as I tape it in place.

I pull back and an exhale eases out of my lips. He's the first person I've intentionally touched outside my family for the last six years. "I would still consider getting stitches."

He closes the kit and wipes a droplet of blood off the lid. "Did you see my father inside?"

"No." My phone beeps from my pocket and I read over the text message. "I have to go. My mom's waiting out in the car. Are you sure you'll be okay?"

"I'll be fine." He doesn't glance up at me as he picks up the towel and heads toward the back room. "All right, I'll see you later, I guess."

No, you won't. Putting my phone away in my pocket, I depart for the door. "Yeah, I guess I'll see you later."

"Thank you," he instantly adds.

I pause with my hand on the doorknob. I feel terrible for leaving him, but I'm too chicken to stay behind. "For what?"

He deliberates for an eternity and then exhales a sigh. "For getting me the first-aid kit and icepack."

"You're welcome." I walk out the door with a heavy feeling in my heart as another secret falls on top of it.

As the gravel driveway comes into view, my phone rings from inside my pocket. "I'm like two feet away," I answer.

"Your brother is out here and he needs to get home. He's got to be at the airport in eight hours." My mother's tone is anxious.

I increase my pace. "Sorry, I got sidetracked...but you sent me in to get him."

"Well, he answered his text, now come on," she says frantically. "He needs to get some rest."

"I'll be there in like thirty seconds, Mom." I hang up as I step out into the front yard.

Daisy, Kayden's girlfriend, is out on the front porch, eating a slice of cake as she chats with Caleb Miller. My insides instantly knot, my shoulders slouch, and I shy into the shadows of the trees, hoping they won't see me.

"Oh my God, is that Callie Lawrence?" Daisy says, shielding her eyes with her hand and squinting in my direction.

12

"What the heck are you doing here? Shouldn't you be like hanging out at the cemetery or something?"

I tuck my chin down and pick up the pace, stumbling over a large rock. *One foot in front of the other.*

"Or are you just running away from the piece of cake I have?" she yells with laughter in her tone. "Which one is it Callie? Come on, tell me?"

"Knock it off," Caleb warns with a smirk on his face as he leans over the railing, his eyes as black as the night. "I'm sure Callie has her reasons for running away."

The insinuation in his voice sends my heart and legs fleeing. I run away into the darkness of the driveway with the sound of their laughter hitting my back.

"What's your problem?" my brother asks as I slam the car door and buckle my seatbelt, panting and fixing my short strands of hair back into place. "Why were you running?"

"Mom said to hurry." I fix my eyes on my lap.

"I sometimes wonder about you, Callie." He rearranges his dark brown hair into place and slumps back in the seat. "It's like you go out of your way to make people think you're a freak."

"I'm not a twenty-four-year-old who's hanging around at a high school party," I remind him.

My mom narrows her eyes at me. "Callie, don't start. You know Mr. Owens invited your brother, just like he invited you to the party."

My mind drifts back to Kayden, his face beaten and bruised. I feel horrible for leaving him and almost tell my mom what happened, but then I catch a glimpse of Caleb and Daisy on the front porch, watching us back away, and I remember that sometimes secrets need to be taken to the grave. Besides, my mom has never been one for wanting to hear about the ugly things in the world.

"I'm only twenty-three. I don't turn twenty-four until next month," my brother interrupts my thoughts. "And they're not in high school anymore so shut your mouth."

"I know how old you are," I say. "And I'm not in high school either."

"You don't need to sound so happy about it," my mom grimaces as she spins the steering wheel to pull out onto the street. Wrinkles crease around her hazel eyes as she tries not to cry. "We're going to miss you and I really wish you'd reconsider waiting until fall to go away to school. Laramie is almost six hours away sweetie. It's going to be so hard being that far away from you."

I stare at the road that stretches through the trees and over the shallow hills. "Sorry, Mom, but I'm already enrolled. Besides, there's no point in me sticking around for the summer just to sit around in my room."

"You could always get a job," she suggests. "Like your brother does every summer. That way you can spend some time with him and Caleb is going to be staying with us."

Every muscle in my body winds up like a knotted rope and

I have to force oxygen into my lungs. "Sorry, Mom, but I'm ready to be on my own."

I'm more than ready. I'm sick of the sad looks she always gives me because she doesn't understand anything I do. I'm tired of wanting to tell her what happened, but knowing I can't. I'm ready to be on my own, away from the nightmares that haunt my room, my life, my whole world.

Chapter One

#4: **Wear a Shirt with Color.**

4 months later...

Callie

I often wonder what drives people to do things. Whether it's put into their minds at birth, or if it is learned as they grow. Maybe it's even forced upon them by circumstances that are out of their hands. Does anyone have control over their lives or are we all helpless?

"God, it's like spazzville around here today," Seth comments, scrunching his nose at the arriving freshmen swarming the campus yard. Then he waves his hand in front of my face. "Are you spacing off on me again?"

I blink away from my thoughts. "Now don't be arrogant." I nudge his shoulder with mine playfully. "Just because we both decided to do the summer semester and we know where everything is, doesn't make us better than them."

"Uh, yeah, it kind of does." He rolls his honey-brown eyes at me. "We're like the upper-class freshmen."

I press back a smile and sip my latte. "You know there's no such thing as an upper-class freshman."

He sighs, ruffling his golden blond locks, which look like he gets them highlighted in a salon, but they're actually natural. "Yeah, I know. Especially for people like you and me. We're like two black sheep."

"There are many more black sheep than you and me." I shield my eyes from the sun with my hand. "And I've toned it down. I'm even wearing a red T-shirt today, like the list said to do."

The corners of his lips tug upward. "Which would look even better if you'd let those pretty locks of yours down, instead of hiding them in that ponytail all the time."

"One step at a time," I say. "It was hard enough just letting my hair grow out. It makes me feel weird. And it doesn't matter because that has yet to be added to the list."

"Well it needs to be," he replies. "In fact, I'm doing it when I get back to my room."

Seth and I have a list of things we have to do, even if we're scared, repulsed, or incapable. If it's on the list, we have to do it and we have to cross off one thing at least once a week. It was something we did after we confessed our darkest secrets to each other, locked away in my room, during my first real bonding moment with a human being.

"And you still wear that God-awful hoodie," he continues,

jerking on the bottom of my gray faded jacket. "I thought we talked about that hideous thing. You're beautiful and you don't need to cover up. Besides, it's like eighty degrees outside."

I wrap my jacket around myself self-consciously, gripping at the edge of the fabric. "Subject change please."

He loops arms with mine as he leans his weight on me, forcing me to scoot over to the edge of the sidewalk as people pass by us. "Fine, but one day we're going to talk about a complete makeover, in which I will supervise."

I sigh. "We'll see."

I met Seth my first day at UW during Pre-Calculus. Our inability to understand numbers was a great conversation starter and our friendship kind of grew from there. Seth is the only friend I've really had since sixth grade, besides a brief friendship with the new girl in school who didn't know the "Anorexic, Devil-Worshipping Callie" everyone else saw me as.

Seth abruptly stops walking and swings in front of me. He's wearing a gray T-shirt and a pair of black skinny jeans. His hair is stylishly tousled and his long eyelashes are the envy of every girl.

"I just have to say one more thing." He touches the tip of his finger to the corner of my eye. "I like the maroon eyeliner much better than the excessive black."

"I have your approval on that." I press my hand dramatically to my heart. "I'm so relieved. It's been weighing on my mind since this morning."

He makes a face and his eyes scroll down my red T-shirt

that brushes the top of my form-fitting jeans. "You're doing great in every department, I just wish you'd wear a dress or shorts or something for once and show off those legs of yours."

My face plummets along with my mood. "Seth, you know why... I mean, you know... I can't..."

"I know. I'm just trying to be encouraging."

"I know you are and that's why I love you." I love him for more than that actually. I love him because he's the first person I felt comfortable enough with to tell my secrets to, but maybe that's because he understands what it's like to be hurt inside and out.

"You're so much happier than when I first met you." He tucks my bangs behind my ear. "I wish you could be this way around everyone, Callie. That you would stop hiding from everyone. It's sad no one gets to see how great you are."

"And vice versa," I say, because Seth hides as much as I do.

He takes my empty Styrofoam cup from my hand and tosses it into a garbage can beside one of the benches. "What do you think? Should we hit up one of the tours and make fun of the tour guide?"

"You know the way to my heart." I beam and his laughter lights up his entire face.

We stroll up the sidewalk in the shade of the trees toward the front doors of the main office, which is a few stories high with a peaked roof. It has a historical look to it, tan brick with a lot of wear and tear, like it belongs in an older era. The yard that centers all the buildings looks like a triangular maze with randomly placed concrete paths that cross the lawn. It's a pretty place to go to school, lots of trees, and open space, but it took some getting used to.

There is confusion in the air as students and parents attempt to find their way around. I'm completely distracted when I hear a faint, "Heads up."

My head snaps up just in time to see a guy running straight for me with his hands in the air and a football flying at him. His solid body collides with mine and I fall flat onto my back, cracking my head and elbow against the pavement. Pain erupts through my arm and I can't breathe.

"Get off me," I say, writhing my body in a panic. The weight and heat off him makes me feel like I'm drowning. "Get off now!"

"I'm so sorry." He rolls to the side and quickly climbs off me. "I didn't see you there."

I blink the spots away from my eyes until his face comes into focus; brown hair that flips up at the ears, piercing emerald eyes, and a smile that will melt a girl's heart. "Kayden?"

His eyebrows furrow and his hand falls to his side. "Do I know you?" There's a small scar below his right eye and I wonder if it's from where his dad hit him that night.

A tiny prickle forms in my heart that he can't remember who I am. Getting to my feet, I brush the dirt and grass off my sleeves. "Um, no, sorry. I thought you were someone else."

"But you got the name right." His tone carries doubt as he scoops the football off the grass. "Wait, I do know you, don't I?"

"I'm really sorry for getting in your way." I snag Seth's hand and haul him toward the entrance doors where there's a big "Welcome Students" banner.

When we're in the corridor by the glass display cases, I let go of him and lean against the brick wall, catching my breath. "That was Kayden Owens."

"Oh." He glances back at the entrance as students swarm inside. "*The* Kayden Owens? The one you saved?"

"I didn't save him," I clarify. "I just interrupted something."

"Something that was about to get ugly."

"Anyone would have done the same thing."

His fingers seize my elbow as I attempt to walk down the hall and he pulls me back to him. "No, a lot of people would have walked by. It's a common fact that a lot of people will turn their heads in the other direction when something bad is happening. I know this from experience."

My heart aches for him and what he went through. "I'm sorry you had to go through that."

"Don't be sorry, Callie," he says with a heavy-hearted sigh. "You have your own sad story."

We make our way down the slender hallway until it opens up and there is a table stacked with flyers and pamphlets on it. People are standing in line, staring at schedules, talking to their parents, looking scared and excited.

"He didn't even recognize you," he comments as he works through the crowd to the front of the line, cutting in front of everyone, and grabs a pink flyer.

"He barely recognized me ever," I shake my head when he offers me a cookie from a plate on the table.

"Well, he should recognize you now." He picks up a sugar cookie, scrapes the sprinkles off, and bites off the corner. Crumbs fall from his lips as he chews. "You did save his ass from getting beat."

"It's not that big of a deal," I say, even though it does stab at my heart a little. "Now, can we please change the subject to something else?"

"It is a big deal." He sighs when I frown at him. "Fine, I'll keep my mouth shut. Now come on, let's go find a tour guide to torture."

Kayden

I've been haunted by a nightmare every single God damn night for the last four months. I'm curled up near the pool house and my dad's beating the shit out of me. He's madder than I've ever seen him, probably because I did one of the worst things imaginable to him. There's murder in his eyes and every ounce of humanity is gone, consumed by rage.

As his fist hammers against my face, warm blood pours along my skin and splatters against his shirt. I know this time he's probably going to kill me and I should finally fight back, but I was taught to die on the inside. Plus I just don't seem to care anymore.

Then someone appears from the shadows and interrupts us. When I wipe the blood from my eyes, I realize it's a girl terrified out of her mind. I don't quite understand it, why she intervened, but I owe her a lot.

Callie Lawrence saved my fucking life that night, more than she probably realized. I wish she knew, but I never could figure out how to tell her, nor have I seen her since it happened. I heard she went off to college early to start her life and I envy her.

My first day on campus is going pretty well, especially after my mom and dad left. Once they drove away, I could breathe for the very first time in my life.

Luke and I wander around the busy campus trying to figure out where everything is, while tossing a football back and forth. The sun is bright, the trees are green, and there's so much newness in the air it gets me pumped up. I want to start over, be happy, live for once.

On a particularly long throw, I end up running over a girl. I feel like an asshole, especially because she's so small and fragile looking. Her blue eyes are enlarged and she looks scared to death. What's even weirder is she knows me, but takes off running when I question how she does.

It's bugging the hell out of me. I can't stop thinking about her face and the familiarity. Why can't I figure out who the hell she is?

"Did you see that girl?" I ask Luke. He's been my best friend since second grade when we both realized how mutually screwed up our home lives were, although for different reasons.

"The one you just ran over?" He folds up the schedule and tucks it into his back pocket of his jeans. "She kind of reminds me of that quiet girl we used to go to school with—the one Daisy was dead set on torturing."

My eyes move to the entrance doors where she disappeared. "Callie Lawrence?"

"Yeah, I think that was her name." He blows out a stressed breath as he turns around in the middle of the lawn trying to get his bearings. "But I don't think it's her. She wasn't wearing all that black shit around her eyes and Callie had a haircut that made her look like a guy. Plus, I think that girl was thinner."

"Yeah, she did look different." But if it is Callie, I need to talk to her about that night. "Callie was always thin, though. That's why Daisy made fun of her."

"That was one of the reasons she made fun of her," he reminds me and his face twists with repulsion at something behind me. "I think I'm going to go find our room." Luke hurries off toward the corner of the school building before I can say anything.

"There you are." Daisy comes up from behind me and I'm overwhelmed by the smell of perfume and hairspray.

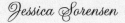

Suddenly I understand why Luke ran off like there was a fire. He doesn't like Daisy for many reasons; one being that he thinks Daisy is a bitch. And she is, but it works for me because she allows me to stay detached from feeling anything, which is the only way I know how to live life.

"I sure hope you weren't just talking about me." Daisy wraps her arms around my midsection and massages my stomach with her fingertips. "Unless it was something good."

I turn around and kiss her forehead. She's wearing a low-cut blue dress and a necklace that rests between her tits. "No one was talking about you. Luke just went to find his room."

She bites down on her glossy lip and bats her eyelashes at me. "Good, because I'm already nervous about leaving my ridiculously hot boyfriend. Remember you can flirt, but you can't touch." Daisy gets bored easily and says things to start drama.

"No touching. Got it," I say, holding back an eye roll. "And again, no one was talking about you."

She twines a strand of her curly blond hair around her finger with a thoughtful expression on her face. "I don't mind if you talk about me, just as long as it's good."

I met Daisy when I was in tenth grade and she moved to our school. She was the hot new freshman and was very aware that she was. I was pretty popular, but hadn't really dated anyone, just messed around. I was more focused on football, like my dad wanted me to be. Daisy seemed interested, though, and a couple of weeks later, we were officially a couple. She's self-involved and she never asks where all my bruises, cuts, and scars come from. She brought it up once, the first time we fucked, and I told her it was from a four-wheeling accident when I was a kid. She didn't question the fresh ones.

"Look, baby, I got to go." I give her a quick kiss on the lips. "I have to check in and unpack and figure out where the hell everything is."

"Oh, fine." She pouts out her bottom lip and runs her fingers through my hair, guiding my lips back to hers for a deep kiss. When she pulls away, she smiles. "I guess I'll go back home and try to fill up my time with boring old high school."

"I'm sure you'll be fine," I say to her as I back toward the doors, maneuvering between the people flooding the sidewalk. "I'll be back for homecoming."

She waves as she turns for the parking lot. I keep my eyes on her until she's in her car and then I go into the school. The air is cooler inside, the lights are faint, and there's a lot of shouting and disorganization.

"We don't need a tour." I walk up to Luke, who's standing near the sign-up table, reading a pink flyer. "And weren't you going to find your room or was that your excuse to escape Daisy?"

"The girl drives me fucking crazy." He rakes his hand through his short, brown hair. "And I was headed there, but then I realized it'd be much easier if I went on a tour so I know where everything is."

Luke is a very structured person when it comes to school

and sports. It makes sense to me since I know about his past, but from an outsider's point of view, he probably looks like a troublemaker, who failed out of school.

"Fine, we'll do the tour." I write our names down on the paper and the redhead sitting behind the table smiles at me.

"You can go join the one starting now," she says shamelessly pushing her cleavage up with her arms as she leans forward. "They just stepped into the hallway."

"Thanks." Grinning at her, I strut off with Luke toward where she directed us.

"Every time," he says amusedly as he sidesteps around a smaller table with plates full of cookies on it. "You're like a magnet."

"I don't ask for it," I reply as we approach the back of the crowd. "In fact, I wish they'd stop."

"No you don't," he states with a roll of his eyes. "You love it and you know it. And I wished you'd act on it, so you could ditch the bitch."

"Daisy's not that bad. She's probably the only girl who doesn't care if I flirt." I cross my arms and stare at the nerdy tour guide with thick glasses, scraggily brown hair, and a clipboard in his hands. "Do we really need to do this? I'd rather go unpack."

"I need to know where everything is," he says. "You can go to the room if you want."

"I'm fine here." My eyes zone in on a girl across the crowd;

the one I ran over. She's smiling at a guy next to her who's whispering something in her ear. I find myself entertained by the naturalness of it, no pretenses like the ones I'm used to seeing.

"What are you looking at?" Luke tracks my gaze and his forehead creases. "You know what? I think that might be Callie Lawrence. Now that I think about it, I remember her dad mentioning something about her going to UW."

"No way…it can't be…is it?" I take in her brown hair, her clothes that show her thin frame, and her blue eyes that sparkle as she laughs. The last time I saw her, those blue eyes were clouded and weighted. The Callie I knew held more darkness, wore baggy clothes, and always looked sad. She shied away from everyone, except for that one night when she saved my ass.

"No, it's her," Luke says with confidence as he flicks his finger against his temple. "Remember she had that small birthmark on her temple just like that girl does. It can't be a freakish coincidence."

"Fuck me," I say loudly and everyone looks at me.

"Can I help you?" the tour guide asks in an icy tone.

I shake my head, noticing Callie is staring at me. "Sorry man, I thought a bee landed on me."

Luke snorts a laugh and I suppress my laughter. The tour guide huffs in frustration and continues his speech about where all the offices are as he points at each door.

"What was that about?" Luke asks in a low voice as he folds a paper neatly in half.

"Nothing." I skim the crowd, but Callie's nowhere. "Did you see where she went?"

Luke shakes his head. "Nope."

My eyes travel across the hallway, but there's no sign of her anywhere. I need to find her, so I can thank her for saving my life, like I should have done four months ago.

Chapter Two

#28: Invite Someone You Don't Know to Dinner.

Callie

"What are our plans for tonight?" I fold up a shirt and place it into the laundry basket on top of the dryer. "Are we going out or staying in?"

Seth hops onto one of the washing machines with his legs dangling over the edge as he pops a piece of gum into his mouth. "I'm conflicted. On one hand, I want to stay in and catch up on *The Vampire Diaries*, but there's this really awesome restaurant I've been wanting to try out."

"Ew, not that one with the sushi bar." I frown, pulling a flimsy sheet of fabric softener off one of my shirts. "I don't like sushi and I don't really feel like eating out tonight."

"No, you've never had sushi," he corrects. "And just because you haven't tried something doesn't mean you don't like it." He stifles a laugh by sealing his lips together. "I know this from my own factual evidence."

31

"I'm sure you do." My phone vibrates as it lights up from on top of the stack of shirts. "Dang it, it's my mom. Give me a second."

"Hi, Mom," I answer, shuffling to the corner to get away from the rattle of the washing machines.

"Hi, baby girl," she says. "How's your first day of classes?"

"First day of class is on Monday," I remind her, pushing my fingertip against my ear to block out the rattle of the machines. "Today's just the day when everyone's checking in."

"Well, how's that going?"

"I already know where everything is, so I'm catching up on my laundry with Seth."

"Hi, Mrs. Lawrence," Seth shouts, cupping his hands around his mouth.

"Tell him hi for me, honey, okay?" she replies. "And that I can't wait to meet him."

I cover the receiver with my hand. "She can't wait to meet you," I whisper to Seth and he rolls his eyes.

"Tell her she can't handle me." The washing machine stops and he jumps off to open the lid.

"He says he can't wait to meet you either," I tell my mom. "In fact, he's really excited."

Seth shakes his head, tugging a jacket out of the machine. "Moms are not my thing. You know that."

"What did he say?" my mom wonders.

"Nothing, Mom." The dryer beeps. "I have to go. I'll call you later."

"Hold on, sweetie. I just want to say that you sound really happy."

"I am happy," I lie through a thick throat, because I know that's what she wants to hear.

Seth drops his hang-dry only shirt on the edge of the basket, puts his hands on his hips, and narrows his eyes at me. "Don't lie to your mother, Callie."

"What's going on?" my mother asks. "I can hear a bunch of noises."

"I have to go." I press the end button before she can say anything else.

"My mom is not like your mom." I open the dryer door and scoop the rest of my clothes out with my arms. "For the most part, she's nice. Well, at least when I'm behaving."

"But you can't tell her things—really important things." He flexes his arm that was in a cast when I met him. "Just like my mom."

"You told your mom." I bump the dryer door shut with my hip. "It just didn't go well and I don't tell my mom, because it will crush her. She's such a happy person there's no use cursing her with dark thoughts." I drop the clothes into the basket as one of the washing machines chugs and bangs against the cement wall. "We can try that new restaurant, if you really, really want." Picking up the basket, I prop it against my hip. "I'll add it to my list of new things I'm going to try."

He grins from ear to ear. "I love that list."

33

"I do too…sometimes," I agree as he gathers a stack of clothes. "And you were brilliant for thinking of it."

The list was made in the shadows of my dorm room when he admitted to me how he broke his arm and where the scars on his hands came from. He'd been walking home from his last day of school and a bunch of football players drove up in a truck. They jumped him, beat him, and tried to break him into a thousand pieces that they could dust under the rug. But Seth is strong, which is why I told him my secret, because he knows what it's like to have something ripped away from you. Although I omitted the gory details because I couldn't say them aloud.

"I'm a very brilliant man." He steps aside to let me through the doorway first. "And as long as you hold on to that notion, you'll be okay."

We laugh and it's real, but a dark cloud hovers over us once the sound is stolen by the wind.

Kayden

"This room is the size of a box," I remark, taking in the very small dorm room. We're in the Downey residence hall, one of the four buildings they stuff the freshmen into. There are two twin-size beds and a desk in the far corner. I can cover the space between the beds in two strides and the closet on the far wall barely holds three boxes. "Are you sure you don't want to get an apartment? I saw some that are really close to campus on my way in."

Luke rummages through a large box labeled "Junk." "I can't afford an apartment. I need to find a job just so I can buy my books and stuff."

"The scholarship didn't pay for that?" I grab a heavy box and drop it onto the mattress of my bed.

He balls up some tape and throws it on the floor. "That only covered tuition."

I peel the tape off the top of the box. "I can help out . . . if you need some extra cash."

He shakes his head quickly with his attention immersed in a box. "I'm not a charity case. If you want an apartment, then go get one. You don't have to stay in the dorms just because I am." He pulls out a headless bronze statue and his face reddens. "What the hell is this?"

I shrug. "I didn't pack your boxes, man."

"Well, I did and I didn't put this in there." He chucks it across the room and it dents the wall. "God fucking damn it, she's trying to mess with my mind."

"Don't let your mom get to you. You know she's just trying to get you to come home so she doesn't have to deal with things on her own." I pick up the broken statue and step out into the hall to toss it in the garbage just outside the room.

On my way back, I spot Callie walking in my direction with the guy she was with earlier and she's smiling again. I

pause in the middle of the hallway and wait for her to reach me, forcing the traffic of people to move around me. She doesn't notice me, but her friend sees me and he whispers something in her ear.

Her head whips in my direction and she stumbles back, like she's afraid I'm going to attack her. Her friend puts his hand on the small of her back in a comforting gesture.

"Hi," I start off awkwardly, thrown off by her skittishness toward me. "I don't know if you remember me—"

"I remember you," she interrupts, her blue eyes flickering to the scar on my cheekbone. "How could I not remember you? We've known each other since we were kids."

"Right," I say, unsure how to respond to her offish attitude. She didn't act this way that night. "That was just my way of starting the conversation."

Her lips form an "O," then she stands silently, fidgeting with the strap on her oversized jacket.

Her friend glances at her and then extends his hand toward me. "I'm Seth."

I shake his hand with my gaze still on Callie. "Kayden."

"You'll have to forgive Callie." Seth gently pats her shoulder and she winces. "She's feeling a little off today."

Callie's eyelids descend as she narrows her eyes at him. "No, I'm not. I feel fine."

Seth presses her with a relenting look and grits through his teeth, "Then maybe you should say something. Perhaps something nice."

"Oh." She focuses her attention back to me. "I'm sorry... I mean..." She trails off, cursing under her breath, "Oh my God, what is wrong with me?"

Seth sighs, like he's used to her awkward behavior. "You're just starting school today?" he asks me.

"Yeah, I'm here on a football scholarship." I eye him up, questioning if he's ever touched a football.

He arches his eyebrows, rocking back on his heels, feigning interest. "Aw, I see."

Callie's bangs flutter away from her forehead as she lets out a slow exhale. "We have to go. We have dinner plans. It was nice talking to you, Kayden."

"You could come with us," Seth offers, ignoring the glare Callie targets at him. "If you want. It's just this new place we're going to check out."

"It's sushi." Callie meets my gaze for the first time. Sadness and diffidence possess her pupils and I almost reach out to hug her pain away. It's an odd feeling, since I've never hugged anyone, other than Daisy and I only hug her when I have to. "I'm not sure it'll be good."

"I like sushi." I look over my shoulder at the open door to my dorm. "But I'd have to bring Luke, if that's okay? Luke was the running back for the Broncos."

"I know who he is." She swallows hard. "He can come, I guess."

"Just a second. Let me see if he's up for it." I duck back into the room where Luke is sitting on his unmade bed, sifting

through a stack of papers. I brace my hands on the doorframe as I stick my head in. "Are you down for some sushi?"

His eyes elevate from the papers to me. "Sushi? Why?"

"Because Callie Lawrence just invited us," I say. "Or well, her friend did...do you remember her being offish?"

He tucks the papers away into a dresser drawer, but crumples up a small one and throws it into the trash. "Yeah, she got that way around sixth grade. It was like one minute she was normal and then the next minute she was fucking weird."

My hands fall to my side and I lean back, glancing out into the hall at Callie who's whispering something to Seth. "I don't remember that. I mean, I remember her being kind of normal and then not really remembering her at all. She didn't really hang out with anyone, did she?"

"Not really." He shrugs. "What's with the obsession with her now?"

"It's not an obsession." He pisses me off with the accusation. "I don't ever get obsessed with anyone. They just offered and I accepted to be polite. If you don't want to go, then we don't have to."

He stuffs his wallet into his back pocket. "I don't care if we go. If I can make it through tons of freaking dinners with Daisy, I'm sure I can make it through a dinner with some girl we went to school with that barely says a word."

I feel like an asshole. He seems to remember more about Callie than I do and I should know the girl who saved me in so many ways that I don't know if I'll ever be able to explain it to her.

Callie

"I'm so mad at you," I hiss under my breath at Seth as we walk across the dark parking lot toward the restaurant that's lit up by fluorescent lights. The four of us drove to the restaurant in the same car and the silence was enough to make me want to pull my hair out. "Why did you invite them?"

"To be polite." He shrugs and swings his arm around me. "Now relax, my lovely Callie, and let's cross off being more social from our list. In fact, we can cross off inviting someone to dinner."

"I'm going to burn that list when we get back." I jerk the glass doors open and step through the doorway into the stuffy atmosphere of the restaurant. Most of the booths are empty, but the bar is rather loud, with a group of girls wearing feather boas and tiaras, like they are at a bridal party.

"No, you're not. Now relax and try to make small conversation," he replies and struts up to the hostess, resting his arm on top of the counter. "Hi, are there any seats available at the bar?"

She giggles, twisting a lock of her red hair around her finger as she scrolls through a list, completely smitten by Seth. "Let me check."

Seth pops a mint into his mouth and rolls his eyes at me from over his shoulder. "Wow."

I smile at him then turn toward Luke and Kayden, but can't find anything to say. I don't do well with guys, except for Seth. I wish I did, but my memories just won't let me.

Luke plucks a waxy leaf off the artificial plant near the door. "I thought Laramie was supposed to be more of a party town then it seems to be."

I point at the window to my right. "It is farther down that way. There's a lot of clubs and stuff."

With his buzzed brown hair, a tattoo around his forearm, and intense brown eyes, Luke always looks like he's about to start a fight and it makes me want to cower back. "So you know where they are?"

"I've heard of where they are." I peek out of the corner of my eye at Kayden. He's listening to me intently as he leans against the door with his arms crossed over his chest. Why is he looking at me like that? Like he's actually seeing me. "But I haven't been to many of them."

"Yeah, you were never really a party girl, were you?" Luke flicks the leaf to the floor.

"Actually she kind of was at one time," Kayden intervenes with a proud expression on his face. "I remember now. It was the beginning of sixth grade and my mom was supposed to bring the cake, but she forgot or something...I think it was your birthday."

"I was turning twelve." My voice is breathless as the images of balloons, confetti, and pink frosting surface, but then bleed away into a pool of blood. "And that doesn't make me a party girl, just a little girl who wanted a birthday party... that's all I wanted."

They stare at me like I've lost my mind and I try to mentally summon my lips to form words, but they are bound together by the painful memories crushing my heart.

"Okay, I got us a table, but it's not at the bar." Seth strolls up and drapes his arm around my shoulder. "What's up? You look sick."

I blink several times and then force a smile. "I'm just tired."

He knows I'm lying, but won't bring it up in front of Kayden or Luke. "Then we should probably get you back early."

The hostess ushers us to our table and leaves the menus for us to look over, along with four glasses of ice water, flaunting Seth a grin before she heads back to the front. My vision is clouded by dark thoughts I've tried not to think about in a while, and I can't see a single word on the list. I press the palms of my hands to my eyes and blink.

"I think I need to admit something," Kayden announces. When I glance up at him, a slow grin turns up at his lips. "I don't like sushi. In fact, it kind of creeps me out."

"Me, too," I agree with a timid smile. "It's weird that it's not cooked."

"She's never had it," Seth divulges, turning the page of his menu. "So technically, she can't put in her opinion."

41

"I think she can offer her opinion." From beneath the table, Kayden's knee brushes mine, whether accidental or not, I'm unsure. It sends a hot flow of heat up my body that makes my stomach somersault. "It seems like a valuable opinion."

I don't know how to take his compliment, so I keep my lips fastened.

"I'm not saying it's not valuable," Seth explains. "Only that she may like it if she tried it. A code that I live by."

I'm sipping my water and I snort a laugh, choking on a piece of ice. "Oh my God."

Seth pats my back with his hand. "Are you going to make it?"

I nod, pressing my palm to my chest. "Yeah, no more jokes while I'm drinking, though, okay?"

"It's what I live by." There's a sparkle in his eyes as he grins devilishly at me. "But I'll tone it down."

"Shit, I left my phone in the car," Luke slaps his hand on top of the table and our water glasses shake. "I'll be right back." He gets up from the booth, strolls down the aisle, and exits out the front doors.

We return to our menus when Seth jumps up from the booth. "I locked the car. He can't even get inside it." He rushes off toward the door, taking his keys out of his pocket.

"Luke actually went to smoke," Kayden tells me, spinning the saltshaker between the palms of his hands. "He just doesn't like to admit it to people he doesn't know. He's weird about it."

I bob my head up and down, not looking at him. "So did

Seth, probably. He usually does it in the car, but he was being polite."

"He could have." Kayden laughs and it lights up his eyes. "Luke's been smoking in my car since we were sixteen."

Unable to help myself, I smile at the idea as I fiddle with the edge of a napkin.

"What's so funny?" Kayden folds his arms on top of the table and the bottom of his sleeves rise up. Tiny white lines cover the back of his wrists and he swiftly jerks his sleeves down to hide them. "Come on, share whatever's making you smile like that."

"It's nothing." I raise my gaze back to him. "I was just thinking about what my dad would have said if he ever found out his running back was a smoker."

"I think he knew he was." Kayden leans over the table, moving closer to me. "He always seemed to know everything that we did wrong, but never said it."

"Yeah, maybe he did, I guess. He did catch my brother smoking once and grounded him for a very long time." Why am I talking to him like this? It's not like me. I tip my chin down and concentrate on the list of appetizers.

"Callie, I'm sorry," he says abruptly, flattening his palm on the table as he glides it toward mine. As his fingers brush my knuckles, I nearly choke to death.

"For what?" I sound strangled.

"For not saying thank you . . . for that night." He covers his big hand on top of mine.

43

For a second, I like how his warmth feels, but then I'm thrown back to the place locked inside my mind, trapped and powerless.

"It's okay." I yank my hand away and hide it under the table. My pulse races as I stare at the menu. "You were having a rough night."

He doesn't say anything as he moves his hand away. I don't look up at him, because I don't want to see the disgusted look in his eyes.

"If I asked them if I could have a hamburger, do you think they'd make me one?" he asks, nonchalantly changing the subject.

I flip the page of the menu, with my eyebrows furrowed. "Does it say they have hamburgers?"

"No, I was kidding." He observes me from across the table. "Can I ask you something?"

I nod warily. "Sure."

"How come you left for college early?" he asks. "Most people want to stay home for the summer and party."

I shrug. "I didn't really have anything left for me there except for my parents and it just seemed like it was time to go."

"You didn't have a lot of friends, did you?" Recollection masks his face as he starts to put the pieces of my sad life together.

Thankfully, Seth and Luke join us at the table before he can try to dig up more details. They smell like smoke and look euphorically happy.

"Nah, they don't really have many on campus." Seth says to Luke as he sits down and unrolls the napkin from around the silverware. "And if they do, security usually breaks them up."

Luke swivels a small plastic display with pictures of the beer beverages on it. "Yeah, that shit happened all the time at our school. Like this one time we had this huge bonfire, and the cops showed up and busted everyone."

"What kind of trouble did you get in?" Seth asks, checking the watch on his wrist.

"Not too much." Luke pops a toothpick into his mouth. "The cops in our town usually go easy on football players."

"Figures," Seth mutters, giving me a sidelong glance, and I offer him a sympathetic smile.

Kayden's foot keeps bumping mine from below the table and I want to ask him to stop, but I can't even make eye contact with him. I grow flustered because part of me likes it. I'm losing control over my feelings and I desperately need to get a hold of them again.

The waitress returns and jots down our orders. I try to do my best and order a whole meal with the intention to eat it all. When the food arrives however, my stomach clenches, and I can tell right away that I'm going to do it, just like I always do.

Chapter Three

#52: Take a Chance, for God's Sake.

Kayden

It's been a week since school started. Classes are a pain in the ass. I was warned that college would be harder, but I never prepared myself for how much solo work was required. Between that and practice, I've had zero time to focus on anything else in my life.

I've crossed paths with Callie twice since we ate at the restaurant and each time she avoids me. She's in my Biology class, but sits in the back, as far away from anyone else as she can, focusing on her pen and paper. The girl has to have a whole notebook full of notes with how fixated she is with them.

I try not to stare at her, but most of the time I can't help it. It's fascinating to watch how oblivious she is to everyone. It would be nice to get lost in my thoughts, instead of always worrying about shit.

I'm getting ready to go to class, telling myself that I need to leave Callie alone, when I get a phone call from my dad.

"You left your shit in the garage," is the first thing he says to me.

"Sorry," I apologize, forcing myself to breathe as I grab my books. "But I thought Mom said I could."

"Your mom has no say in these things," he says sharply. "If you wanted to keep your shit here, you should have asked me. God, how many times do you have to screw up before you stop?"

I want to argue, but he's right. I screw up more than I don't. I let him chew my ass off for over fifteen minutes, and he makes me feel like a fucking kid again.

After I hang up, I stare at the mirror above the dresser, analyzing every scar on my face until it just looks like one big scar. Suddenly, all this anger pours out of me and I kick the shit out of the dresser until one of the drawers falls out. Luke's stuff scatters all over the floor; lighters, photos, a few tools, and a razorblade. He hates it when his shit gets disorganized and is going to go nuts if he comes back to this mess.

I quickly put everything back inside, trying to make it look orderly, and pretend not to notice the white elephant staring me in the face as I scoop it up off the floor. But it's all I can think about as I hold it in my palm, begging myself not to use it.

My hand shakes as my mind drifts back to a time when I wasn't like this; where I thought that maybe, just maybe, everything didn't have to center around pain.

My older brother, Tyler and I were messing around in the garage. He was about sixteen and I was eight. He was working on a motorcycle he had bought with the money he'd saved up from his summer job.

"I know it's kind of a piece of shit," he said to me as he grabbed a wrench from the toolbox in the corner. "But it'll get me places—away from here, which is all I fucking want."

He'd been fighting with my dad all day and had a giant bruise on his arm and cuts on his knuckles. I'd heard them arguing and then they were hitting each other. It was normal though. Life.

"Why do you want to leave?" I asked, wandering around the bike. It wasn't shiny or anything, but it looked like it could be fun. And if it could take anyone away from here, then it had to be something special. "Is it because of Dad?"

He tossed the tool back into the box rather hard and raked his hands through his long brown hair, which made him look like a homeless person, or at least my dad said so. "One day, buddy, when you get a little bit older, you're going to realize that everything in this house is one fucking big lie and you're going to want to get the hell away from here, no matter what it costs."

I stepped up on a crate and climbed on top of the bike, grabbing on to the handles as I swung my short leg over it. "Will you take me with you? I want to leave, too."

He rounded to the back of the bike, squatting down to check the tires. "Yeah, buddy, I will."

I pushed the throttle, pretending to drive away, and for a second I saw the possibility of a life without pain. "You promise?"

He nodded as he messed with the air pressure gauge. "Yeah, I promise."

It turned out my brother was a liar just like everyone else in the house. He ended up moving out, and leaving me behind because he'd rather be drunk than deal with life. A few years later, my other brother, Dylan, graduated and moved out of the house. He changed his number, never told anyone where he was going, and no one has heard from him since, although I'm not sure how hard anyone looked.

I was twelve at the time and the only kid left in the house, which meant I was the main focus of my dad's rage, something he made clear to me the night Dylan packed his shit and left. The beatings before that weren't too severe; slaps across the face, lashings with his belt, and sometimes he would punch us or kick us, but would hold back just enough that it hurt like hell but could be hidden.

I watched Dylan pull away from the driveway and drive down the road into the dark, pressing my face to the window, wishing I were in the car with him, even though Dylan and I had never been close. My dad walked in from outside, bringing in the cold night air with him. He'd yelled at Dylan all the way to the car, telling him he was a fucking moron for giving up his football scholarship and refusing to be on the team.

"What the fuck are you looking at?" He slammed the

front door so hard the family portrait above the mantel fell to the floor.

I turned around on the couch and sat down, staring at the portrait on the floor. "Nothing, sir."

He stalked toward me, his pupils swallowing his eyes, and I could smell the alcohol on his breath from clear across the room. He was bigger than me, stronger than me, and he had a look on his face that let me know he was about to use it to his full advantage and there was nothing I could do about it.

I knew the drill. Get up and hide, otherwise he wouldn't have time to cool off. But I couldn't move. I kept thinking about my brothers who were gone and had left me behind like an old T-shirt. We used to be in this together, now it was just me. I started to cry, like a stupid fucking baby, and I knew it was only going to piss him off more.

"Are you crying? What the fuck is wrong with you?" He didn't slow his momentum as he raised his fist and slammed it into my shoulder.

The pain that spread up my neck and down my arm sucked my oxygen out in one swift snap of a finger and I crumpled to the floor, blinking the black spots away from my eyes.

"Get up!" He kicked me in the side, but I couldn't get up. My legs had given up on me and with each slam of his shoe, something died inside. I didn't even bother tucking my legs in to protect them. I just let the pain take over, allowing it to numb the pain of being left behind. "You're so useless! At least your brothers fight back. But what are you? Nothing! It's all your fault!" Another kick, this time against my gut and the pain shot up into my head.

"Get up! Get up. Get up…" His boot slammed into my gut and his voice took on pleading. As if it was all my fault and he wanted me to make it stop. And maybe it was my fault. All I had to do was get up. But even something so simple I couldn't get right.

It was the worst beating I ever had, like he had channeled all his frustration with my brothers and directed it all on me. My mom kept me out of school for two weeks while I healed, telling the school, family, friends, neighbors—anyone who asked that I had strep throat and was highly contagious.

I lay in bed almost the entire time, feeling my body heal, but my mind and will to live died, knowing it would never get better, that this was it for me.

I blink the thought away as I sit down on the floor and lift up my shirt. I vowed when I went to college that I'd give it up—stop the fucking habit. But I guess it owns me more than I thought.

❧

The next day in Biology I'm trying to hold as still as possible to keep the pain on my stomach contained, but I keep glancing behind me at Callie, who seems oblivious that I'm turning into a stalker.

Professor Fremont takes his sweet time wrapping up his lecture. By the time I make it into the hall, it's crammed with people. I'm blocking the doorway, trying to determine whether I want to skip my next class or not, when someone slams into my back.

"Oh my God. I'm so sorry," Callie apologizes, backing away from me like I'm a criminal. "I wasn't paying attention to where I was going."

"You don't have to apologize. I promise I'm perfectly fine, even though you ran into me." I flash a grin at her as I move to the side, so people can get by. As my midsection turns, my muscles burn.

"I'm sorry," Callie repeats and then shuts her eyes, shaking her head at herself. "I just have a bad habit of saying sorry."

"It's okay, but maybe you should work on breaking it," I suggest, bracing my hand on the doorframe. Her brown hair is pulled up and thin wisps hang around her face. She's wearing jeans, a plain purple T-shirt, and minimal makeup. Her tits aren't hanging out of her top and her jeans aren't skintight to show off her curves, like how Daisy dresses every day. There's nothing to check out, yet I find myself really looking at her.

"I'm trying, but it's hard." She looks down at the brown carpet, so shy and innocent. The girl looks like she needs a thousand hugs to erase all the sadness she's carrying around on her shoulders. "Habits are very hard to break."

"Can I take you out somewhere?" I ask without even thinking about what I'm doing or what the consequences will be. "I really want to say thank you for, well, you know, for what you did."

Her eyelids flutter open and my heart skips a beat. That's never happened before and it tosses me into a momentary state of vertigo. "I'm actually supposed to meet Seth in just a few minutes, but maybe some other time," she says evasively and starts down the hall, swinging her bag over her shoulder.

I fall into step with her. "You know, he's an interesting person. I have him in my English class and he always raises his hand, just to give the wrong answer."

A faint smile touches at her lips. "He does it on purpose."

Pressing my palm against the glass, I hold the door open for her. "Why?"

She blocks the sun from her eyes with her hand as she steps outside. "Because it's on the list."

I pause just outside the doorway, cocking an eyebrow. "The list?"

"It's nothing." She waves her hand at me dismissively. "Look, I have to go."

She picks up the pace, her thin legs moving quickly as she leaves me in the campus yard, her head tucked down and her shoulders hunched as if she's doing everything she can to be nonexistent.

Callie

My dorm room is located in the McIntyre building, which is the tallest of the residence halls. I swipe my ID card to get into the hall and then push a code to enter my room. From out the window, the people look tiny, like I'm a bird seeing everything from an aerial view.

I pull out my journal that I keep hidden beneath my pillow and grab a pen. I started writing in it when I was thirteen, as a way to put my thoughts down on paper. I wasn't planning on making it a lifelong hobby, but I feel so much better when I write, like my brain is finally free to say whatever it wants.

The edges of the cover are tattered and some of the pages are falling off from the spiral. I sit down with my legs crisscrossed, and press the tip to a clean sheet.

It's amazing how the things you remember forever are the things you'd rather forget and the things you desperately want to grasp on to seem to slip away like sand in the wind.

I remember everything about that day, like the images have been burned into my brain by a branding iron. But I wish they would blow away in the wind.

There's a knock on my door. Sighing, I hide the notebook back under the pillow before answering the door. Seth strolls in with two iced lattes and he hands one to me.

"You sounded like you could use one of these." He shucks off his jacket, drapes it over a chair that's in front of the desk, and sinks down on the bed. "Okay, spill your guts."

"I don't know why he's talking to me and asking me to go places." I pace the floor in front of my bed and sip on the straw. There are sketches and a poster of Rise Against on my roommate's side of the wall, and her bed is covered in dirty clothes. "He's never really talked to me before."

"Who, Kayden?" Seth asks and I nod. He flops onto my bed and scrolls through my playlists on my iPod. "Maybe he likes you."

I stop in the middle of the room and shake my head, the ice swishing in the cup. "No, that's not what it is. He has a girlfriend—a super slutty girlfriend who he can touch."

"He would probably touch you, if you'd let him," he says and my breath catches in my throat. "Okay, so we're not there yet."

Setting the coffee on the desk, I sink down on my bed and tuck my hands under my legs. "I'm not sure I'll ever be there. I think I've come to the conclusion that I won't ever be able to handle going that far with anyone. I may end up being one of those old ladies with a thousand cats and eating cat food straight out of the can."

"First of all, gross, I would never let you turn into that. And second of all, we should add it to the list." He sits up and reaches for a pen on my nightstand.

"Just because it's on the list, doesn't mean it will happen," I say as he stands up and marches to the board on the back of the door where our list is written.

"Yes, it does, Callie." He grins, flipping the cap off the pen with his thumb. "Because it's a magical list, full of possibilities."

"I wish that were true." I stare out the window at the people flooding the campus yard. "I really do."

The pen squeaks as he scribbles something down. When

I return my attention to him, he's added, *#52 Take a Chance, for God's Sake* to the bottom of the list. He clicks the cap on, cocks his head, and smiles with pride at his cleverness.

"I do amaze myself sometimes. I'm going to have to add this one to my copy of the list when I get back to my room." He tosses the pen onto the dresser and sits down on the bed. "So what's your chance, Callie? Because I know you're strong enough to at least try one."

"But what if I take a chance and everything crumbles?" I ask. "What if I trust someone again and they steal something away from me. I don't really have that much left before I'm hollow."

"Take an easy chance," he singsongs. "Come on, Callie, do it."

"Are you trying to peer pressure me?"

"Yeah, is it working?"

"Not really, since I don't know what you want me to do."

He rubs his hands together with a devious gleam in his eyes. "I have an idea. You should call Kayden and take him up on his offer."

"No, Seth." I pull my knees up and rest my chin on them. "I can't be around people like him. They make me nervous and remind me too much of high school. Besides, soon it's going to dawn on him how much his girlfriend hates me and he's going to back off."

"He seems nice." Seth removes his cellphone from his

pocket and checks the screen. "I even have his phone number in my phone."

My brows knit. "How?"

"Because I'm scandalous." He swipes his finger over the screen to turn it on. I dive for him with my arm out, but he jumps out of my reach and runs for the door. "Here we go."

I stand up and put my hands on my hips, digging my fingers into my skin as I hunch over and force air through my lungs. "Seth, please don't. I can't. I don't do well around guys."

He puts the phone up to his ear with a stern look on his face. "Callie, you have to remember that not all guys are him...Hello, is this Kayden?" He pauses. "Yeah, this is Seth. Hold on just a second. Callie wants to talk to you." Covering the mouthpiece with his hand, he extends the phone toward me. "Take. A. Chance."

I remove my hands from my hips and my skin is dotted with red-crescent moon marks from my fingernails. I take the phone from him, my pulse erratic through my fingers, my wrists, and my neck as I raise it to my ear.

"Hello," I say, my voice barely a whisper.

"Hi," he replies, sounding lost, but intrigued. "Did you need something?"

"Hey, I was thinking that maybe...I could still take you up on that offer to go somewhere," I explain, and Seth motions his hand at me encouragingly. "We don't have to do anything right now, but maybe later."

"I was just getting ready to leave to explore the town," he says as I bite on my fingernail. "Do you want to go with me?"

I nod, even though he can't see me. "Yes, that sounds nice. Should I meet you outside or something?"

"Do you know what Luke's truck looks like?" he asks.

"Is it that rusted one he used to drive in high school?"

"Yeah, that's the one. Why don't you meet me by it in like ten minutes? It's parked near the side entrance of the quad."

"All right, sounds good." I hang up and scowl at Seth.

He claps his hands and does a little dance. "See, taking a chance isn't so bad. In fact, it can turn out really good."

"What if I panic, though?" I hand him the phone back and grab a hoodie from my dresser drawer. "What if I do something really weird? I've never been alone with a strange guy before."

"You'll be fine." He puts his hands on my shoulders and looks me in the eyes. "Just be the Callie I know."

I zip up my jacket. "Okay, I'll try my damn hardest."

He laughs and then encloses his arms around me, drawing me in for a hug. "And if you need anything, you can call me. I'll always be here for you."

❧

Kayden isn't out in the parking lot. As I wait by Luke's truck, I watch the other students hurry to and from class and I almost bolt. As I step up onto the curb to head back to my dorm, Kayden exits out the side doors of the building. He's talking to a girl with wavy black hair that runs all the way down her back.

He's wearing jeans that hang low on his hips and a long-sleeve, dark gray Henley. The way he moves is captivating. He's got a lot of swagger in the movement of his hips, yet his shoulders bend in and his whole stomach area looks stiff, as if walking causes him pain.

I step back to the truck and wait with my arms crossed over my chest. When he sees me, his lips turn upward and he waves good-bye to the girl, who I think is in my Philosophy class.

"Sorry I'm late." He hitches his thumb over his shoulder at the girl walking away. "Kellie needed help with an English assignment. Were you waiting here a long time?"

I drop my arms to my side then fold them over my chest again, unable to figure out what to do with them. "Not for too long."

He steps off the curb and I begin to recoil as he reaches toward my side. But he grips the door handle and I relax, side-stepping so he can open it.

"Are you okay?" He pulls the door open and the hinges creak as bits of rust fall off the edge.

Nodding, I put one foot up on the floor of the truck, and hop in. The vinyl fabric of the seat is frayed and pokes through my jeans, scratching at my skin. He slams the door and I wring my hands on top of my lap. It's the first time I've been alone with a guy in a car before, except for Seth, and my heart challenges my chest to endure its wrath.

"Callie, are you sure you're okay?" he asks with his hands on top of the steering wheel. "You look a little pale."

I force my eyes to concentrate on him, trying not to blink too much. "I'm fine. I'm just a little tired. College wears me out."

"I completely agree on that." He offers me a smile that crinkles around his eyes as he starts up the engine. It chugs and then backfires. "Sorry, Luke's truck is a piece of shit."

I spread my sweaty palms flat on my knees. "What happened to your car? The one you used to drive to school. Did you leave it at home?"

His neck muscles work to swallow a lump in his throat. "My dad has a rule that once we leave the house, we're on our own. The car was bought by him, so therefore it's his."

I nod, reaching over my shoulder to grab the seatbelt. "I don't have a car either. My parents offered to give me my brother's old car, but I declined."

"Why?" He shoves the shifter into gear and the tires roll forward. "It seems like life would be easier if you had one."

I click the buckle into the lock and then watch the leafy trees zip by as we pull out onto the street and away from the campus. "It seemed like too much responsibility, I guess. Besides, I wasn't really planning on leaving the campus very much."

He turns on the wipers to wash the grime off the windshield. "I kind of have a question and feel free not to answer it." He dithers. "How come you never hung out with anyone in high school? After I started thinking about it, I just don't remember you doing anything."

I scratch at the back of my neck until it stings. "That's because I didn't do anything."

He watches me, waiting for me to elaborate, his eyes on me instead of the road, but I can't tell him anything. It's my secret and I'll take it to the grave of shame.

"There's this really awesome place I heard about where you can stand up on the hills and see the whole town," he says. "I was thinking we could go there. It's not too far of a hike."

"A hike?" I question. "Like we would walk up a mountain?"

He laughs and I feel like a moron. "Yeah, like we'd walk up hills and everything."

I scrunch up my nose at my brown boots that fold down at the top. They're a size too small and just walking around campus gives me blisters. "Okay, I guess we can go on a hike."

His lips part as he starts to say something, but his phone rings from inside his pocket. His brows decline as he reads the name on the glowing screen. "Can you be quiet for a second?" he asks with a guilty face.

I nod, eyeing his phone. "Sure."

"Hey baby, what's up?" he answers and I can hear Daisy's voice on the other end.

"Then don't say that to them and maybe they won't get mad." Kayden pauses. "Yeah, I know. I miss you, too. I can't wait until homecoming. . . . No, I haven't got a tux yet."

A hint of jealousy burns in my heart. When I was younger, I dreamt of going to prom and wearing a pretty dress with lots of sparkles on it. I even wanted a tiara, which seems silly now.

"I love you, too," he says flatly and then quickly hangs up the phone.

My jealousy lifts and I let out a breath I hadn't realized I'd been holding.

He tosses the phone onto the seat between us. "That was Daisy . . . you know Daisy McMillian, right?"

"Yeah, a little."

"By your tone, I'm guessing you don't like her."

"Why would you guess that?"

His hands grip the wheel as his eyes evaluate me. "Because most people don't."

"If that's the case, then why do you date her?" I ask, wondering where the forwardness is coming from.

He shrugs, his jawline rigid. "She's a nice girlfriend. She keeps me happy for the most part."

"Oh, sorry. I'm being pushy, aren't I?" I grip the edge of my seatbelt as he turns onto a dirt road with large potholes and a very sharp drop-off on the side of it. It weaves up into the mountains that are green with trees and grass.

"You weren't being pushy. I was asking you questions first." He grinds his jaw and his fingers tighten on the wheel.

We're quiet for the rest of the drive and I can tell something must have upset him. The wheels in his head are turning as his mind sorts through something complex.

A ways up the hill, he cranks the steering wheel to the right and veers the truck toward a turnout. A long ditch sections across the entrance and he gradually slows down. The truck bumps and then slants as he pumps the gas again and ramps back up, jolting us from left to right. When we're on flat land again, he directs the bumper at the trees and inches it forward until it's close, then shoves the shifter into park and turns the engine off.

A steep hill slopes up in front of us and there is graffiti on the side of a rock in various colors marking dates, lyrics, poems, and declarations of love. There are other vehicles parked next to us and on the road. People are on the path and up on top of the hill. I'm glad we're not alone, but don't like that there are a lot of people. It's kind of problematic.

He flips the handle and prods the door open with his elbow. "I promise it's not that far. At least that's what I've been told. If it ends up being intense, just let me know and we can turn back."

"Okay, I will." I push my door open and swing my feet out, avoiding a puddle. I meet him around the front of the truck and tuck my hands into my pockets that are lined with soft fabric and the feel of it brings me comfort, because it reminds me of a teddy bear.

We walk up the dirt path and pass by a couple sitting on a boulder in hiking boots with backpacks on. They wave at us and Kayden returns the wave while I stare up at a rock that is stained with paint.

"What is that?" I wonder aloud and read one of the quotes. *"Seize the day, take hold of it, and make it whatever you want."*

He dodges to the side of the path to avoid a large hole and his shoulder accidentally bumps into mine. "I guess it's a tradition for the seniors at UW to come up here and write words of wisdom to all future seniors."

"Rock on and prosper." I glance at him, my lips quirking. "That's very deep."

He laughs and lines form around his mouth. "I never said they were all words of wisdom, only that I heard that's what they are supposed to be."

I scoot over toward the rocky hill to gain a little distance between us. "It seems like a good idea, kind of. To mark the end with whatever you want."

"It does, doesn't it?" He hops over a massive rock, his lengthy legs stretching as he lands on top of it, and then leaps off the other side. He's panting, smiling, and proud of himself. "It's kind of like the whole bonfire thing back in Afton, where we write down our thoughts on a piece of paper and then burn it."

"I never went to that," I admit, clenching my hands into fists. If I had, I would have been tortured by people whispering that I was a devil worshiper who never ate anything. Because my hacked hair job, excessive black eyeliner, and antisocial behavior could have only been the work of the devil.

"Oh." He examines me for a while as I pretend not to

notice. "Callie, I'd like to get to know you. I mean, you saved my ass and I barely know anything about you."

I pluck a leaf off a bush and peel at the waxy edges. "There's not much to know, really. I'm kind of a boring person."

"I doubt that's true." He kicks a rock over the ledge of the cliff. "How about I'll tell you something about me and then you can tell me something about you?"

"What kinds of things?"

"Whatever you want."

We halt as we reach the end of the path. It widens to an area bordered by hills and boulders and there's an enormous cliff paved by edges that look like stairs. It's steep, but climbable.

"How do we get up?" I drop the leaf onto the ground and tip my head back to look at the top.

Rubbing his hands together, he grabs a hold of one of the stairs and props his shoe onto the lower one. "We climb up." With a bounce of his knee, he jumps up, like he's ascending up a rock wall. Once he's halfway up, he looks over his shoulder at me. "Are you coming?"

I glance behind me at the path curving down the hill, and then back up at the cliff. *Take a chance for God's sake.* Even though I'm afraid of heights, I grip the coarse edge, bounce onto my toes, and heave myself up. Positioning each of my feet on a ledge, I maneuver my way up to the next one, getting light-headed the higher I climb. When I look down, I freeze with the fear of splattering against the rocks below. The wind sneaks through my hair and pieces slip loose from the elastic.

"Are you going to make it?" He stands at the top with his hands on his hips like he's the king of the world, which would be an awesome job, if it existed. I could wear a crown and everyone would have to listen to me. If I said stay away, then they would.

I inhale through my nose and move my hand to the next step. "Yeah…" As my fingers slip, I squeeze my eyes tightly and my back bows inward. I'm not going to fall, but it makes me feel helpless and I can't move.

"Fuck, Callie," he says. "Give me your hand."

My fingers snag another ledge and I dig them in as my airflow decreases. Dizziness swarms through my brain and my knees tremble, about to buckle underneath me.

"Callie, open your eyes," Kayden says in a soft, but commanding voice and I crack an eyelid open. He's climbed down and his feet are just above my head with his long arm stretched toward me. "Give me your hand and I'll help you get up."

I eye his hand like it's the devil, because that's what hands can be; they can own you, pin you down, touch you without permission. Biting my lip, I shake my head. "I can do it on my own. I was just thrown off for a moment."

He sighs and the muscles in his arm relax. "You're afraid of heights, aren't you?"

I lean inward until my body is pressed against the jagged rocks. "Slightly."

"Give me your hand," he repeats, his voice is soft, but his eyes are demanding. "And I'll help you to the top."

The wind increases and dust stings at my cheeks. My body heats with my nerves as I shut my eyes and place my hand into his. Our fingers entwine, a shock zips through my arm, and my eyes lift up to him.

Tightening his grip, Kayden hoists me up, the muscles of his arms flexing until I'm on the next stair. I plant my shoes against it and he gives me a moment before tugging on my arm again and lifting me to the next one. When he reaches the top, he lets go, but only to heave himself up. Then he extends his hand over the ledge and I grab it, trusting him again as he pulls me up. I stumble and my shoes scuff against the dirt as I work to regain my steadiness.

His hand comes around my back and touches me just above the waist to steady me. My body stiffens as a mixture of emotions gust through me. I like that he's touching me, the gentleness of his fingers, and the warmth of his nearness. But then my mind flashes back to a big hand shoving at my back until I land on a bed.

I whirl around with my eyes amplified as strands of my hair float in front of my face. "Don't touch me, please."

"It's okay," he says with his hands out in front of him and a cautious look on his face. "I was just helping you get your balance."

I reach up to secure the elastic in my hair. "I'm sorry...

it's just that... that had nothing to do with you, I swear. I just have issues."

He lowers his hands to his side and watches me for the longest time. "I don't want to be pushy, but you seem kind of jumpy. Can I...Do you care if I ask why?"

I aim my gaze to the view over his shoulder. "I'd rather you not."

"Okay," he says simply and faces the opening of the cliff.

I move up beside to him, leaving a small gap between us. The hills roll for miles; green, flourishing, dotted with trees and hikers. The blue sky is endless and the sun illuminates through the thin white clouds. There's a breeze coming upward and also across and as they collide it makes me feel as if I'm flying.

"It kind of reminds me of that painting Mr. Garibaldi had on his wall." Kayden rubs his scruffy chin thoughtfully.

"The one he was so proud of? And talked about all the time?" I leave my hands at my hips but bring them out a little and put my palms flat as I imagine what it's like to be a bird, flying up high and free.

He laughs and his head falls forward, his hair falling across his forehead. "Did he tell that story to every class?"

I roll my tongue around in my mouth as I restrain a smile. "I think it was a tradition. It was his way of bragging that there was a time in his life where he wasn't stuck in a classroom."

He raises his head back up and exhales gradually. "How long do you want to stay up here?"

I shrug and turn for the ledge. "We can go back, if you want."

"I don't want to go back," he says and I pause. "Unless you do?"

I glance back out at the hills. "I'd like to stay here longer if that's okay?"

"It's perfectly okay." He sits down in the dirt and crosses his legs as he stretches them out in front of him. Then he pats the spot next to him.

I stare at it for a long time before I drop to the ground and cross my legs, too. My muscles constrict at the fact that our legs are so close, but I don't move over.

"I kind of hate football," he reveals as he pulls one of his legs up and drapes his arm on top of his knee.

"Oh, yeah," I say, startled. "How come?"

His finger trails along the scar that runs down half his cheekbone. "The violence sometimes gets to me."

I rest back on the palms of my hands. "I don't like football, either. There's only one purpose and that's to dominate."

He laughs, shaking his head. "I wouldn't go that far, but I get your point. I'm the quarterback, though, so all I really do is throw the ball."

I drag my pinkie back and forth in the dirt. "I know what position you play and what a quarterback does. My father's a coach and therefore I got to listen to a recap of every game and practice when we were eating dinner."

"Your dad's a nice guy, though," he states, cutting me a sideways glance. "I like him."

I know I shouldn't ask, but I can't help it. It's been bothering me for months that I just left him after he'd been beaten up. I never really believed that it was the only time his dad hit him. That much rage doesn't just come once and then dissolve.

"Kayden, what happened that night? That night I was at your house...and your dad, well, when he hit you. Did that ever happen before?"

"I think it's your turn to tell me something about you," he evades the question, his hands balling into fists, and his knuckles are so white the scars on them blend away.

"I don't have much to say about myself." I refuse to look at him as I shrug. "Nothing particularly interesting anyway."

He raises his hand, making a pinching position with his finger and thumb. "Come on. Just one tiny detail. That's all I'm asking for."

Frowning, I rack my brain for an intriguing detail about me that won't be very personal. My shoulders rise up and down as I shrug. "I like to kickbox down at the Tune-up Gym sometimes."

"Kickbox?" he questions, his forehead creasing. "Really?"

I pick the dirt out of my cracked fingernails. "It's a good way to relax."

His eyes scan my body from my toes to my face and my cheeks heat. "You look too tiny to be a kickboxer. I can't picture those little legs of yours being able to do very much damage."

70

If I were braver, I would challenge him to a match right here, just to prove him wrong.

I angle my chin up to the sky and place my hand in front of my eyes to block out the brightness of the sunlight. "I don't do it for sport, just for fun. It's a good way to . . . I don't know . . ." I trail off because the rest is too personal.

"To take your inner anger out," he says it more to himself than me.

I nod. "Yeah, kind of."

"You know what?" He looks at me with a smile expanding at his full lips. "The next time you go, you should call me. My coach, who's kind of a dick compared to your dad, has been hounding me to get into better shape. Then you can show me how much damage that little body of yours can do. I'll even tone it down and give you a chance to pin me down."

I bite on my lip to keep from smiling. "All right, but I don't go that often."

"Only when you feel like kicking some ass?" he teases with a crook of his eyebrow.

My lips twitch to a tiny smile. "Yeah, something like that."

He turns sideways so he's facing me and crisscrosses his legs. "Okay, I have another question. I actually just remembered this. I think it was back in fifth grade and your family was over at my house for one of those stupid barbecues my dad has every Super Bowl. Somehow a collector football disappeared from my dad's display case and everyone thought it was my brother Tyler that did it, because he was acting weird, but really he was just wasted. But I swear to fucking God I saw you walking out to your car with it under your shirt."

I tuck my feet under my butt as I cover my hands over my face. "My brother told me to do that. He said if I stole it for him he wouldn't tell my mom that I was the one who broke one of her silly little collector unicorns." I pause and it gets really quiet. Finally, I work up the courage to peek between the cracks in my fingers. "I'm really sorry."

He scrutinizes me and then a slow smile forms on his face. "Callie, I'm just messing with you. I don't care if you did it. In fact, it's kind of funny."

"No, it's not," I say. "It's horrible. I bet your brother got into trouble."

"Nah, he was eighteen." He draws my hand away from my face. "And when my dad started being a douche, he just left."

"I feel like a douche. I think my brother still has it in his room. I should make him give it to you."

"No way." He's still holding my hand as he guides my arm toward my knees. I'm very aware of his fingertips touching my wrist right above my hammering pulse and I'm conflicted on whether or not to pull away. "My dad can go without some of his shit."

"Are you sure?" I can't take my eyes off his hand on my arm. "I swear I can give it back."

He laughs softly and then his fingers graze the inside of

my wrist, causing my entire body to shiver. "I promise. No harm, no foul."

"I'm really sorry," I repeat.

He looks at me with this strange expression, like he's conflicted about something. He licks his lips and then presses them together, holding his breath.

I've often wondered what a guy would look like when he was about ready to kiss me. Would it be the same as my first and only kiss; a glimmer of conquer blazing within the pupils? Or would it be something else entirely different? Something less terrifying? Filled with more passion and desire?

Turning back to the cliff, he frees my wrist and his hand begins to tremble. He flexes it, elongating his fingers and letting out a sigh.

"What's wrong with your hand?" I ask, struggling to maintain a steady voice. "Did you hurt it climbing up?"

He balls it into a fist and places it on his lap. "It's nothing. I just broke a few bones a while ago and it gets that way sometimes."

"Does it affect how you play?"

"Sometimes, but I can handle it."

I stare at the scars on his knuckles, remembering the night when they were split open. "Can I ask you a question?"

He stretches out his legs and leans back on his hands. "Sure."

"How did you get the scars on your hand?" I reach out to touch them, the need to feel him so intense it temporarily overpowers my doubts, but life catches up with me and I swiftly move my hand away.

Putting his weight on one arm, he elevates his hand out in front of him. At the bottom of each finger is a thick white scar. "I punched a wall."

"Excuse me?"

"Not on purpose," he adds, and then makes a path with his finger along each bump and groove. "Accidents happen sometimes."

I recollect his dad slamming his fist into his face. "Yeah, I guess they do, but sometimes bad things happen on purpose by the hands of bad people."

He nods, then gets to his feet, and dusts the dirt off his jeans. "We should head back. I got a killer Literature paper I have to write." He offers me his hand to help me up, but I just can't bring myself to take it.

I turn over onto my hands and knees and push myself to my feet. "Now I just have to make it back down," I say with a sigh as I walk toward the cliff and peek over the edge.

He laughs quietly as he follows behind me. "Don't worry. I'll help you down, if you'll let me."

My eyes broaden at his words and then at the cliff. What a dilemma. But I trusted him once and I decide to do it again. I just pray to God he doesn't shove me down and break me, because I'm already in too many pieces and I just don't know how much more breaking I can take.

Kayden

I'm nervous helping her scale down the cliff and not because I think she's going to fall. My arm is around her back and her weight is against me. She's safe and I'm glad she is.

The problem lies inside me. The entire time we're climbing down, my heart is thumping in my chest. I want to reach over and feel her skin, suck on her lips, even let my fingers graze her ass. I've never wanted anyone like this before and it's fucking scary as hell. For a second, I considered kissing her while we were up on the cliff, but it would have been wrong of me. Not only because I shouldn't be kissing someone as nice as Callie, but also because I have a girlfriend and it wouldn't be fair to anyone.

Even though our conversation on the cliff was a minor moment in time, it held more depth than any other conversation I've had. When I talk to Daisy, it mostly focuses on shallow things, like homecoming, what she is going to wear, and where the parties are going to take place. That's how I want my life. Simple. I already have enough complexity locked away inside me to shadow the whole world with darkness.

"Are you sure we're not going to fall?" Callie grips at my upper arm, delving her fingertips into the fabric of my shirt as she blinks her eyes at the ground. "It feels like you're going to drop me."

"I'm not going to drop you. I promise." I tighten my arm

around her back and gently tug her closer. "Just relax. We're almost there."

I slide my foot down along the rock toward the next ledge, resisting the urge to grab her ass, and place my hand on her lower back. She reaches her hand down, holding on to me as she stretches her leg toward the lower ridge. Once her foot touches it, she relaxes as she steps down on the one below.

I let go of her as her feet touch the bottom. "See, I told you I wouldn't drop you."

Showing off a little, I jump down the rest of the way and land in front of her, ignoring the pain in my calf muscles. "Remind me never to take you somewhere up high again."

She makes an apologetic face as she brushes the dirt off the front of her shirt with her hands. "I'm sorry, I should have warned you. Although, climbing like that doesn't seem very natural. It felt like we were trying to be lizards or something."

Unable to help myself, I laugh at her. It's been a while and it feels good. "So for future planning, what kind of places do you like to go?"

She looks about as lost as I feel. "I have no idea."

"Well think about it." I start down the path toward where the truck is parked and Callie follows me. "And the next time I ask you if you want to hang out, you can tell me where."

Her forehead creases as she stares out at the hills to the side of us. "Is there going to be a next time?"

"Sure," I say casually. "Why wouldn't there be?"

She looks at me and shrugs, looking unconvinced. "I don't know."

It seems like she knows a lot of things, which is why I should be running away from her, before she finds out about me. But like my father always says, I was never that bright, and I have a feeling I'm not going to be able to stay away.

Chapter Four

#43: Don't Take Shit from Anyone.

Kayden

I'm having a good dream. Callie and I are climbing down the cliff. As I help her to the bottom, she bites at her bottom lip, stumbling back against the rocks, looking nervous as hell.

With my eyes locked on her lips, I place my hands on the rocky wall, so her head is trapped between my arms. Her body trembles as I tip my head down and breathe against her neck. I love that she's shivering and I want to make her shiver more.

The palms of my hands slide down the rocks, the jagged edges scraping against my skin. It's a combination of pain and fucking want and my adrenaline pumps through my body. Gripping her hips, her lips part as her head falls back and she moans.

"Tell me you want me," I say, because I have a feeling she's never told anyone that.

"I want you," she breathes.

Lifting her up, my lips come down on hers as I press up against her, wanting nothing more than to rip her clothes off and bury my dick deep inside her.

"Wake up, lover boy." A warm hand pats my cheek and I fling my arm at them because they're ruining my dream.

"Come on, sexy boy." Someone bounces on top of me. "You have a present waiting for you if you wake up."

I blink my eyes open to a pair of blue eyes and a lot of curly blond hair hanging in my face.

Daisy is straddling my lap, wearing a short denim skirt, and a white lacy top. "Surprise."

I rise up on my elbows, feeling deflated and wanting to go back to my dream to see how it ends. "What are you doing here?"

Her eyes narrow at me. "Way to welcome the love of your life. God, Kayden, you can be such an asshole sometimes."

I sigh and put on my plastic smile. "Sorry, I'm just tired. Between school and practice, I barely have time to sleep."

She scrunches the ends of her hair with her fingers. "Well, wake up. You need to take me out somewhere before I have to go home. I'm only here for like an hour."

"Why are you here?" I ask with caution as I sit up and lean against the headboard.

She shakes out her hair and adjusts her top over her stomach. "My mom drove here to go shopping. It's the closest place where she can buy shoes that don't have generic brands on them."

I arch my eyebrows, feigning interest. "Oh yeah?"

She nods and then walks her fingers up my bare chest that's covered up by a sheet. "I thought I'd come with her and see you. You can take me out and then maybe you'll get lucky."

"I have class," I say. "And where's Luke? I'm guessing he let you in? But who let you into the building?"

"I have my ways." She slips her leg off me and gets to her feet. "Luke let me into the room and then left. I don't get what his deal is with me. I mean, if I so much as look at him, he runs in the other direction."

"He's just quiet." I sit up and the sheet falls off my chest.

She takes in the white lines that run in every direction along my skin likes she's forgotten they were there. "You know they have laser treatments that can fade scars away? Maybe you should look into it." She traces her fingernail down my cheek. "You'd be perfect if you didn't have those scars."

I slide away from her, take a red T-shirt out of the dresser, and put it on. "There. Now you can't see them."

She crinkles her nose. "I didn't mean to be rude. I was just telling you the truth."

I grab a pair of jeans off the floor, pull them on, and fasten the button before slipping on my shoes. "Where do you want to go?"

She taps her lip thoughtfully. "Surprise me. Just as long as it's somewhere nice."

I swipe up my wallet and phone and then open the door for her. "You know I don't have my car."

"Duh." She rolls her eyes as I shut the door. "That's why I made my mom let me use hers. She's stuck at the mall so we have to make this a quickie. Although, you better make sure I enjoy it." She flashes me a grin and sways her hips as she struts down the hall. Her skirt barely covers her ass and her long legs stretch with confidence. A few guys walking down the hall check out her ass.

When she approaches the door, she waits for me to open it for her and then we step out into the sunshine. The campus yard is packed with people heading to and from class with books in their hands.

We start down the path beneath the trees, and Seth and Callie emerge at the end. Callie has a long-sleeved purple shirt on and her hair is pulled up. My mind drifts back to my dirty dream and how it felt to have her in my arms.

She's talking to Seth with a serious expression on her face and Seth is waving his arms in the air animatedly. When her eyes meet mine, they light up for a split second then she looks over at Daisy. Callie is the sweetest girl I've ever met, but the look on her face is filled with hatred.

I start to wave, when she extends her arm up toward me with an ID card in her hand. "I'm supposed to give this to you." Her tone is flat.

I take my card from her, offering her a small smile. "Thanks. How did you end up with this?"

She shrugs. "Luke said he grabbed it by accident. He stopped me after class and asked if I could stop by your dorm and give it to you, but since I ran into you, here you go."

Daisy gives Callie a once over. "Who the hell are you?"

Callie's eyes are as cold as ice. "Callie Lawrence."

Daisy sneers maliciously. "Oh my God. It's the Anorexic Satan Worshipper. Different clothes, but the same skinny body. Starve yourself much?"

"Daisy," I say in a tight voice. "Back off."

Seth's eyes widen, which means Callie must have told him about Daisy. But why? Am I missing something?

Daisy glares at me. "Maybe I should ask you what the fuck you're doing? Hanging out with someone like her."

A light turns off in Callie's eyes as she starts to step around us, but Seth whisks forward and gets in Daisy's face.

"I don't know what you're being so cocky about, girl," he says. "Take away that push-up bra, fake tan, dyed hair, and fancy clothes, and all you'd be is a slightly overweight girl with a really bad nose job."

Daisy gasps and covers her nose with her hand. "I didn't get a nose job."

"Whatever you say." He smirks at her, links arms with Callie, and waves to me. "See you later, Kayden."

Callie doesn't look at me as they dart around us and hurry off toward the front entrance of the campus.

Daisy places her hands on her hips and purses her lips. "Why were you talking to that girl?" she asks. "You remember who she is, right?"

"Yeah, she's Callie Lawrence." I shrug and head up the sidewalk. "She was in my grade at school and was really quiet."

"She was also a freak." She laces her fingers through mine and it sends a feeling of numbness through my body. "She's anorexic and used to wear all those baggy clothes. She had that God-awful haircut and never talked to anyone."

"She's not anorexic or a Satan Worshiper." I shake my head. "And she wasn't always like that, nor is she like that any-more. She's pretty normal." And sad. And every time I look at her it rips at my heart. "Besides, she's helped me out with some stuff."

"What kind of stuff?" she questions, giving me a hard stare, like she's about to claw my eyes out. "Are you sleeping with her? Because if you are, that's disgusting and pathetic."

For a second I consider telling her that I am, then stand there and watch her walk away, ridding her from my life. But then what the hell would I do? Date someone else? Date Callie? As much as my mind loves the idea of that—and my dick—she's too good for me and even from the few moments I've spent with her, I've felt everything way too much.

"No, I didn't sleep with her. She's just someone I talk to sometimes," I say, and it's the partial truth, because that's who Callie needs to be to me.

Callie

There's no one else at the library, except for the librarian who's pushing a cart around, putting books back on the shelves. I wonder if she lives alone, has cats—I wonder if she's happy.

"So how much time has to go by before we can talk about what happened?" Seth asks, fanning through the pages of a textbook.

I feel terrible, like a child, only I'm not anymore. I'm a grown woman, in college, yet I reacted like I'm in high school. I hate that crossing paths with someone from my past can throw me back to the darkness and sadness that may always be a part of me.

I shrug, highlighting a note on a page with a bright yellow marker. "What's there to talk about?"

He snatches the marker from my hand and it leaves a yellow streak along the paper. "The fact that you just let that damn bitch walk all over you and the fact that Kayden barely said anything."

"Why would he? He never did before. I'm not his problem." I peek up at the window where a trail of sunlight streams in. "What happened out there was the story of my life. Soon she'll be gone and I won't have to think about her."

He drops the marker onto the table and gazes out at the trees. "What happened with that girl is not okay. You need to grow some confidence and stand up for yourself. Next time she does something like that, pull those tacky extensions out of her hair."

"She wears extensions?" I ask and he nods. I smile, but then shake my head. "If it were the people who tortured you in high school, would you have been able to be so confident?"

"We're not talking about me," he presses with hard eyes.

He shuts his book and crosses his arms on top of it. "We're talking about you."

"I don't want us to talk about me anymore. It's giving me a headache." I collect the marker from the table and put the cap on. "How about we call it a day for studying. There are some other projects I need to work on."

He sighs and gathers his books into a stack, before pushing away from the table. "Fine, but when I get back to my room, I'm adding *Don't take fucking shit from anyone* to the list."

Kayden

It's been a week since I talked to Callie. The last time was during Daisy's random visit that ended in a meaningless fuck and a halfhearted good-bye. I can't tell who's avoiding who when it comes to Callie and I, but the more time we spend apart, the more I think about her.

My mom also made a sporadic stop at my dorm yesterday when she came to visit the town, which is the bullshit lie she uses whenever she's taking a break from her drinking to go to a spa and sober up. She has a thing for painkillers and a whole lot of wine. It has been that way for as long as I can remember, which might be why she never stopped the fights. I tried to tell her once about my dad but she didn't seem too eager to do anything about it.

"Well, you're just going to have to try harder," she had said, taking a sip of her wine. Some of it spilled down the front of her shirt, but she didn't seem to notice. "Sometimes we just have to deal with things the best that we can. It's called life, Kayden. Your dad's a good man. He puts a roof over our heads and gives us more than a lot of guys would. Without him, we'd probably be on the streets."

I stood at the end of the table, clutching my hands into fists. "But I'm trying my hardest and he only seems to get madder."

She turned the page of her magazine and when I looked into her eyes, she seemed like a ghost, absent, as lost as I was. "Kayden, there's nothing I can do. I'm sorry."

I left the room, pissed off, wishing she could be the other person for two damn minutes; the one who hosted parties and charity events and smiled. The one that wasn't a fucking zombie dosed up on pain meds.

⁓

"What the hell is your problem today?" Luke chucks the football down the field near the field post so it's far out of my reach. We're in our uniforms, sweaty, and exhausted, but I can't calm the fuck down.

"Can we please call it a day?" His cheeks are red from underneath his helmet and his shirt is soaked with sweat. "I'm fucking tired. Practice ended two hours ago."

"Yeah, I guess." I kick one of the cones and it dents before flying over toward the bleachers. Kellie and another girl are sitting on the bottom row, with books in front of them, observing us as they talk and pretend to study.

I glance up at the gray sky and around at the bleachers that enclose the field. "How late is it?"

He shrugs as he starts across the green field toward the tunnel that leads to the locker room, taking off his helmet. "I don't know, but it's pretty damn late and I'm done."

I follow after him, but out of the corner of my eye, I see Callie sitting in the grass below a tree at the far end of the field, on the other side of the fence. There are papers spread out in front of her and she's chewing on a pen as she reads over them.

I realize that maybe I'm the one avoiding her because she makes me feel things I'm not used to; the dirty dreams, the protectiveness, the way my stupid heart starts to beat like it's finally alive. Unlatching the strap below my chin, I slip off my helmet as I make my way over to her. She's so absorbed in whatever is written on the papers that she doesn't notice me. Gripping the top of the fence, I swing my legs over it and land on the other side. Adjusting the sleeves of the shirt under my jersey, I stop just a few feet away from her.

Her hair is twisted up in a messy bun and she has a short-sleeve shirt on with a jacket tied around her waist. She stops biting on her pen to examine one of the papers closely but when my shadow casts over her, she glances up and her whole body spasms. For a second, I think she's going to leap to her feet and run off.

She catches her breath and puts her hand over her heaving chest. "You scared me."

"I can tell." I drag my fingers through my damp, sweaty hair and then crouch down in front of her slowly, so I won't scare her again. If I've learned anything, it's that she doesn't like people getting into her personal space without forewarning. "What are you doing out here?"

She looks at the papers and then up at me again. "Homework.... I like hanging out here sometimes." She gazes out at the field with recollection on her face. "It kind of reminds me of when I used to hang out with my dad while he coached."

"I don't remember you ever being there," I say, feeling like a dick again for not remembering her. "How old were you when you did that?"

"I did it for years." She swallows hard and focuses on her papers. "Besides, I can't do my homework in my dorm a lot of the time. My roommate...well, sometimes..." Her cheeks blush and I find myself smiling at how cute she looks, in a really innocent way. She sputters, "She has guys over a lot."

I scratch my nose to stop myself from laughing at her. "I see. So you have to give her the room for a few hours."

She puts a hand on each side of the row of papers and rearranges them together until they form a stack. "Yeah."

I pause and an apology slips from my lips. "I'm sorry."

Her brows knit as she elevates her chin to meet my eyes. "For what?"

"For not telling Daisy to shut her fucking mouth," I say. "I should have. She was being a bitch to you."

She shrugs, staring at the field. "You don't need to stick up for me. She's your girlfriend. You should be on her side."

I kneel down on the grass, getting closer to her. "No, I should have stuck up for you. I owe you that much."

She presses her lips firmly together, returning her attention to me. "You don't owe me anything, I swear. What I did that night wasn't that big of a deal. If I would have walked away from the situation then it would have been a big deal."

I do owe her though, so much. Because of her, I have fewer scars. I wish I could take away whatever makes her look so sad all the time. I set my helmet on the grass and pick up her books for her as she reaches for her bag over by the bottom of the tree trunk. "What are you doing tonight?"

She stuffs her papers into her bag, crinkling the edges, and then I hand her the books. "I'm probably going to just stay in and watch a movie or something."

"How much longer is your room preoccupied?" I ask and smile as her cheeks turn even redder.

"I don't know." She rises on her knees, shifts her bag onto her shoulder, and gets to her feet. "I'll probably just go hang out with Seth until her friend is gone."

I scoop up my helmet and follow her as she heads down the line of the fence. "Why don't you come out with Luke and me? He wants to go check out this club down in the Town

Center. It might end up being a complete shithole, but it's better than just sitting around in your room."

She halts, adjusting the handle of her bag on her shoulder, and bites her bottom lip so hard the skin around her mouth turns purple. "I don't think I can."

"Why?" I ask in a playful tone as I grin at her. "Am I that bad to be around?"

Her arms fall to her sides and her eyes fasten on mine. "No."

I rub the sore muscles on the back of my neck. "Okay, then come with us. It'll be fun and if it's not, we can go do something else."

She balls her hands into fists and then stretches her fingers back out. "Okay."

I'm shocked. I'd been flirting with her out of simple fascination with how she gets flustered, but I didn't think it would work on her. "Okay, meet us at Luke's truck at like nine-ish?"

She nods and turns her back to me, walking away so quickly, it's like she's terrified I'll stab her in the back. She seems afraid of everyone, except for Seth. But why?

Callie

I remember pink and white birthday balloons floating around the room, red streamers hanging from the ceiling, and gold wrapping paper balled up on the floor. The way the flames of the candles danced and the trail of smoke flowed up to the ceiling. My mom on the other side of the table, with a camera in her hand and a smile on her face as she clicked the button over and over again.

The flash hit my eyes and I kept blinking, wishing she'd stop taking pictures that would forever mark this God damn day.

"Make a wish, sweetie," she said and the camera flashed again, lighting up the faces of the people who surrounded the table.

I stared at the pink frosting, the "Happy Birthday Callie." Make a wish?

A red balloon floated over the table, slowly, up and down, up and down.

"Make a wish, Callie," my mom repeated as the balloon moved over her shoulder.

Everyone was watching me, like they could see that I wasn't whole anymore.

Make a wish? Make a wish?

The balloon popped.

There are no such things as wishes.

My roommate, Violet, enters the room as I finish writing the last line. She's tall, with black curly hair streaked with red. Her nose is pierced and she has a tattoo of a star on the back of her neck. She has a pair of plaid pants on, a torn black T-shirt, and combat boots.

"Have you seen my leather jacket?" she asks as she shuts the door and tosses a bag onto her unmade bed.

I close my journal and slide the pen into the spiral. "I haven't."

She sighs as she collects her books from the desk in front of the window. "I think I might have lost it at the club. Fuck."

"I'll keep an eye out for it." I tuck the journal underneath the pillow and get up from the bed.

She opens the drawer of the desk and glances over her shoulder at me as I slip my shoes on. "Are you heading out?"

I nod, easing my arm through the sleeve of a gray hoodie. "I am."

I hear a bottle of pills rattle as she shuts the drawer and holds up a red scarf. "I might have someone over tonight. I'll put this on the doorknob if I do."

Again? What does this girl do? "All right." My fingers wrap around the doorknob. "I'll make sure to check first."

"You better," she says, her hand hovering near the drawer. "Otherwise you're going to see something you don't want to."

Sighing, I walk out the door, wishing I had my own dorm room.

❧

"I think I just got myself in over my head," I tell Seth as he lets me in his room. "Like really bad."

Seth pauses the television screen, sits down on the bed, and pats the spot beside him. "Come sit down and spill your problem."

I let my bag fall to the floor and sink down onto the bed. "Kayden asked me to go to a club with him and Luke tonight, and I accidentally said yes."

"How do you accidentally say yes to something like that?"

I huff out a breath of frustration. "He kept smiling at me and getting me all flustered and I couldn't think straight."

Seth grins and a giggle escapes his lips. "Oh my God, you have a crush on him."

I shake my head, getting flustered just by the thought. "No, I don't."

The mattress curves beneath me as he bounces up and down like a little kid with too much sugar in their system. "Yes, you do. You have your very first crush, Callie. How exciting!"

Still shaking my head, I sit up and smooth my hair away from my forehead. "I don't have a crush on him. Is he good-looking? Of course. And he's known that since we were in third grade." I pause, getting agitated. "And I've had crushes before, just not for a very long time."

"You so have a crush on him." He picks up the remote and turns off the television. "This will be good, and then we can cross number five off on the list."

"I'm not dancing," I argue, cringing. "Dancing equals touching and getting close to people. I just can't do it."

"Yes, you can. You've done it with me like a hundred times," he encourages. "I mean, think about when we first met. You would barely talk to me and you always looked like you were going to stab me with a pencil or something. Now look at you. You're sitting on my bed in my room, just you and I. You've come so far, my little Callie girl."

"But you're you." I sigh, discouraged. "I trust you."

"Yeah, but I had to earn it."

"I know and I'm so sorry for making you do that. I'm surprised you stuck around like you did."

He hops off the bed and opens the top dresser drawer. "Whatever. You were so worth it."

I swing my feet over the edge of the bed. "You seem really happy today."

He takes out a green button-down shirt with a front pocket and holds it out in front of him. "You remember that guy I was telling you about? The one in my Sociology class?"

I nod. "The one with the really soft-looking hair and pretty blue eyes?"

"That's the one." He walks over to the mirror, fussing with his hair as he inches his face closer to the reflection. "He talked to me today and I mean really talked to me for more than five minutes."

I scoot off the bed and pick up a marker from a cup on his nightstand. "Do you think he likes you?"

He shrugs, clamping his jaw shut to keep from smiling. "It's hard to tell who he likes, but maybe if I talk to him more."

I work to get the cap off with my teeth and then spit it out on the bed. "Are you going somewhere?"

He tugs the shirt over his head, wiggling his arms through the sleeves and then rearranges his hair back into place with his fingers. "Yeah, with you to a club."

My shoulders relax as I go over to the board on the back of the door with a very long list drawn on it, with very little numbers crossed off. "Are you going to be okay? I mean,

I know how you feel about football players, considering what happened to you."

He fastens a leather watch to his wrist. "That Luke guy seems pretty nice. At least he was during our ten-minute conversation when we were out smoking and I think he knows about me."

I put the tip of the marker up to the board. "Why would you think that?"

"I just got a vibe," he says. "It seemed like he didn't care."

I scratch off number five very slowly and the marker squeaks. "But I'm only dancing with you."

"Sounds like a great plan to me." He offers me his elbow and I link my arm with his, feeling safe with him by my side as we saunter down the hall to go outside.

It's late, the sky is black, and the stars look like pieces of shimmering glass. Crickets chirp in the damp grass and there's a couple sitting on one of the benches kissing each other fervently. It makes me blush a little because for a split second I picture Kayden and I in their places.

"Why do you have that look on your face?" Seth wonders observantly.

I look away at the road. "What look?"

He sighs, but doesn't press. When we reach the grass, he stops moving his feet and pulls me back, his eyes darting to my face. "Wait a second."

I touch my hair self-consciously. "What's wrong? Do I have something in my hair?"

He slants his head to the side and then his hand snaps out, his fingers snagging my hair. With one swift yank, he's torn the elastic from my hair and strands fall to my shoulders. "There we go. Let that freaking hair of yours down."

I gather my hair behind my head and stick out my hand. "Give me that back, Seth."

Batting his eyelashes, he raises his hand and stretches the elastic on two of his fingers.

"Don't," I warn, lunging for him. "Please, Seth, don't do this."

He flicks his thumb so the elastic flings through the air into the darkness. "Whoops."

I drag my fingers along my face as I hunch over and search the damp grass for the elastic. "Where the fuck is it?"

Seth laughs. "Holy shit, the swear words are coming out."

I stand up and glare at him with rage burning in my eyes as I work to tie the strands of my hair into a knot. "I need to get my hair up. Please help me find it." Tears sting at the corners of my eyes. "God damn it, Seth, where the fuck is it?"

His expression falls and his skin drains of color as he realizes he might have pushed the wrong button. "I don't think we're going to be able to find it."

I shake my head as tears bubble out of my eyes and trail down my cheeks. "I can't breathe," I gasp.

"You're hair smells so good, Callie," he says, twisting a strand of my long brown hair around his finger. "Like strawberries."

My chest constricts as I start to sob. In three short strides, he has his arms encircled around my shoulders and is drawing me into him. "I'm so sorry. I didn't realize the hair thing was that big of a deal. I thought it was more of a complex."

I wipe the tears away with my fingers and suck in a slow breath through my nose to regain control over my fear. "I'm sorry, it's just...it brings back things I don't want to remember."

He leans away and threads his fingers through mine, squeezing my hand. "You'll be okay, I promise. I'll be right by you the whole time."

"Maybe I have time to run back to my room." I glance at the doors, right as Kayden and Luke come strolling around the corner of the dorm building.

Luke is a little smaller than Kayden, with shorter hair, and a face without scars. He has a plaid shirt on, a pair of faded jeans with a black leather belt and boots on his feet. Kayden's hair is tousled with stray pieces hanging in his eyes and he has on a hooded black thermal shirt, with dark jeans that ride extremely low on his hips. I bet when he raises his arms above his head his stomach will show.

"Callie, you're staring," Seth hisses under his breath and prods me in the ribcage with his elbow.

"What?" I blink at him as I wipe the last of the tears away from my cheeks, surprised how calm I've become.

He presses his lips together, containing a smile. "You were staring at a particular someone."

"No, I wasn't," I deny. "Was I?"

He nods his head once and then hisses through his teeth, "You were and your mouth was hanging open."

"Hey," Kayden says and his forehead creases at my tear-stained face. "Were you two just arguing?"

I shake my head and glance at Seth. "No, we were just talking heatedly."

"Okay…" He eyes me with skepticism. "Should we get going?"

Nodding, I step aside so him and Luke can walk between us and lead the way.

Seth pulls his cigarettes out of his pocket and pops one into his mouth as we trail behind them. "Are we riding with them?"

"No." I swing my gaze over to the rusted single-cab truck where no other vehicles are parked. "Not unless they want to ride in your car."

"Well, let's offer to drive then," he says. "And then you can be our DD since you never ever drink. Although, you should try it tonight. It'll probably calm you down."

"I drank a beer that one time," I protest. "And it didn't relax me."

"Oh, my naïve little Callie." He sighs, retrieving his lighter from his pocket. "One beer isn't going to do much to you. You need something with a kick. Something potent."

"We can't drink at the club," I say as he flicks the lighter with his thumb. Cupping his other hand around the flame, he lights the end of the cigarette and the paper burns and crinkles. "Remember what happened the last time you tried that at a club?"

He sucks in a breath, inhaling the smoke, before puffing it out in front of his face. "Yeah, excellent point. Don't want to go back into the holding cell again."

"You're lucky it was your birthday and they let you off the hook."

"I also flirted with one of the officers." He grins as a thin trail of smoke snakes out of his lips.

"So, who wants to sit on whose lap?" Kayden asks with his hand on the open door of the truck. His eyes are on me and there's a hint of amusement on his lips. "Personally, I think there's only one option here."

I point at Seth's black Camry parked a few spots down. "I think we're going to take Seth's car. You guys can ride with us if you want."

Luke tosses the keys up in the air like a baseball and then catches them in his hand. "Sounds good to me. That way, I don't have to be responsible for driving."

I was kind of hoping they wouldn't ride with us so Seth could give me a speech of encouragement and I could put my hair up with something because the way it touches my shoulders and the smell of it is driving me crazy. I have the urge to run back to my room and hack it all off again.

As we walk over to Seth's car, I comb my fingers through my hair trying to get it manageable and out of the way. I reach for the passenger door, but Luke's arm extends out and he opens the door for me. Moving to the side, I elude him like I'm dancing, when really it's just to keep my distance.

"Thank you." I catch Seth's eye over the roof of the car and he arches an eyebrow as we climb in.

Seth slams the door and I jolt in the seat. "Relax, Callie," he whispers as he turns the key and the engine purrs to life. Rolling down the window, he puts his hand outside so the smoke doesn't fill the cab. "You're going to be fine."

Luke and Kayden hop into the backseat from opposite sides of the car and their doors slam simultaneously. Seth turns the stereo on as we buckle our seatbelts. "Hurt" by Nine Inch Nails turns on and he presses on the pedal, ripping the tires against the wet pavement. The car lurches forward and I grab on to the door handle. Seth is a crazy driver. He has a drawer full of tickets and when he was a teenager, his parents took away his car twice, because he kept wrecking it. He always seems to be in a hurry, like he kind of is with life.

Luke leans forward, bracing his hand on the back of my seat, and I angle my head to the side. "Can I smoke in here, man?" he asks Seth.

Seth raises his cigarette, which is burnt almost to the end. "Of course."

A smile curves at Luke's lips as he slumps back in the seat.

Seconds later there's a flick of a lighter, the window rolls down, and a cool breeze blows in.

After Luke gives Seth directions, no one speaks for a while and I worry that the night is going to end in a tragic silence. Then Kayden scoots forward and props his arms on the console.

"Luke and I have this brilliant idea," he says and the glow from the buildings reflects in his eyes. "You remember that rock we climbed up to? The one that all the seniors go and tag?"

I revolve sideways in the seat and bring my leg up onto the leather. "Yes, I remember."

He leans his weight on his arms, slanting even closer to me, and my heart leaps in my chest. "Well, we want to go up there and tag it."

"But you're not seniors." I adjust my seatbelt on my shoulder. "Well, duh, I guess you already knew that."

He laughs at me in an amused tone. "We do know that, which makes it fun."

Luke peeks over the top of the seat with his arm to the side so the trail of smoke is blowing out the window. "We used to crash senior parties all the time back in high school. It was a blast because they weren't too fond of it."

"You liked upsetting them?" I ask and he tilts his head sideways so he won't blow smoke in my face.

"Yeah, it was pretty fun." Luke sticks his cigarette out the window, brushes the pad of his thumb on the bottom, and the ashes blow outside. "To mess with someone's mind instead of being the one messed with."

It's like he's told me an unsolvable riddle and I glance to Kayden for an explanation.

"It is pretty entertaining," he promises me with a wink. "We were thinking we could drive up to the rock and put something on it tonight."

"But it's late." I glance at the bright red numbers on the clock and then at Seth.

"We'll be okay." Seth veers onto a slender side road that squeezes between two-story brick buildings.

There are people walking up and down the sidewalk. Most of the girls are wearing skimpy dresses and high heels, and the guys have on nice jeans and shirts. I look down at my converses, my black skinny jeans, and the fitted white T-shirt beneath my unzipped jacket. I feel underdressed and silly for being here.

Seth turns into a small parking spot and squishes the car into it. It's a tight fit and I have to crack the car door open and maneuver out. Luke rolls down his window, sticks his head out, and putting his hands onto the roof, heaves his body out the open window.

"You're a lot skinnier than I am." He props up on his toes and jumps to the ground. "My dumb ass would have gotten stuck in the door.

Smiling, I walk around to the front of the car where Seth is waiting for me with his elbow extended out. There's a lanky guy with sores on his face and long black hair leaning against a lamppost near the street.

He eyes me as he sips from a beer bottle and when he moves it away from his lips, the look he gives me sends a chill through my body. "Hey there, sexy," he slurs, stepping away from the curb before stumbling right back. "You look fucking fine tonight."

I start to run back to the car, but Seth's fingers enclose around my elbow. "Are you talking to her or me, because I just can't tell," he smarts off to the guy.

The guy's dark eyes turn cold with the need to conquer someone. I've seen that look before and it makes me gag; filling my body with a toxic feeling of revulsion, distrust, and shame.

The drunken man shifts his body forward and wobbles toward us. "I'm gonna fucking kick your ass for that."

I jerk on Seth's arm, ready to run, jump into the car, lock all the doors, and cower on the floor. "Please let's just go back to the car, Seth."

Kayden steps up beside us, his fingers brushing up the inside of my arm, and the man's eyes rise to meet his. His shoulders stiffen as he halts, his shoes scuffing against the gravel on the sidewalk.

"Shut your fucking drunken mouth, turn around, and go home," Kayden orders calmly pointing his finger down the street.

The man's chapped lips part, but then he fastens his jaw

shut as he takes in the sight of Kayden's broad shoulders and height. He tosses the beer bottle out into the street where it shatters into pieces across the asphalt and then he drags his feet as he staggers toward the corner.

Seth and I blow out a breath of relief, our eyes wide as we stare at each other in shock.

Seth turns to Kayden. "You're like a knight in shining armor."

I catch a faint hint of Kayden's musky scent mixed with cologne. From now on, whenever I smell it I'll come back to this moment when I felt protected. "Thank you," I tell him.

He smiles, leaning down so his face is near mine. "You're welcome."

We head up the sidewalk with Seth and me in the front and Luke and Kayden in the back. Luke keeps whispering to Kayden and then suddenly we hear a grunt. When I turn around, Luke is hunched over, cradling his gut.

"You fucking asshole," he growls and he collapses onto his knees.

My eyes bulge as Luke stands up straight and prowls toward Kayden, raising his fists. Kayden does nothing but stand there with a stoic look on his face.

"Oh my God!" I cry, instinctively stepping for him as the memories of that night when his father beat the shit out of him surface.

Luke surrenders his hands out in front of him and steps back from Kayden. "Callie, I was just messing with him."

"Oh, I'm sorry." I cover my hand over my mouth, feeling

like an idiot. The drunken man has put my nerves up way too high.

Kayden shoots a piercing look at Luke as he edges toward me. "It's okay," he says cautiously. "Luke was just giving me a hard time about something so I hit him in the stomach as a joke. The whole thing was a joke."

I free a breath imprisoned in my chest. "Okay, I'm sorry. I just thought he was going to hurt you."

"You don't need to be sorry." He glances at Seth then back at me and his shoulder shifts forward as he wraps an arm around my shoulder.

I tense from the rush of his touch and the fear of it. It feels so much more personal than when we were climbing up the cliff, because there's no point to it except to touch each other.

I look to Seth for help, but he mouths, *Relax and breathe.*

I order my erratic heart to shut the hell up and even though it doesn't listen, I manage to make it all the way to the door of the club with Kayden's arm around my shoulder. It's something new, fresh, and raw. While being insignificant, it's momentous and a contradiction in itself.

Kayden

Callie is the most skittish person I've ever met, which says a lot since every time my dad would raise his voice, my brothers and I would scatter around the house and hide while we were being hunted.

Luke was giving me shit about checking out her ass, which I was, but I couldn't help it. She's so tiny and the way she swings her hips is captivating and kind of sexy, although she's probably not doing it on purpose.

"You're going to get yourself into a lot of trouble," Luke remarks as we walk just a ways behind them.

I transfer my gaze off Callie's ass and scowl at Luke. "Why?"

He points a finger at Callie with an accusing look on his face. "Because of her right there. Do you know what Daisy would do if you ever cheated on her?"

"Move on to the next guy that told her she had nice tits." I stuff my hands into my pockets and step around a pole.

"Okay, you're probably right on that one," he says and aims his finger at Callie again. "But do you know what Daisy would do to Callie if she ever found out there was something going on between you two?"

"There's nothing going on between us."

"Yet."

I shake my head, frustrated. "She's not like that. She's sweet and...innocent."

"That's a dangerous combination for someone like you." He reaches for the pack of cigarettes in his front pocket. "I'm totally rooting that you find someone else, because I fucking hate Daisy. Just break up with her first and don't bring Callie into it. She seems sad." He swallows hard. "She kind of reminds me of Amy."

Amy is Luke's older sister, who took her own life at the age of sixteen. He was never the same after her death. I wonder what happened to bring Amy to the bottom, what made her want her life to be over.

"I promise I'm not going to bring Callie into anything." I kick an empty cup across the road.

"Just think with your head." He smirks. "And not with your dick."

I swing my arm out to my side and my elbow smashes into his gut, hard enough that it'll annoy him, but not hurt him. "I'm not breaking up with her and there's nothing going on between Callie and me."

He lets out a grunt as he clutches his stomach. I'm about ready to laugh at him when Callie spins around looking terrified. I feel like an asshole. It only gets worse when Luke charges at me, and she just about jumps in between us. I question if she was thinking back to that night that she saved me or if she's the kind of girl that just wants to save everyone.

I want to comfort her so I do something I shouldn't. I put an arm around her shoulder and her muscles constrict so tightly that I worry she's going to crumble to the ground. It's different from the cliff because there are no excuses, yet she lets me hold her like that until we get into the club, then she quickly steps away as the music and smoke engulf us.

"It's so loud in here," she remarks, as she gapes at the people dancing in the middle of the room, writhing their hips, and pressing their sweaty bodies together. Neon lights flash across their horny faces and it's practically like watching porn.

It's a little much even for Luke and me, but we still go search the room for a vacant table, pushing our way through the mob of people. Seth and Luke instantly light up once we're settled in a corner booth.

"I'll go get the drinks," Luke says sliding toward the end of the seat. "Since I'm the only one with an ID, unless you have yours on you."

"I told you my dad found it while we were packing up my stuff." I pick up the menu that's in the middle of the table. "He cut it up."

From across the table, Callie peers up at me. I flip open my menu to avoid her penetrating gaze. "What do we want to order? Should we get an appetizer or something?"

"I have to use the little girls' room," Seth announces and Callie giggles at him. "Come with me, Callie."

She takes his hand and follows him without even questioning. It leaves me scratching my head. She trusts him so much and everyone else so little. For a brief moment, I picture what it would be like for someone like her to trust me, but I have too many twisted secrets locked away inside me for that to ever happen.

Callie

"Holy Jesus." Once we're inside the restroom, Seth whirls around and places his hands on his hips. "That was ridiculously sexy."

I turn on the faucet and place my hands underneath the warm water. "What was?"

He walks up beside me, capturing my gaze as he clears his throat accusingly. "The way he stepped up to save us."

I shut off the water and wave my hand in front of the paper towel device. "It was very nice of him."

"Callie Lawrence, you let him put his arm around you," he states. "It was more than nice for you. God, I'm so jealous."

I grab a paper towel and run it along my hands. "He made me feel safe for a minute," I admit, tossing the towel into the trashcan.

"And that's a big step for you," he says.

I nod my head an excessive amount of times. "I know it is."

His lips spread to a massive grin. "Should we go out and have some fun?"

One of the stall doors swings open and a fortyish-year-old woman walks out tucking her shirt into her jeans. Her heavy lined eyes land on Seth. "This is the women's restroom." She points a finger at the door. "Can't you read?"

"Can't you see that everyone in this club is about twenty years younger than you?" Seth retorts, turning to the mirror.

With his pinkie, he messes with his bangs. "Now if you'll excuse us, we're going to have some fun."

He grabs my arm and I offer the woman an apologetic smile before stumbling over my own feet as I hurry to keep up with Seth. He bangs his hand against the door and shoves it open, moving us to the outside. The smoke and noise instantly shatter around me as his fingers leave my arm.

"Can you believe her," he says, patting his pocket for his cigarettes. "What a bitch!"

I don't argue with him. He has a thing with being treated as an equal. "I think you left your cigarettes at the table," I tell him.

We wind our way around the dance floor where an erotic song is playing. People have their hands all over each other, skin to skin, and watching it gives me a headache.

At the table, there are four shot glasses filled with clear liquid. Alongside each shot is a taller cup full of a brownish liquid with a lemon slice floating on the top.

"I didn't know what everyone wanted to drink," Luke explains as Seth lifts the shot to eye level and peers through the distorted glass. "So I just ordered vodka shots and Long Island Iced Teas. So we have intense and semi-intense."

Seth glances at me from the corner of his eyes. "Looks good to me." He raises the shot glass in the air. "Should we make a toast?"

I direct my attention to the dance floor so I won't be

scrutinized and watch a girl jump up and down with her arms in the air, trying to maintain her balance in the neon pink stilettoes on her feet. The guy she's with is shaking his head at her, laughing.

"Callie, did you hear what Luke asked you?" Seth's concerned voice flows over my shoulder.

Ripping my gaze away from the dance floor, I concentrate on Seth's bloodshot eyes and the small glass in his hand. "No, what?"

"He wanted to know if you were going to join us?" he asks with pressing eyes.

I shake my head. "I don't think so."

Luke smacks his hand on the table and the vibration tips over the salt and pepper shakers. "There's an unwritten rule that you have to make a toast if it's proposed."

I stand the shakers back up and sweep the spilt salt off the table. "Someone has to drive us all home."

"We'll get a cab," Luke proposes. "Easy fix."

I stare at the alcohol in front of me, wondering what the big deal is with the stuff, because with the beer I felt nothing. "But then you can't go spray paint the rock."

Kayden targets a warning at Luke. "Just let her be, okay? If she doesn't want to, then she doesn't have to."

Setting the glass down, Seth chimes in. "We can have the cabdriver drop us off and pick us up later." He leans over and cups his hand around my ear. "If you want to, then just do it.

Pick up the glass and have some fun for once in your life, but if you really don't, then shake your head."

My hair is down, I let Kayden touch me, and I'm sitting in a place bursting with sexual tension. It's the most challenging night I've had in terms of facing my fears, so I wrap my fingers around the glass and lift it up in front of me.

"What the hell," I say over the music. "We'll get a cab."

Seth claps his hands and scoops up the shot. "Hell yeah!"

Kayden laughs at Seth and then inclines over the table toward me. "Are you sure you're good? You don't have to."

I nod with assurance. "I'm okay. I promise"

Seth levels his arm so his glass is just above the center of the table, right below the domed light. "Bottoms up."

Luke puts his hand up, and Kayden and I follow.

"Shouldn't someone say something like meaningful or something?" Seth asks. "That's what toasts are for."

Luke cocks his head to the side, tapping his fingers on the table. "To getting away."

Seth grins at me. "To acceptance."

Kayden bites at his bottom lip with his eyelids lowered. "To feeling alive."

The three of them fasten their eyes on me and I glance to Seth for help.

"This is your thing, Callie," he tells me. "Whatever you want to say, just say it."

I suck in a breath and release it out gradually. "To being able to breathe."

There's a moment that passes between Kayden and me as our expressions match. Then the four of us clink glasses.

"Fuck." Seth spills some of his on his hand and he licks it off. Tipping his head back, he pours the shot into his mouth. Then he slams the glass down and points at it. "I'm already ready for round two."

Kayden watches me as he moves the glass to his lips, arches his neck back, and gulps it down. I observe his neck muscles as they move to force the alcohol down. He lifts his head back up and licks his lips with his gaze attached to mine.

Inhaling deeply, I position the rim to my mouth, and the stench burns my nose as I let my head fall back and suck out the drink. The hot liquid spills down my throat and the heat is almost unbearable. As I bring the glass away from my mouth, my gag reflex kicks in and I choke on the burn, but keep my lips sealed, forcing the alcohol down. My shoulders heave as a strangled sound bursts from my lips.

"Are you gonna make it?" Luke wonders, setting his glass down on the table.

Seth gives me a gentle pat on the back. "Are you okay?"

"Yeah, I'm fine," I choke, with my palm pressed to my chest.

"Callie is a newbie," Seth explains as he takes a swallow of the Long Island Iced Tea.

"You've never drank before?" Kayden gapes at me. "Really?"

I feel stupid as I shrug my shoulders. "No, nothing this hard anyway."

"Then why did you do it tonight?" he asks, looking guilty. "Did we pressure you too much?"

"No, I wanted to try it." I wipe my lips with the back of my hand.

His eyebrows furrow and a hint of a smile curves at his lips. "Was it on your list?"

"What?" Seth exclaims over the loud music, slamming his hand on the table. "You told him about the list?"

"I told him *of* the list," I explain, stirring the straw around in my drink, watching the lemon go around and around. When I peek up through my hair, Kayden is observing me curiously.

"What list?" Luke wraps his lips around the straw and sips his drink.

Seth and I trade a glance and then he shoos me with his hands to move off the seat. "How about you and I go dance?"

"All right, I'm in. Just don't do any of those weird moves again. Last time I fell on my butt." I adjust my shirt over my stomach as I get to my feet.

Laying a hand on the small of my back, Seth steers us toward the dance floor. He's done this a couple of times with me, so he understands what he's in store for; lots of panicking and a whole lot of clinginess.

He selects a section at the side of the dance floor where there are less people and the atmosphere is mellower. A slow song plays from the speakers and the lights stop flickering and settle to a pale glow. Seth looks ghostly white underneath them and his honey-brown eyes look black as he puts his hands on my hips.

"I'm sorry if I pushed you too hard, baby girl," he whispers. "I feel bad."

I reach for his shoulders and step closer to him so the tips of our shoes are touching. "You didn't pressure me, although, you could have warned me that it was going to burn that bad. Then I would have tried harder not to choke and not look like a complete moron."

"Trust me, neither of them think you're a moron." He laughs, like he knows a secret. "I don't want to lose all that trust I've earned with you."

"You didn't lose anything." I squeeze his shoulders with my fingertips, inching in as a guy in a fedora rams into my back. "The day you told me all your secrets was the day I knew we'd be friends forever. You're the bravest person I've ever known."

He smiles brightly and draws me closer. "Are you feeling okay?"

"I feel fine," I tell him and rest my cheek against his. "Although, I'm a little iffy on going up to the cliff with them."

"People go up there all the time. We won't be the only ones there. You need to stop thinking of every guy as being like *him*, otherwise, he'll always own you."

I blow out a breath. He's right. I need to let go of my fears

115

and rid my brain of the guy who instilled them, but how can I let go of the one person who holds such a huge part of me?

Kayden

I can't take my eyes off the dance floor. Even when my phone vibrates from inside my pocket, I slip my hand into it and press the off button on the side.

"Don't do it." Luke plucks a piece of ice out of his drink and pops it in his mouth.

"Do what?" I ask, distracted as my heart thumps when Callie throws back her head and laughs.

A hand knocks against the side of my head and my hand shoots up. "Okay, what the fuck was that for?"

"That's payback for when you hit me back on the curb," he says and his eyes roam to a girl with long red hair strutting by our table in a short black dress. "And it was also to distract you from doing something really stupid."

"It's not what you think," I say. "I was just watching people dance."

He rolls his eyes. "Do everyone a favor and send Daisy a text to break up with her. Then you can do whatever you want."

"You want me to break up with her in a text?"

"Like you care. You don't care about her even though you tell her you love her."

"What is your problem with her, besides the fact that she annoys the shit out of you?"

He tosses his straw onto the table, grabs the cup, and pours the rest of the Long Island Iced Tea down his throat. "I'm going to go buy another round."

I let him out, and then start to lower myself back into the booth, but my eyes find Callie again. She's smiling as she talks to Seth. I've never been that happy before about anything. It makes no sense to me and maybe that's why I'm drawn to her.

Even though I shouldn't, I move across the dance floor, turning sideways to fit through the couples dancing, and getting rubbed on by a couple of girls along the way. Seth's eyes locate me first and he whispers something into Callie's ear.

Turning her head, she looks at me and her eyelids lift slightly. Her pupils look huge below the hazy lights, her skin pale, and her hair soft.

"Mind if I cut in?" I ask over the music.

Seth lets go of her hips. "Be my guest." He winks at Callie and walks backward off the dance floor, turning as he arrives at the edge, where the crowd closes in.

Callie's gaze lingers in the spot he vanished from, her shoulders stiff and her fingers tucked into her palms.

I put my lips beside her ear. "You don't have to dance with me, if you don't want to."

Her shoulders jolt upward and she rotates her tiny body to face me. Her gaze scrolls up my legs, my stomach, and it makes

me kind of uncomfortable. She knows where my scars are hidden and she's the kind of person who wonders things.

"It's fine. We can dance." Her nerves show through the shakiness of her voice.

I hold out my hand and she wavers before placing her palm on top of mine. Enclosing my fingers around her hand, I slowly lure her body toward mine with my eyes fixed on hers. She's looking at me helplessly, like she's praying I won't hurt her. It takes me back to a time when I was younger and my father was furious with me because I'd knocked a vase off the shelf. He came at me with a belt in his hand and rage in his eyes as I dove under the table trying to hide. The cuts from the previous day's beating hadn't healed yet, and all I could do was hope he didn't kill me.

"Can I put my hand on your hip?" I ask and she nods.

I spread my fingers around her waist and her eyes get a little wider, especially when I position my other hand on her side. I listen to my heart thud inside my chest, louder than the music. I'm feeling things I haven't felt before and I might be getting in over my head. What if I continue to get to know her and the feelings amplify? I don't deal with feelings.

She unwinds a little as her hands glide up my chest and hook around my neck, her head angling back so she can look up at me.

"I don't really like to dance," I admit. "I kind of developed a fear of it when I was little."

Her lips twitch upward. "Why's that?"

Digging my fingertips gently into her hips, I draw her toward me so our feet touch and I feel the heat of her breath on my neck. "When I was ten, my mom went through this dance faze where she took all kinds of dance classes and when she practiced at home, she liked to use my brothers and I as her partners. I've hated dancing ever since."

She smiles. "That's cute that you danced around with your mom."

My fingers inch around her back and graze the sliver of skin between the top of her jeans and the bottom of her shirt. "You can't tell anyone that. I have a reputation to uphold. At least I did back home. Here I'm not so sure."

Her smile expands as her head tips forward and pieces of her hair veil her face. "It can be our little secret."

I laugh softly as she looks back up at me. She seems happy. As the music shifts to an upbeat rhythm, I decide to show off, just to keep her smiling.

"Hold on," I warn.

She bites down on her lip, and the urge to kiss her compresses at my heart. Suddenly, I can't decide whether to leave her there on the dance floor, or continue to show off.

Shoving her away, I glide my hand up her arm until our fingers interlace. Her eyes widen as I yank her back toward me and twist her around, before colliding her body into mine. Her lips are inches away from my mouth as her heaving chest brushes against mine.

"Do you want more?" I ask in a low voice, hoping to make her shiver.

She doesn't shiver, but she nods with excitement gleaming in her blue eyes. My palm slides down her back possessively, feeling the heat of her skin emitting through the thin fabric of her shirt. I pull her hand forward and tip her body backward. Her hair dangles to the floor, her back arches, and I have the perfect view of her tits and the sliver of skin peeking out from the bottom of her top. Taking a deep breath, I glide my hand up her back, until she's standing upright with her chest pressed against mine again.

"Don't tell anyone about that either," I whisper in her ear with my arms around her waist.

"Okay," she says, breathless, her fingers gripping my shoulder blades.

I continue moving with her in my arms until the end of the song, and then we let go of one another and go back to the table as if nothing happened. Something did, though, but I'm not sure whether to pursue it or run like hell.

Chapter Five

#3: ~~Try to be Happy.~~
#3: Be Stupidly, Drunk Happy.

Callie

I'm happy, like stupidly happy. I don't know if it's because I have a buzz or because it has been a good night. I've accomplished what I thought was impossible and I am so proud of myself that I practically skip to the cab. I danced with Kayden, let him touch me in a way no one ever has—at least with my permission—and I liked it!

Seth and I take the backseat in the van and Kayden tells the cabdriver where to go. The inside smells like old cheese overlapped with a pine scent. The cabdriver is a round guy in his fifties who doesn't look that thrilled to have four loud eighteen-year-olds in the car. There is some eighties music playing in the background and Seth keeps giggling about the lyrics, telling me they are secretly dirty and talking about pussy.

121

Luke overhears him and rotates around in his seat. "Is it really talking about that?"

Seth points at the speakers. "Listen to them."

We sit quietly, staring at the speaker, listening to the lyrics. Seth balls his hand into a fist and puts it up to his lips like a microphone as he begins mouthing the words.

"How do you know this song?" I wonder. "It's not the kind of music that you listen to."

He grins, leaning in, finishing out the lyrics. "My dad is a total eighties freak. He has the mullet and everything."

I giggle as he does this weird jiving movement with his hips.

"It is talking about pussy, isn't it?" Luke declares and the cabdriver cranks up the stereo to muffle out our conversation.

My cheeks heat and I turn my head toward the window, pulling the top of my shirt over my nose to hide my laughing. I shouldn't think it's funny, but I do.

"Oh, Callie's drunk," Seth announces as he lets his hands fall to his lap. "Did you finish off the Long Island Iced Tea?"

I shake my head and let my shirt fall off my nose. "Only half."

"Lightweight," Kayden teases me with a grin and my blush magnifies.

"Hey, it's her first time," Seth protests in my defense, patting my head like I'm a dog. "She did good. In fact, she did great."

I turn toward the window, knowing what he means, and loving him for saying it.

❧

"I feel like we're going to get robbed," Seth whispers as we head toward a store that is located near the foothills of the mountains. We decided to stop and get some flashlights and spray paint before proceeding with our plan, otherwise, it'd be a pointless journey.

There's a group of guys in front smoking cigarettes. They watch the four of us walk across the parking lot, through the sliding glass doors, and into the store.

"Everything's supposed to be a dollar in here." Luke grabs a shot glass on a display just in front of the doors and peers at the bottom. A piece of glass falls from the rim and he hastily sets it down. "Yeah, I can see why."

There's some funky music playing from the ceiling and Seth bobs his head as he walks to a shelf and picks up a hideous orange and brown scarf.

"Oh, I think I remember my grandma wearing something like this." He shawls it around his neck and skips up the aisle, examining the shelves.

"We should split up," Luke states. "And look for flashlights and spray paint. It'll make it faster."

"Or we could just ask the cashier for some help." I peek over my shoulder at a register where a tall, thick-necked guy with the hardest look on his face watches us. "Or not."

"Let's make it a race," Kayden announces, jumping up to

slam his hand against one of the red sale banners on the ceiling. I can't tell if he's drunk, because I don't know him well enough, but he seems a little off balance. "First person to find the stuff is the winner."

"That's a fantastic fucking prize," Luke remarks sarcastically, peering down an aisle. "How about loser has to buy drinks the next time we're out."

"Sounds like a plan to me." Seth joins us, untying the scarf and tossing it aside on the shelf. "I say we do this."

Kayden and Luke raise their hands above my head to high-five each other and then aim their palms at me. I gently tap my palms against theirs and Kayden laughs at me as my arms fall to my sides.

"What's so funny?" I wonder, but he just shakes his head.

"All right, so here are the rules." Luke marches back and forth in front of us like he's a director. "The rules are that there are none except to be the first one up to the checkout stand with four flashlights and a can of paint. Last one up there is a loser."

I try not to laugh. Is this what people do to have fun?

Luke stops walking and his eyes darken. "Ready, set, go." He says it quickly and then sprints off down the main aisle, his boots skidding against the linoleum before any of us can react.

Seth skitters down one of the side aisles and Kayden dashes down the one to my right. I'm left standing in the main aisle alone. I begin to walk up it, swinging my arms and reading the signs above each row.

When I reach the third one, Kayden crosses the other end and then backs up, smiling at me.

"You're not trying very hard," he says. "In fact, it looks like you're not trying at all."

I point above my head at the aisle number sign with the list of items. "I'm trying for a different approach other than running around looking like a lunatic."

He faces me and cups his hands unnecessarily around his mouth. "Now what's the fun in that?"

I giggle. "I don't know."

He moves his hand to his ear. "Huh? I can't hear you. You're going to have to speak up."

Feeling silly, I cup my hands around my mouth. "I said, I don't know."

He lowers his hands, still smiling. "Come on. You run down that side and I'll run down this one. Let's see who can beat the other one to the end."

I shake my head. "No way. You'll win. You're the football player. You run around all the time."

He considers what I said and then snatches a roll of paper towels off the shelf. "I throw more than I run." He backs up, raises the paper towel roll over his shoulder, and then flings it in my direction. It spins through the air right for me.

I stick out my arms and catch it effortlessly. His arms drop to his side as he gapes at me. "Well, someone has a hidden talent."

I lift the paper towel roll over my shoulder and throw it

back at him. "My dad *is* a coach." He catches it and slants his head, looking at me with interest as I continue, "I started playing catch with him and my brother when I was like three."

Keeping his eyes on me, he returns the roll of paper towels to the shelf. "All right, let's see how you can run." He darts to the side and disappears behind the shelf.

I sidestep, moving to the next aisle, where he's waiting at the other end. Before I can say anything, he hurries out of my view again and I take a couple of rushed steps until I'm at the end of the next aisle. He's not there, so I practically run to the next one, catching him right as he's taking off again. I start running as laughter escapes my lips. Every time I reach the end of the aisle, he's vanishing to the other side. Finally, I spot the paint aisle and make a hurried turn down it, just as Kayden appears at the other end.

We both stop and glance at the spray paint on the bottom row in the middle of the aisle.

"Seems like we've run into a bit of a problem," he says, a little winded as he meets my eyes.

My gaze skims back and forth between him and the paint, and then I sprint off toward the paint. His shoes squeak against the floor as he runs down the aisle. We arrive at the section at the same time and crash into the shelf, inadvertently knocking off a bunch of cans. I laugh as my feet stumble over the cans rolling over the floor and grab on to the shelf as I lose my balance.

"No way." Kayden's long fingers wrap around my wrist as he pulls my hand away. "You're so not winning this."

I reach toward the shelf, but he captures my hand and pulls me toward him. I twist my arms trying to get away without laughing and my foot stomps down on the floor. There's a hiss as green paint sprays over the white linoleum and my shoe.

I freeze, my eyes widening at the mess on the floor. "Oh my God."

Kayden's lips press together as he tries really hard not to laugh at me. "That was your own fault."

"It's not funny." I bend my knee and raise my foot up. "What am I supposed to do?"

He sets the can in his hand down on the shelf and inches around the mess on the floor. His fingers link with mine as he tows me toward the end of the aisle.

"Okay," he says, peeking around the corner. "We're going to walk out of here like nothing happened."

I look back at the paint and the green footprints my shoe left on the floor. "I'm leaving a mess all over the floor."

"Take your shoe off, then."

I slip my hand out of his, noting how sweaty my skin is, and wiggle my foot out of the sneaker. Picking it up by the shoelace, I hold it behind my back and we walk out of the aisle side by side.

Seth and Luke are near the checkout stand, looking at the candy section, with a can of paint and flashlights in their hands.

"Where are you two going?" Luke asks and one of the flashlights falls from his arms onto the floor.

The cashier guy surveys us like a hawk as we hurry toward the doors.

Seth turns away from the candy, following us with his eyes. "Why does Callie only have one shoe on?"

"We're going out to the car," Kayden says with a wave. "See you out there."

We take long strides toward the doors and rush out into the night, laughing our asses off. The cement is cold through my sock and I quickly put my shoe back on. The black fabric is speckled with green paint. I try to wipe it off by dragging my shoe along the ground, but it's not working very well.

Kayden watches me with amusement. "I don't think it's going to come off."

I frown at my shoe. "Man, these were my favorite pair."

He glides the door of the taxi open, we hop in, and the cabdriver shoots us an annoyed look. I scoot into the back and Kayden slams the door as he sinks down beside me.

He rests his hands on his knees as he looks at me through the dark. "You know Luke is going to call it a tie and make us both pay for drinks the next time we go out."

"That's not too bad," I say. "Then, at least, it's half the money."

He drapes his arm over the back of the seat and pulls his leg up. "Nah, he'll just order more drinks."

I attempt to focus on anything else other than the fact that his knee is touching the side of my leg. "Oh yeah?"

He nods and his eyes travel up to the front seat. "Yeah, so be prepared."

I stare out the window at the dark lines of the mountains. It catches up with me. The night. The easiness. Everything. My mind drifts to thoughts I didn't know existed, like what his lips taste like, and how his muscles would feel under my fingertips.

"Callie."

I glance at Kayden, blinking my thoughts away. "Yeah?"

His gaze flickers to my lips as his mouth opens, but then he cinches his jaw shut and a slow smile curves up on his lips. "That was fun."

I smile back at him. "You know what? It really was."

❧

"It is so fucking dark out here," Seth complains as we hike up the road. "And dirty."

Luke has his flashlight in front of him. Seth dropped his almost the moment we got out of the cab and mine was a dud, so we are down to two.

The cab is waiting at the bottom of the path. The driver said we have twenty minutes before he leaves without us. He didn't like that we made him drive up to a mountain area where there is obviously an illegal party going on.

"It's the mountains," Kayden says to Seth, sweeping his flashlight from side to side. "What did you expect?"

The rocks crunch under my shoes as I hold on to Seth's arm. The air is a little bit chilly and there's lightning zapping across the sky.

When we arrive at the bottom of the rock, Luke hands me the flashlight and shakes the paint can. "So, who is the bastard who gets to climb up there? It's not that far, but I'm pretty wasted."

Seth sticks his hand in the air dramatically. "Well, since I really am a bastard, I'll do it."

I shine the light at his face and he has the deer-in-the-headlights look in his eyes, surprised I didn't know this about him. "I thought you said your dad listens to eighties rock and has a mullet?"

"My stepfather," he clarifies and extends his hand toward Luke. "Give me the can. I would love to put my two cents down on that rock."

Luke drops the can into his hand. "It's all yours, buddy."

Shaking the can, Seth strolls up to the steep rock that inclines up to the flashing gray sky. Propping his boot on a lower rock, he bounces up, grabbing on to a small lip on the side. He shifts his other foot onto the next rocky step, so both his feet are on the cliff. Tucking the spray can under his arm, he puts his other hand on the ledge and hoists himself onto it. Rolling onto his back, he stands up.

I beam the light at his back as he stares up at the rock. "Are you okay up there?"

He peers over his shoulder. "I'm just thinking of some- thing infamous to write. Oh wait, I got it." Lifting the can up, he holds down the nozzle and begins to move his hand in swirls and circles. Red paint slowly stains the rock, forming letters until it's finished and then he lowers his hand.

"You can suck it," I read his words, shivering from the cold as goose bumps dot my arms. "That's what you're going to write?"

He turns around with his hands on his hips. "It's what I already wrote, and if you want something better, then you can drag that tiny little ass of yours up here and write it yourself. You're the writer."

Kayden spins toward me, his hair nearly black in the pale light of the moon. He aims the light between our feet. "You write?"

I shrug, aiming the flashlight over his shoulder. "In a journal."

He's intrigued by this information for some bizarre reason. "I can actually see that about you."

I run my hand up and down my arm, trying to erase the goose bumps. "Why?"

He shrugs, kicking the toes of his shoes at the dirt. "You always look like you're thinking deeply...Are you cold?"

"I'm okay," I say through chattering teeth, wishing I hadn't left my jacket in the cab. "It's just a little bit chilly."

He reaches around to the back of his neck and pulls the

collar of his shirt over his head, taking it off. The black T-shirt he has on underneath rides up a little and I catch a glimpse of the jagged scars on his lower abs.

Tugging down the bottom of his shirt, he stretches his arm out to me with his thermal shirt in his hand. "Here, put this on."

"You don't have to give me your shirt."

"But I want to."

Hesitantly, I take it and the fabric is soft against my fingertips. I pull it over my head as Kayden runs his hands through his hair. The shirt dwarfs me and I feel small.

"Better?" he asks as I insert my arms through the sleeves.

I nod, wrapping my arms around myself, enjoying the warmth, and the smell of his cologne. "Thank you, but aren't you going to get cold?"

He smiles like he finds me amusing. "I'll be okay, Callie. I promise. A little cold air is nothing."

"Callie!" Seth hollers and I jump, whirling toward the cliff with the flashlight darting across the rocks. "Get your ass up here and write something poetic."

I sigh and trudge toward the cliff with the light pointing just in front of my feet. The circle of light shows the way around the rocks and to the base of the cliff.

"Toss me your flashlight," Seth yells with his hands around his mouth. "I'll point it at you while you climb up."

"If you miss it, it'll break," I call out, standing up on my tiptoes.

"Just do it," he says in his silly, drunk voice as he skips from side to side on the ledge, swinging his arms.

I'm worried he's going to fall. "Be careful!"

Kayden moves up beside me with his hand held out to the side. "Here give it to me. I'm an excellent thrower." I put the flashlight in his palm and he tips his shoulder back, raising his arm. "Go long."

"Huh?" Seth says as Kayden's arm whips forward. He releases the flashlight and it soars through the air like it's a football.

Seth screeches as he sticks his hands out in front of him to catch the flashlight, which flickers like a firefly as it lands in his hands. It bounces out of them, hitting the ground and shuts off.

"Where is he?" I ask as Luke comes up behind us and beams the light at the rock above. It's silent for a moment. The yells and laughter of the party below travel up to us.

Seth pops up from the rock, stretching his arm in the air with the flashlight in his hand. "I got it."

"Maybe you should come down," I advise. "I'm worried you're going to fall."

"Only after you tag the rock." He flips on the flashlight and the glow illuminates across the writing behind him. "Now come on."

I trek up to the rock, roll up the sleeves on Kayden's shirt, and place my hands onto the nearest ridge. Tilting my chin, I look up at the top as I bend my knee and brace it on a lower rock. Bouncing up and down on my toes, I prepare to climb up, but I hear someone move up behind me.

"Let me help you," Kayden whispers in my ear, and for the first time in my life I actually shiver from the nearness of a guy.

"Okay." Since I've never been drunk before, I'm not sure if it's the alcohol relaxing me or what, but even when he places his hands onto my hips, I'm okay. In fact, I'm more than okay.

With the guidance of his hands, I stretch my body out and reach up to the next ledge. The rock is rough like sandpaper against my palms as I drag myself up and Kayden's hands slide down my back as he pushes me higher. Swinging my leg up, he gives me one last shove by cupping my butt, before pulling away.

My eyes widen as I roll on top of the ledge and stare up at the sky. The spots on my skin where he touched me tingle and a shiver courses through my body.

Seth appears above me, the silver bolts of lightning reflecting in his eyes. "Are you okay?"

I flip over onto my stomach and use my hands to push myself to my feet. "I'm okay. No scrapes or cuts."

He beams the flashlight below his chin. It illuminates his face and causes his eyes to look like coals. "I wasn't talking about the climb. I was talking about the fact that he just grabbed your ass."

"You saw that?"

"Of course I saw that. He basically just groped you."

I place my hands on my hips and pace the length of the narrow cliff, kicking up dirt with the bottom of my sneakers. "I'm okay. Really. In fact, I feel more than okay."

"I think that might be the alcohol talking." Seth holds out the spray can.

"You think?" I take it from him and shake it.

He nods guiltily. "I think just a little bit. I just hope you don't have an *oh my God* moment when you wake up tomorrow morning."

"I'll be okay. This is the most fun I've had in a very long time." Walking toward the rock, I consider what to write. I read along the vague words of wisdom others have written and the declarations of love.

"Jesus, it's high up here," Luke declares as he hoists himself over the edge. He gets to his feet and peers over the cliff, popping his knuckles. "I'm not a fan of heights."

"Me neither," I tell him as Kayden ascends over the top, dragging himself up with his arms, and then he lies on his stomach. Panting, he rolls onto his back. "Yeah, I remember," he says, turning his head toward me and grinning.

I target the nozzle at a bare spot on the rock. As I press down on the top, I pretend I'm an artist tracing the most beautiful painting, the lines blending together to put everything into meaning. When I'm finished, I step back, breathing in the air, which is potent with paint fumes.

Kayden moves up next to me and drapes his arm around

my shoulder. *"In the existence of our lives, there is a single coincidence that brings us together and for a moment, our hearts beat as one."* He looks at me. "I'm impressed."

I hand him the paint can and his fingers graze my knuckles. "I actually wrote that a while ago." I lower my voice and lean in. "Right after that night at the pool house."

His expression plummets as his hand drops from my shoulder. He tosses Luke the can. "We should get going or the cabdriver will leave our sorry asses and there's no way I'm walking back."

My mood sinks as I realize that what I said upset him. As I watch him climb down, I feel my happy night drift away to the sky and the lightning.

❦

When we return back to the dorms, Kayden leaves without saying good-bye. It hurts inside and confuses me to no end.

"What happened between you two?" Seth asks as I swipe my card and open the door to my residence hall.

I shrug as I step inside. "I think it's because I brought up the pool house. I don't even know why I did it."

His eyes look red under the lights as we make our way up the hallway toward the elevators located next to the lounging area. "It's because you aren't thinking very clearly tonight."

I swerve us to the right as two bulky guys, wearing football jerseys, walk down the hall toward us. "I know. Being drunk is weird."

136

He covers his hand over his mouth to stifle his laughter. "Oh my God. I love you so much. Especially when you say stuff like that."

"Like what?"

He shakes his head, still smiling as we enter the elevator. "Nothing. Never mind. Although I'm dying to know why your shoe is green."

I crane my neck to look over my shoulder at the heel of my sneaker as he pushes the button to my floor. "I stepped on a spray can while Kayden and I were fighting over one."

"I'd have loved to see that."

"I'm sure you would have."

The elevator doors open and we turn down the hall, stopping at the very end in front of my door. There is some giggling and thumping on the other side and the air smells like smoke.

Seth unties a red scarf from the doorknob and holds it up in front of my face. "What's this for?"

"It means I can't go inside." I take the scarf from him, dangle it over the knob, and sigh tiredly. "I'm so tired."

"Is she having sex or something?"

My skin warms. "I don't know...maybe."

His fingers wrap around the top of my arm and he hauls me toward the elevators. "Come on, let's go get you to bed."

I hurry to keep up with him. "Where are we going?"

"To bed."

When we reach the bottom floor, he steers us away from the noisy lounge, heading outside and around the corner toward his building. "You're going to sleep in my room. My roommate is never there anyway, so I'll take his bed and you can sleep in mine."

I want to hug him, but I'm afraid if I let go of him, I'll fall over from the sleepiness taking over my body. "Thanks. I'm so tired."

When we get to his room, he punches the code to unlock the door and pulls me inside as he flips on the light. His roommate's bed is empty and piled with dirty laundry. Seth's side is orderly, expect for a row of empty energy drinks on top of his computer desk—Seth is addicted to energy drinks.

"He never sleeps here?" I ask, kicking an empty soda can out of the way.

He shakes his head, shucking off his jacket. "I think he's afraid of me."

I pout my lip as I tuck my hands up into the sleeves of Kayden's shirt. "I'm sorry. For what it's worth, he's a moron."

"You don't need to be sorry, baby girl." He empties his change and wallet out of his pockets and drops them on top of the dresser beside a lamp. "You're the most understanding person I've ever met."

He starts to unbutton his shirt and I enfold my arms around him. "You're the greatest person ever."

Laughing, he pats my head. "Yeah, we'll see if you still think that when you have your very first hangover in the morning."

I gladly collapse onto his bed. Fluffing the pillow, I turn to my side, and stare at a picture of him and a guy with dark hair and bright blue eyes. "Seth, is this him? In this picture."

It takes him a minute to respond. "Yeah, it's him. That's Braiden."

Braiden looks like a football player; strong shoulders, a lean chest, and well-defined arms. He has his arm wrapped around Seth's shoulder. They look happy, but deep down one of them isn't. One of them will out the other one when accusations of their love start to swarm around the school like a cluster of bees. One of them will watch as the other one is beaten. I want to ask him why he kept the photo—why he has it on the wall—but I can tell he's growing uneasy with the subject.

He shuts the light off and from across the room, the bed squeaks as Seth lies down. It's quiet between us and I curl my body into a ball, nuzzling my face into the pillow and shutting my eyes.

"Can I ask you something?" Seth suddenly asks.

My eyelids open. "Sure."

He pauses. "Do you ever have nightmares about what happened to you?"

I squeeze my eyes shut, inhaling the scent from Kayden's shirt. "All the time."

He lets out a breath. "Me, too. I can't seem to escape it. Every time I shut my eyes, all I see is the hate on their faces and fists and feet coming at me."

I swallow hard. "Sometimes, I swear, I can still smell him."

"I can still smell the dirt and taste the blood," he whispers. "And feel the pain."

He grows silent and the need to comfort him overtakes me. I roll to my side, climb off the bed, and sink down on the mattress beside him. He turns toward me; his face just an outline in the moonlight.

"Maybe we won't have nightmares tonight," I say. "Maybe things will be different."

He sighs. "I sure hope so, Callie. I really do."

For a minute I have hope. The night has been great and I feel like anything is possible, but then I close my eyes and it's all stolen away from me.

Chapter Six

#8: Challenge Yourself.

Kayden

After we leave the rock, I go back to my dorm, wanting to run away from everything I'm feeling. The bathroom is occupied, so I end up going to bed, staring up at the ceiling while rain splashes against the window. From across the room, Luke is lying facedown on the bed, snoring.

As the alcohol lifts from my system, every emotion rushes through me like a stream full of needles. I have to turn it off. It is the only way I know how to deal with life.

I roll to my side, raise my fist, and ram it into the headboard as hard as I can. My knuckles crack and Luke jumps up from his bed.

"What the fuck was that?" He blinks around the room as silver lights flash from the lightning outside.

"It was the thunder," I lie and turn over, shutting my eyes

and holding my hand against my chest as the burning pain explodes up my arm. Moments later, I fall into a deep sleep.

"Don't sit down here all night by yourself," Luke says, walking across the room to the mini fridge in the corner. He takes out a beer and pops off the tab. *"You've been acting weird since the graduation ceremony."*

I lie down on the couch, flexing my hand over and over again, staring at the veins flowing through it. *"I'm just feeling a little bad about leaving."* Honestly, I'm just feeling weird about life. I want to leave, go away to college, be free, but the idea of being out in the open, surrounded by things I don't understand is fucking terrifying.

"You should go get yourself fucking laid, but by someone other than Daisy." He opens the door and the music from upstairs flows into the room. *"That's what I'm going to do."* He shuts the door and leaves me alone, trapped in my own thoughts.

He's right. I should just go upstairs and screw the first girl I come across. It's the best way to pass time and get through life, but I can't stop thinking about my hand and my fucking future.

Finally I get up from the couch. Walking toward the wall, I glance at the door. Then I lift my fist and hammer it into the wall as hard as I can. The sheetrock and paint crumble and my skin separates a little, but that isn't enough. I punch it again and again, forming holes in the wall, but causing very little damage to my hand. I need something harder—I need brick.

142

I turn toward the door, but it swings open and my dad walks in. He takes a look at the holes in the wall and then at my hand cut up and bleeding all over the carpet.

"What the fuck is wrong with you?" He shakes his head as he stalks toward me, staring at the Sheetrock and paint on the ground.

"I have no idea." I cradle my hand to my chest as I hurry around him and rush outside.

Inside the house, people are laughing, screaming, singing to the music and the lights gleam through the darkness. I walk around to the backyard, hearing him at my heels, knowing he's going to catch up with me and he's madder than hell.

"Kayden Owens," he says as he darts in front of me, panting and his eyes are full of anger. His breath smells like whiskey and the wind is blowing leaves everywhere. "Were you trying to mess up your hand on purpose?"

I don't speak as I make a detour toward the pool house, unsure where I'm going but feeling like I have to move.

When I reach the door, he snags my elbow and forces me to turn around. "Start explaining. Now."

I stare at him blankly and he starts yelling at me, telling me what a fuck up I am, but I barely hear him. I watch his lips move, waiting for it. Seconds later, his fist collides with my face, but I hardly feel it. He does it over and over again as his eyes drift into a state of blankness. I fall to the ground and he kicks me as hard as he can, wanting me to get up. I don't. I'm not sure I want to. Maybe it's time for it to be over; there isn't that much to be over anyway.

I listen to my heart beat calmly inside my chest, questioning why it doesn't react. It never does. I wonder if it's dead. Maybe it is. Maybe I am.

Then, out of nowhere, a girl suddenly shows up behind my father. She's small and looks terrified, like I should be. She says something to my dad and when he looks at her, I think she's going to run away. But she stays with me until my dad leaves.

I sit on the ground confused and at a loss for words, because that's not how things go. People are supposed to walk away, pretend this doesn't exist, let the strange excuses make sense.

Her name is Callie and I know her from school. She's standing above me and looking at me with horror in her eyes. "Are you okay?"

It's the first time anyone's asked me that and it throws me off. "I'm fine," I say more sharply than I'd planned.

She turns to leave, but I don't want her to leave. I want her to come back and explain to me why she did it. So I ask her and she tries to tell me but it doesn't make sense.

Finally, I give up on trying to understand and ask her to get a first-aid kit and an icepack. I go into the pool house and take my shirt off, trying to clean up the blood on my face, but I look like shit. He hit me in the face, something he does only when he's really pissed.

When Callie comes back, she seems nervous. We barely speak to each other, but then I have to ask her for help to get the kit open because my hand won't work.

"You really need stitches," she tells me. "Or you're going to have a scar."

I try not to laugh. Stitches aren't going to help. They fix skin, cuts, wounds, heal stuff on the outside. Everything broken with me is on the inside. "I can handle scars, especially one's on the outside."

"I really think you should have your mom take you to the doctor and then you can tell her what happened," she says refusing to give up.

I start to unwind a small section of gauze, but using only one hand, I drop it like a dumbass. "That'll never happen and even if it did, it wouldn't matter. None of this does."

She picks it up and I expect her to hand it back to me, but she unravels the gauze around her hand. She puts the gauze over my wounds, eyeing my scars, noting them and the wrongness they carry. There's something in her eyes that looks very familiar, like she has something trapped in her. I wonder if it's what I look like.

My heart begins to beat loudly inside my chest for the first time in as long as I can remember. It starts off as subtle, but the longer her fingers are near my skin, the more deafening it gets until I can't hear anything anymore. I try not to panic. What the fuck is wrong with my heart?

She steps back with her head tucked down, like she wants to hide. I can barely see her face with my swollen eye and I want to see her face. I almost reach out and touch her, but then she's leaving, double-checking to make sure I'm okay. I pretend not to care, but my heart keeps hammering inside my chest, louder and louder and louder.

"Thank you," I start to tell her. For everything, for not letting him beat me, for stepping in.

"For what?"

I just can't get there. Because I'm still not sure if I'm thankful.
"For getting me the first-aid kit and icepack."

"You're welcome."

*Then she walks out the door and the God damn silence is back
again.*

⌒

My hand has to be taped up for the next week and I got my ass
chewed off by my coach because it's fucking up the way I play.
Things aren't going as well as I planned. I thought now that I
was finally away from home, I'd get over the darkness that pos-
sesses me, but I was wrong.

It's been over a week since Callie painted those beautiful words up on the rock. They meant more to me than she
probably understood. Or maybe she did know, which is why
I needed to pull back. That kind of emotion I can't deal with.

Near the end of the week, I'm feeling really down and my
body is paying for it. I'm lying in my bed, getting ready to go
to class, when Daisy sends me a very vague text.

Daisy: Hey, I think we should see other people.

Me: What? Are you drunk or something?

Daisy: Nope. I'm completely sober. I'm just bored and
   sick of being by myself all the time. I need more.

Me: I can't give you more when I'm in college.

Daisy: Then guess u don't luv me as much as I thought.

Me: What do u want me to do? Drop out?

Daisy: I don't know what I want, but it's not this.

At the very same time I get another text and I switch screens.

Luke: I just got a text from D Man and he said he thinks Daisy cheated on you with Lenny.

Me: Are you fucking serious? Lenny?

Luke: Yeah, he said it happened during Gary's banging out the new school year party or whatever the fuck he calls it.

Me: The banging out party took place before she came to visit.

Luke: Yeah…I know. Sorry man.

Me: Yeah, later.

I turn off my phone, not bothering to text Daisy back. I don't really feel upset about it, but it feels like I should. It seems like I should be pissed off, but I feel empty.

During my Public Speaking class, I'm listening to a girl give a speech on women's rights. I take some notes, but mainly stare out the window. I'm eyeing the football stadium in the distance, wishing I could be out running laps and releasing all this pent-up energy.

Suddenly, I see Callie walking across the lawn with a bag on her shoulder. She's on her phone, her hair is down, and her legs move rapidly to take her wherever she's going. She's wearing black yoga pants and a hoodie. She crosses the parking lot and yells something out when Luke appears on the sidewalk, heading for her. He's limping and glancing around like he's doing something wrong.

They meet up under a large oak tree where leaves are piled. Callie says something and then hands Luke her phone. She pulls pieces of her hair out of her mouth as Luke punches some buttons on her phone. She laughs as he says something and it leaves me scratching my head.

When he hands her the phone back, they give a parting wave to each other and walk off in opposite directions. Callie disappears between a row of cars in the parking lot and Luke limps off toward the back area of the school. He never mentioned that he was hanging out with her. Why is he hanging out with her? Why is this fucking bothering me?

Reaching into my pocket, I slip my phone out and turn it back on.

Me: Why were you just talking to Callie?
Luke: Where the hell r u? I was fucking texting u and
    then suddenly ur phone was off.
Me: In class...I saw u out the window.
Luke: Ok...Why does it matter what we were doing?

Me: It doesn't. I was just wondering.

Luke: We were just talking. Gotta go. Class is starting.

It drives me crazy, which makes no sense. I should be more upset about my girlfriend of three years dumping me, but it's a glitch compared to the idea that Callie and Luke could be going out or something.

Finally I shove up from the desk, making a scene as I storm out of class right in the middle of the poor girl's speech. Bursting out the doors, the sunlight blinds me as I stomp toward the benches in the quad. Slumping down onto one, I lower my head into my hands and take a deep breath. I can't react this way about anyone. Ever. It's a rule of mine. Never drag anyone into my own shit. Callie is the last person who needs it on her shoulders.

The longer I sit there, the more worked up I get, and I realize the only way to sort stuff out is to actually figure out what's going on. I text Luke and ask him if I can borrow his truck. He says yes, but to be back by two because he needs to go somewhere, and he lets me know that the keys are on the dresser.

I drive off toward the Tune-up Gym, where Callie said she kickboxes. She was dressed like she was going to work out so I assume that's where she's heading, however, when I arrive I can't determine if I want to be right or wrong about my assumption.

I climb out of the truck and stare at the small brick building. "What the hell am I doing here?" I mutter to myself, turning back to the truck. That's when Seth hops out of the car a few rows down.

He waves at me with a cigarette in his hand and a puzzled look on his face. "Hey."

I wind around the front of the truck toward him. "Are you working out?"

He glances down at his jeans and button-down shirt. "Nah, I just come with Callie to keep her company."

I nod, feeling like a fucking idiot for coming down here. Since when do I chase down girls? "I see."

He flicks his cigarette to the asphalt and stomps on it with the tip of his boot. "Why are you here?" He eyes my dark jeans and plaid shirt.

I shrug. "I have no idea. I really don't."

He points a finger at the glass doors of the gym. "Callie's inside. I'm sure she'd love to talk to you."

I pop my knuckles, even the ones that are taped up. It hurts, but it calms me down. "Okay, I'll walk in with you for a second."

He grins and we weave around the cars toward the entrance of the building. There's a big guy walking in with a bag over his shoulder and Seth moves up to hold the door open for him.

"Can I ask what happened?" He nods his head at my hand as we step inside.

I lift my taped hand up in front of me. "I hurt it during practice."

"That sucks." He leads the way around the treadmills to

the back area where mats are set up. The room stinks of salt and heat and is filled with clanking noises from the weight machines. There's upbeat music blasting through the speakers to pump everyone up.

Callie is near the back of the mats, kicking at a bag that dangles from the ceiling. I don't like how happy I am to see her, or how happy my body is to see her. Emotions and want rip through me like a fucking wave.

She's bouncing around on her toes with her jacket off. She has a tank top on and her hair is pulled back. It's the most skin I've seen her show and I enjoy the view; the freckles on her shoulders, the arch of her neck, her collarbone. The tight pants she has on give me a great view of her ass and her legs.

"Don't hurt her," Seth says, leaning in my face. "I fucking mean that."

I blink at him. "What are you talking about?"

He backs toward Callie. "Don't hurt her," he repeats, and then spins on his heels, putting his back to me. He whisks up to Callie, and says something to her.

Emotions flood her face as her gaze darts to me. She timidly waves her hand and I walk over to her with my hands tucked in the pockets of my jeans.

Her white bra is showing through her shirt and she crosses her arms over her chest. "What are you doing here?" she asks, tracing the toe of her shoe back and forth across the mat.

"I was just driving by and saw Seth's car out front," I lie. "So I thought I'd stop in and say hi."

"Hi." She presses her lips together.

I shake my head and chuckle under my breath. Circling around the punching bag, I give it a little shove, and then dodge to the side when it flings back at me. "You really weren't kidding about the kickboxing thing."

She tightens the elastic around her ponytail. "Did you think I was saying it to try and impress you?" She flutters her eyelashes as she steps to the side. I question if she did it on purpose, to try and flirt with me. I doubt it. I'd be surprised if she knew how to flirt.

"Well, I was hoping you were." I punch the bag with my good hand.

Her gaze flickers to Seth who's messing around with small dumbbells, shaking his hips as he sings to the song on the radio. "Nope, this is what I do for fun."

"Are you any good?" I eye her tiny frame with doubt.

Pieces of her damp hair frame her face as she places her hands on her hips, trying to look tough, but all I'm focused on is her bra showing through her shirt. "You want to find out?"

"Oh, big words for a little girl." I'm flirting with her and I know it's wrong for so many reasons, but it's the most alive I've felt in a long time. I pick up one of the gloves from the corner of the mat and put it on before positioning my hand out to the side. "Give it your best shot."

Her eyebrows dip together. "You want me to kick you? Really? What if I hurt you?"

"I absolutely want you to kick me," I say and then trying to get her riled up, add, "I'm not worried about getting hurt."

Her blue eyes turn cold, her expression serious as her fists rise in front of her. She angles her body sideways, stepping back on her foot. She's got pretty good form, but she's so little that I know it won't hurt.

She pivots her hips, springing up on her toes, and the bottom of her sneaker collides against the glove. My arm shoots back and my foot slides along the mat. Fuck. It stings. A lot.

She grins as she returns her foot to the mat. "Did it hurt?"

"Kind of," I admit, shaking my hand. "You know, you're as sweet as can be, but give you permission to kick me, and holy hell, you're ruthless."

"I'm sorry." The laughter in her voice says otherwise. "I didn't mean to kick you so hard."

"I think you did." I pick up another glove and wiggle my fingers into it. "All right, let's see what else you got."

She gapes at me with her hands out to her side. "Are you joking? You want me to fight you."

I punch one glove into the other. "I won't fight back, but I'll try to stay out of your wrath."

She laughs and it makes my heart jump alive inside my chest. "All right, but don't say I didn't warn you."

I grin at her as I move forward. "Give it your best shot."

She attempts to look dangerous, her lips a straight line, her eyes unblinking, but it's more entertaining than anything. She steps to the side, and I think she's going to pop her foot up and kick, but she keeps overlapping her feet as she circles me. I turn with her, curious what she's doing and then out of nowhere, she springs up and slams her foot into my hand. I barely block it and she lowers her foot, giving me hardly any time as she twirls around on her toe and jabs her shoe into my other glove.

She stations her foot onto the ground with a cocky look on her face. "Had enough yet?"

I shake my head as I reposition my feet. "Okay, if you want to play dirty, then let's play dirty."

She bounces up on her toes, getting ready to jump up and kick me. Before she finishes it, I dash forward, wrap my arms around her waist and flip her around, pressing her back against my chest.

I freeze, wondering if she's going to panic, but she swings her arm up toward me as she tries to squat down and slip out of my arms. I strengthen my hold on her and pin her against my chest.

"This isn't fair," she says. "You're breaking the rules."

"Come on," I tease her as she tries to kick me in the shin and I jump back, keeping my grip on her. "You acted all tough when you were the one having all the fun."

Her body suddenly stills. Then she reaches up, grabs my arms and with no warning, flings them off her. Trying to keep a hold of her, because I was enjoying the feel of her warmth against me, I seize the bottom of her shirt. She stumbles back into me and our legs entangle together. Spinning around, we trip over each other's feet and tumble to the mat on our sides. She quickly hitches her leg over my midsection and mounts on top of me, pinning my arms down with her small hands.

Her ponytail has partially fallen out and her hair touches my cheeks as she hovers over me. Her chest heaves up and down, her skin damp, and her eyes stern.

"I win," she says, shifting her weight.

The feel of her on top of me, the way she smells, the way her legs are spread around my hips is intoxicating. I'm starting to get turned on and she's going to feel it pressed up against her.

"You're vicious when you fight," I state. "I really didn't think you had it in you."

Her forehead creases. "Me either."

I let a few more seconds pass, even though I should be moving out from under her. My gaze zones in on her lips and I almost glide my hand up her back, tangle it through her hair, and pull her down for a kiss.

"Okay, as much as I hate to interrupt this beautiful moment here," Seth says as his face appears over us. "I'm going to have to. Miss Callie here has somewhere to be."

She blinks, her cheeks turning pink, like she's coming out of a daze, and she swiftly hops off me. "I'm sorry. I got a little carried away."

I prop up on my elbows. "Where are you heading?"

"Umm...." She slips the elastic out from her hair and refastens it into a tight ponytail. "I'm meeting Luke somewhere."

"Luke, as in, Luke?"

She nods, glancing at Seth. "Yeah, that's the one."

I push up from the ground and wiggle my hands out of the gloves. "Why?"

She runs her arm across her forehead. "I can't tell you why."

I toss the gloves onto the ground near the corner, irritated. "Okay."

"I want to tell you," she hurries and adds, "but I can't."

"It's fine. I have to head out anyway. I have some stuff I need to do." I walk away from her, knowing it's for the best, but wishing I was the one she was going to see.

Chapter Seven

#27: Offer to Help Someone Without Them Asking.

Callie

I feel weird going with Luke, for various reasons, one being that I barely know him. I have no idea how I got into the situation. Actually I do. I was walking around the back end of the campus, because I like how quiet it is there.

As I was pouring some M&M's into my mouth, I rounded the corner and nearly stepped on Luke. He was sitting down on the ground, in the dirt, with his head lowered and his legs bent up in front of him.

"Oh my God." I jumped back, pressing my hand to my heart. "What are you doing back here?"

He had on shorts and a white T-shirt and his brown hair was damp. He lifted his face up and his skin was paler than snow. "Callie, what are you doing?"

I balled up the candy wrapper in my hand. "I walk this

way after my English class is over. I was actually getting ready to meet up with Seth to go to the gym."

He bobbed his head up and down and sweat was beading his forehead. "Oh."

I turned to leave, but decided I couldn't leave him looking so terrible. "Are you okay?"

He scratched at his arm. "Yeah, I was working out and started feeling like shit so I came back here to take a breather for a minute."

I crouched down in front of him, keeping enough distance to make me comfortable. "Are you sick or something? You look..."

"Like shit," he finished for me as he got to his feet and sighed.

My gaze snapped down to his leg, swollen twice its size, blotchy and red. "What happened to your leg?"

He released a slow exhale as he inclined against the brick wall of the school. "I may or may not have forgotten to take my insulin for the last few days."

"You're a diabetic?"

He put a finger to his lips and shook his head. "Don't tell anyone. I don't like to show weakness. It's a weird thing with me."

"Why haven't you been taking your shots?"

"I ran out and never picked up more. It's another weird thing with me...I sometimes can't bring myself to stab a needle into my body."

I didn't press as I eyed his leg, inflamed from the knee down. "Do you need me to take you to the doctor? Or go find Kayden?"

He shook his head, stepping forward and then stumbled back, banging his elbow into the wall. "Don't tell Kayden. When I say no one knows, I mean *no one* knows."

I adjusted the strap of my bag higher up on my shoulder. "I think you need to go to the doctor."

"I know I need to go to the doctor." Putting some weight on his leg, he hobbled toward me. "Look, don't you have stuff you don't want people to know?"

I nodded warily. "Yeah."

"Okay, well for me, this is one of those things," he said. "So can you keep quiet about it?"

I nodded again. "As long as you let me take you to the doctor."

He shut his eyes, breathed in through his nose, and his chest expanded out from underneath his shirt as he opened his eyelids. "Okay, we have a deal. Let me go change my clothes, make an appointment, and then I'll meet you out front in like twenty minutes."

"Maybe you should just go to the ER," I suggested. "You look terrible."

"ER trips cost a lot of money," he replied, limping toward the metal doors. "Money I don't have."

"Okay, I'll meet you out front," I told him and then he stepped inside, letting the door slam shut behind him.

As I headed for my dorm to drop my stuff off, I had no idea how I'd gotten myself into the situation. I'd spent the last six years trying to stay away from guys, but it seems like that's all I've been around lately, but I wasn't going to bail out on him.

When I met him out front twenty minutes later, it turned out he couldn't get into the doctor for another two hours, so we exchanged numbers and I promised him I'd be back from the gym in time to take him.

Two hours later, we're sitting in the office. Luke jiggles his knee up and down as I read through a copy of *People* magazine while finishing off a piece of licorice. I changed out of my workout clothes into jeans and a T-shirt. I'm surprised how well I'm handling what I did at the gym with Kayden. Sitting on top of him like that was strange, but my body liked it. A lot. Seth teased me about it the entire drive home and I kept waiting for it to crash into me, yet I still feel fine.

Luke's skin looks almost yellow beneath the lighting of the waiting room. I flip the page and then tilt my head to the side to try and make out what I'm looking at.

"Don't you hate doctors' offices?" Luke says abruptly.

I glance up and his brown eyes are huge as he stares at a man across from us, hacking into his hand. "I guess so."

He scratches agitatedly at his temple until there are red streaks on his skin. "It's so fucking unsanitary."

I close the magazine and drop it on the table. "Maybe if you didn't think about it so much, then you'd relax a little."

He pauses and his foot quits tapping. "I just really hate needles."

It makes no sense, since he's probably had to take insulin shots for a while. The fear in his eyes makes me wonder if there's more to his phobia than just the needles, though.

"Okay, think of something else." I scoop up a copy of *Sports Illustrated* from off the table beside me. "Read this. It'll help take your mind off stuff."

His eyebrows furrow as he takes the magazine from me and studies the girl on the cover. "You know, I don't remember you being this way in high school. You were really quiet and everyone..." He trails off, but I know what he was going to say; that everyone made fun of me, picked on me, teased and tortured me. "I'm sorry. I shouldn't bring that stuff up."

"It's fine," I assure him, but memories explode through my brain like shards of glass.

"You know, you remind me of my sister, Amy," he says. "I don't know if you remember her. She was a couple of years older than us."

I shake my head. "I don't. Sorry."

He opens the magazine and flips the page. "She was a lot like you. Quiet, nice, but sad."

I notice he said *was*. I press my lips together as the glass in my head multiplies as it shatters into more pieces. "Will you excuse me for a second?"

I get up from my chair and scurry down the hall to the bathroom. My shoulders start to hunch over as the ache in my stomach builds. Thankfully, the bathroom is empty, otherwise I would have done it in the hall and everyone would have known my little secret. The one thing that makes me feel better during the darkest times of my thoughts. The one thing that belongs to me and no one can take it away.

"I think I should take you there as a thank-you," Luke says as we drive by a carnival set up in the fairgrounds. The sun is descending behind the mountains and the sky is gray with splashes of pink and orange. Neon lights and music take over the land.

"I haven't been to one since I was like eleven," I admit. "I was never really into the rides, especially the ones that went high."

"Didn't you ever go to our town fair?" he asks, pausing at a stoplight.

I shake my head. "I stopped going when I turned twelve."

He looks at me, waiting for an explanation, but what would I say? That my childhood kind of ended at twelve when my innocence was stolen? That after it happened, cotton candy, balloons, games, and rides made me wish for a time I'd never have again?

"Well, then I'm taking you," he says as the light changes and a green glow reflects across his face. He releases the clutch and the truck rolls forward.

"Oh, you don't have to do that," I tell him. "I was happy to help you, especially since you no longer look like you're going to drop dead."

"Did I look that bad?"

"You looked like shit."

He shakes his head with a small smile on his face. "Still, I think we should go hang out. It's better than going back to the campus and sitting in the dorms. I've barely gotten out of my room since school started." He pauses as he spins the wheel and makes a right into the dirt parking lot at the side of the white tents and the neon glow of the rides. "You can call Seth and invite him." He considers something as he shuts off the engine. "I'll call Kayden and see if he wants to come."

I pick at my fingernails as I try to stay calm and not get all giddy like a silly girl. "I guess we could do that."

I pull my cell phone out of the pocket of my jeans while he grabs his off the cracked dashboard. While I call Seth, he talks to Kayden. I hear Luke being vague as to why we're together and I wonder if Kayden's still mad.

"Seth's in." I raise my hips to shove my phone back into my pocket. "And he said he was going to call Kayden to see if he wants a ride . . . if he's going."

Luke repeats what I say to Kayden, and then he snaps his phone shut, rubbing the back of his upper arm where he got the insulin shot. "Kayden says he's in, too." He opens the door and hops out, slanting back into the cab to snatch the keys from the ignition. "I told him we'd meet him over by the Zipper."

I climb out, push the door shut with my hip, and meet him

around at the other side of the truck. I take in all the crazy, spinning rides. "The Zipper? That one sounds interesting."

He chuckles as we hike across the parking lot toward the gated entrance. "Yeah, we'll see if you're still saying that when you see it."

❧

We're waiting in line for a ride that has a long metal center with cages attached to it. Each cage flips around as the middle section whips in a circular motion, so there is double the spin. The lights twinkle and some heavy rock music plays so loudly I can barely hear the screams from inside the cages. I watch it spin around and around, psyching myself out while Luke texts on his phone.

"Are you going to make it?" Kayden's breath caresses my neck as his voice touches my eardrum.

I turn my head and his lips nearly touch mine. The abrupt closeness throws him off as much as it does me and we both take a step back at the same time.

He's wearing a loose fitted pair of jeans, boots, and a long-sleeve black shirt. His dark hair looks a little wet, like he just got out of the shower before he came here.

He's gorgeous, I admit to myself. It's the first time I've been able to admit that about a guy in a very long time.

"You look freaked out," he shouts over the music as he leans closer. "Are you seriously considering riding that thing?"

"Maybe…" I slant my neck back, tipping my head up at the ride. "But it goes so high up."

Pink and yellow lights dance across his face as he glances at the ride and then looks me in the eyes. "How about we share a cage?"

"I don't think that's such a good idea," I say. "In fact, I think it's a very bad idea."

"What's that supposed to mean?" The corners of his lips quirk as his gaze darkens. "Don't you trust me?"

"Yes, I trust you," I say. "But I don't want to end up throwing up on you."

"You'll be okay," he assures me, nudging his shoulder into mine and then he winks at me. There's something different about him tonight; he's freer and I think he might be flirting with me. "I promise I won't let anything happen to you. In fact, you can hold my hand the entire time."

Where was he during my twelfth birthday? Probably playing hide-and-seek with the rest of the kids.

"All right, I'll ride with you," I say with hesitation. "But don't say I didn't warn you."

"Warning taken and rejected." He interlocks his fingers through mine as he jerks me forward with the moving line.

"I'm sitting this one out," Luke calls out as he drifts over to the bench with his attention on his phone. "I got some stuff I got to take care of."

"Where's Seth?" I ask, glancing around at the booths, the

games, and the trailers with food, trying not to make a big deal that Kayden's holding my hand.

But it's all I notice.

"He went to meet up with someone." Kayden steps forward and I move my feet with him. "He said to tell you that he would catch up with us in a little bit and to relax and have fun."

I scrunch my nose at the ride. "And this qualifies as fun?"

"Oh yeah." He tugs me toward the guy running the ride, who's dressed in a blue polo shirt, old jeans, and a trucker's hat. "You'll have a blast."

I show the guy the stamp on my hand and then Kayden puts his arm in front of me to show him the stamp on his. As he pulls back, his hand unintentionally grazes my boob and I blink at the tingling sensation it elicits.

The ticket guy unlocks the gate for us and we walk up the ramp. Kayden lets go of my hand so I can hop into the cage. Once I'm in the seat with my feet planted firmly on the bottom, he joins me. Without any preparation, the ticket guy slams the door shut and locks the cage from the outside. There are padded bars on the inside that push against my shoulders and secure me back into the seat. It's a tight fit and Kayden's leg is pressed against mine; scorching hot through my clothes.

He angles forward, meeting my eyes and a slow smile spreads across his face. "It's snug in here."

I nod my head and it bumps against the back of the seat. "Too snug. If it flings off the hinges, it'll be crushed into a ball when it hits the ground and smash us right along with it."

166

"Stop psyching yourself out," he says in a carefree tone, then jerks his shoulders forward and rocks the cage.

"Don't," I beg, my fingers tightening around the bars. "Pretty please. Can't we just stay stationary?"

He shakes his head as the ride progresses forward and halts so the cage in front of us lines up with the ramp. "Now what would be the fun in that?"

"It would be fun because I would be able to hold in all that candy corn I ate," I say innocently.

He stops rocking the cage. "Oh, come on, Callie. It won't be fun if we don't rock it. In fact, the more we rock it, the better it'll feel." His voice drops to a deep whisper. "We can rock it nice and slow or really, really fast."

His words make my cheeks flush, but luckily it's dark. "And what if I get scared? Or my gag reflex gets a little too excited?"

"I'll tell you what." He maneuvers his hand around the bar and squeezes my knee with his fingers, sending a shot of warmth between my legs. "If you feel like you're going to throw up and you get freaked out of your mind, yell, *Kayden is the sexiest man alive* and I'll stop."

The cage jerks backward and I grip the bars as we begin to ascend to the top. "That is seriously what you want me to yell?"

"Absolutely." He pauses as our cage reaches the highest point and the ride comes to a standstill, swaying in the breeze. "Do I have your permission to rock away and give you the ride of your life?"

Why does it feel like he's secretly talking dirty to me? "Yeah, go ahead, rock it nice and hard," I say without thinking, then bite down on my lip as the dirty section of my brain catches up with me. Honestly, I didn't even know that side existed.

"Wow." He releases a slow breath with wide eyes and then shakes his head. "Okay, are you ready?"

I intensify my grip around the bars and press the tips of my shoes to the floor. "Yep ... I think."

He flings his body forward as the ride takes off. Our cage starts to spin gradually at first, but the more weight he puts into his rocks the faster it goes. The lights from outside flash all around and the music picks up. I hear the roar of other rides; people laughing, screaming. The wind blows against my cheeks and the air smells like salt and cotton candy.

The faster it goes, the more I lose sight of what's up and what's down as we go around and around. The hinges squeak and I hear Kayden laugh as I let out a little squeal. Surprisingly, I don't freak out, nor does Kayden get a lap full of candy corn. I'm having fun, even though it feels like my face is being sucked back into my skull and my brain is rattling around.

When the ride stops, we're at the top and the breeze sneaks in between the holes in the door.

Kayden opens his eyes and a confused look rises on his face. "I thought you passed out or something with how quiet you were."

"I was just enjoying the ride," I say breathlessly. "It was actually pretty fun."

"Well, I'm glad I'm that good," he says, resting back in the seat.

I turn my head away to hide the smile on my face, because he's just having fun and I'm enjoying it way too much. He has a girlfriend. A very pretty girlfriend, who isn't up to her neck in problems. One that he can touch and rock away with or whatever.

We don't speak until our cage reaches the ramp. When the ticket guy opens the door, Kayden hops out and I follow, stumbling over my own feet as the world sways from my dizziness. My shoulder slams into his broad chest. He laughs at me as his fingers grip my waist and he guides me closer to his side. Between the rush of adrenaline and the feel of his hands holding me, it seems like it's going to be a good night.

And I've been looking for one of those for a while.

Chapter Eight

**#17: Let Something Amazing Happen,
Without Question or Hesitation.**

Kayden

I know what I'm doing is wrong, but I can't seem to stop. I'm flirting with her, looking for excuses to touch her and make her laugh. I've never laid it on this thick before with anyone, including Daisy. Daisy was easy. All I had to do was say something nice about her and life was good. Not with Callie. With her I have to earn it.

"No one ever wins these games, especially the top-shelf prizes," Seth declares as we roam along the row of booths. He's got his arm around Callie and they keep whispering to each other. I want to exchange places with him, but don't know the right way to go about it.

"It's a trick, I tell you, to steal all your money." He makes an evil villain mixed with a pirate laugh and Callie buries her face into his chest, her shoulders heaving as she laughs hysterically.

"Did he seriously just say that?" Luke asks as he maneuvers around an older man handing out flyers.

I nod, my gaze tracking the booths. "I think he did."

Luke's neck cranes to the left as he checks out a tall brunette, wearing tight jeans and a shirt that covers half her stomach. "I think you might have to prove him wrong."

"Are you trying to tell me that you can win that?" Seth points at a booth where darts have to be thrown at balloons. Then, he aims his finger toward the ceiling where there are massive teddy bears hanging by strings. "And I'm not talking about those silly little prizes on the bottom row. I want one of those big ones up there."

I crack my knuckles and my neck. "Okay, first off *when* I win one, it's not going to be for you. It's going to be for that beautiful girl right there." I point at Callie, then want to take it back, even though it's true.

Callie glances up at me through her eyelashes, trying to hold back a blush and Seth clears his throat. "All right, manly man," he says. "Go prove that you're a man."

I slip my wallet out of my back pocket, while Luke ambles off toward the rides, lighting up a cigarette.

"You do realize he's the quarterback, right?" Callie says to Seth as they walk behind me and it makes me smile for some stupid reason. "He practices hitting a target every day."

"So what?" Seth argues. "I'm still calling his bullshit. These games are unwinnable."

Callie stands to the side of me as I hand the guy in the booth some money in exchange for five darts. He lays them down on the counter and backs into the corner, returning his attention to his dinner.

I pick one up, raise it over my shoulder, and squint at a balloon. Callie crosses her arms, studying me, and I lower the dart, but keep my eyes on the balloon. "Are you trying to make me nervous?"

"No, why? Am I?" she asks uneasily.

"Kind of," I admit, looking at her. "I can feel your intense gaze burning through the side of my head."

"Sorry, I'll stop," she sputters and begins to turn away.

I catch the bottom of her white T-shirt and my knuckles graze her soft skin. "No, keep looking at me like that. It makes it more challenging."

She glances down at my hand and then her gaze glides up me. "Okay."

I tear my eyes off her, lift the dart back up as she focuses on me, and fling it at a red balloon on the top row. It pops and Callie flinches. "One down, four to go." I grin at her, but note that she's growing nervous.

I pick up another dart and throw it, then repeat the same move. Each one pops a balloon and when I'm done, the top row is nothing but deflated pieces of latex. The guy behind the counter comes over with a frown on his face.

"Congratulations," he says in a monotone voice and points his finger at a row of teddy bears dangling from the ceiling. "You get your choose from one of those lovely prizes up there."

I glance at Callie who's staring at the balloons with a frown on her lips. "I said if I won, it was for you."

Callie sighs, her shoulders slumping as she fixes her eyes up at the bears. "They seem so big. I think my roommate would be pissed if I brought it back to our tiny room."

"We have to take the prize," Seth says with a serious expression on his face as he puts his hands on the counter and tilts his head up to look at all the prizes. "You don't turn down a top-shelf prize."

She dithers, twisting the end of her ponytail around her finger. "Okay, I'll take the pink one with the torn ear."

The guy behind the counter scratches his neck. "Are you being serious?"

Her face is stoic. "Absolutely. I never kid about teddy bears."

Seth and I laugh at her and the guy pierces us with a look, before he marches over to the wall and grabs a metal pole. Pointing it up to the tent ceiling, he unhooks the bear Callie selected. Then he takes it off the end and tosses it on the counter before he stomps away, muttering, "I need a fucking smoke break."

Callie picks up the bear, which is half the size of her, and assesses it with distaste. "I still don't think I should bring it back to the dorm." She glances up at me. "Maybe you should take it with you. You did win it."

I shake my head. "There is no way I'm going to drag a giant, deformed, pink bear across campus and take it to my room."

"Okay, maybe we could give it to a little kid," she suggests, flicking her fingers at the bear's nose and making a face. "They'd probably love to have it."

We peer around at the crowd and then Callie giggles as she stares at a booth that is set up with display cases that hold sunglasses. "Or we could dress it up and put a *Wanted: In need of a home sign* in its hand and leave it somewhere for someone to pick up."

I poke my finger at the teddy bear's eye and it falls out. "I actually like that idea and the sunglasses can hide the fact that it just lost an eye."

"Oh, can we buy it a tiara?" Seth asks, glancing around excitedly. "Please let me put one on its head. It can cover up its missing ear."

"Okay, you go get a tiara and I'll go get it some sunglasses." She lugs the bear up in her arms as Seth takes off toward a red and white tent that's set up at the end.

I fidget with the bear's good ear as Callie pushes her way through the crowd, practically using the bear as a shield. "It's a sad-looking thing, isn't it?"

She stops at the sunglass booth and drops the bear to the ground. "I like it. I just don't think my roommate would like it." She cocks her head at the bear. "When I was younger, I would have kept it in a heartbeat. In fact, I had a whole collection of them."

I arch an eyebrow at her. "You collected broken, smelly carnival bears?"

She laughs and I love that it was me that made her do it this time, not Seth. "No, but I had a collection of broken stuffed animals. Like a cat with no whiskers and a puppy with no nose."

"What did you do?" I joke. "Torture them and tug off their limbs?"

She places her palms on the table that holds a display case full of glasses. "No, I just never wanted to throw them away. Even if they were broken, I still loved them." She peers down into the case, completely oblivious to how much her words mean to me.

Slowly, I place my hand on the table and inch it toward hers, finally covering it with mine. Her chest rises and falls as she pretends that nothing's going on and I trace my finger along the folds of her hand, my eyelids starting to shut.

"Which ones were you looking at?" An older woman with beads on her wrists and a long flowing skirt waltzes up to us.

I jerk my hand away and let it fall to my side as I lean over Callie's shoulder to look through the glass. "Which ones were you thinking?"

She slants her head to the side and her hair touches my cheek. "How about the sparkly blue pair that are shaped like stars?"

"Sounds good to me." I barely pay attention to what she's saying, because I'm smelling her hair like a fucking weirdo.

What the hell is wrong with me? Strange feelings clench at

my chest, ones I was taught to shut off. It's literally hurting me, like a knife to the chest, and all I want to do is fucking leave and go turn it off the only way I know how.

❧

"Are we already moving on from the *Wicked Witch of the West*?" Luke asks as I circle around the ticket booth, searching the grass for the glasses Callie accidentally dropped somewhere.

"We?" I stand up straight. "I didn't realize it was something we were doing together and I'm not trying to do anything with Callie. We're just friends."

He flicks the button on his lighter with his thumb, ignoring my comment. "You know, if you want, I can get her in a situation with you where you'll have your chance to do whatever you want with her."

"You know I just broke up with Daisy, right?"

He rolls his eyes. "And you seem so sad about it."

I find the glasses near the trashcan and pick them up, plucking off the grass stuck in the cracks of the frames. "I'm not sure I want to do anything with Callie."

He pulls his unlit cigarette out of his mouth and stares at it. "I can't remember where I left my pack." He pats his pockets and then turns in a circle, looking at the ground.

Luke has this thing with losing stuff, especially his cigarettes. Nicotine is his sedative and without it, he flips out. "Where the fuck did I…" He trails off walking backward toward a bench and sighs as he scoops up the pack. He tucks it into his pocket and shuts his eyes, like he thought he just lost an arm. "We could do a challenge."

I open and close the ends on the glasses. "We haven't done that since sophomore year."

"When you started dating Daisy," he points out. "Man, I miss those days."

I stare off at the rides whipping around in various directions. "Yeah, I don't think I can trick Callie into going under the bleachers with me. It'd feel wrong."

Luke thrums his fingers on the side of his leg to the beat of the rock song playing nearby as his gaze roams to the jungle gym ride in the corner. It's dark inside and no one's standing at the gate. "Hang on. I got an idea."

"Care to share the details of your idea?" I ask. "I don't want to walk into this blind."

"Think challenge to the max." He walks backward across the dry grass toward the exit gates. "I'll be back in five minutes. All you need to do is follow my lead and, as a thank-you, you can let me drive that motorcycle you don't let anyone touch when we go home for Thanksgiving."

"No fucking—"

He disappears out the gates, waving me off. Shaking my head, I return back to Callie and her bear, feeling guilty. But deep down, I know I'm going to go through with Luke's plan, because I want to, more than anything at the moment.

Callie

As Seth puts the finishing touches on the bear, Luke comes strolling up with an unlit cigarette between his lips. He has a jacket on with the hood pulled over his head and the front pocket is bulky.

"What the hell is that thing?" He squints down at the cardboard sign in the bear's hand. There's a glittery tiara on its head, sunglasses covering the eyes, and a string of beads around its neck. He reads the sign aloud, *"Will be ridiculously cute in exchange for a loving home, food, water, and a little cuddle time."* He flicks the ear with his fingers. "What the fuck is this?"

I laugh, biting down on the top of the pen. "We made it so it would get adopted and so none of us has to take it home."

Luke glances at Kayden, who shrugs. "I thought it was kind of funny. And be thankful. For a while, Callie was trying to get me to take it home."

Luke scrunches his forehead, takes the cigarette out of his mouth, and sticks it into the bear's mouth. "There, that's much better."

Kayden rolls his eyes at him and stuffs his hands into the pockets of his jeans. "So what's next on the list? And I'm speaking figuratively, not about your actual list."

I look over my shoulder at the rides twirling, twisting, and sparkling against the night. "We could ride some more rides, I guess."

"I actually have a better idea." Luke strolls off without finishing his thought and the three of us trade glances before hurrying after him. He marches toward a jungle gym made up of ropes, ramps, netting, and bars. There are three levels and a short gate borders the bottom. I think the point of the ride is to get to the top and then down to the bottom again.

"I don't think it's open," I say as Luke reaches for the latch on the gate.

With his hand in his pocket, he checks over his shoulder and then nudges the gate open with his foot. "Oh look at that. It is now." He walks inside and signals us to follow. "Come on. It's nothing but a giant playground. Besides, we're celebrating."

"Celebrating what?" Seth and I ask at the same time.

He grins and then glances at Kayden. "The end of the Wicked Witch." He starts humming a tune from the *Wizard of Oz* as he backs toward the curtain entrance of the ride.

I step in first, since I've been on such a roll lately. "Who's the Wicked Witch?"

"I think I'll let him explain it to you." Luke looks at Kayden before ducking through the curtain into the entrance of the ride.

I glance over my shoulder at Kayden. "What's he talking about?"

Kayden shrugs as he closes the gate. "Luke's excited that Daisy and I broke up."

"Oh." I try not to smile and finally have to bite down on my bottom lip, hard. "I'm sorry."

"Don't be sorry." He reaches his arm over my shoulder and draws back the curtain for me. "It really isn't that big of a deal."

It seems like it should be. They've been dating forever, but he appears really content.

I lower my head and step into the ride, holding my breath as the curtains brush against the top of my hair. It's nearly pitch black and the sounds of screams and soft music envelop around me.

"Where are you?" I hiss, with my hands out in front of me, my elbows locked. "Hello?"

A lighter flickers and then Luke's face appears above the flame. "There we go."

Seth strolls up next to me, just a shadow in the dark, and thrums his fingers together in front of him. "Oh, are we going to do a séance?"

Luke looks at Seth like he's nuts as Kayden moves up on the other side of me. I'm very aware of his nearness and the smell of his cologne. It makes me nervous, yet excited at the endless possibilities.

"So, what's the ingenious plan?" Kayden asks, his breath flowing across the back of my head. "Are we going to trash the place?"

"We're going to—" The lighter falls from Luke's hand and darkness takes over. "Ah, fuck! That's hot."

Seconds tick by and then Seth turns on the screen of his cell phone, which casts a blue glow over our faces. Luke nods as he picks up his lighter and drops it into the pocket of the hoodie, taking out his own cell phone to use for a light. He dips his hand into his other pocket and draws out a bottle filled with a golden liquid.

"Tequila? Where the hell did you get that?" Kayden's fingers brush the lower section of my back, and I stifle a gasp clawing at my throat.

"I bought it off one of the carnies." He unscrews the cap and sniffs the inside of the bottle, pulling a thoughtful face. "All right, who's ready to get this party started?"

Seth's gaze skims over the three of us. "What kind of party are we talking about? Because honestly, I was trying to work something back at the ticket booth, but got a little distracted by the bear."

"Really?" I ask excitedly and he nods with pressing eyes.

I want to hug him, but I'll save it for later when he can give me the details. Seth hasn't dated anyone since Braiden and I hope he's ready to finally move on.

Luke takes a swig from the bottle and his shoulders twitch as he swallows it. "I want to do a challenge."

"No challenges tonight," Kayden grimaces, but there's a hint of amusement in his voice. "We have practice early in the morning and challenges always end in pain."

My head snaps toward him. "Pain?"

"Good God," Seth says with a dramatic sigh. "Please explain what this challenge thing is."

"It's a long story." Kayden waves us off with his hand and faces Luke. "Just know that you don't want to do it."

"You're just pissed off because you lost last time," Luke says in a taunting tone. "Besides, I bet Callie would totally be into it. She seems tough for a tiny girl."

"Hey," I start to protest as Luke takes another mouthful. "I'm not that tiny."

Kayden pinches my side and I flinch. "Actually, you are really tiny, but it's cute."

I cross my arms over my chest and inhale quietly, uncertain how to respond.

"Relax, Callie," Kayden says, looking a little remorseful. "Now, if you want to do the challenge we can, but don't say I didn't warn you."

I've never been much of a curious person. I just did what I had to and stuck to myself, at least since my twelfth birthday, but curiosity sparkles inside me.

"I am kind of curious to see what your challenges are," I say and Kayden seems extremely pleased, the corners of his lips quirking as he struggles not to smile, even though he'd just been protesting it.

Luke takes another mouthful of tequila and wipes his lips with his arm as he passes the bottle to Kayden. "Usually we set up an obstacle course, like running and jumping and shit." He gestures his hand at the net above us. "But we got a prebuilt one right here."

"So what? You just race?" I ask as Kayden hands Seth the bottle, moving his arm around my back. "And what does the winner get?"

Seth tips his head back and takes a long, loud gulp. "Damn that's good."

"The satisfaction of winning." Kayden exchanges a look with Luke.

Luke stares up at the top. "I say first one to the top and back is the winner."

"I say that this time the winner owes the other one a favor." Kayden steps around me and steers me to the side by the shoulders. "Like letting the other one borrow their truck whenever they want."

"That's fine," Luke retorts. "Just as long as when I win, I get to ride that motorcycle that hasn't left your garage, when we go home for Thanksgiving."

"That's my brother's," Kayden states with a noticeable rise in the pitch of his voice.

"You drove it once before," Luke protests.

"And I got in deep shit for doing so." His breathing is ragged and tension swirls in the air.

He lets out a breath as Luke takes another drink with a challenge in his eyes. I've heard the expression "too much testosterone," but never witnessed it until now.

"Fine, you got a deal." Kayden jerks the bottle from Luke's hand and throws his head back, pouring in a mouth full of tequila. "But I'm not letting you win."

"Yeah, we'll see." Luke steals the bottle back and wraps his lips around the top, knocking back a shot.

"You know what?" Seth shuffles toward the exit, staring at

his phone. "I think I'm going to go find the person I was talking to."

"No way." Kayden steps toward him. "You got to stay down here and call the winner."

Seth waves his hand at him, brushing him off. "Nah, Callie can do it."

Kayden shakes his head. "Callie's in the challenge, remember?"

I cringe, wondering what I've gotten myself into. "Maybe I should just stay here."

Kayden lowers his face toward mine and strands of his brown hair tickle my forehead. "I thought you were going to prove to us you weren't little?"

I glance up at the nets and ropes with doubt. "How am I supposed to do that? I see no possible way of me winning anything against you two."

He positions his fist in front of his chest with a wicked glint in his emerald eyes. "With your awesome kickboxing skills."

Luke snorts a laugh as he spills some tequila onto the ground. "What?"

Kayden lowers his fist, biting on his lip, with a look in his eyes that's very overpowering. "What do you say? Can you handle it?"

I nod, even though I don't think I can. "All right, so I just try to beat you guys to the top?"

Kayden rubs his jawline. "Absolutely."

I follow them to the bottom step as they line up with their hands out to the side and their feet positioned to run. I feel short and small standing between them.

Seth stands near the curtains, checking the clock on his screen. "Do you want me to just say go?"

Kayden nods, without taking his eyes off the tunnel in front of us. "Yep, whenever. We're ready to go."

Seth glances at his clock again and then sighs. "On your mark, get set, go!"

I skitter to the side as Luke shoves Kayden and then runs down the tunnel. Kayden recovers and dodges back onto the steps, sprinting down and disappearing into the darkness. I glance at Seth and he gestures for me to get my butt moving.

I walk quickly, ducking my head, and listening to the sounds of their footsteps that are already above me. Hunching over, I exit out of the tunnel and onto a wooden stairway. I step up, getting a little uneasy at how dark it is, but when I approach the next level the glow from the rides flows inside.

I hear the sound of Kayden's voice as he shouts something and I pick up my pace toward a bridge. It has netted sides and a rope for a railing. There are boards that pave the way to the other side and the floor sways underneath my feet as I step onto it. It's gone quiet and my adrenaline soars.

"Okay, why did I agree to this?" I mutter to myself. Then I answer my own question. "Because Kayden looked at you with those sexy eyes." I step forward with my palms flat against the net to secure my balance.

"Callie," Kayden suddenly whispers. "What are you doing?"

I glance over my shoulder and then grab on to the rope as the bridge rocks underneath my feet. "Where are you?"

"I'm over here." His voice sounds close.

I squint through the darkness and then jump back. He's right on the other side of the net, watching me, which means he probably heard me talking to myself and calling him sexy.

"How long have you been standing there?" My voice sounds high.

He lets out a low laugh and it sends a shiver through my body that coils into my stomach, bursting heat downward. The sensation knocks me off balance and my cheeks heat.

"You think I have sexy eyes." His fingers thread the net as he stares at me through the dark from the other side.

"You heard that?" My head falls forward to conceal my mortification.

"Callie." His voice is deep and husky. I've never had a guy use that kind of a voice on me.

I raise my chin up and encounter his intense gaze. "I'm sorry. I thought I was alone." I shift my weight and the unsteadiness of the ground hurls me forward. I reach for the wall, lacing my fingers through the net and my knuckles brush his. Our faces are inches away. I can feel his breath and the heat from his body. If I leaned forward slightly, our lips would touch.

"Stay there," he says in a low whisper and removes his fingers from the net.

I watch the outline of him move through the dark as he walks down the side and turns the corner so he's standing at the end. The floor ripples under his steps and he holds on to the railing, heading straight for me.

I have no idea what he's going to do when he reaches me, but the intensity in the air and the way his long limbs move with determination, make me think it's going to be something I've never experienced before.

I rotate my body to face him and lace my fingers through the holes of the net, with my back to the wall, and my arms bent up beside my head. It's dark enough that I can only see the outline of his face, but every once in a while the moving lights from outside shimmer in his eyes.

We're breathing wildly, our chests heaving as he halts in front of me.

"I have a confession to make." He places a hand at the side of my head and grabs on to the net. "This was a setup."

I lick my lips nervously. "What was?"

"The whole challenge thing. I did it to get you up here alone." His other hand grips the net so my head is confined between his arms. My heart dances inside my chest as he whispers, "I'm really sorry."

He leans in, shutting his eyes, and for a second I contemplate running. I keep my eyes open until the very last second, and then suck in a breath as his lips touch mine. My knees buckle as his tongue delves deep inside my mouth and I clutch on to the net to keep from falling down.

Without question or hesitation, I untangle my fingers from the holes, and slide my hands up his chest, wrapping them around his neck. His hot breath is mixed with passion and tequila and his chest crushes against mine. A gasp escapes from my lips as his searing hot palms move down my back. He thrusts his tongue deeper into my mouth and grabs at my hips, drawing me closer as the floor sways under our feet.

It's my first real kiss; one that wasn't taken away from me and held inside someone else's hand. I thought I'd be more terrified, but if anything the nerves flying through my body are driven by the thrill of his tongue inside my mouth.

His hands slide from my hips to the perimeter of my butt. I flinch, starting to panic, but he intensifies the kiss, his tongue moving faster and with more determination. His fingers tangle through my hair, pulling my head back, so he can search my mouth more thoroughly, and I get lost in the moment. His fingers glide underneath my thighs, and grip tightly at my legs as he tugs me up and presses my back against the net wall. He urges my legs around his waist and I cross my ankles around his back, latching on to him.

My bottom lip quivers as I feel his hardness between my legs. It's mind blowing. And scary as hell.

Kayden

She's more inexperienced than I thought. Her hands are shaking as she knots her fingers through my hair and her bottom lip trembles as I massage it with my tongue. I've totally gone AWOL with my plan to stay away from her, but that decision was made the second Luke suggested the stupid challenge plan we used to do to trick girls into going under the bleachers to make out with us.

I realize the moment my lips touch hers that the day she came running up to the pool house to save my ass with her legs trembling, but her voice confident, something changed inside me. I have no idea what it is, but I know I want her, so fucking bad and I've never wanted anyone. Not like this. Want equals dependency and that is not what I'm looking for in my fucked-up life.

I feel my way down her body, sucking her tongue into my mouth, and she lets out the sexiest moan I've ever heard as she traces her fingers down the sides of my neck and grips at the fabric of my collar. I move my mouth away from hers, but only to trail soft kisses from the corner of her mouth, down her jawline, to the arch of her neck. My dick is pressed up against her and her warmth is radiating through my jeans. It feels so fucking good.

"Oh my God..." She lets out a plea combined with a moan as my hand glides up to her breast and grips it. Her small body trembles in my arms and I swear I'm going to lose it right then and there. I've never felt like this before, with anyone. It's against the rules of surviving.

"Callie," Seth's voice drifts up from somewhere. "We gotta go!"

I'm not ready to let go of her yet and allow the world to

catch up with me. I clutch at her waist, wishing we could just stay up here, in the quiet. My head is tipped down as I breathe heavily against her neck with her chest heaving in my face as she tries to regain her breathing.

"Kayden." Her voice is soft, cautious, like she senses something's wrong. "I think we need to go back down."

Nodding, I inhale through my nose, and elevate my face away from her chest. I lower her legs to the ground and we head back across the bridge without talking to each other. When we reach the bottom and duck out of the curtain, Seth and Luke are waiting with a couple of guys in ratty T-shirts and torn jeans.

"You can't be up there," the tallest one says, spitting something nasty onto the ground.

"We were just leaving," I mutter as I shove by them and march for the parking lot, taking strides that are as long as possible, wanting to leave it all behind.

By the time I reach the truck, the night crashes into my chest; the flirting, the games, the way she felt when I touched her, and how she reacted. I feel everything and I need to get it out of me.

Chapter Nine

#43: Face Your Fears Head-on and Tell Them to Fuck Off.

Callie

I drive home with Seth from the carnival. Kayden looks like he's going to be sick, so I don't ask too many questions when he says he needs to ride back with Luke and call it a night.

When we get to my door, the red scarf is on the knob again and I frown. Seth and I don't say anything as we walk across the campus yard in the chilled air and go into his empty room. He sinks down on his bed and starts to unlace his boots as I slip off my sneakers.

I stand there in the middle of the room, recollecting every detail that happened. The way Kayden's hands touched me, the feel of his lips, how it felt so incredibly good.

"Do you want to share what that weird look on your face is about?" Seth kicks his boots into the corner and lies down on his bed with his hands tucked behind his head.

I lie down next to him and rest my cheek on the pillow. "You really want to know?"

He glances at me from the corner of his eyes. "Heck yeah. You look like you're high." He pauses, propping up on his elbow as he pivots to his side. "Wait a minute. Is that what you were doing up there? Were you getting high?"

I swat his arm. "No . . . we were . . . kissing."

He laughs at me. "You say that like it's so wrong."

I shrug, picking at my fingernails. "It feels like it should be wrong . . . the last time someone kissed me that's how it felt."

He shakes his head and sighs. "That's because the last time it was wrong, but not this time. This time it was right and both of you wanted it. Right?"

I nod slowly, trying to hold back a smile, but it sneaks through. "It was a really nice kiss."

He springs up on his knees and puts his hands on top of his legs. "Okay, tell me how it went. What were you doing? And how did it happen?"

I sit up and lean against the wooden headboard. "He said that whole challenge thing was a setup to get me up there."

Seth rolls his brown eyes. "Well, duh. I got that they were up to something."

"Really?" I feel stupid. "I thought they were just being guys."

"Oh they were," he assures me. "Relax, it was all for fun and he got to kiss you just like he was trying to do the whole night."

I pull the pillow onto my lap, reliving it over and over

again in my mind. "Yeah, but did Kayden seem a little offish when we left?"

Seth shrugs. "He seemed tired, but not offish."

I yank the elastic out of my hair, gather the strands into a messy bun, and secure the band around it. "What happened with that guy you were talking about?"

He reaches his hand into his pocket and takes out his phone. Flicking the screen with his finger, he shows it to me. "I got his number."

"I'm so happy for you." I incline back against the headboard. "Are you going to go out with him?"

"Maybe." He drops the phone onto the desk at the foot of the bed and then lies back down, glancing at the picture on the wall. "God, it was such a great night."

I slide my body down and lay flat on the bed, staring up at the ceiling. "It really was."

And at that moment, I mean it.

❧

I wake up in the middle of the night dripping in sweat, unable to tell where the hell I am. The sound of heavy breathing drifts up from the warm body lying beside me. I sit up, blinking around the dark, clutching at the blankets, panting feverishly, trying to shake my dream.

"Callie, listen to me," he says. "If you tell anyone about this, you're going to get into trouble and I'm going to have to hurt you."

My small body trembles, my muscles are sore, and my body

and mind is bruised. Tears stain my eyes as I blink up at my bedroom ceiling with my hands lifeless at my sides, my fingers clutching the comforter.

"Callie, do you understand me?" His face is getting red and the tone of his voice is sharp.

I nod, unable to speak, gripping the blankets tighter.

He climbs off me and zips up his pants, then backs away to the door, putting his finger to his lips. "This is our little secret."

When he disappears out the door, I gasp for air, but my lungs won't work. I can't breathe. Letting go of the blanket, I stumble off the bed and run to the bathroom, leaning my head over the toilet bowl. I heave my guts out until my stomach is empty, but I still feel dirty inside, spoiled, rotten, foul. It's killing me, gnawing away at my insides and I need to get it out.

I shove my finger down my throat, desperate to get rid of it. I push and gag until my throat bleeds and tears slide down my cheeks. My shoulders shake as I stare at the trail of blood on the floor and listen to the sounds of the kids just outside, laughing and playing hide-and-seek.

I gasp for air, dragging my fingernails down my neck. "Go away. Go away," I whisper and Seth lets out a loud snore.

I hop out of bed and search the floor for my shoes, needing to get rid of the feelings beginning to surface. But I can't find my shoes. It's too dark. I yank at my hair wanting to rip it out and scream.

Finally, I give up and sneak out the door bare foot. The hallway is vacant and I run to the end of it where the bathrooms are. Locking myself in the farthest stall, I kneel down on the cold hard tile floor, lean my head over the toilet, and jab my finger down my throat.

As the vomit surfaces I start to feel better. I keep pushing and pushing until I reach the end and my stomach is empty. Calmness settles over me as I take back control.

Kayden

The next morning, after Callie and I made out in the jungle gym, I wake up with my mind crammed with a lot of shit. I climb out of bed and start packing a bag, shoving in a few shirts and an extra pair of jeans. Then I zip it up and swing the handle over my shoulder.

Luke is lying on his bed, face down and I shake his shoulder. He rolls over with his fists up, ready to take a swing at my face. "What the hell?"

"Hey, I need a favor." I collect my wallet and phone off the dresser.

He relaxes. "What favor? And why do you have a bag packed?"

"I need to borrow your truck." I adjust the bag higher on my shoulder. "For a few days."

He blinks again, still out of it as he reaches for his watch on the nightstand. "What time is it?" He rubs his eyes and then gapes up at me. "It's six o'clock in the fucking morning. Are you crazy?"

"I need to get away from here for a while," I say. "I need to clear my head."

Sighing, he scoots up so he's sitting. "Where are you going?"

"Back home," I say, knowing it's stupid to go back, but it's all I know. There is nowhere else for me and staying here means dealing with shit I just can't deal with and Callie deserves better. "I thought I'd go check up on my mom and make sure everything is okay there."

He rubs his forehead and glances at the sun rising over the mountains. "You know I'm going to be stranded here if you take my truck? What am I supposed to do? Stay here for the entire weekend?"

"You can borrow someone else's car." I turn around, looking for his keys and then scoop them up from off the desk.

"I guess I can get a ride from Seth." He frowns. "God damn it. This better be important."

My stomach tenses. "It is. In fact, it's kind of a matter of life and death." I walk out the door without saying another word, the bandages beneath my shirt hidden, but I feel the pain. It's all I feel.

⤳

Driving back home is a fucking downer, but if I hang around the campus, I'm going to want to be near Callie and it's unhealthy for both of us. I do the only thing I know. I go back home, hoping I can clear my head of her.

When I park the truck in front of the two-story house, though, every single memory rushes back to me. The fists, the beatings, the yelling, the blood. It's all connected to me, like the veins under my skin and the scars on my body, along with this house, and what's inside it—it's all I have.

It takes me a second to work up the courage to open the truck door. My boots land in a puddle as I step out. Leaning back inside, I grab my bag from the passenger seat, and slam the door. Draping the strap over my shoulder, I head up the path lined with red and green Venus flytraps. The leaves from the trees have fallen, and the neighbor's son is out raking them up from the grass.

Each year, my mom pays someone to come clean them up, because my dad hates them in the yard. They're dead and pointless and look like shit, he says.

I wave at him as I trot up the stairs to the front porch. Freezing in front of the screen, I take a deep breath and step inside. It's exactly the same as when I left. There is no dust on the pictures in the foyer or on the banister leading upstairs. The floor has been polished, the glass on the windows are wiped clean. I walk up to a family portrait hanging on the farthest wall and squint at it.

My mom and dad sit in the center, and my two older brothers and I stand around them. We're smiling and look like a happy family. But Tyler has a tooth missing from where he banged his face on the table when my dad was chasing him. Dylan has a brace on his wrist from falling out of a tree when

he climbed up it to hide from my father. Even though it isn't visible in the picture, I have a bruise on my shin the size of a baseball from getting kicked by my dad after I accidentally spilled cereal all over the floor.

I wonder why no one questioned our injuries, but maybe that's why we were always playing sports. As soon as we turned the right age, we were thrown into soccer, T-ball, and when we got a little older, basketball and football. These were good excuses that my mom gladly passed around.

I thought about telling someone a few times when I got old enough that my brain could grasp the idea, but the fear and embarrassment stopped me. Besides, I shut down at an early age. After that pain was just pain. I can do pain. That's the easy part of life. It's everything else, happiness, laughter, love, that's fucking complicated.

Callie

"I'm nervous about seeing Kayden," I admit to Seth as he walks me to my room. Neither of us have class this morning, so we decide to go out to breakfast, just him and me so we can talk.

Fortunately, the scarf isn't on the doorknob and when I open the door, Violet isn't in the room. Although, she's left soda cans everywhere and there's a nasty-looking sandwich on the desk.

"Can I make a suggestion?" Seth says, observing Violet's unmade bed. "Please spray disinfectant everywhere."

"Suggestion taken." I grab a plaid shirt and a pair of jeans out of the dresser. "Can you step out so I can change?"

Nodding, he backs out the door. "Hurry up though, I'm starving."

When he shuts the door, I slip out of my shirt that smells like cotton candy mixed with cigarette smoke. I inhale the scent, remembering how it felt when Kayden kissed me, before I toss the shirt on the bed and insert my arms through the sleeves of the plaid shirt. I pull on a pair of jeans and then grab a brush to put my hair up, but pause, thinking about my fears and how Seth told me this morning that I should tell them to fuck off.

After the incident last night, before I returned to Seth's room and went back to bed, I promised myself it would never happen again. When I woke up, I felt better.

I slip the elastic out and let my hair hang down to my shoulders. "You can do this," I mutter, grabbing my bag. "You made out with a guy, for God's sake."

When I step out the door, there's a smile on my face, but my happiness vanishes when I see Seth talking to Luke, and neither of them look happy. Luke is wearing black jeans and a black fitted T-shirt. It's a lot of black, but it works for him

When Seth catches my eyes, his expression is filled with sympathy and pity.

My eyebrows furrow as I stroll up to them. "What's wrong?"

Luke has a guilty look on his face as he turns around. "Hey, Callie, what's up?"

I fiddle with the strands of my hair, tucking them behind my ear. "Nothing much. Seth and I are just heading out to get some breakfast."

"Yeah, we were just talking about that." Luke hurries backward down the hall, like he's desperate to get away from me. "I was asking Seth if I could borrow his car, but I'll just find someone else."

"Why? Where's your truck?" I ask, and his shoulders stiffen as he pauses in the center of the hall.

"Kayden took it somewhere." He waves at me, before spinning on his heels and hurrying off. "I'll catch up with you two later." He disappears between a group of cheerleaders, dressed in their uniforms.

I turn to Seth, confused. "What was that about?"

He stares at me contemplatively, then sighs and loops his arm through mine. "We need to talk."

We step out into the crisp autumn air and beneath the cloudy sky. The liveliness of the campus yard surges around us and yellow and orange leaves skitter across the dying grass.

"Are you going to tell me why you're looking at me like you're about to tell me my dog died?" I wonder as we step off the curb of the sidewalk and down onto the asphalt of the parking lot.

He looks left and right, before we hurry over to his car. "I have something to tell you and I don't know how you're going to take it." He frees my arm and we part ways, going to opposite sides of the car.

When we get in and shut the doors, he turns the key in the ignition and pauses as he scrolls through his playlists on an iPod. "Kayden borrowed Luke's truck." A song pops on as he places the iPod back into the stand on the dashboard. "To go back home for a few days."

I fasten the seatbelt over my shoulder. "Okay, why are you acting weird?"

He shoves the shifter into reverse and looks over his shoulder as he backs out of the parking space. "Well, because he didn't say anything to you." He straightens the wheel and merges the car out onto the road. "Wait a minute. Did he tell you?"

"No, but why would he? We barely know each other."

"Callie, you made out with him last night and let him feel your boob."

"Hey, I told you that in confidence."

He raises his fingers up from the wheel. "Relax, I'm just pointing out that that was a big step for you—an important step. You wouldn't just do it with any guy."

"I like Kayden," I admit. "But it doesn't mean he has to tell me everything he does. I'm not his girlfriend."

"So what?" Seth turns down the volume of the stereo. "He should have said something instead of just taking off. He knew you'd probably want to see him. You know his darkest secret, Callie, which is the hardest part about getting to know someone."

He's quoting his Psych 101 on me, so I fold my arms and

stare out the window, watching the leaves blow across the street and into the gutter.

∾

When I get back to my room later that day, I write until my hand hurts, needing to get it out, but only daring to tell it to a blank sheet of paper. There are no accusations with writing, no judgment, no shame, only freedom. As the pen touches the paper, for a moment, I'm alive.

The day I changed is like a scar. It's there, a memory in my mind, something I always remember and can never erase. It was the week after my birthday party. I'd locked myself in the bathroom and stared in the mirror for an eternity. I used to love how I looked, the length of my hair, perfect for braiding. I had always been tiny for my age, but suddenly I wanted to be smaller— invisible. I didn't want to exist anymore.

I grabbed a pair of scissors out of the drawer and without even thinking, began hacking off my long brown hair. I didn't even bother trying to make it look nice, I just cut, even shutting my eyes sometimes, letting fate take over, like it had done with my life.

"The uglier the better," I whispered with each snip.

When I was finished, I didn't look like myself. I hadn't been sleeping very well and my blue eyes had dark circles under them and my lips were chapped from dehydration from all the vomiting. I felt ugly and the thought formed a tiny smile on my face, because I knew no one would look at me and want to come near me again.

When I walked into the kitchen, with my brother's jacket on

202

and the baggiest pair of jeans I could find, all the color drained from my mom's face. My father had been eating his breakfast at the table and looked up at me with horror in his eyes. My brother and Caleb stared at me, too, making repulsed faces.

"What the fuck happened to you?" my brother said with wide eyes.

I didn't reply. I just stood there, blinking at him, wishing I could be smaller.

"Oh my God, Callie," my mom breathed, her eyes so wide they looked like marbles. "What did you do?"

I shrugged and grabbed my bag off the doorknob. "I cut my hair."

"You look...you look." She took a deep breath. "You look hideous, Callie. I'm not going to lie. You've ruined yourself."

I'm more ruined than you think, I wanted to tell her. But she kept looking at me in disgust, like she wished for a second I didn't exist and I felt exactly the same way. I bottled everything up, knowing I could never tell; that she would look at me with even more hate and revulsion if I told her.

For the first few years of my turmoil, she tried to understand. And I give her credit for that. She asked questions, took me to talk to a counselor, who told her that I was acting out because I needed more attention. He was a small-town shrink and had no idea what he was talking about, although I didn't try to help him understand, either. I didn't want him to know what was living on the inside. At that point, all the good and clean had been spoiled and was rotten like eggs left out in the sun.

The thing about my mother is she likes things happy. She hates seeing bad things on the news and refuses to watch it. She won't read the headlines of the newspapers and doesn't like talking about the pain in the world.

"Just because the world is full of bad things, doesn't mean I have to let them bring me down." This is what she would say to me all the time. "I deserve to be happy."

So I let my shame own me, kill me, wilt me away into a thousand dead flakes, knowing if I kept it all in, she would never have to learn the dirtiness that was forever inside me—the bad, the ugly, the twisted. She could go on living her happy life, just like she deserved.

Eventually, she stopped asking me so many questions and started telling everyone that I was suffering from teenage angst, just like the therapist told her.

I heard her tell the neighbor once, after he accused me of stealing his garden gnomes, that I wasn't that bad of a kid. That one day, I would grow up and look back at my silly little time spent locked away in my room, writing dark words, wearing excessive eyeliner and baggy clothes as something I wished I'd never done. That I'd regret my lonely adolescence, learn from it, and grow into a beautiful woman who had a lot of friends and smiled at the world.

But the thing I regret—will always regret—is going into my room on my twelfth birthday.

Chapter Ten

#49: Tell the Truth to Yourself.

Kayden

I've been at my house for two days now, and I've almost returned to the place I ran away from. My dad hasn't hit me yet or anything, but I'm afraid of him, just like when I was a child.

"Why the fuck did you leave that piece of shit truck parked out front?" he asks when he walks into the kitchen. He's wearing a suit, even though he doesn't have to work today. He just likes looking important.

"Because the garage is full." I butter my toast as quietly as possible because my dad hates the noise the knife makes against the dry bread.

"I don't give a shit." He opens the cupboard and takes out a box of cereal. "You need to get it out of here. It's leaking oil all over the driveway."

"Fine." I bite into my toast. "I'll find somewhere to put it."

He steps in front of me and I freeze. His green eyes are harsh, his jawline taut, his expression indifferent. "I think you forgot something."

I force the bread down my throat. "Fine, sir, I'll find somewhere else to put it."

He eyes me with intimidation for a second longer, before stepping back. "And you better come back and clean those crumbs off the counter."

I inhale through my nose as I move for the doorway. "Yes, sir."

He takes out a bowl from the dishwasher and I hurry out of the house. Why can't I just hit him? I thought about it a few times when I was younger, but was always afraid he would retaliate twenty times harder. By the time I got older and bigger, something had died inside me and I didn't really care. I let him kick me, hit me, wishing he'd finally go over the edge and it'd all be over.

That is until the night he almost did and Callie showed up and saved me.

My phone rings and I retrieve it from my pocket as Daisy's name pops up on the screen.

"What?" I answer, jogging down the steps of the front porch.

"Hey," she says in the high-pitched voice she uses when she's around her friends. "How's my favorite guy?"

"Fine."

"What? Aren't you excited to hear from me?"

"I heard from you a few days ago," I say. "When you

made it very clear we weren't a couple anymore. Or actually, Luke did when he told me you were fucking around with someone else."

"God, he has such a vendetta against me," she snaps. "It's like he wants us to break up. I never got why you were friends with him. He's not even like you."

"What do you want, Daisy?" My tone is clipped as I hike across the grass toward the old truck, stuffing the last of the toast into my mouth.

"I want you to take me to homecoming, like you promised."

"I promised that when we were together."

She sighs dramatically. "Look, I know you're mad at me, but I don't have a date and I've been nominated for homecoming queen. The last thing I want to do is be alone when they call my name."

"I'm sure there's a ton of guys that would love to take you."

And get into your pants.

"But I want you to take me," she complains. "Please, Kayden, I need this."

The phone vibrates and I pause at the end of the lawn, quickly switching the screen to text messages.

Callie: I wanted to see if u were okay. Luke told me u had to go home. If u need anything let me know.

I shake my head at her sweet message. She's worried about me. No one has ever been worried about me before.

"God damn it, I can't do this," I mutter, kicking at the dirt. "I can't be with you."

"Yes, you can," Daisy says. "All you have to do is pick me up at seven."

I wasn't talking to her, but it doesn't matter. I need a distraction. "Fine, I'll take you, but I'm not going to the party afterwards."

We hang up and I have the most sickening feeling in my stomach. As I pull the truck onto the street, I almost head east to the freeway, toward the campus. But as I glance down at the scars on my knuckles, I head west, toward town to park the truck somewhere and then walk back home to take Daisy to the prom.

Callie

"It's Saturday night," Seth says and he runs some gel through his hair. "You have to go out with me. There is no way in hell I'm going to let you stay in."

"I'll be fine." I lift up a stack of textbooks in search of my notebook. Honestly, I'm feeling a little down after Kayden never returned my text. He's probably just busy, though. "You're totally looking into this Kayden thing too much."

He sits down in front of the computer, swiveling the chair as he scrolls through his Facebook page. "You haven't been the one looking at your sad puppy-dog eyes for the last two days."

I drop the stack of books and put my hands on my hips. "Where the heck did I leave my notes?"

"You left them in your room," he says. "Remember we dropped them off while…" He trails off and then promptly shuts the screen down. When he swivels the chair around to look at me, his brown eyes are enlarged. "I have a brilliant idea. Why don't you and I just go out? I can blow off Greyson and you and I can go see that silly movie you've been wanting to see."

I flop down on his bed. "No way. I'm not going to ruin the first date you've had in almost forever."

"Please, Callie, just come out with me and have some fun."

I prop up on my elbows. "What's wrong with you? You're acting like a weirdo."

"That's because I am a weirdo." He stands up from the chair without looking at me and shoves boxes aside with his foot so he can open the closet door. "I think I need to tell you something that you might be upset about, but that I feel you need to know."

"Okay…what is it?"

He removes a hanger from the bar and takes his jacket off it. "You know what, let's just go out and do something crazy."

I ease out of bed and stand up. "Seth, please tell me what's going on. You have me worried."

He sighs, leaning back into the closet to put the hanger back on the bar. "Please don't let this ruin your progress, but while I was on Facebook, I saw that Kayden had tagged himself with Daisy McMillian at the homecoming dance."

I bite down on my tongue until it hurts. "Okay."

He zips up his jacket and picks up the keys off the desk. "Do you want to change first, before we go out?"

I grab my bag off the bed. "I think I'm just going to go back to my room and study."

"Callie I—"

"Seth, I'll be okay. Now go on your date and have a lot of fun for the both of us."

I dash out of the room before he can try to persuade me. I'm not sure how I feel about Kayden. I thought I was getting somewhere with my life. I thought I could smell the possibilities in the air.

Guess I was wrong.

Kayden

I slip into my dorm room in the middle of the night, still wearing the tux with my bag in my hand. When I turn on the light, Luke sits up, blinks his eyes, and shakes his head.

"Okay, we have got to come up with a system where you quit waking me up." He studies my tux. "So that tag was right? You really went with her?"

"No, I picked her up and while I ran inside to pay for the gas, she took my phone and did that herself."

"You didn't go to the dance with her? You just what? Wanted to get dressed up for fun?"

I tug the bowtie off my neck. "No, I made it to the parking lot, before I had a revelation."

He glances over at the clock. "I've heard those are pretty life changing."

I shuck off my jacket and toss it on the floor. "This one might have been . . . maybe. And you'll be pretty happy about it."

"Why's that?"

"Because part of it was that I realized Daisy is a bitch."

He grins. "Finally. Took you long enough. You know, you're kind of slow."

I sit down on the bed and start to untie my shoes.

The revelation was actually simple. During the drive to the school, Daisy had been yammering about how the manicurist messed up her nails. She kept rambling on and on and I started noticing little details about her, like the way her nose scrunched when she was talking or the dryness of her hair. She kept making her voice sound ditzy and when she reached over to touch my leg, I felt like flinging it off my lap.

She kept insulting everyone, so I tried to change the subject and make a joke, but she didn't laugh. In fact, she looked at me for a second like she was wondering what she was doing with me. Then I began wondering what I was doing with her.

I dropped her off at the school and shoved the shifter into park. "Have fun."

She gaped at me. "What? You're not coming in?"

I shook my head with a small smile on my lips. "I should have never been here to begin with."

She threatened me with everything she could think of, before getting out of the car. I drove away, picked up my bag from the house, and headed back to the campus, feeling a weight lift from my shoulders.

"You're right. I am kind of slow." I pick up my shoes and drop them into the closet. "Hey, did you see Callie at all while I was gone? I found an earring in your truck and I think it's hers."

He's quiet for a moment and then shifts in his bed. "I have to ask you something about her. Just how much do you like her?"

I shrug, because I really don't know. "She's nice and interesting." I shrug again, conflicted. "Why are you asking me such a fucking weird question?"

"Well, tonight, I ran into Seth out in the parking lot," he says. "And he informed me that Callie found out you were at homecoming with Daisy."

I grab my jacket and head for the closet to get a hanger, my steps slowing down as I realize what it means. "Did he say if she was upset?"

"*He* sure was," Luke replies. "He yelled at me for like ten minutes."

I insert the ends of the hanger through the sleeves of the jacket. "I should probably go talk to her." I grab a T-shirt and some pajama bottoms from my bag and walk back to the closet to change so Luke doesn't see my hideous scars.

"Yeah, good luck with that." Luke collapses back onto the bed, yawning. "Because I'm pretty sure Seth isn't going to let you anywhere near her ever again."

My heart constricts inside my chest at the idea. Even though I keep telling myself to stay away from her, it hurts thinking that it might actually happen. I admit the truth about my feelings for the first time in my life. I actually have them. And I have them for Callie. Now what I'm supposed to do with them I have no fucking idea.

❧

The next morning I wake up early because I can't sleep. I have this reoccurring dream where I'm back at the pool house and my father is beating me. This time though, Callie doesn't show up, and his fists continue to smash into my face over and over again until I black out.

I get dressed and walk over to the shop across the street to get a coffee. I'm on my way back to the campus when Callie appears at the end of the sidewalk. She has a book in her hand, reading while she heads in my direction, oblivious to the people and cars moving by her. Her hair is braided to the side, with loose strands framing her face, and her jacket is zipped halfway up. Her tight jeans show how breakable she is.

I wait for her by the street post and she doesn't glance up at me until the last second.

"Hey," I say, trying not to worry about the fact that she's stopped several feet away from me. I move over to her slowly, taking a sip of my coffee. "What are you reading? You looked totally into it."

Her gaze lingers on me and I squirm. She lifts the book up and taps the cover where the title is.

"Sister Carrie," I read aloud.

She lowers the book to her side with her finger in the binding to mark the page. "It's for my American Literature class, which I'm supposed to be at in an hour. I was supposed to read it last night, but I couldn't find the book."

"Oh, I see." I'm at a loss for words hearing the tightness in her voice.

She punches the crosswalk button on the pole with her thumb. "Did you have a nice trip back home?"

"It was okay," I say, waiting for her to call me out.

She hitches her thumb under the strap of her bag and scoots it higher on her shoulder as she watches the crosswalk sign in front of her. "That's good."

It grows silent as she returns to reading. I watch her lips move along with the words as she reads silently; the lips that I know are ridiculously soft and barely touched. I could tell that hardly anyone had kissed her and something about that draws me to her even more, like she trusted me enough to be one of them. Probably not now, though.

"Hey, I think we need to talk," I say. "There's some stuff I want to tell you."

The light on the sign changes and she glances up at it. "I can't talk right now. I have to get a coffee and stop by the library before class."

She starts across the street, and I grab her sleeve. "Callie, I owe you an explanation."

Her muscles stiffen as she glances down at my hand on her arm and then up at me. "No, you don't. I promise. I didn't think we were dating or anything." She wiggles out of my grasp and hurries across the street.

I start to call out to her that she's wrong, that I owe her everything, but she starts to run, like she wants nothing more than to get away from me.

Chapter Eleven

#3: Do Whatever the Hell You Want for Once Instead of What You Think You Should Do.

Callie

I'm avoiding him. I told myself a thousand times that he didn't do anything wrong, but I'm "unstable" as Seth so pleasantly told me during History class. He also told me that I cut my ties with Kayden because when he left, he took some of my "trust" with him.

"Why do you keep making air quotes?" I ask, picking up my bag off the floor.

Professor Jennerly glances back at us from the front of the classroom and then continues on with his lecture, pacing in front of the class with his hands behind his back.

Seth leans over the desk and whispers, "Because I'm quoting what it said in my Psych book."

"Your Psych book talked about my problem?" I put my bag on my desk and unzip it.

"Not specifically, but it was close." He sticks the end of the pen in his mouth as he returns upright in his chair.

I drop my books into my bag and by the time I'm finished packing, class is being let out. We wait until the room has almost cleared before we head down the stairs.

Professor Jennerly, a tall man with salt-and-pepper hair and thick-framed glasses, waits for us by the door. "My classroom is not for outside chitchat," he says. "If you two want to talk, then I suggest you stay out of my class."

"We're sorry," Seth says and then rolls his eyes at me. "It'll never happen again."

We walk down the packed hallway. Outside the windows, the football stadium stretches in the distance and the metal gleams in the sunshine.

"Are you thinking about him?" Seth asks.

I tear my gaze away from the window and scoot over for a group of guys taking up half the hall. "Thinking about whom?"

He angles his head to the side with a pucker at his brow. "Callie, you need to just forget about him or talk to him. You can't keep avoiding him, yet wanting him."

"I don't want him," I lie and when he frowns at me, I sigh. "All right, fine. Yes, I think about him. A lot. But I'll get over him. God knows I barely know him."

"Yet you two have shared a lot," he says and presses his hand flat on the door to push it open. "You saved him. He

was the first guy you ever trusted. He gave you your first real kiss."

"I trusted you first." I rummage through my purse for my gum as the breeze whisks through my hair.

"That's not the same." He releases the door and it clicks shut. "I'm a friend. Kayden is more to you than that."

"I don't know if that's true." I take out the gum and wiggle a piece out of the pack. "I don't know what I feel for him or if it is good or bad. In fact, sometimes I just feel like a scared little girl who doesn't know what to do with anything."

He looks at me with pity as we amble underneath a canopy of bare branches with the sunlight shimmering through them. "Well, maybe you should just do whatever the hell you want, instead of what you think you should do."

I stab a finger at him with accusation in my eyes. "You just quoted that from the list."

He laughs wickedly, throwing his head back and his blond hair falls out of his eyes. "That's because it's the quote of the day. Didn't you get the memo?"

I shake my head, laughing at him. "Darn it. I forgot to check my messages today. I must have missed it."

He swings his arm around my shoulder. "The question is: what do you *want* to do? And I mean really, really want?"

I stop in front of the bench, considering what he asked, and staring out at the large stadium in the distance. "I want to have fun."

Kayden

"I'm not really in the partying mood." I spray some cologne onto my shirt and click the cap back on. "I'd rather just stay in and catch up on sleep. I feel like shit."

"That's because you're depressed." Luke pulls open the dresser drawer and searches through his shirts, finally selecting a long-sleeved one. "Over someone who I can't mention or else you're going to look at me like you want to kill me."

I run my fingers through my hair. "That's such a fucking lie."

He loops a belt through his jeans with an exaggerated eye widening. "We should just walk, right? That way, no one will have to be responsible for driving back."

"You do realize the party is three blocks down at Campus Habitat. We'd be stupid to drive."

"I thought it was at one of the apartments farther down?"

I check my messages and then hold down the side button, locking the screen. "Nope, it's only a few streets over from this one."

He grabs his jacket off the back of the computer chair. "That makes the DD situation even better."

We lock up and head outside. It's late, the stars are out, and the lampposts gleam against the concrete. There are a group of girls in tight dresses and high heels, traveling in the same direction we are.

We end up behind them and Luke's wheels are turning

as he eyes the tallest one's ass. "I think a challenge would be lovely right about now."

"Or you could just go hit on her. That always works, too."

"Only when you're my wingman." He glances at me, testing my reaction. "What do you think?"

I shrug, even though I don't want to. "I can go up there with you."

He rolls his eyes. "All right, if that's the way you want to be."

We strut up to the girls and Luke starts making conversation with the girl he was checking out. A shorter one with blond curls, wearing a red dress, starts talking to me, but I barely hear her. I'm preoccupied by thoughts of Callie and what I'd be doing if I were actually with her.

"I'd definitely not be going to a party," I mutter to myself. "That's for sure."

The girl that's been chatting to me blinks confusedly. "What?"

"It's a really nice night," I say and she laughs, but her eyebrows knit.

There's a lot of noise coming from the hot tub that's around the side of the three-story apartment that the party is taking place at. I hold the door open for everyone to walk in.

Luke is making a joke as he enters and the other two girls walk in behind him, whispering and giggling to each other. It's annoying me to no end, and by the time I'm knocking my fist against the door, I can't wait to get inside and ditch them.

One of the members of the football team, Ben, is throwing the party. He's a nice guy, although I don't really know him. When he swings the door open, however, it would appear that we're best friends.

"Kayden, man." He sticks out his hand to pound fists.

I bump mine against his and arch my eyebrows. "Hey, man."

He looks over my shoulder at Luke and the girls. "You brought guests." Grinning, he steps aside so we can come in.

The apartment is much bigger than my dorm. Music plays from the stereo and there's a fold-up table in the corner where a poker game is going on. Alcohol bottles line the counter inside the kitchen, along with cups, chips, and a bunch of other food. In between the couches a horde of people are dancing.

My eyes zero in on a girl with her brown hair pulled up in a clip, wearing black jeans with a pair of lace-up boots and a purple tank top. She's talking with a guy, laughing and shaking her ass as she really gets into the music.

"Callie." No matter how many times I blink, it doesn't seem real.

"Do you want to get a drink?" The girl I walked in with coils her hair around her finger as she gazes up at me, biting her bottom lip.

I shake my head and my attention returns to Callie. "Maybe in a minute."

She's dancing with Seth, who's really getting into the music as they shout out the lyrics with the crowd and then laugh, raising their hands in the air.

"What are they doing here?" Luke wonders as he steps up beside me. "This doesn't seem like their scene."

Seth notices us and leans forward to say something in Callie's ear. She turns her head and looks at us. Her face lights up and she weaves around people toward me with Seth at her heels. For a second, I wonder if I've fallen asleep and this is all a dream because she looks really happy to see me.

When she reaches me, she flings her arms around my neck, and I can smell the vodka on her breath. "Kayden's here," she says, hugging me so tightly it kind of hurts.

My breathing speeds up a little as I put my hand on her back. "Are you drunk?"

She draws away, looking me in the eyes and nodding. "A little."

"No, she's wasted," Seth explains as he pushes through the last of the crowd and joins us in the entrance, shoving up the sleeves of his black, button-down jacket. "And I mean fucking trashed."

Keeping my hand on her back, Callie rests her face on my chest. "I thought she didn't drink that much?"

He's distracted by a guy in the corner of the room, who is sipping a drink and talking to a girl with really short auburn hair. "She doesn't, but tonight she did. Look, can you watch her for just a little bit? There's someone I need to talk to."

I nod, tracing my fingers down her back. "Sure."

"Make sure to keep your hands to yourself," he warns, backing away with his finger pointed at me. "She's drunk enough that she won't remember a thing, which makes any touching on your part wrong."

I shake my head at him. "What kind of a guy do you think I am?"

He shrugs with judgment in his eyes. "I have no idea."

Callie blinks up at me with hardly any awareness on her face. "Who are the girls you're here with?"

The blonde standing to my right shoots me a dirty look and puts her hands on her hips.

I keep my eyes on Callie. "Hey, let's go into the kitchen and get you some water."

She nods her head up and down. "I am really thirsty."

The innocence in her eyes and the way she clings to my shirt as I guide her toward the kitchen makes me uneasy. She trusts me at the moment and I'm worried I'm going to fuck it up, like I always do.

Ben is in the kitchen talking to a girl with long, curly brown hair, a tight pair of jeans, and a low-cut red top. When he sees us, a curious expression crosses his face.

"Who's this?" he asks me, nodding his chin at Callie.

"It's Callie Lawrence." I move my arm away from her to grab a plastic cup off the top of the stack on the counter. "She goes to school here. Her dad was actually my coach back in high school."

Callie lets go of my waist. With her hands out to the side of her, she attempts to control her balance as I turn the faucet on to fill up the cup.

"So, your father is a coach?" Ben leans back against the

223

counter as the girl he was talking to wanders over to the bar to fill up a glass.

"Yeah, he's been one for like twenty years or something," Callie says with a slight slur to her speech.

"Did he teach you stuff?" Ben asks, crossing his arms. I don't like the teasing tone in his voice. "Like what the plays are or how to throw and catch a ball?"

I turn around with a glass of water in my hand as Callie rolls her eyes at him. "Obviously, like I know that you're the receiver." She blinks her eyes, mockingly. "Which means you catch the ball."

"Well, aren't you just adorable." Ben takes a step toward her with a look of fascination on his face.

My hand goes up against his chest to push him back. "No way. She's off limits."

Ben looks at me apologetically as I hand the glass of water to Callie and she tips her head back, downing it. "I'm sorry. I didn't realize you were dating her."

I don't bother to correct him, for many reasons, some of which are really fucked up. When he leaves the kitchen, Callie moves the cup away from her mouth and licks the water off her lips, making me think dirty thoughts I know I can't act on.

"He's kind of an asshole," she says, handing the cup back to me.

I crush it and toss it in the trashcan. "And you're kind of feisty when you're this drunk."

When I face her again, she's chewing on her bottom lip

with her gaze boring into me. "Do you like that I'm feisty? Does it make you want me?"

Oh, fucking shit. She is wasted. "How about we get you home?"

She shakes her head, backing toward the counter with unsteady legs. Gripping the edge, she hops onto it and bumps her head on the cupboard. "I want to know." She rubs her head, shooting a dirty look at the cupboard like it did something wrong. "When I'm like this, does it make you want me?"

I glance over my shoulder, praying to God Seth will walk in here and save me from this uncomfortable conversation. "I don't know, Callie."

She pouts out her bottom lip. "It's because you don't want me at all, isn't it?"

Sighing, I put my hands down on the counter so she's in between my arms. "No, it's not that. Trust me. It's just that I don't want to have this conversation with you when you're not going to remember it."

She leans forward, reducing the gap between our faces. "I'll remember it. I promise."

I try not to laugh at her, clenching my hands into fists to resist the urge to slide them onto her hips. "All right, you want the truth?" I ask and she bobs her head up and down. "No, I don't like you better this way. I like the sober Callie, the one that I can talk to. The one that is so sweet it's fucking adorable." I dip my face forward and breathe on her neck, moving toward the no-touching line, but not crossing it. "The one that trembles just

225

from the feel of my breath. The one that I want to kiss and touch so fucking badly it drives me crazy. The one that makes me feel things…" I trail off and incline away, glad to see that her eyelids are only half open. That way I know I'm still safe.

"I'm tired." She yawns, stretching her arms above her and I catch a glimpse of her bare stomach; flat, tiny, and firm. "Can you find Seth so he can take me home?"

I tuck a strand of her hair behind her ear. "Yeah, you come with me, though. I don't want to leave you here alone."

She nods, hopping off the counter, and I drape my arm around her back to hold her steady. We search the house, but Seth isn't anywhere. I find Luke at the poker table, playing a hand, cheating just like his father taught him.

"Hey, man, I'm going to take Callie home," I say as he glances up at me from his cards. "If you see Seth, would you tell him?"

Luke nods and then his eyes dash to the red and blue chips in front of him. "Yeah, man will do."

Callie buries her face into my shirt as we walk out the door and into the quiet hallway. She leans her weight on me and I guide her down the stairs and out the doors. The air is chilly and she shivers against me.

"Where's your jacket?" I ask, rubbing my hand up and down her arm.

She shrugs as she stumbles over the curb and I catch her with my arm. Her eyes are barely open and she keeps sighing. Finally, I give up and stop in the middle of the sidewalk.

She blinks up at me. "What's wrong?"

I let go of her and speak slow because I know she's struggling to comprehend anything that's going on. "I'm going to pick you up and carry you back. Is that okay?"

She eyes my hands and then reverts her gaze to me. "Okay."

I step cautiously toward her. "Put your arms around my neck."

She obeys, sliding her hands up my chest and hooking them around my neck. She rests her head against my chest as I wrap my arm around her back. Bending my knees, I put my other arm underneath her legs and scoop her up into my arms. She nuzzles her face into my chest as I start up the sidewalk. I take my time because I love how it feels to carry her, the way she needs me, the way I need to protect her.

By the time I reach the McIntyre residence hall, I'm working really hard not to panic that I have to put her down. "Callie, where's your ID card?" I ask. "I didn't bring mine."

"In my pocket," she murmurs, reaching for it, but her arm falls slack to her side. "I'm too tired to get it out."

"Try again, okay?" I practically beg but she's nonresponsive.

Emptying my mind of any potential dirty thoughts, I brace her against my chest and slip my fingers into her pocket, quickly pulling her card out. Swiping it through the lock, the door unlocks and I get us inside. I take the elevators to the upper floor and find her room. When I extend my hand for the doorknob, she wakes up and grabs a hold of my arm.

"No, don't open it," she says, nodding at the red scarf tied around the doorknob. "That means my roommate is… she's…preoccupied."

I try not to laugh at the fact that even when she's drunk, she has a hard time saying it. "Where do you want me to take you?"

She drops her head back against my chest. "You can just keep carrying me. It's very relaxing."

"What about Seth's room?"

Her eyelids are shut and her warm breath flows through my shirt. "You'll have to go get him…"

My shoulders slump as I shift her body inward toward my chest and start down the hall to my right. When I step outside, I walk across the grass to the Downy building and take the elevator to my room.

"Callie, I have to set you down while I get the door open," I whisper in her ear.

She nods and I carefully lower her feet to the ground. She leans back against the wall, her eyelids closing. I tap my fingers against the lock, pushing the code, and then shove the door open. Flipping the lights on, I step back and pick her up, carrying her inside. Kneeling down on the bed, I lower her onto the mattress, gently setting her down. She rolls to her side as I stand back up and figure out what I'm going to do. I could sleep in Luke's bed, but he'll chew my ass out when he shows up.

"Where are you going to sleep?" She eyes me as I kick off my boots into a corner.

"That's what I was trying to figure out." I stare at her with hesitance. "Is it okay if I lie down by you?"

Her eyes enlarge a little and hesitantly, she wiggles her body, scooting over toward the wall. I lie down on my side, keeping space between us as her eyelids close.

"I've never shared a bed with anyone besides Seth," she mutters. "I can't sleep when I'm lying by someone else."

I start to roll out of the bed. "That's okay. I'll go find somewhere else to sleep."

Her fingers wrap around my arm. "You don't have to go anywhere. I feel safe with you."

I pause. "Are you sure?"

"Yeah, you make it seem like everything he did doesn't exist."

"Callie, what are you talking about?"

"It doesn't matter." She yawns and inches a little closer to me, tucking her hands under her cheek and curling her knees up. "I'm tired."

My hand shakes a little as I reach out and smooth her hair back from her forehead. "It's okay. You can go to sleep."

She nods her head and seconds later, the sound of her soft breathing surrounds me. Without even thinking, I lean over and gently kiss her forehead, wondering what the hell I'm going to do when morning rolls around.

Chapter Twelve

#12: See How Far You Can Go with Something You're Afraid Of.

Callie

When I open my eyes, my skull feels like it's cracked and my brain is throbbing. I'm aware right away that I'm not in my room. There are guys' clothes all over the floor, a PlayStation on a shelf near a flat-screen television, and the blankets pulled over me smell like the cologne Kayden wears.

My eyes widen as I sit up in the bed, racking my brain for details of what happened last night. I remember Seth asking me what I wanted to do and I told him I wanted to have fun. So he took me out and we ended up getting drunk. After that, everything becomes hazy, but for some reason I can picture staring up at the stars while someone carries me.

The door to my right squeaks as Kayden enters the room holding two coffee cups. He's wearing a hooded black thermal shirt that shows off his lean arms and his jeans hang at his hips.

He does a double take when he sees that I'm awake. "For a while, I thought you were going to sleep all day."

Sunlight flickers through the window as I glance at the clock hanging on the wall above the bed. "Holy crap, it's almost dinnertime?" The thought of food squeezes at my stomach.

He hands me a coffee and I gladly take it. "Seth told me that you love lattes."

I nod, taking a swallow. It tastes divine. "God, my head hurts so badly."

He balances the other cup on the nightstand. "That usually happens when you drink too much."

I lower the cup away from my face. "Kayden…I can't…I don't know what happened."

He sits down on the bed beside me and the mattress curves under his weight. "Well, I only got the privilege of witnessing the last half of the night, but from what I heard, Seth said you drank a ton of vodka. By the time I met up with you at Ben's party, you were trashed."

I wince. "Did I do anything…weird?"

"Not really. You had to sleep here because I lost track of Seth and there was a red scarf on your door."

"Where did you sleep?"

He tenses, looking guilty. "Next to you."

I lick the froth from my lips and stare out the window

at the clear blue sky. "If I remember right, you had to carry me?"

He nods. "You could barely walk…I didn't mind doing it, though."

I pull the blanket off my body and slide my feet over the edge of the bed. "I should probably go take a shower and try to eat. Although, I feel like puking my guts out."

He places a hand on my leg, enfolding his fingers around my knee. "I actually want you to come somewhere with me. There's something really important I need to tell you…It's about what happened that night at the pool house." There's heaviness in his eyes and stiffness in his voice.

"Okay," I say. "Do I have to go with you now? Or can I shower first? I feel really gross."

He laughs at me. "You can shower first. I'll wait for you out on the benches."

I get to my feet with a sudden urge to hug him. "All right, I'll make it quick." I head for the door, but pause as I turn the knob. "Kayden, thank you for taking care of me last night."

"It's not that big of a deal." He hesitates. "I owe you a lot more nights of that before we'll ever be even."

Kayden

I hardly slept last night. I lay in bed, listening to Callie breathe, trying to match my own breathing to the rhythm.

Part of me wished she'd just stay asleep, so I could continue to lie next to her.

By the time the sun rose above the mountains, I decided it was time to tell her the truth, so she knew what she was getting into. Then she can decide if she really wants me, because I can't seem to stay away from her.

I'm nervous as fucking hell as I drive up the mountain where we took our first hike together. I park the truck near the tree line and we hop out, walking below the blue sky toward the hills.

"We're really going to climb up there again?" she asks, staring up at the top of the cliff as we approach it. Her hair is scattered across her back and her arms are crossed over her chest.

I mount onto a boulder that's on the side of the path and gaze out at the view. "It's quiet today." I sit down on the rock and pat the spot next to me. "Come sit down by me."

She shuffles toward me and I offer her my hand to pull her up. She situates beside me, rests back on her palms, and gazes out at the hills in front of us. I shut my eyes for a moment, feeling everything, knowing it's going to go either good or bad when I tell her.

"That night you showed up and my father was beating my ass," I start before I can back out, "wasn't the first time that he hit me."

She doesn't act surprised. "How many times has he hit you?"

I watch a leaf float in front of us, drifting up and down, before blowing out across the spacious land. "I don't know... I lost track around the age of seven or something."

She sucks in a sharp breath and her head angles to the side so she's looking at me. "He hit you like that when you were little?"

I shrug, like it's no big deal. "It's just something he did, you know? More when he was drunk, although he did do it when he was sober. He didn't like things that we did and instead of grounding us or taking away our toys, he would hit and yell at us."

She stays silent for a long time as she studies the clouds in the sky. "What did you do to make him mad that night?"

"I hurt my hand." I flex my fingers out in front of me, not telling her that I did it on purpose. I'm not ready for that. "He was worried I was going to ruin my football career."

She grows quiet again. "Why did you never do anything about it? Tell someone? Or fight back?"

And there it is. What I was waiting for. She's realizing how fucked up the situation is. "I don't know. At first I guess it was because I was too young to understand and by the time I got old enough to do something about it, I just didn't care. Sometimes it feels like I've died inside." I shrug and then shrug again, forcing myself to look at her.

She arches her eyebrows at me, confounded, but there's no judgment in her eyes. "You didn't care that he hit you?"

I shut my eyes and inhale the cool air. "That's why I'm telling you this. I just don't do feelings very well and I'm probably going to shut down and do a lot of fucked-up things. You need to just stay away from me."

It's silent and I open my eyelids, half expecting her to be gone, but she's watching me, her chest rising and falling with her breathing. She stares at me and then shifts her weight, scooting toward me and I tense. Kneeling up, she hitches her leg over my lap and encloses her arms around my neck, resting her head against my shoulder. She hugs me tightly and my eyes widen, my whole body constricting as I try to keep my hands off her, not knowing what to do or how to react. After a while her scent and warmth get to me and my hands slide up to the bottom of her back. Shutting my eyes, I hug her back with everything I have in me.

Callie

There is something about someone trusting you enough with their secrets that it makes it easier to trust them. It's like they're opening their heart and in return yours should open up to them, too.

Kayden opened up to me and I wanted to open up back, but I couldn't. Not completely anyway. I want to. I want him so much that I don't know what to do with myself.

I want him. I want him. I want him.

No matter how many times I write it, it still doesn't feel real. None of this does, because I never believed it would happen.

Someone knocks on my door and I climb off the bed to answer it. Kayden is on the other side with a football cradled

under his arm. Instead of wearing his uniform, he's dressed in a nice pair of jeans and a gray T-shirt. His brown hair flips up beneath a black baseball hat.

"I have a favor to ask you." It's been a couple of weeks since he told me about his father and we've hung out a lot as friends, but there's something in his eyes tonight that's different, lighter.

"Okay..." I back away from the doorway and let him in. His eyes instantly go to the open notebook on my bed. I lunge for it and tuck it under my pillow.

"Was that the journal?" He grins as he switches the ball's position to beneath his other arm.

"Can you pretend you didn't see that?" I put my hands out in front of me, overlapping my fingers. "Pretty please."

He smiles. "Is there stuff in it about me?"

I pretend to itch my eye to conceal the blood rushing to my cheeks. "No."

"Callie, you're blushing," he teases, taking a step forward so he can withdraw my hand from my face. "Don't hide it. It's cute."

I roll my eyes, more at myself, because his comment only makes my cheeks heat more. "So what's the favor?"

"I need you to come help me practice." He wanders around the room, taking in everything, passing the ball back and forth between his hands. "Luke's busy with some girl he's been dating for a week and he won't come with me."

"I can do that," I say. "But you don't look dressed for practice."

"This will be a mild practice." He faces me. "Just a little throwing."

"And you think I can help you?" I question, my gaze scaling up his very sturdy body.

"I saw you at the store. It looked like you were more than capable. Besides, you were bragging to Ben at that party about how awesome your football knowledge is."

"I did not. Did I?"

He nods. "You did."

It makes me wonder what else I said. Sometimes it feels like I said stuff to him that he keeps from me.

"All right." I grab my keys from my desk and slip my feet into my Converses. "I will do my best to challenge you."

He chuckles under his breath as he turns for the door and I wonder if he's thinking about the night we kissed like I am.

❧

When we get to the stadium, the lights are shining down across the green field. The bleachers are empty and the only sign of anyone is the janitor out front emptying the garbage cans.

We walk into the center of the field and I spin in a circle, looking at all the bleachers, feeling small because of the massive size of my surroundings. The sky is dark, the stars are out, and the moon orbs fully.

Kayden tosses the football up in the air as I button up my jacket. "You know, ever since that day at the store, I've been really curious to see you throw again. I'm wondering if it was a fluke."

I position my hands on my hips and target a glare in his direction. "Hey, what's with the insulting?"

"I'm just trying to get you worked up." He starts to run backward with the ball in his hand. "It'll make you play better." He launches the ball at me and I catch it, wincing when the leather scrapes my palms.

"That stung." I pretend to be hurt, cradling my wrist.

His arms fall to his side and he strides toward me. "Callie, I'm so—"

I fling back my arm and throw the football as hard as I can in his direction. He runs backward, jumping just in time to catch it.

When his feet touch the grass again, he shakes his head. "You play dirty."

I shrug, not arguing. "It was how I was taught. My dad takes the game very seriously."

"Oh, I know that. Do you know how many times he chewed my ass off for messing up? It was a good thing, though." He throws the football to my side and I have to move quickly to catch it. "He kept me on my toes and pushed me. If it wasn't for him, I probably would have never gotten the scholarship."

I hold the football in my hands. "I don't want this to come out rude, but couldn't your family afford to pay for your tuition if you wouldn't have received the scholarship?"

"My dad wouldn't," he says, swallowing hard. "He used to tell us all the time, either we found our own way out of the house, or we'd be stuck there...I didn't want to be stuck there." I start to open my mouth, but he claps his hands and then holds them out in front of him. "Here, throw it to me."

I toss it back to him and he catches it easily with a grin on his face. "All right, this time I'm going to throw it to you and then try to tackle you."

My eyes widen as my jaw drops. "Are you being serious?"

He chucks it high up in the air. "I never kid about football. So, go long. It'll give you more of a chance to outrun me."

I back down the field, still doubting he'll actually chase me and tackle me to the ground. When I'm fairly close to the touchdown zone, I stop and face him. "Are you really going to chase me down? Or, are you just trying to make me play better?"

He's a ways away, but the deviousness masking his expression is evident. "Trust me, I'm not joking. In fact, I'm kind of looking forward to it."

My heart skips at the gruffness of his voice. "Fine, throw the ball, but I'm going to win."

He looks momentarily stunned, but then he backs up, his feet picking up momentum, before his arm swings forward

and the ball spirals through the air toward me. My feet move quickly as I sprint backward with my hands up in the air. At the last second, I give a little jump, and snag the ball in midair. When my feet touch the grass, I hesitate, still unsure if he's going to chase me down.

As soon as I'm steady, he runs at me, like *really* runs. I whirl around on my toes and take off down the field. Thankfully, I'm close because there's no way my tiny legs are going to be able to outrun his long ones for very long.

He's laughing as he chases me and his heavy footsteps are approaching rapidly. My eyes zone in on the yellow poles at the end and the white line I need to make it over. When my foot crosses it, I spin around with my arms above my head.

Kayden slows to a jog, shaking his head and panting. "Okay, I think I might have underestimated you and given you too much of a head start."

A grin spreads across my face as I throw the football at the grass. "What is it you guys do when you get a touchdown?" I put my finger to my chin, pretending to think deeply. "Oh, yeah." I skip backward, waving my hands in front of me, doing a silly little dance.

He laughs, his eyes crinkling at the corners. "Wow, you have a cocky streak in you."

I pick up the football, grab the pole with my free hand, and spin around it, feeling alive and weightless. For a second, I shut my eyes and enjoy the cool breeze against my cheeks, owning the moment. When I open my eyelids again, Kayden is walking toward me, taking leisurely strides with his hands tucked into his pockets.

I slow down, still holding on to the pole, watching him narrow the distance. He doesn't say a word, his emerald eyes fastened on me with confusion and intensity in them. As he reaches me, I lean against the pole, fighting to keep my breathing steady against the desire flowing off him.

He takes the ball out of my hand and throws it over his shoulder toward the end of the field. "Let's get rid of that stupid thing."

"I thought that's why you brought me here?" I say with an uneven voice, unable to take my eyes off his lips as he licks them. "To help you practice."

His lips part, like he's going to say something, but then he presses them together and rotates his hat backward so the visor is behind his head. Inclining his body toward me, my back brushes the pole as his lips hover above mine. He deliberates, putting his hand on the pole next to my head, and then he kisses me.

It starts off soft, a light brush of our lips, but then his other hand grabs the pole and his body moves in until it presses against mine. Our legs tangle, our chests collide, and the tip of his tongue runs along my lips until I open my mouth and let him in.

A breathy noise escapes the back of my throat and at first I'm mortified, but it seems to encourage him. Desire and heat radiates through the entwining of our tongues. One of his hands grips my waist, just beneath the bottom of my shirt and my nerves jumble. His other hand travels down my side, his thumb tracing my ribs, before resting on my hip. Tightening his fingers around me, he lifts me up. Gasping, I hook my legs around his waist in a vise grip.

My mind is flying about a million miles an hour. I'm afraid. Not of him, but everything connected to what he's doing. Do I want this? Do I? The answer is yes. I want it. Badly.

I hope he doesn't notice the anxious tremble of my body as his fingers slip underneath my shirt and he sketches his finger-tips along my stomach. As he nips at my bottom lip, I let out an uncontrollable whimper.

He draws back, putting a sliver of space between our faces. His pupils are huge and shiny beneath the stadium lights and his untamed breath caresses against my cheek.

"Callie, I don't want to…" He pauses, tucking a strand of my hair behind my ear. "I don't want to push you."

It's like he can read my inexperience all over my face. I bite down on my lip, working to hide my embarrassment. "It's fine."

He wavers. "Are you… are you sure?"

I nod my head swiftly. "Yes."

Without any more reluctance he crashes his lips against mine and a gasp falters from my throat at the heat his kiss brings to my body. His tongue enters my mouth again as his hands stay under my shirt, his palms touching my stomach. It's the most frightening and most wonderful experience of my life. I don't ever want to forget it.

Daringly, I slip my hands underneath his shirt as I breathe ravenously. He winces as my hands wander along his well-defined abs covered with the bumpy lines of his scars.

I worry he's going to reach up and tug my hands out of his shirt, but instead his hand explores higher up to the edge of my bra. His lips leave mine and touch the corner of my mouth, trailing kisses down my cheek, along my jawline, to the side of my neck where my pulse is racing. My head falls to the side uncontrollably as his palm moves over my breast just outside my bra. Sucking in a deep breath, I wait for it to catch up with me, but all I can think about is him exploring my body more. I want to find out what it's like to be touched by someone I trust; by someone I give my permission to.

His fingers start to move below my bra and my insides quiver as he strokes his thumb across my nipple. Heat blazes through my body and I grab on to his sides, grasping on to him with everything in me; feeling his scars, while he feels mine.

He lets out a groan as he sucks on the bottom of my neck and my body curves into his. "Callie," he whispers. "If you want me to stop, just tell me."

I don't want him to stop. At all. It feels too good. "I don't—"

There's a deafening click and within seconds, every light flips off and darkness smothers us. I freeze, grabbing on to

Kayden, as he pulls his mouth away from my neck. I feel his chest heaving where my fingers hold on to him and for a moment, we're silent.

Then, Kayden starts to laugh. "Well, this is fun."

"Can you see anything?" I whisper, turning my head and squinting.

He shakes his head. "Hold on."

He removes his hand from my breast and I think he's going to put me down, but instead he wraps his arms around my lower back, interlocking his fingers to hold up my weight. He walks through the dark, carrying me, and I tighten my legs around him, wishing I could see his face, because I want to know what he's thinking.

His shoes scuff the grass and then we move up onto concrete. Seconds later, we exit out of a tunnel and into the parking lot, which is mostly vacant except for a few cars along the back row, which is lit up by lampposts.

The brightness stings at my eyes. "Why did that happen?"

His emerald eyes sparkle as he shrugs his shoulders. "I wonder if that was by accident, or if it was done intentionally to get us off the field?"

I adjust my hands a little so my arms are looped around the back of his neck. "Were you not supposed to be playing there?"

"Technically, no." His smile grows like he's enjoying the moment. "But I'm extremely glad I did."

I let my head fall forward into his shoulder, breathing in his scent. "Now what do we do?"

He's quiet for a while and I finally lean back to look him in the eyes. He appears conflicted by something and then he sets me down on the ground, lacing his fingers through mine.

"Should we see where the wind takes us?" he asks.

I stare at my hand in his and then look up at him. "That sounds good to me."

Chapter Thirteen

#9: Dance in the Rain.
#13: Live in the Moment.
#15: Be Yourself.

Kayden

I'll admit it. I had the whole thing planned and it ended up going where I hoped it would go. Ever since I told Callie about my father, we'd been getting close as friends. Which was fine, except I'm extremely fucking attracted to her, a revelation that came to me during an intense moment in the library.

She'd been helping me study for an English exam and when she showed up, she'd had a jacket on. As she was reading me some of her notes, she took off the jacket. Underneath it, she had on a white T-shirt and I could see the outline of her bra through it and her nipples poking up through the fabric. She probably didn't realize it because she is not the kind of girl that would do that on purpose. In fact, if I pointed it out to her, her cheeks would get red and she'd run off.

"Kayden?" she asked, looking at me perplexedly. "Are you listening? You kind of look like you're spacing off."

I was leaning back in the chair with my arm on the table and a pen in my mouth as I chewed on the end. "I kind of was."

She let out an exhausted sigh. "Do you want me to read it again?"

I nodded my head, barely paying attention. "Sure."

She started reading from the book and my mind went back to dirty thoughts of what it would be like to touch her all over and make her moan underneath me as I rocked into her. I wondered if she'd let me if I tried. The friend's thing seemed to be working for us. She made me laugh and smile and I was enjoying myself. My dark thoughts and problems had been contained more than they had in a long time.

It seemed like I should just let things be, but the more I watched her lips read the words from the book, the more I wanted to bite on them.

Her eyes rose up from the book and she was trying to look angry. "You're not listening to me, are you?"

I shook my head, unable to stop myself from grinning at her. "Not really. Sorry. I'm kind of distracted."

"With what?" she asks with uncertainty. "Do you want to talk about it?"

It took a lot not to smile and whisper in her ear every single detail about the very vivid images running through my mind. "No, that's okay. Trust me. You probably don't want to hear about it."

Her forehead wrinkled as she tried to figure out why I was so happy. "Do you need a break?"

"Nah, you can keep reading. I'm enjoying the sound of your voice."

She sucked her bottom lip in to stifle a smile and that nearly threw me over the edge. I decided that I needed to be with her just a little bit more so I conjured up my lovely football plan.

After the lights shut off at the field, we end up back at my room. I'm surprised how willingly she went with me. I almost backed out a few times on our way there, when my emotions were getting a little too intense for me.

She walks around the small space in between the beds, glancing at my stuff, and picks up a DVD case, reading the back. "You recorded all your games?"

I pull a face as I take my hat off and toss it onto the bed. "No, my dad did. He liked to make me watch it afterward, so he could point out everything I did wrong."

She sets down the case and turns to me. "I'm sorry."

"No, I'm sorry," I say, raking my fingers through my hair. "For talking about this stuff with you."

Her eyes fix on me as she inches toward me. "I want you to talk to me about it. I would have never asked you questions if I didn't want to hear the answers...I can't just forget what I saw that night. I don't think I ever will."

I remember the night she was drunk and how she muttered about a guy doing something to her. "You can tell me stuff, too, if you want. I'm a great listener."

She turns her face toward the window, her chest rising and falling. "You know, I'm surprised at how much warmer it is here than back at home."

She's hiding something. I decrease the gap between us and her shoulders tense. I start to open my mouth to press her, but she tilts her head toward me with a strange look on her face, like she's scared out of her mind. Before I can even register what she's doing, she leans in and seals her lips to mine. Her body trembles as she grips at the bottom of my shirt, waiting for me to kiss her back.

I wasn't planning on taking it any farther tonight, but the feel of her lips is overwhelming. Without even thinking, my mouth opens and my tongue enters hers, devouring her.

"Oh, my God," she moans as my hands slide around to her back and I pull her closer, moving my lips deliberately against hers. I'm savoring every inch, every spot, memorizing it.

Suddenly the intense kiss shifts to desperation. I spin us around and back us toward the bed, my feet getting entangled with hers. My hand snaps out to catch us as we fall onto the mattress. Rolling her onto her back, I hold up my weight with my arms, but allow enough closeness that her heat radiates into me and her breasts brush my chest every time she breathes.

I loosen up a little and start to explore her body with my hands, feeling the soft skin of her stomach, her ribs, the bottom of her breast. Before I know what I'm doing, I have my hand underneath her bra again. I stroke my finger across her nipple and she gasps as her legs constrict around my midsection. It

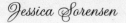

feels good—way too good. I need to stop, otherwise it's going to break apart on me.

I start to turn to the side, but her body follows mine and her leg hitches around my hip, so my thigh is pressing between her legs. As my fingers dig into her waist, her body bows forward and she rubs herself along my thigh. Her head falls back as her glazed eyes open and she begins to quiver.

Fuck. I've never been so turned on before. I begin moving my leg against her and lean forward to grab her lip between my teeth, nipping it softly as I cup her breast with my hand. Clutching my shoulders, her entire body shakes with her nerves.

Should I stop? It's pretty clear she's never gone this far before and I don't want to be the one responsible for pushing her where she's not ready to go.

"Callie," I say, but her fingers tighten around my shoulder blades, her nails piercing my skin through the fabric of my shirt as she lets out a moan and I know she's close. I put my hand between her legs and rub her the rest of the way, her body bucking against my hand.

Moments later, she blinks her eyes as her body relaxes. I watch her in complete awe as she works to reclaim control of her thoughts. As she settles down, her whole face sinks and my chest tightens as she stares over my shoulder.

"Hey?" I graze my finger along the small birthmark on the side of her eye. "Are you okay?"

She blinks at me and I can tell she's trying not to cry.

"Yeah, I'm fine." She squirms out of my arms and starts to climb over me. "Can you just give me a few moments?"

I'm worried. The sadness that washed away from her eyes momentarily has returned and is magnified. "Where are you going?"

"I have to . . ." She trails off as she stands up and pulls her bra and shirt back into place.

I sit up, reaching for her arm. "Callie, I'm sorry. I shouldn't have—"

She throws the door open and runs out without so much as an explanation.

"God damn it." I flop down on the bed, dragging my fingers across my face. Usually, I'm the one who bails out of these kinds of situations, which makes me wonder what she's running from.

Callie

I have no idea what just happened. Well, actually I do. I had my first orgasm, simply by rubbing up against Kayden's leg and then he finished it off with his hand. It felt so good, my mind could scarcely comprehend anything else, but when it's over, everything piles on my shoulders like cracked bricks. Suddenly, I see *his* face instead of Kayden's.

He's looking at me with concern as I jump off the bed and race out of the room. Once I'm in the bathroom, I lock the door and collapse onto my knees in front of the toilet. I lift the lid, feeling the pain burn in my stomach. I want it out. So badly. I drop my head down, jab my finger down my throat, and with a sharp shove, I force everything to exit my body. My shoulders jerk as I hack on my finger and the vomit tears at my throat. My eyes water and my nostrils burn as I lean away and take my finger out of my mouth. The tip has a little blood on it and I wipe it off on a piece of toilet paper.

I rest my back against the cold tile wall and my head falls back. Hot tears spill out of my eyes and stream down my cheeks as I smear the vomit and sweat off my face with the sleeve of my shirt, my chest twitching fitfully as I work to breathe.

"I don't want to be this way," I whisper as my eyes fill up with tears. "I don't want to be this way." I yank at my hair and scream through my teeth, fucking hating the guy who did this to me with every single ounce of strength that I own. "I fucking hate you. I fucking hate you … I fucking…" My cries overwhelm me and I surrender, bawling my eyes and heart out.

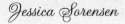

I can't stop thinking about Kayden and the way it felt when he touched me, how good it felt. I want to do it again. I just wish I could stop associating it with that one fucking time. That God damn time I wish I could forget.

I go back to the memory a thousand times, wishing I'd be able to see what was going on beforehand. I really thought he just wanted to give me a birthday present.

I followed him down the hallway so easily and into my room, actually glancing around at my bed and floor, searching for the present.

"Where is it?" I had asked him, turning around.

He was locking the door. Why was he locking the door?

❧

A week goes by and I avoid Kayden at all costs. I ignore his calls, skip out on the one class I have with him, and don't answer my door when he knocks. I feel bad, but I'm too embarrassed to face him. I assumed after what happened he'd just walk away, but it's not the case.

At the end of the week, I sneak off to the library when I know he's in Biology class to find some books for a paper I have to write about depression. The campus is fairly quiet since it's so close to the holidays. My mom and dad are flying out to Florida to see my grandparents for Thanksgiving, so I'm not going home. I can't afford the plane ticket to fly there with them, either.

While I'm searching a shelf, my phone buzzes in my pocket. "Hey, I thought you had class," I answer.

Seth says, "Shouldn't I be saying the same thing to you?"

"I'm taking a break today."

"A break from what, though?" he asks with insinuation.

"Life." I skim my fingers along the titles, feeling the worn spines of the books. "Besides, I'm using my time to catch up on assignments. By the sound of that music playing in the

253

background, I'm taking it that you're watching reruns of *Pretty Little Liars*."

"Hey, I'm not planning on spending all day in my room," he argues. "In fact, I'm going to head out right now to see you. Where are you?"

I sigh, standing up straight. "I'm in the library trying to find this damn book on depression. The catalogue said it was in, but it's totally not on the shelf."

"What section are you in?"

"I'm in the back corner, near the window that shows the stadium." I swallow the lump in my throat that forms when I think of Kayden.

"Are you going to be there for a while?" he asks and the television shuts off. "I'm heading out now."

Standing on my tiptoes, I peer up at the top row of the shelf. "Probably. I'm too short to see the top."

"All right, Callie girl, one knight in shining armor is on his way." He hangs up and I put my phone into my back pocket.

I search the nearby aisles for a stepstool I've seen around a few times. Finally, I give up and go back to the spot. Propping my foot on the second shelf up, I check from left to right and climb up the shelf.

"There it is," I say and grab the book from the row. I hop down and sense someone move up beside me. When I glance up, suddenly Seth's little comment about a knight in shining armor makes sense. Kayden is in front of me, wearing jeans and a black hoodie, his brown hair disheveled.

"Hey." His shoulders are rigid and his voice is tight. "You've been avoiding me."

"Yeah," I admit, fiddling with the corners of the pages. "I'm sorry about that. There was just some stuff going on."

"You don't need to be sorry, Callie." He rests his arm on one of the shelves and leans his weight against it. "I'd just liked to know what's going on... Did I... did I push you to do stuff?"

I shake my head. "Nothing about any of this is your fault, I promise. I wanted to... everything that happened, I wanted."

His shoulders unstiffen. "Then why did you run off?"

"It's complicated," I say, staring at the spot on the floor in front of my feet.

He angles his body forward and lowers his face to capture my gaze. "You could talk to me about it. Maybe I can help. I'm pretty good at understanding complicated."

"It's not anything that can be helped," I say. "It's just something I've got to work through."

He lets out a gradual breath. "I completely understand that."

"I'm really sorry for freaking out on you. I shouldn't have just run off and avoided you for the last week. I just didn't know what to say and felt stupid. I'll try not to do it again."

"Is there going to be another time for you to try to not do it again?"

I didn't realize what I was saying. "I don't know. What do you want?"

He chuckles softly. "I think I've been pretty clear on what I want. So it's really up to you. What do you want, Callie?"

My eyes travel up his long legs, his tight chest, and land on his eyes that care about nothing more than to hear my answer. *I want him. I want him.* I've scribbled it down in my journal many times because it's the truth.

"I want…" I pause trying to figure out the best words. "I want to spend more time with you."

His smile broadens and his posture loosens as he cracks his knuckles. "You were making me nervous there for a minute."

I can't help but smile at him. "I was just trying to think of the right words."

His eyes move over my shoulder to the window where the sky is starting to turn pink as the sun descends below the hills. "I have to be at the stadium in like five minutes, but can you do something for me?"

I tuck the book under my arm. "Sure. What?"

"Can you come watch me play?" he asks. "I need someone to cheer me on."

"Isn't that what cheerleaders are for?" I joke.

"Cheerleaders are overrated." He reaches toward my face, hesitates, and then grazes the pad of his thumb along my bottom lip. "Besides, I have a feeling you'll bring me a lot of luck."

I have to force my eyelids to stay open from his touch. "All right…I'll be there."

The sky is gray, the lights are bright on the green field, and the metal bench beneath my butt is colder than a freezer. There are clusters of people around me, yelling, laughing, and waving their hands in the air. It makes me antsy, but I work through it.

"So what is it with football that makes people crazy?" Seth observes the field with wide eyes and then squints at the red digital timer on the board. "I really don't get what the big deal is. I never have. I've even been to games before—watched... Braiden play—but I still don't get it."

"Maybe it's fun to watch guys run around wearing tight pants," I suggest with a shrug.

"You know what? You just made an excellent point." His brown eyes sweep the field where the players are lined up as he tugs the hood of his jacket over his head.

Kayden is easy to spot because he's one of the tallest. Of course the "Owens" on the back of his brown and yellow jersey is kind of a dead giveaway, too. I think he's glanced up at me a few times, but it's hard to tell for sure.

Five minutes later Seth grows restless, tapping his fingers on his bouncing knee. "I feel like I need to get up and dance or something. Liven up this party."

I motion my hand in the air. "Dance away."

He cocks his head to the side at the round man sitting next to him, wearing a beanie and a hooded sweatshirt, and stuffing his face with peanuts. "I wonder what this guy would do if I did."

I laugh, tucking my hands between my legs. "Probably throw those peanuts at you."

He pulls a face and then exaggeratedly rubs his belly. "Good, I hope he does. I'm starving."

I glance up at the timer. "There's only two more minutes left."

"And are we winning or losing?"

"The score is twenty-eight to three."

He raises his hands to the side, aiming me a "duh" look. "And who's twenty-eight?"

I point at my chest. "We are. We're winning by a lot."

He bobs his head from side to side, eyeing the woman in front of us, inhaling a hamburger. "God, I'm so hungry."

I sigh, pointing at the stairway. "Then go get something to eat. There are some booths outside."

He stares at the stairs skeptically. "Will you come with me? Sports people are intense."

Laughing, I get to my feet and he follows me. I say excuse me at least ten times while I accidentally step on people's toes. When we are on the stairs, I let out a breath of relief at the open space and follow Seth as he trots down to the bottom.

"You're not leaving, are you?" I hear someone shout over the rustle of the crowd.

Kayden is standing at the sidelines, looking extremely sexy in his uniform, his emerald eyes locked on me.

I shake my head, wrapping my fingers around the cold railing, and lean over it. "No, Seth just needs to get something to eat!"

"Good, because I don't want you to take your luck with you!" he shouts with a wink and a smile.

I try not to let a big silly grin surface on my lips. "Don't worry! I'll be back!"

Wait for me afterwards, he mouths, his lips moving slowly from beneath his helmet. Mesmerized, I nod and he turns back to his team with a spring in his walk.

I return my attention back to the aisle and almost run into Seth. "I thought you kept walking." I brace myself against the railing and step back.

He gapes at me unfathomably. "I can't believe this."

I inch to the side out of a man's way. "Believe what?"

He shakes his head in awe. "You're in love with him."

I roll my eyes, almost laughing. "I am not. Now can we please go get you something to eat before the game ends and we get taken out by the crowd."

Shaking his head, he backs toward the last flight of stairs, still thinking the same absurd thought, but he's wrong. I'm not in love with Kayden. I barely know him and love requires a lot of time, a lot of trust, and a lot of other things I don't understand.

❧

Seth leaves me in the tunnel, just outside the locker room. He has a date tonight with Greyson and he walks off toward his car with a skip in his walk. After the crowd clears, I sit down on the concrete and check my text messages.

Mom: Hey sweetie. I've been trying to call you for the last few hours. I wanted to know if you were coming home for Thanksgiving. I know it's kind of late notice and I already told you we're going out of town, but our plans changed and we are going to be home. Call me.

I sigh at the thought of going home to the memories and the lies. I put my phone in the pocket of my jacket and direct my concentration to the side as rain begins to pour down from the sky and flood the sidewalks and streets. The streetlights flicker through the raindrops and I inhale in the scent, closing my eyes.

"Holy fucking hell." Kayden's voice rises over the noise.

I open my eyes. He's standing just in front of me, dressed in a gray Henley, dark jeans, and boots. His hair is damp and his eyes are locked on the rain. I push to my feet and brush the dirt off the back of my jeans.

"I was right about your luck," he says. "We totally kicked their asses."

I shake my head. "I think that was all you guys. Not me."

His legs stretch toward me as he closes the space between us. "No way, that was all you. I played better than I ever have because I knew you were watching and I was trying to impress you."

"You know I've seen you play before, right?"

He tilts his head to the side. "When?"

I shrug. "Sometimes my dad would make me go with

him to practice because my parents thought I needed to get out of the house more. I would hang out under the bleachers and watch." He looks at me sadly as I tuck my hands up in my sleeves and change the subject. "What are we going to do about the rain? Luke didn't happen to drive, did he?"

His eyes wander to the veil of rain pouring down from the roof. "No, we always walk over. I could go ask someone for a ride. I think a few people drove here."

I watch the rain splatter against the concrete, knowing if Seth were here he'd make me go out there. "There's a thing on the list that says I have to dance in the rain."

Kayden's eyebrows furrow as he redirects his concentration back to me. "You want to go out there and dance?"

I look at him, deciding. "No, but I think I'm going to run home. I'll meet you back there."

Before he can respond, I run out of the tunnel, putting my arms over my head, shivering as the cold droplets soak through my jacket and drip down my face. Puddles splash underneath my shoes as I race down the sidewalk, feeling invigorated and alive. Thunder booms from the sky and the rain lashes down harder, but I let my hands fall to my side, letting go and being myself as I live in the moment.

Kayden

I was pumped up the entire game. Something about Callie being up there, not judging me, only being there for me, lightened the pressure my dad always put on me. She brought the fun back to it and I played better than I ever have.

After I change out of my uniform, I head out of the locker room. She's sitting on the ground with her face turned to the side and her eyes shut. I stare at her for a moment, taking in her parted lips, her long eyelashes that flutter every time the thunder snaps, and the way her chest moves as she breathes. I finally look over at the end of the tunnel and holy fuck, it's raining hard.

As I try to figure out a way to get us back to the dorms without getting drenched, she says something about dancing in the rain being on her list and then takes off into the rainstorm. I'm stunned as she sprints down the sidewalk, splashing in the puddles with her hands out to the side like it's one of the best moments of her life.

"Fuck it." I take off after her. When the water hits my body it's like ice. It's hard to keep my eyes on Callie because the rain is so thick. I shield my face with my arm and keep my chin tucked down.

She slows down when she reaches the street to check for cars and I catch up with her, panting loudly.

"Are you crazy?" I ask as beads of water fly everywhere. "It's fucking colder than hell out here."

She jumps back, startled as rain streams down her body and her hair sticks to her cheeks and neck. "I didn't know you followed me. You didn't have to."

I lace my fingers through hers and we jog across the street, water soaking our clothes and dripping in our hair. I hold my arm above her head, protecting her from as much rain as possible. Cars zip up and down the street as we sprint up the sidewalk toward my dorm building. When we reach the trees in front of it, I guide her toward the side entrance, but she slips her hand from mine and jumps out from under the trees into the downpour of the rain.

"Callie, what the hell are you doing?" I call out as icy raindrops shower from the branches and down the back of my neck and face.

She closes her eyes and spreads her arms out to the side of her, tipping her head back as she spins in circles, and her wet clothes cling to her body. Rain pours down on her face and drips from her hair, which has slipped loose and hangs down her back. Her jacket falls from her shoulders and the water cascades down the bare skin of her arms.

I inch forward, unable to take my eyes off her. The way she moves, the way the rain covers her body—I'm enthralled by it. Ducking my head, I step out from the shelter of the tree and into the rain with her. I don't understand it, but I need to be near her. I've never felt this way before and it's exhilarating and fucking terrifying because I've never needed anything from anyone.

I stop in front of her in the middle of the muddy grass and her eyelids lift open, her lashes fluttering against the raindrops. She starts to raise her head up, but I cup her face in between my hands, holding her in place. I tip my head forward and bring my mouth to hers. Sucking the rain from her bottom lip, I taste her slowly, feeling the warmth of her breath against my mouth.

"Kayden," she murmurs, shutting her eyes as her fingers travel up my back and knot through my hair.

I open my mouth and slip my tongue deep inside hers as my hand tangles through her wet hair. My other hand slides down her neck, leaving a hot trail as I feel my way along her wet clothes and body down to her hips. I scoop her up and she gasps as her legs latch around my waist. The heat of our bodies warms up the coldness from our wet clothes as we cling to each other. Holding her tightly, I secure my arms underneath her ass and kiss her fiercely as the rain nearly drowns us. Heading across the grass, I crack my eyelids open every once in a while to make sure I'm traveling in the right direction of my dorm building.

I luck out and someone is walking inside as we reach the entrance. I catch the door with my foot, before it closes, maneuver it open, and get us into the hallway without putting her down. There are people inside, watching us curiously, but I don't stop. This is one of those moments that it would nearly kill me if I pulled away.

As my hands wander across her body, I feel everything. The way my heart jumps inside my chest, the way her hands in my hair make my breathing rapid, the excitement to get her in my room, the eagerness to touch more of her, to make her moan, the way she clings to me, trusting me, needing me.

No one has ever needed me before because I've never let anyone that far in.

Callie

I'm dancing in the rain, just like I'm supposed to. It's cold, yet it feels wonderful because it was my choice. As I'm spinning around in circles, Kayden walks up to me with fear and want in his eyes. The look scares me and excites me. I don't know if I'm ready for what waits on the other side of that look, but I want to find out.

He cups my wet cheeks and kisses me deliberately, like he's memorizing every second. It's the perfect kiss and I pretend it's my first, kissing him the way I want to.

He picks me up, with his lips fastened to mine as he carries me toward his room. I grip on to him, telling myself that I can make it farther this time, that I just need to trust him.

He somehow gets the door to his room open without putting me down and he stumbles inside and shuts the door. Laughing against my lips, he kicks something out of the way and it hits the wall with a thud. I lower my feet to the floor as his hands sneak under my shirt and his palms are cold against my skin. I trace my fingers through his wet locks, down his broad shoulders and to the bottom of his shirt, along his lower abs.

He winces at my touch and I recoil my hand. "I'm sorry," I say.

He blinks at me and then reaching over his shoulder, he tugs his shirt over his head and discards it on the floor. I saw him with his shirt off once, at the pool house. This is different though. The light emphasizes every single white scar, small and big, on his lean chest, his arms, his firm stomach. Some are as tiny as my fingernail, some bigger, and there is one that tracks all the way down the front of him.

Impulsively, I lean forward, shut my eyes, and touch my lips to the middle of his chest above his heart, my breath feathering his skin.

"Callie," he says as his muscles stiffen. "I don't think..." He trails off as I begin to place kisses all over his chest, making sure to touch each scar, wishing it would take the memories of them away, but knowing memories that dark don't go away.

My head travels upward to his collarbone, his neck, his chin. I don't know what I'm doing or what I'm feeling, but it's new and raw and sends adrenaline through my body. When I reach his lips, I place a kiss on them and then move away.

His eyes are amplified, his breathing erratic, and his face is filled with agony. I tense, worried I've done something wrong, but then his expression softens. He cups his hand around the back of my neck, his fingertips pressing into my skin as he leans in to kiss me with so much passion it rips away all the cold inside my body.

He backs us toward the bed, slipping the jacket off my shoulders and reaching for the bottom of my shirt. I tell myself I can handle it; that he's not going to hurt me as I raise my arms and he lifts it over my head.

A big step and it scares the shit out of me, but he crashes his lips into mine before my thoughts can catch up. I clutch his biceps as he unhooks the clasp of my bra and it falls off my arms. I barely breathe at the feel of his bare skin touching mine. It feels good. And bad. It feels like everything I've wanted, but didn't think I could have.

His lips leave my mouth and move downward across the hollow of my neck, pausing at the top of my chest. My eyes roll shut at the first touch of his mouth against my nipple. I fist my hands, unsure where to channel the helpless energy as he slides his tongue along the curve of my breast. A pleading cry flees my lips as my knees start to give out. He grips at my waist, his palms scorching with heat as he steadies me, and makes a path of kisses across my chest. A tingly sensation spreads between my thighs and I cry out, grabbing handfuls of his hair as my heart throbs inside my chest.

"You're so beautiful," Kayden murmurs as I struggle to stay on my feet.

"You're so beautiful," he mutters as he pins me down. I struggle to break free, but his knees press down on my shins and his fingers wrap around my wrists, trapping my arms above my head.

It all comes crashing down like the rain and the lightning outside. My eyes snap open and I jerk away, folding my arms across my chest. "I-I'm sorry. I-I can't do this."

He blinks his eyes, shocked. "What's wrong?"

I turn in a circle, searching the floor. "It's nothing. I just need my shirt." I kick some of the clothes on the floor out of the way, my lungs squeezing tightly, constricting my oxygen flow. "I just need my shirt."

His fingers graze my arm and I flinch, sucking in a deep breath, forcing back the tears. "Tell me what's wrong," he begs.

"It's nothing." I shrug off his hand as tears spill from my eyes. "I just need to go."

His hands come down on my shoulders and he forces me to face him. I keep my eyes locked on the floor, refusing to look at him. He hooks his finger under my chin and elevates my face upward.

He scans the tears and his eyes widen. "Oh my God, I thought you were okay with going that far. I'm sorry."

"It's not you or that." I wrench my face away from him and back toward the door with my arms still covering my chest.

"Then, what is it?" He steps toward me, searching my eyes desperately for an answer. "Callie, you're really freaking me out right now. Please tell me what's wrong."

I shake my head, backing away, my shoulders curling inward in humiliation. "I can't tell you. I just need to go."

As the foul feeling in my stomach begins to build, owning me, controlling me, I reel for the door, ready to run out without a shirt on. He hurries in front of me, blocking my way with his body.

"You can't walk out there like that," he says, his eyes skimming my bare chest.

"I need to get out of here," I choke, clutching at my stomach.

"I feel like I did something wrong...Did I hurt you or something?"

268

My shoulders lurch as I choke through the sobs. "You didn't do anything. He did."

"Who did?" He steps toward me and I'm verging on shoving my finger down my throat right there in front of him because I can't hold it in.

I skitter to the side, trying to dodge around him, the walls closing in on me. I need air. "I need to get out of here."

His fingers snag my waist. "I can't let you go out like that. Just trust me enough to tell me."

"No! You can't handle it."

"Callie." He's freaking out. I'm freaking out. The entire situation is a mess. "I can handle anything you tell me."

I shake my head as my knees buckle and his arms hold me up. "No, you can't." The vomit burns at the back of my throat as my ears ring and my eyes blur over with more tears. I'm hyperventilating and dizziness floods through my body. "No one wants to handle hearing about a twelve-year-old being raped...I have to keep it locked away. I have to..." I trail off, knowing I'll never get it back.

I jerk from his arms, feeling ashamed, but he grabs my hand and yanks on my arm, crashing me against him. He cradles my head, smoothing my hair as my shoulders shake and my tears soak his scarred chest.

Chapter Fourteen

#34: Let ~~Someone~~ Kayden Get Close to You.

Kayden

If I could hold her forever, I would. I wasn't expecting that to come out of her mouth. I knew she had something dark hidden inside her, but not that. It hurts deep inside my chest and I have a hard time not busting my fist against the headboard again. The only thing that stops me is I don't want to take my arms off her.

She cried forever and each sob nearly ripped me in two. It was like stitches coming apart. Eventually she fell asleep curled up against me with her head tucked against my chest. I trace lines on her bare back, staring off into empty space, wondering how anyone could have done that to her.

I don't know if I can handle it. The longer I lay there, the more worked up I get as feelings of anger consume me. I flex my hands, stab my nails into my skin, fight to stay still.

Callie begins to stir and peers up at me with her swollen, bloodshot eyes.

"Are you okay?" I ask, brushing her hair back from her forehead.

"I'm fine." Her voice is hoarse, her cheeks red, and her pupils are dilated.

I pause, not sure what question is the right question, or if one even exists. "Callie, what you told me...who else knows about this?"

"No one." Her bare shoulders rise and fall as she fights to breathe. "Except for Seth."

I hesitate, my fingers still in her hair. "Not even your mom?"

The sadness in her eyes nearly kills me. "Only you and Seth." She tucks her head down, hiding her face.

I want to ask her who it was, so I can hunt them down and fucking beat him to death. Thousands of ideas flood my mind, but I never knew her well enough to make assumptions. I could ask her, but at the moment she might break if I do. I know because I've been at that point most of my life.

"I think we should get you dressed." I lift my head and glance over her shoulder at the clock on the nightstand.

"I'm sorry. You probably have stuff to do and I'm sitting here, holding you up." She slants her head to the side to slip out from my arm, but I flex my arms and hug her against me.

"I only said that because Luke's going to be home soon," I

explain, inching her face closer to mine. "Not because I want you to get dressed and leave."

"Oh." She relaxes a little, the locks of her hair spreading across my chest as she lowers her face down.

I sweep some of her hair to the side, which smells faintly of rain, and kiss her gently on the lips. When I pull away, she seems surprised.

"Kayden...I-I..." She struggles for words. "You don't have to be with me because you feel sorry for me. I didn't even mean to tell you that. I just got caught up in the moment."

I gaze down at her, astounded. "I'm with you because I want to be with you."

She swallows hard. "Even after what I told you?"

I brush my finger along her cheekbone. "Callie, I feel the exact same way about you now as I did an hour ago. Nothing's different."

She fights back tears as she blinks her eyes. "Are you sure? Because sometimes...sometimes I'm a mess. What happened just barely wasn't a one-time thing. I get that way when I remember things."

I nod, scared as hell. I want to be with her, more than anything at the moment. I just hope I can handle it, for her sake.

Callie

I didn't mean to drop it on him like a giant bomb, but the need to get away from him so I could rid the vile feeling in my body was too overpowering. I let it slip out, hoping he'd freak out and let me go, but he did the opposite. He held on, allowing me to cry, letting me break apart, and giving me more than he'll ever know.

Saying it aloud to him was liberating, like I took hold of a part of my life again. I just hope it stays that way.

He doesn't let me go as I sit up, his body rising up with me. He releases me briefly to climb over me and pick up my bra from off the floor. I loop my arms through the straps and my hands tremble as I reach around to fasten the clasp. He gathers up my shirt next, shaking it out, then slips it over my head. I elevate my arms as he pulls it down over me to cover me up.

"What do you want to do for the rest of the day?" he asks and glances at the window. "Or, should I say night?"

I pull the shirt over the last of my stomach and flip my hair out from under the collar. "I should probably go back to my dorm and get caught up on my homework. I have a lot of papers to write still."

"You know break starts in a few days, right?

"I know, but I missed a lot of classes when I was...avoiding you."

He grabs a red shirt from his dresser and pulls it over his head, ruffling his hair into place. "Do you want me to walk you back?"

"If you want to," I say, feeling guilty for making him do something else for me. He's already done enough for the night.

A small smile touches at his lips. "I'll walk you back."

We head outside together and I feel strange, especially when he places his hand over mine. The lights of my building glimmer in the distance and all I can focus on is getting there.

"Are you going home for Thanksgiving?" he asks as we cross the wet grass and duck beneath the trees, where rain showers down on us.

I shrug. "I wasn't planning on it, but maybe. My parents were going to fly to Florida for Thanksgiving, but I got a text from my mom earlier today saying they were staying home and that I should come home."

"You should ride with Luke and me," he suggests as we cross the street, through the puddles, and hop over the curb. "We're heading back in a few days or so."

There are many reasons why I don't want to go home; one being that the guy who ruined my life could be staying at my house. "I'll think about it and let you know."

"You know it could be fun," he says with a quirky smirk. "You could hang out with Luke and me, and we could show you the nonexistent fun times of our life."

I offer him a half smile, because his words remind me of my life back home and how much I hate it. "Maybe."

He licks his lips, looking like he might kiss me, and even though I want him to, I still worry that he's doing this for the wrong reasons. I reach for the handle of the door to my dorm building. "Thanks for walking me home." I slip my fingers out of his and hurry down the hall, leaving him stunned. I try not to look at the bathroom as I pass by it, but it's all I can think about, and I end up backtracking.

Once I'm finished, I can breathe again.

Kayden

I can't stop thinking about what happened to Callie. I think she thought telling me would scare me off, but it's had the opposite effect. I want nothing more than to be with her and protect her, like no one ever did for me. I want to make sure nothing else bad happens to her.

It's getting close to the holidays and I'm preparing to go back home. Honestly, I don't want to go back there, but where else am I going to go? I don't have anyone but my mom and dad, as shitty as they may be. And my mom practically begged me, saying that Tyler would be home and I haven't seen him in years. I wonder what he's like now, after years of drinking.

Callie and I have spent the last few days together, watching movies and talking, but it's been strictly a friend thing. Not because I want it to be, but because I have no idea how to try and take it farther.

I'm walking back to my dorm from my last class before I head home when I spot her wandering around through the trees, reading a book. Her hair is down to her shoulders and she has a long-sleeved gray shirt on and black jeans.

"Reading anything good?" I ask, stopping in front of her.

Her head whips up and she snaps the book shut, which actually is her journal. "Hey, what are you doing?"

I eye the notebook and then cock my eyebrow. "You know one day you're going to have to let me read some of the stuff you put in there."

She shakes her head quickly, hugging the notebook against her chest, the blood rushing to her cheeks. "No way."

Her reaction makes me want to read it even more.

We walk across the grass together with no real direction other than to make it to the sidewalk.

"Have you decided if you're going home yet?" I ask, stuffing my hands into my pockets. "You know I really want you to."

She frowns. "So does my mom, but I don't know...I'm just not a fan of being at home. It reminds me of too many things."

"Mine does, too," I agree. "And that's why we should go together. We can take off every day and hang out. Luke's not a fan of his home either, so I know he'll give us a ride wherever."

She peeks up through her eyelashes with a skeptical look on her face. "Okay, I'll think about it."

"You sound skeptical."

"It's just that...it seems kind of unbelievable that you, Luke, and I would hang out like that."

"Why wouldn't we?"

She shrugs, her shoes scuffing against the mud at the edge of the lawn. "Because we never did before. We've known each other for years and the only time we've talked is while we've been here. Away from Afton."

I reel in front of her and she almost runs into me. "You think I'd ditch you because we were back home?"

Her shoulders shift upward as she shrugs again and stares at the ground. "It's kind of inevitable. People will be there and a lot of people you hang out with don't like me."

I secure my finger under her chin and incline her head up, looking into her sad blue eyes. "You're referring to Daisy?"

"Daisy, her friends, everyone we went to school with," she says miserably. "But it doesn't matter. I just don't feel like going home."

She swipes her card through the lock and I open the door to her building. The warm air encircles us as we walk down the unoccupied hallway. "Then what are you going to do? Stay here by yourself?"

"I'm a big girl," she says as we get onto the elevators and then shakes her head when I begin to smile. "I don't mean in the literal sense."

The elevator rises up and I stay quiet as I try to figure out a way to persuade her into going with me. When we reach her bedroom door, I begin to panic. The thought of leaving her here by herself is ripping at my heart.

"Okay, I'm going to be completely honest here." I take a deep breath, because what I'm about to say is very real and more honest than I've ever been. "I don't want to be away from you for that long."

She sucks her bottom lip into her mouth and bites on it. "I'm sure you'll be okay." She extends her hand toward the lock and punches the code. She starts to turn the knob, but I catch her wrist.

"No, I won't," I assure her with an unsteady voice. "I'm becoming attached to our little talks and…and you're the only one that really knows everything about me."

Her shoulders sink as she looks at me with empathy. "I'll have to talk to my mom first and ask her a few things. I'll let you know tomorrow."

I release her and step back, feeling somewhat better. "Promise me you'll really think about it."

She nods, twisting the doorknob. "I promise."

She takes a step inside, but I can't let her go yet. My fingers snag her sleeve and I pull her back out into the hall.

"What are you—"

Before either of us can protest, I seal my lips to hers, stealing our breaths away. My hand touches her face and I hold her cheek in my palm while my other hand presses against her lower back, arching her body against mine. I slip my tongue into her mouth, just a quick kiss, but it conveys all the hunger I feel inside. Our legs give out and my hand snaps out, bracing us against the wall before we fall to the floor. She lets out a soft moan and I pull away, knowing if I go any farther it's going to be that much harder to let her go.

She blinks her eyes wildly as I back down the hall with a grin on my face. "And remember, you promised."

With a dazed look in her eyes, she walks inside her room, and tosses her notebook onto her bed, before shutting the door.

❧

"Do you have your old yearbook with you?" I ask Luke when I enter our room.

"I think so," he says, looking away from the television for a split second. He's playing a racing game, totally zoned out as his fingers hammer at the control buttons. "Why?"

"Can I look at it for a second?" I grab a can of soda out of the mini fridge.

He points at the closet door, his eyes returning to the screen. "I think it's in my trunk in there."

Setting the can down on the foot of my bed, I go into the closet. Unlatching the locks of the trunk, I raise the lid and search through the books until I find it tucked in the side. I fan through the pages until I get to the "L" section and find "Callie Lawrence."

The girl in the picture is not the Callie I know. Her hair is to her chin and choppy, like she cut it herself. She has on a baggy jacket that hides her slim shoulders and heavy black eyeliner that swallows her beautiful blue eyes. The same sadness is there, though; haunting her.

I scan some more pages for her, but it's like she barely existed. I get to my feet, put the book back, and shut the trunk, wondering what it would have been like if we had been friends in high school. For some reason, I think that maybe things would have been a little easier and the pressure on my shoulders would have been a little bit more bearable.

Callie

Seth wakes me up the next morning by nudging me a ton of times in the ribs. He has iced lattes in his hands, his blond hair is a little messy, and he has a determined look on his face.

"I had this dream," he starts, lowering himself onto the edge of my bed, "that you may need to talk to me. In fact, I have this really bad feeling that you've been keeping something from me."

He's right. I haven't told him how I broke down in front of Kayden. He's been really happy lately, going on dates with Greyson, and I didn't want to ruin his mood with my dark thoughts.

I sit up and take the iced coffee, nearly downing it in just a few sips. "I thought you were heading home this morning?"

He nods, sipping on his straw. "I am, but I'm giving Greyson a ride, so I have to leave a little bit late."

I guide my legs to my chest and rest my chin on my knee. "Is he going home with you?"

He shakes his head with a look of astonishment on his face "No way. Could you imagine if I brought a guy home to meet my mom? Besides, I barely know him."

I elevate my chin away from my knee and chew on my

straw. "But how long do you have to know someone before it means something?"

He sits down on my bed and rests his arms on my knees. "That's for the people who are in the situation to decide, which brings me to part of the reason I stopped by."

I fake a pout. "It wasn't to say good-bye to your best friend?"

"That's part of the reason," he says in a serious tone. "The other reason is that I ran into Kayden this morning. Now, typically we have quick little chats about really stupid stuff, but today, he kept asking me about you. He wanted to know if I knew what you were doing for Thanksgiving and if I'd checked on you lately. Now would you like to tell me anything?"

I frown. "Do I have to?"

He nods, placing the plastic cup on the ground beside his feet. "Did something happen between you two?"

I dither. "Maybe."

He waits patiently for me to explain. Sighing, I finally spill it out to him leaving out a few of the more intense details but giving him enough that he gets the gist of it.

"You told him?" he says, his brown eyes huge. "Like told him, told him? Why did you not tell me this earlier? That is the kind of info that should be divulged to me as soon as it happens."

"Because you were happy and because I don't even know how I feel about it. I mean, I told him by accident." I throw the

blankets off me and scoot over to the edge of the bed, swinging my feet to the floor. "During a freak-out moment on my part."

"Because he was touching you?"

"No, that wasn't it. I liked that he was touching me, he just said something that reminded me of...it."

He stirs his straw around in his drink. "Kayden was okay with you? He didn't hurt you or make you feel like shit after you told him?"

"He seemed okay." I grab my drink and the condensation dampens my skin. "But he could have been doing it because he felt sorry for me."

Seth thrums his fingers on his knee. "Or because he understands what it's like to have someone hurt him."

I wipe my wet hand on the front of my pants. "That might be, but I don't want him to have to deal with my problems. He has so many of his own."

"Or maybe, it's that he scares you because he makes you feel things your uncertain about," he points out.

"Are you Psych 101ing me again?" I ask, getting to my feet.

He shrugs. "Maybe, but the thing is I think he really cares for you. You should have heard him that day when you were in the library and I called you so he could find out where you were. He was really worried about you."

I grab a rubber band from the box on top of my dresser and fasten it around my hair, leaving pieces out around the front of my face. "Probably because I ran out on him after I..." I trail off.

"Had an orgasm?" he finishes. "Orgasm. Orgasm. Orgasm. It's not a bad word, Callie."

"I know that." I finish off the last of my drink, sucking the whipped cream off the straw before tossing the empty cup into the garbage.

"Okay, then." He stands up, smoothing out the wrinkles on his skinny jeans. "Here's what I suggest. You should go home for Thanksgiving. Ride with Kayden and Luke, go back and have some fun. Don't sit around here by yourself. It makes me nervous."

"I want to go with them," I admit. "But what if *he's* there?"

He hands me my phone. "Call your mom and find out."

I snatch my phone from him. "I'll send a text."

Me: Who all is going to be staying at our house for Thanksgiving?

Mom: No one so far. Your brother said he wasn't coming back and Grandma and Grandpa canceled. Please tell me you're coming home sweetie.

I hesitate and let out a frustrated grunt.

Me: I'll come home, but I need to see if I can catch a ride still.

Mom: Dad can come get you if you need him to.

Me: I might be able to ride home with someone.

Mom: Who?

Me: Someone

Mom: Callie Lawrence, what are you keeping from me? Is
it someone I know?"

Me: I don't know.

Mom: Callie, just tell me. Please. I'll bake you your
favorite pie.

Me: Gotta pack. C u soon.

"Wow," Seth mutters as he reads the text from over my
shoulder, blowing his coffee breath on me. "She's super
obsessed."

"She's not use to me having friends." I change my ringer to
vibrate and put my phone into my back pocket. "She probably
knows it's someone from back home."

A conniving grin expands across his face as he taps his fingers together. "What do you think she'll do when she finds out
who it is?"

I shrug, grabbing a bag from under my bed, and then dramatically wave my hands in front of me. "Freak out. Jump up
and down and go, 'Oh, my God! Oh, my God!'"

He giggles. "But you're going?"

I nod with my heart squeezing inside my chest. "Yeah, I'm
going. Just as long as Kayden will give me a ride."

He covers his mouth with his hand to muffle his laughter.
"I bet he would love to give you a ride."

I press my lips together, holding back a smile. Pretend all

I want, the idea makes my body tingle. I begin putting my clothes in a bag, ignoring his remark.

"Do me a favor." He steps in front of me and looks me in the eye with a stern expression. "Let him get close to you if he wants to, okay? In fact, you can cross off number thirty-four on the list."

I fold up my jacket and set it in the bag. "That's let *someone* get close to you and I already have—you."

"Well, I'm crossing it off and putting Kayden's name up there." He backs toward the door, pausing before he walks out. "Call me every day so I don't worry."

"Yes, sir," I say firmly with a salute and he laughs. "And vice versa."

Once he's gone, I finish packing and sink down onto the bed to dial Kayden's number.

"Hey," he answers and something thumps in the background.

"Hey...are you getting ready to head back home?"

"Yeah, we're carrying our stuff out to the truck right now. I was actually just getting ready to come over to your dorm."

"Why?"

He chuckles into the phone. "To make sure you were getting packed to go back home."

I peel away at my thumbnail. "Who said I was going?"

"I saw Seth this morning and he promised me he'd talk you into it," he says. "And I knew he would."

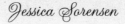

"Seth's kind of turning into a traitor," I reply, lying back on the bed and staring at the poster on the wall across from me.

"Callie, if you don't want to go, you don't have to." He pauses. "But I really want you to."

I'm still not sure I want to. "Okay, I'll be ready in a few minutes."

I hang up and stare out the window at the leaves and dirt splattered against the grass, put there by the wind. How could the direction of my life change so fast? I'm doing things I wouldn't normally do, trusting people, feeling things, living life. I wonder how long it will last.

Chapter Fifteen

#21: Let Yourself Be Bored.

Callie

It's been two days since Kayden and Luke dropped me off at my house. Luckily, it was at night, so my mom didn't run out and embarrass me. I've heard from Kayden quite a few times through texting, but we haven't hung out.

The entire drive home, I had an out-of-body experience. I was riding in the truck with Kayden and Luke and it was surreal, like I was watching it happen to me instead of living it. I've had a few similar moments, but they were never good like that. They were bad and full of images I wish I could have been blind to.

It's a couple of days before Thanksgiving and my mom and I are in the kitchen. The cupboards are stacked with food, the stove with pans, and the sink with dirty dishes. There are orange and brown leafy decorations along the tan walls, in the center of the table, in the windowsill, framing the doorway—my mom has always been a big holiday decorator.

"I still can't believe how much you've changed." My mother beams at me and I shake my head, chopping an apple on a cutting board. She touches my hair, noting the length of it. "And you stopped cutting your hair. I'm so glad. I've wanted it longer since the day you cut it off."

"I'm not sure if I'm a fan of it," I lie, angling my head sideways and moving it away from her. I'm a fan when Kayden's touching it, which he did during most of the drive here, but that's it. "In fact, I think I'm going to chop it off again."

She puts her hands on her hips and narrows her hazel eyes. "Callie Lawrence, you will do no such thing. You look so beautiful, honey. A little skinny, but that's probably because you're not wearing all those baggy clothes."

I fidget with the corner of my fitted black T-shirt. "I'm as skinny as I've always been."

She reaches behind her back and refastens the tie on her apron with little apple patterns on it. "Well, we're going to fatten you up a little. I'm making food galore."

I set the chopping knife down and reach for another apple. "Why? If it's going to be just you, me, and Dad."

"Oh, we're going over to the Owenses' this year." She takes a wooden spoon out of a drawer, tucking a strand of her long brown hair behind her ear. "They've invited a lot of people, like they did a couple of years ago."

I frown as I recollect the dinner she is talking about. That was the year Kayden started getting serious with Daisy and she made that dinner for me a living hell. "Who's going to be there?"

She shrugs and starts humming to the song playing from the stereo. "Should we go get our hair done that day before the dinner? Wouldn't that be fun? To get all dressed up?"

I'm about to tell her no, and that it sounds like the last thing I want to do, when my phone beeps, announcing there's a text message waiting.

Kayden: Did you know that Mrs. McGregor is having an
    affair with Tom Pelonie?

Me: Um...what?

Kayden: Or that Tina Millison is getting a new Mercedes
    for Christmas?

Me: Should I know this? Because I'm really confused.

Kayden: I think my mother needs a friend. She's been
    following me all over the house, telling me the latest
    gossip. She even wanted me to take her to get her
    nails done.

I snort a laugh, but quickly erase it when my mom looks at me questioningly.

Me: I guess she misses you.

Kayden: No, she's bored and needs to lay off the wine. I
    think my dad's been on a lot of trips while I was gone

and the empty house has made her lose her sanity more than she already had before I left.

Me: Mine wants me to go get my hair done with her.

Kayden: Yeah, but you're a girl.

Me: Oh, I forgot for a sec. Thanx for reminding me.

Kayden: I haven't forgotten at all. In fact, it's all I think about all the time.

Me: That I'm a girl???

Kayden: That ur a girl I very badly want to touch right now.

I press my lips together, uncertain how to respond. We've barely kissed once since I dropped my secret on him and suddenly he's talking dirty to me.

"Callie, what's wrong?" my mother asks with concern. "You look flushed."

I glance up from the message at her worried eyes. "I'm fine."

She reaches for my phone. "Who are you texting?"

I turn my back on her and walk to the table, so she can't see my face.

Kayden: Did I scare u off?

Me: No, I was just thinking about something.

Kayden: About me touching you?

"Callie, the pans are boiling over," my mom says. "Can you turn the temperature down?"

Me: I have to go. My mom's having a cooking crisis

Kayden: Okay, I'll text u later. Be prepared to give me an
   answer ;)

My skin is hot as I run over to the stove and turn the knobs
to low. Steam fills the air as I take a lid off one of the pots and
stir the noodles in the water.

"So, about getting our hair done." My mom picks the conversation up right where we left off. "What do you think?"

"I think I'm going to go up to my room," I evade her question, wiping my hands on a paper towel. "I've got a lot of stuff
to do."

"But it's break time," she says. "We're supposed to be
spending time together. What are you going to do up there
besides be bored?"

My mother has always wanted me to be things I'm not,
even before I changed. When I was six she wanted me to be a
ballerina and I wanted to be a football player. When I was ten
she thought it would be neat if we bought me a whole ward-
robe of dresses for school and all I wanted was to pierce my
ears. When I was eleven I decided I wanted to learn how to
play the guitar. She signed me up for beauty pageant lessons.

"Being bored isn't all that bad." I put the knife in the sink
and walk toward the back door. "I'll come back in a little bit."

It's cold outside as I head for the garage, a light frost glaz-
ing the windows and railing. While I was away at college, my
mom and dad put a ton of boxes in my room, along with my

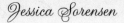

dad's football memorabilia. I could either sleep on the couch in the living room or stay in the apartment above the garage. I chose the garage for privacy reasons. Plus I like that I don't have to stay in my room, haunted by memories that will keep me awake all night. Up here it's peaceful and quiet—my mind is somewhat clear from the storm.

I climb the stairs and shut the door behind me, cranking up the two space heaters before grabbing my journal out of my bag. I take out my iPod and put my earbuds in, scrolling to "Seth's Awesome Playlist." Seth has a very broad taste in music and I wonder what's going to turn on when I click on the first song. "Work" by Jimmy Eat World flows into my ears as I flop down onto the mattress and kick my feet up on the metal headboard.

I open my journal and put the pen to the paper, my heart and mind racing wildly.

I've been wondering over the last few days what it would be like to be with Kayden. Like really, really be with him. The more I explore the idea, the more I wonder about it. Sometimes, it feels wrong thinking about this stuff, but other times, I enjoy my thoughts and very vivid images. It's like I'm not me anymore, like he's changed me into a girl who thinks about the possibilities of life and love.

I was daydreaming the other day in the living room, picturing his mouth on my breast, like it was that night before I flipped out, when my mom came into the room.

"You look so happy," she said, sitting on the couch beside me. "It's been so long since I've seen you smile like this."

I looked at her, and I mean really looked at her for a moment. Did it ever once cross her mind, even for just a split second, that maybe something terrible happened to me? Did she wonder, but the idea was so dark that her mind couldn't grasp it?

A warm hand touches my shoulder, startling me, and I wrench my arm away as I bolt upright, dropping my pen and notebook on the bed.

Kayden takes a step back, putting his hands up in front of him as I breathe profusely, kneeling up in the bed. He's wearing a pair of cargo shorts, a black hoodie, and sneakers. His hair is tucked under a beanie and his mouth moves as he says something.

I quickly tug on the cord of my earbuds. "What are you doing here?"

"Your mom told me you were up here." He glances around at the tiny room that has no carpet and only Sheetrock for walls, his gaze lingering briefly on the unmade bed. "Is this your room or a guest room or what?"

I set the iPod down on the bed and stand up. "It's supposed to be a guest house. My parents have been working on it for years, but this is as far as they got."

He smiles at a small hole in the wall that needs to be spackled. "My parents would flip if any part of our house was like this."

"Mine get sidetracked with other stuff; sports, town meetings, pie baking contests, trying to beg my brother and I not to go so far away for college. They have attachment issues."

"So they would rather do life. I like that." He faces me, his emerald eyes sparkling. "Your mom seems nice. I know I've met her before and everything, but she seemed really chatty this time."

I internally cringe. "What did she say to you?"

He pulls the beanie off and tousles his hair with his fingers so the bottom ends flip up and wisps hang over his forehead. "Not too much."

I aim a doubtful look at him and arch my eyebrows. "Really? Because I kind of doubt it. In fact, I bet she said a lot to you."

He's working hard not to smile. "She was completely nice." He circles around me, and I twist my body to face him. "She said she was so excited that we were hanging out and that she's so glad we're good friends."

"I didn't tell her any of that," I tell him, feeling embarrassed. "She just assumes things."

He steps around behind me and I start to turn to follow him again, but he wraps his fingers around my upper arms to hold me in place, pressing his chest to my back. "Why wouldn't you tell her that?"

I shrug, shivering a little from his breath on my neck as he leans his head over my shoulder. "Because I don't tell her anything. I-I don't..." I drift off as his mouth moves beside my ear and grazes the tip of it.

"If we're not good friends, then what are we, Callie?" He pulls my earlobe into his mouth and drags his teeth gently along the skin. "'Cause I would really like to know."

"I don't know," I breathe, wondering where the hell this is coming from.

"I couldn't stop thinking about that text and I decided I just needed to come here and hear your answer," he whispers, his voice husky. "I actually would have come over sooner, but my dad's been making me work out. He said...he said I let myself go a little while I've been gone."

His rock-hard chest that is pressed up against my back indicates just how big of a liar his dad is.

"Are you...okay?" I ask cautiously. "I mean, your dad hasn't...done anything to you, has he?"

"I'm fine. He's barely been there. I guess he's been going to a lot of town meetings and charity events. My parents always were good at putting on a great appearance for the outside eye." He pauses. "Are you okay? We haven't really talked much about stuff. I wanted to talk to you in the car, but Luke was there."

"It's okay," I say. "I don't really feel like talking."

He hesitates, breathing in and out, my back rising and falling with the steady movement of his chest. "Then what do you want to do?"

What I was writing about in my journal. "I don't know..." A soft whimper flees from my throat as he bites softly on the spot below my ear.

His arm snakes around my waist and up my stomach, between my breasts, and up to my neck. Pressing his fingers against my jawline, he turns my head toward him while holding my body in place. Up close, I notice there's a scratch on the side of his cheek and a little bit of stubble on his chin.

"Are you okay?" I reach up and trace my fingers gently down his cheek. "Where did this come from?"

"It's just a tiny cut." His pupils shrink as his eyes open wider. "I'm okay. I promise."

My chest presses against his arm as my breathing accelerates and his eyes focus on my lips. He inches his mouth closer to mine, and my eyes shut on their own accord as his lips graze mine. His mouth moves leisurely as he keeps one arm across my chest, while his other travels along my stomach, his hand gripping onto the fabric of my shirt. I try to figure out what to do with my hands and finally just grab on to his arms. Letting my lips part, my head falls back as his warm tongue delves into my mouth and it steals the air from my lungs.

Suddenly, he tenses and leans back, looking me in the eyes. "Do you want me to stop? Because you can always tell me if you need me to slow down."

I consider it, but only for a moment and then shake my head. "No."

"Are you sure?" he checks and I nod way too enthusiastically.

Sliding his hands to my sides, he spins me around to face him. I stand on my tiptoes, hooking my arms around his neck, and he pushes on my lower back so my body arches against him. When our lips connect I feel a spark that tickles down my body and I moan ridiculously loud, my knees buckling. My cheeks start to heat, but he lets out a groan, cupping my face between his hands as he steps forward, leading us somewhere. My feet tangle with his as I back up and seconds later, we're falling onto the mattress.

I pray to God that this time the moment will last; that nothing from that day will catch up with me.

His body conforms to mine as one of his hands knots through my hair, his other hand kneading my thigh. I slip my hands underneath his shirt and feel the lines of his muscles and the bumps of his scars. His stomach tightens under my touch, but he continues to explore my mouth with his tongue, the tip running along the roof and then his teeth bite softly at my lip. His fingers begin to drift along the top of my jeans and my insides quiver. I rub my feet together, tightening my legs, trying to figure out how to relieve the tingling between my legs.

"Callie..." he groans and his hand starts to go down the front of my jeans as he rolls us to the side. I'm surprised at how much my body wants him to touch me there, so I keep kissing him while little moans escape my lips and I thread my fingers through his hair. His fingers remain just inside my jeans, like he's testing me, and then finally he slips one inside me.

He inches his mouth away for a second to look me in the eyes. "Are you okay?"

I'm nervous and scared, but it feels so good. "I'm fine," I say and the breathlessness of my voice is all the reassurance he needs.

His finger starts moving as he returns his lips to mine, slipping his tongue inside my mouth as his other hand feels my

breast on the outside of my shirt, making a gasp rush out of me. My hips start to writhe up against him and he slides his hand away from my breast down to my thigh, guiding it over his hip so I'm opened up to him.

My head tips back against the pillow as I work to catch my breath. He leans back slightly, his finger massaging me from the inside, and he watches me in wonder as every single part of my body rises and falls. Something deep within me bursts with heat and I gasp, trying to hold on to it, but seconds later I come back down to reality.

Kayden slides his finger out of me and kisses me gently, his breath hot against my lips. "Are you still good?"

I nod my head up and down, my breathing erratic and my skin damp with sweat. "I'm great."

He smiles at my answer and I would probably blush under normal circumstances, but the high in my body still lingers. He lies down on his back with his arm tucked under my neck, his fingers combing through my hair, as he stares at the ceiling with a puzzled expression on his face. "I have to go meet up with Luke. He kept texting me, saying he needed to get the fuck out of the house. I told him I was stopping by here for a few minutes and then I'd be over."

"Oh. Okay." I'm kind of hurt he's taking off.

"I promise we won't hang out with him for the whole night." He climbs off the bed and extends his hand to me. "We can come back here a little later or maybe go catch a movie."

I take his hand and stare up at him. "You want me to go with you?"

He lifts me to my feet with his eyebrows dipped. "What? Did you think I just came over here to ... to do that to you?"

I feel stupid. "Maybe. You were texting me all that stuff out of the blue." I shrug. "I really don't know what I was thinking."

He keeps holding my hand as he steps toward the door. "Callie, I'm not using you. The whole texting thing was just my sexual tension catching up with me. If you don't want to do stuff, you can say so."

"I want to do stuff," I say. "That night, when that stuff happened, I only panicked because of something you said that reminded me of what happened ... with that other thing. It wasn't because of anything you did."

The worry in his eyes subsides as he brings my wrist to his lips and kisses it delicately. "So we're good to keep going?"

I nod, even though I have no idea where we are going. I'm extremely interested to find out, though, especially after what we just did. I always believed that stuff like that wouldn't be possible for me; that it would remind me too much of what happened, but all I was thinking about the entire time was Kayden. Everything else left my mind.

Chapter Sixteen

#7: Do Something Just Because It's Fun.

Kayden

I'm worried that I'm getting in too deep. I couldn't stop thinking about her after Luke and I dropped her off at her house, which is why I had been staying away. The longer I did, the more intense my feelings got. All I could think about was being with her, especially because my dad has been an asshole ever since I got home. He hasn't hit me, but he doesn't make it easy to be around him, even just a little amount of time.

Finally, I decided to go see Callie because I knew seeing her would make me feel better. I was just going to make it a quick stop, but so many emotions raced through me, I couldn't control myself and things ended up a little heated. When Callie came, I nearly died. All I wanted to do was rip off her clothes and thrust my cock inside her, feel her everywhere—feel everything. But I'm afraid of what will happen if we cross that line. What it will mean to her—what it will mean to me.

My head's so screwed up. I should walk away from her, but I'm too fucking weak.

Callie wanders around the small room in the basement of my house, taking in my trophies and pictures on the wall. She glances at the bed in the corner and then at the leather couches and television. The spot on the wall that I punched has been repaired, like that night never happened. But it did. And part of me is glad it did, because it brought Callie into my life.

"So what is this?" she asks curiously. "Like your bachelor pad?"

I open the side door that leads to the outside to let in Luke, who ran out to the truck to grab a cooler. My dad's gone for the night, thankfully and my mom didn't see us pull in. "I guess that's what you can call it. Really, it's just where my brothers and I use to hide out when we were trying to stay invisible." It's so strange talking to her openly about it.

She sits down on the back of the couch with her legs dangling over the edge. "I wish I had one of these rooms when I was growing up."

"So what the hell are we doing tonight?" Luke stumbles inside carrying a blue cooler, his face is red, and there's dirt in his hair. "Personally, I'd like to try and not relive the last night we hung out here."

"What happened then?" Callie asks curiously.

"Someone got really trashed and ended up getting punched by Dan Zelman." Luke glances at me as he drops the cooler down on the table. "You were really fucking stupid for picking a fight with him."

I wince at the memory, flexing my hand. "Yeah, that one hurt."

Callie looks at me. "Dan Zelman? He's like huge. Why would you pick a fight with him?"

I shrug, joining her on the back of the couch. "I was drunk." I lower my voice to a whisper and lean in toward her ear. "And I was upset that I didn't have the guts to punch someone else earlier that morning."

"Your dad?" she whispers, turning her head and her lips nearly touch mine.

I shift my weight uneasily. "Yeah, pretty much."

Luke opens the fridge and beer bottles fall out onto the floor, the glasses clinking together. "Damn it! That wasn't my fault."

I roll my eyes with exaggeration and Callie giggles. I hop off the couch and go help him pick up the bottles, glad none of them spilled. The last thing I need is for my dad to come down here and find the carpet stained and reeking of beer.

After we get them picked up, Luke takes a bottle of Jack Daniel's out of the cooler. "Shots all around."

Callie shakes her head, sliding her legs off the couch and jumping onto the floor. "No shots."

I flash her a playful grin. "What? Didn't you enjoy the last time you got drunk?"

"I can't even remember anything," she says with a hint of laughter in her voice. "Although, you can. So you tell me. Did I enjoy being drunk?"

Grinning, I tuck a lock of her hair behind her ear. "You seemed to."

"It would be really nice if you just told me what I did and said."

"Nah, it's better if I keep it to myself. Trust me, what you don't know can't hurt you."

"I'll tell you what?" Luke steps forward, unscrewing the cap off the bottle. "We can make it a game. That way, if you're really good, you won't ever have to drink."

Callie glances back and forth between us. "What kind of a game?"

Luke gives me a sidelong glance and I shake my head, knowing where he's going with this. "The rules are pretty easy. Someone says something like, I've never fallen asleep on the front lawn of the next-door neighbor's house, because I was so fucking drunk I thought it was my house." He extends the bottle toward me. "And now he has to drink."

I snatch the bottle from him, let my head drop back, and force a large mouthful down my throat. "Thanks for making me the example."

"So what?" Callie asks. "If you've done what the person has said, then you have to drink?"

I lick the alcohol from my lips. "Yeah, but you don't have

to play. We can just hang out. Luke just thinks everything has to center around alcohol."

Luke yanks the bottle away from my hand, cutting me a harsh look. "That's not true. I'm just trying to cure my boredom. There's nothing to do around here now that everyone's gone."

Callie gives a one-shouldered shrug. "We can play. I haven't done much of anything, so it seems like the odds are in my favor."

"Yeah, but you don't know much about us," Luke says wickedly. "So it'll be tough for you to come up with things to get us with."

She shrugs again with a look in her eye that makes me wonder if she does know something.

We settle on the couch with Callie on one side, and I sit on the other. Luke takes the recliner, kicking his feet up on the coffee table as he takes a drink straight from the bottle.

He sets the bottle down on the table. "So, who wants to start?"

"I will," Callie offers, raising her hand.

"Really?" I ask her. "Because you don't have to. You don't have to be a part of any of this."

She smiles innocently, twisting a strand of her hair around her finger. "I don't mind. I promise."

"Let her go," Luke says, draping his arms on the back of the sofa and relaxing back. "I'm really interested to hear what's going to come out of her mouth."

I motion at the bottle. "Okay, let's see what you got."

She bites on her lip, mulling it over, and then her eyes lock on Luke. "I've never argued with my coach about not being drunk when clearly I was wasted during a game."

Luke's expression falls. "How did you know about that?"

She shrugs. "My dad's the coach and I hear things."

With his eyes fastened on Callie, he tips his head back and gulps more than a shot out of the bottle. "Okay, so now I've got to get back at you."

"Those aren't the rules!" Callie glances at me for help, her blue eyes enlarging with panic. "Are they?"

"They're my rules." Luke taps his finger on his chin as he leans forward. "I've never stepped on a spray paint can and left a mess on the floor for the checkout guy to clean up."

She rolls her eyes with a smile emerging on her lips, showing a competitive side that I wish was directed at me.

Luke dangles the bottle in front of her face, taunting her, and she snatches it from him. Making a disgusted face at it, she puts her lips to the top, leans back, and sucks out a tiny swallow.

Gagging, she thrusts the bottle in Luke's direction with her head turned and her eyes shut. "Oh my God! That's worse than the vodka." She shudders as she blinks like crazy.

Laughing, I scoot closer to her on the sofa and put my arm around her shoulders. "Luke plays dirty, Callie. Since you went after him first, he'll probably go after you a lot."

She sticks out her bottom lip, pouting, and it's glossy from the Jack.

"Hold on, you have something on your lips." I lean forward and suck it off.

Her eyes widen as I slide my tongue along my lips and move back. "You're right, Jack is pretty fucking gross."

"It's terrible," she agrees in an unsteady voice.

"Okay, I have one," I say, clearing my throat. "I've never walked home wearing just a pink robe and a pair of slippers."

Callie snorts a laugh as Luke narrows his eyes. "You're fucking asking for it. I'm going to tell her all your dirty little secrets now, you fucking douche."

I laugh, kicking my boots up on the table. "That was just to get you back for going after her first."

"Can I hear why he had to do that?" Callie asks as Luke takes a shot. "Because I'm really curious."

"He was over at this girl's house," I start, ignoring Luke's death glare. "And while they were having sex, her parents showed up. They'd taken off all their clothes out in the living room, so he had to borrow her robe and slippers because it was the only thing he could fit in."

"It was fucking cold, too," Luke recollects as he drinks from the bottle again. "Although, having sex with Carrie Delmarco made it kind of worth it."

Callie covers her mouth, her chin tipping down, probably to hide her embarrassment. It's fucking adorable and suddenly I find myself wishing Luke would leave so I could be alone with her.

"I have one," Luke declares, shooting a malicious grin in my direction. His eyes are turning red and his speech is a little unbalanced. "I've never told a girl I was the lead singer of Chevelle just so I could hook up with her."

"I'm going to fucking kill you for that one." I reach over the table to confiscate the bottle from his hand. "You know that, right?"

He grins at me as I take a drink and look at Callie. "I was fifteen. I did a lot of stupid things back then."

She doesn't seem bothered, but sometimes she's hard to read. "You don't have to explain it to me."

"All right, I have one." I focus on Luke, wanting to beat his ass. "I've never stripteased on a table in front of an entire room full of people."

His brown eyes are cold as he slams back a shot and then forces the alcohol down his throat with a jerk of his neck. "I've never woken up crying in the middle of the night because I had a nightmare after watching *Halloween*."

"I was like ten," I protest, yanking the bottle from his hand. I knock back a big gulp, starting to feel the alcohol burning in my system. "I've never pissed my pants because I was locked out of the house and couldn't get in."

Luke grabs the bottle from my extended hand, spilling some Jack on the coffee table. "I've never sent a girl a check yes or no letter. 'Do you like me Tami Bentler? Do you think I'm cute?'"

Callie busts up laughing, slapping her hand over her mouth as her shoulders hunch toward her knees. "I don't even know what to do with all this information."

I force another shot down my throat and wipe my lips clean with my sleeve. Even though I'm pissed off that Luke is making me look like a jackass, I'm glad she's happy.

"Oh, you think this is funny?" I ask and she lifts her head up, wiping tears from her eyes, nodding. "Because I can get you easily."

She shakes her head, still smiling. "You don't know that much about me, Kayden, so I'm not too worried. Besides, I already told you I haven't done much of anything."

I lean toward her, putting my lips next to her ear, tucking her hair out of the way. "I've never made out in the rain and had one of the best kisses of my life." I'm fucking drunk and admitting more than I normally would, but my drunken mind doesn't care at the moment.

She shivers from my breath, her shoulders shuddering upward. "But you have, haven't you? Or maybe you haven't. I don't know."

"I love it when you ramble. It's cute." I put the bottle to my lips and slant my head back, sipping a shot, letting her know my answer. I aim the bottle in her direction with my gaze on her. "Your turn, unless it's not true."

Her fingers tremble as she wraps her hand around the bottle. I watch her mouth move as she inclines her head back and takes a deep swallow. I probably shouldn't be staring, but watching her lips move is distracting and turning me on.

She coughs, her cheeks puffing out as she places the bottle on the table and smears the sleeve of her shirt across her lips. "God, it burns so bad."

Luke collects the bottle from the table and gets to his feet. "I have to fucking take a piss." He opens the door of the basement and staggers outside, leaving it cracked behind him.

Callie looks at me bewilderedly. "Why did he go outside?"

"It's a drunk thing with him." I relax back on the couch with my arm still around her. "He likes to go outside and piss."

"Is he going to be okay?" Callie tucks her leg underneath her. "He seems pretty drunk. What if he wanders out into the trees and gets lost?"

"He'll be fine." I wave her off, not wanting to talk about Luke anymore.

We sit quietly for a moment and I watch her out of the corner of my eye, wanting to touch her so badly, like I did earlier in her room.

Callie rotates her body toward me, pressing her lips together, restraining a smile. "So you really made Tami Bentler a yes or no letter?"

"Let me clarify that that happened in third grade." I relax on the couch, grab her shoulder, and guide her down beside me, so we're lying side by side and I wrap my legs around hers.

She bumps her head on the arm of the chair as she gets situated. "Ow...what did she say?"

"Here, lift your head up." I tuck my arm under her, before she lies down, letting her use it as a pillow. "She said no way."

She turns on her side, facing me. "That's so sad. I would have said yes."

"Would you have?" I question. "Because I wasn't as charming as I am now."

She chokes on a laugh and then lowers her head toward my chest. "I kind of had a crush on you back in grade school."

"What?" Fixing a finger under her chin, I elevate her head, so I can look into her eyes. "Really?"

"I think you know that almost every girl did, which makes me surprised Tami said no."

"I think Tami may have taken the letter better if it was from someone like you."

"You mean...she liked—likes girls?"

I shrug, staring up at the ceiling. "That's what I heard, but who knows if it's true." I pause, glancing down at her as she wets her lips with her tongue. "How drunk are you?"

"I'm not drunk at all," she says. "I had two tiny swallows."

I pinch her side and she cradles her arm against her ribs protectively. "Yeah, but you're tiny and a lightweight."

"I'm not that tiny," she protests. "And I promise I barely feel a thing."

I pause, examining her eyes, and then move forward with

caution. "So if I kissed you right now, I wouldn't be taking advantage of you?"

"No, but I might be taking advantage of you. Your breath smells about as bad as the bottle." She smiles and fans her nose.

"Trust me. You can take advantage of me and I won't mind, even when I sober up." I press my lips to hers, feeling my heart thump in my chest as her breath catches.

It grows silent as we lie with our foreheads touching and our breaths mingling. I place my hand on her hip, shutting my eyes, feeling the intensity of the moment like an open wound.

"I have a question," Callie whispers. "How many people saw Luke walking in that robe?"

"You know how every Christmas they do that caroling thing down in the town center?"

"Yeah."

"Well, he walked through there."

She laughs, rolling into me, and nestling her face into my shoulder as her leg slides across my stomach. "There are always a ton of people there. Oh, my God, I bet my parents were even there. They always go."

"I know…" I smell the scent of her hair; shampoo mixed with cigarettes from Luke smoking in the car on our way here. "Callie, I. …" Fucking hell. What the hell is happening to me? "I really want to kiss you right now."

She freezes, her chest grazing against mine as she exhales. "Oh yeah?"

I sweep her hair out of her face and she peers up at me through her long eyelashes. "Can I?"

She stays motionless for a second and then nods her head. "Yeah, you can."

I let out a tense breath and lean toward her, tipping my head to the side as I seal my mouth to hers. Nipping softly on her bottom lip, she lets out a breathy moan that floods my body with a hunger. I dive into the kiss, opening my mouth and caressing her lips with my tongue. She's warm and tastes like Jack and I want more—more than we're probably ready for.

Grabbing her waist, I pull her onto my lap so she's straddling me. "I can't stop myself with you."

A tiny gasp escapes her lips as my hard cock presses against her. "Kayden…" she starts, but trails off as I knot my fingers through her hair and escort her face toward mine. Moving my lips down her neck, I suck on her skin, devouring the taste of her.

"I have to tell you something." The back of my mind screams at me that I need to shut up. That I'm drunk and what I'm going to say isn't good, but I do it anyway. "I've never felt this way about anyone before."

Her body goes rigid, her breath feathering against my neck. "What?"

"You and me…I like it so much. I've never liked the idea of being with anyone before."

Exhaling slowly, she pushes upward and climbs off me. "I think maybe we should talk about something else."

"Like what?" I'm worried I've scared her, like I've done with myself.

"Like something that makes you happy," she suggests. "Or something that you're not going to regret in the morning."

"That's you. Callie, you're the only person that's ever made me feel happy about anything. That night you saved me, you changed something in me—you made me want to live." I tell her the truth, knowing that when morning comes around, it's all going to catch up with me.

Chapter Seventeen

#21: Create Memories That Belong to You.

Callie

Last night was interesting to say the least. Kayden was drunk and saying things to me he probably wouldn't in a sober state, so I stopped it. I don't want him telling me things just because he's drunk. I've seen Seth ramble on about nonsense way too many times and he never means most of it.

I end up falling asleep on the bed in the corner and when I wake up, I have an, "oh shit" moment. My phone is beeping with a thousand messages from my mom. I don't even bother checking any of them. I spring up from the bed and hurry over to the couch where Kayden is lying on his side with his eyes shut and his arm draped over his face.

I glance over my shoulder at Luke, sleeping on the floor with his head on a pillow and then crouch down in front of Kayden. "Wake up. I need a ride home."

He breathes quietly, his chest lifting and falling, so I place a hand on his cheek, running my thumb along the scar below his eye. "Kayden, please wake up. My mom is freaking out."

His eyelids lift, his pupils shriveling as the light hits them, and it looks like he wasn't even asleep. "What time is it?"

I check my cell phone screen. "Almost eleven. Were you awake the whole time?"

He shrugs, sitting up and stretching his arms above his head. His shirt rides up and I try not to stare. "I've been awake for a while. Thinking about stuff."

"Oh." I straighten my legs and search the room for my jacket. "Can you give me a ride? Or should I wake up Luke?"

"That'd be walking into dangerous territory," he says, getting up from the sofa. "Luke is not a morning person."

I slip my arms through the sleeves of my jacket. "I don't even remember falling asleep. One minute, we were talking and the next, I'm waking up in the bed."

He smiles, grabbing Luke's keys off the coffee table. "I think you did that in your sleep. You were lying by me and then you got up and wandered off over there. You looked pretty out of it."

He opens the back door and we step out into the cold afternoon air. The sky is a light blue with a haze covering spots and I can see the pool house to my left. Kayden shuts the door and we start across the grass silently. I don't know what to say. I feel awkward carrying around his words that he doesn't remember.

He stops suddenly at the corner of the house and rakes his hands through his messy hair. "I remember it."

I peer over my shoulder at him. "Huh?"

He takes a few tentative steps toward me. "I wasn't that drunk. I remember what I said. I've been lying on the couch for practically half the night trying to figure out what the fuck to say to you when we were both awake."

I blow out a breath. "You don't have to explain. I've been around Seth enough that I know how the day after goes. Trust me, he's done and said so many things that he regrets."

He shakes his head, with a quizzical look on his face. "But I don't regret it. I just...I just don't know how to handle it. When I said I felt things for you that I never have, I meant it and it fucking scares me, especially because there are still a lot of things you don't know about me—bad things."

I close the gap between us. "I don't believe that. I don't believe that there are bad things about you. Only things that you think are bad."

Massaging the back of his neck, he looks out at the road behind me. "You wouldn't be saying that if you knew what the stuff was."

"You could always tell me," I suggest. "And let me be the judge of it."

He locks eyes with me. "You wouldn't like me if you knew."

I summon a deep breath, ready to say something that terrifies me. "For the last six years, I've been afraid of almost everyone except Seth, but he and I shared this connection and I trusted him fairly quickly. It was the same with you. That day we went up to the cliff, it might have seemed like I was terrified—which I was—but just going there with you and letting you help me get up onto that cliff was a huge step for me. I trusted you and that means something."

"I want to tell you," he says softly. "I do, but I don't know if I can."

"You told me about your dad."

"Yeah, but this is different. This is—"

"Where the fuck have you been?" Kayden's dad comes storming around the corner, dressed in a navy-blue sweat suit, his face bright red, and his hands forming fists. "You were supposed to go..." He trails off when he sees me standing by Kayden. "Who are you?"

I grab Kayden's hand automatically. "Callie Lawrence."

Recollection surfaces in his irate expression. "Oh, you're Coach Lawrence's daughter?"

Déjà vu. "Yeah, we've met a few times."

He stares at me for a while, like he's trying to force me to cower back. Finally he fixes his gaze on Kayden. "We were supposed to be working out this morning. Remember?"

Kayden's hand tightens around mine. "Yeah, sorry. I overslept and I have to take her home, so I can't go yet."

He opens and closes his hands and a vein in his neck bulges. "How long are you going to be?"

Kayden shrugs. "I don't know, maybe thirty minutes or so."

Mr. Owens glances at me, appearing annoyed. "Why can't she drive herself home? We have a schedule."

"No, you have a schedule," Kayden says and then tenses as his dad's face contorts with aggravation. "You just think I'm supposed to follow along with it."

"I'm sorry, are you talking to me?" The intimidation he sends off is terrifying as hell and I want to dive behind Kayden and hide. "Because I think you're forgetting the rules here and what the consequences are for forgetting the rules."

"I have to go." Kayden's breath is ragged as he strengthens his grip on my hand and walks around his dad, towing me with him.

"Kayden Owens," he calls out. "You better not be walking away from me."

Kayden and I dash toward the truck parked in the driveway beneath the trees.

"God fucking damn it!" his dad yells after us.

Kayden helps me in the truck, then jumps into the driver's side and starts up the engine. From the middle of the yard, his dad watches us with a dark look masking his face. My mind goes back to that awful night and what that man can do.

The tires spin as we hit the road and Kayden shifts the truck into a higher gear, the trees on the sides of the road blurring by. An elongated pause passes before Kayden speaks.

"Can you text Luke?" He hands me his cell phone. "And tell him to just hang out downstairs until I get back?"

I nod, taking his phone, and scroll through his contacts until I find Luke's name. "Do you think he'll go down and yell at Luke?" I ask as I send the message.

He shakes his head, his fingers tightening around the wheel. "He only does it to his kids."

I set the phone on the dash and scoot across the seat toward him. "Kayden, I don't think you should go back there. What if he does something to you?"

"I'll be fine. It's nothing I can't handle." His voice is sharp and I recoil, starting to slide back across the seat. "No, stop." He quickly places his hand on my thigh. "I'm sorry. I shouldn't have snapped at you like that. It's just that, it's what I do. I've been dealing with it forever. It's my life."

"Well, make it so it's not your life anymore," I say, my voice taking on a pleading tone.

He turns toward me with doubt in his eyes, like that isn't an option. "And what am I going to do? Never go back? As fucking messed up as he is, he's still my father. That house is where I grew up—it's my home."

"It doesn't have to be anymore. Just leave," I say, trying to understand what I need to say to convince him. "Come stay with me. You don't deserve to be treated like that. There's so much good in you and you deserve better." My voice tremors. "Please, please, just come stay with me."

He swallows hard, his eyes widening. "You would let me do that?"

I nod my head, my heart aching for him as I reach out and touch his arm. "Of course. I don't want you to go back to him. He's...why is he like that?"

"I think that's how his father was with him." He steers the

truck toward my road. "It wasn't quite as bad when we were younger, although it still fucking sucked. He would just get mad at things and yell and sometimes slap us or hit us with the belt. It got worse as we got older, like he knew he could...." He grinds his teeth. "Hit us harder without killing us. My brothers fought back when they got old enough, but when they moved out...and I was alone...Things just kind of fell apart. All his anger was kind of focused on me."

My eyes burn as I blink several times to stop my tears from pouring out, thinking about him alone in that house with that God-awful man. "Don't live with it anymore. Come stay with me. You don't need to be there."

As his eyes search mine, he looks terrified, confused, and kind of like a lost little boy. "Okay, but I have to go pick up Luke."

I can breathe again, my lungs relaxing as the airflow returns to them. "You'll come right back, though? Promise?"

He nods as he turns the truck into my driveway, parking it behind my mom's car. "I promise."

I glance at the window by the back door, where the curtain is pulled back and my mom is peering out. "Do you want me to go back with you? I just need to tell her."

Kayden cups my cheek and rubs the pad of his thumb beneath my eye. "I'll be okay. You stay here and try to calm your mom down."

"Are you sure? Maybe I should get my dad to drive over with you?"

"Callie, I'll be fine. Luke's there. I'm just going to grab my stuff and then come over. Nothing will happen."

My heart knots as I lean over and brush my lips against his. I start to pull away, but he slides his hand to the back of my neck and presses his mouth to mine again, kissing me fiercely, before releasing me. With a heavy feeling in my heart, I climb out of the car and watch him back away, knowing I'll be holding my breath until he returns.

Kayden

I'm scared shitless. I've never talked back to my dad like that and the look in his eyes told me I was screwed, but Callie is right. I don't have to deal with it anymore. All I have to do is walk away. Something I should have realized a long time ago, but for some reason I just couldn't. All I've ever seen in my life, is people leaving, not caring hitting, yelling, telling me to suck it up. But then Callie comes along and tells me I can change it—that I deserve so much better. It's so simple yet her words mean so much to me.

I park the truck behind the tree and send Luke a text to meet me out at his truck in ten minutes, because I need to get my bag. Memories haunt my mind as I walk up the front porch. The atmosphere is dead silent and the front door is agape.

Putting my guard up, I step inside the house. When I was younger, my dad liked to make a game out of the beatings. He

would give us time to hide and then he would come searching for us. If we hid well enough, we'd win. If not, we'd pay. We always ended up paying because he'd never give up looking.

The house seems empty so I hurry up the stairway to my room and toss my clothes into the bag. Swinging it over my shoulder, I trot downstairs, feeling freedom waiting for me as the front door emerges into view. But my dad steps out from beneath the stairway, and stands at the bottom, blocking my path.

He crosses his arms over his chest. "I'm wondering if it was the girl that made you act so stupid or if you've just gotten dumber since you went away to college? You never really were bright."

My mind calculates my options. "Look, I'm sorry, but I'm not going to stay here anymore. I just…" I tread down to the step below.

He inches to the side, getting in my path. "You have a workout to make up for."

"No, I don't," I say, my palms sweating. This is the farthest I've ever pushed him. "I work out enough at school." My foot moves down another step and I'm right in his face. "I'm going to go."

He seizes my arm, squeezing it so firmly the skin burns. "You're going to get your fucking ass in that God damn car and we're going to go down to the field to work out. You will not push me anymore."

I think of Callie sitting back at her house, waiting for me;

actually worrying about me. No one has ever worried about me before. I jerk my arm out of his grip and shove my hands against his chest, shaking with the fear of a three-year-old. Taking the opportunity, I jump down the rest of the steps, but he regains his balance, and comes at me with his fists up and uncontrollable anger in his eyes.

"You fucking piece of shit!" he yells, taking a hit at my face.

I duck my head and his hand slams through the window of the front door, shattering the glass and splitting his knuckles. It doesn't faze him and he rams another jab at me and his fist connects with my jaw. Bones pop and my ears ring.

"Fuck!" I clutch my face as pain explodes up my cheek, but I'm used to pain enough that I shake it off. For the first time in my life, I take a swing at him. My knuckles pop as he ducks and my hand smashes into the wooden banister.

Seconds later, I'm being tackled to the ground, his arms wrapping around me as he throws us both to the floor. Glass stabs through my shirt and into my muscles as I kick my father in the gut. He slides across the floor, bumping his head into the wall, and I throw my hands up in the air as I scramble to my feet.

"I'm done," I say and before he can get up, I run out the door.

Luke is waiting in the truck with the engine running. I don't look back until I'm safely in the cab and the door is shut. Luke's eyes are bulging as he assesses the glass stuck in my skin, the tears in my shirt, and my cheek that's swollen double its size.

"What the fuck?" he says. "He's still doing that shit?"

I shake my head as my dad walks out onto the front porch, eyeing the truck. "Just drive. Take me to Callie's. I don't want to be here."

He reverses the truck onto the main road and I support my injured hand against my chest, keeping my eyes on my father until he disappears out of my sight.

Callie

I can't sit still. I keep sending him texts, but he won't answer. My mom gave me a very long lecture about how worried she was that I was gone all night. I let her ramble on, wondering how concerned she'd be if I told her my secret.

After she's finished, I wait for Kayden in my room above the garage. I feel sticky from last night, like alcohol is coming out of my pores, so I take a shower. Wrapping a towel around me, I comb my fingers through my hair and walk out into the bedroom to get dressed.

Kayden's sitting on my bed with his back turned to me, his shoulders slouched over, and I leap back, surprised. "Oh." I cover my mouth with my hand, stepping toward the door, embarrassed I'm only in a towel.

He turns his head to look at me, and I no longer care. His cheek is puffy and red, he has blood and slashes on his shirt, and his knuckles are coated with dry blood.

Securing the towel in a knot, I rush over to him. "What happened?"

He shakes his head, his eyes skimming my barely covered body. "It doesn't matter anymore. It's done."

"What is?"

He holds his hand out toward me, which is trembling. "I tried to hit him and then I kicked him."

"Your dad?" I ask. "Did he . . . are you okay?"

"I am now." He grabs my hips, shuts his eyes and breathes through gritted teeth as he pulls me onto his lap. My lips part in protest as the bottom of the towel opens up and the roughness of his jeans touches my bare skin, but he rests his head on my shoulder and his body starts to tremble. I fasten my jaw shut, close my eyes, and smooth my hand over his hair, fighting back the tears.

I remain motionless, afraid to move, as he struggles for air. After what seems like hours, he lifts his head and his eyes are red.

"I'm sorry," he says, blowing out a breath as he rubs the palm of his hand against his eye. "It all just caught up with me for a moment."

"I understand completely," I tell him and kiss his forehead.

His fingers seek my cheek and he traces a line across my birthmark on my temple. "I've never stood up to him before. It was fucking terrifying."

He's so much braver than me; standing up to something that's haunted him since he was a kid. I envy him for it.

I lightly stroke his injured cheek and he flinches. "Do you want me to get you some ice? Bandages? Painkillers? My mom has a ton of them in her medicine cabinet."

He crooks an eyebrow at me. "Why?"

I shrug. "I asked her once and she said they were from an old cheerleading injury back in high school."

His eyebrows knit and his swollen eye closes. "Wasn't that like twenty years ago?"

"She's crazy," I say, starting to climb off his lap. "Maybe that's why she's happy all the time."

His fingertips press into my hips, securing me in place and there is panic in his eyes. "I don't want to let you go."

I know that look; the one that begs for someone to help them.

"Please help me, Mommy," I whisper as I feel him shift above me and every single part of my body feels like it's ripping in two. He covers my mouth with his hand roughly, and tears slip from my eyes. Where is she? Why doesn't she come get me? Because she thinks I'm hiding, like the rest of the kids are. That's what I'm supposed to be doing, instead of dying on the inside, although part of me wishes I were dying on the outside, too.

Please, Mommy....

I wrap my arms around his neck and hug him as he burrows his face into my neck, resting his lips against my racing pulse. Shutting my eyes, I breathe through the moment; scared to death, but overwhelmingly wanting it. He kisses my neck slowly, relishing each touch, and my head drifts to the side.

"I'm going to go wash the blood off my hands," he whispers and I lean away. "Just stay right here, okay?"

Gathering the bottom of the towel, I nod, and slide my legs off his lap. He gets up and heads to the bathroom while I lay down on the bed, knowing something's about to happen. I can feel it in the air, in the warm sensation on my neck where he kissed me, and everywhere his hands touched me.

When he walks out of the bathroom, his shirt is off and he has a towel pressed to his broad chest. When he climbs on the bed, I sit up and lower his hand holding the towel so I can look at the cut. It's deep and just across his upper rib; another scar to add to his already torn body. I run my finger up his forearms, noticing the fresh wounds on his skin.

"What happened with these?" I stop on a cut near his bicep and study it. "It looks like someone was cutting your skin."

His fingers enclose around mine and he shakes his head, looking at the wall. "I'm fine. I promise, Callie. This is the stuff I can handle."

I rise to my knees, feeling the towel open at the bottom, but don't bother to close it. I graze my lips to his chest, inching up his neck along a jagged scar. I suck on his skin, run my tongue gently along it, and then engulf the softness of his lips. His head slants to the side and our mouths connect as his fingers envelop around my waist. He lures me closer to him, parting his lips and sucking my tongue into his mouth. I let out a groan as the overpowering emotions burst through me and possess me, erasing away the internal pain.

His fingers find the bottom of the towel, and he touches the bare skin of my waist. I can't think straight as he feels my body, tastes my lips, and steals my torturous thoughts away momentarily. I sit up, pressing my chest against him and he shifts his weight, lying down on the bed. Our legs entwine and his knee slides between my thighs. The feel of the fabric of his jeans sends heat through my body that coils into my stomach.

"Kayden," I moan against his lips as I dig my nails into his shoulder blades.

He inches his mouth away, breathing fitfully, his eyes assessing mine. "Do you want me to stop?"

I tighten my hold on him as I shake my head, my hair falling into my eyes. "No."

Sucking in a breath, he crashes his lips against mine and the soft savoring kisses turn desperate as the towel unwraps from my body and I lie naked underneath him. My nipples stroke his chest with every breath and my legs fall open. My hands are on his cheeks and his warmth gives me reassurance as he reaches toward my arms and his fingers encircle my wrists. Leading my hands away from his face, he puts one on each side of my head as his tongue consumes my mouth.

Abruptly, he releases one of my arms and my body shivers beneath him. "Callie, let me know if I need to stop," he breathes against my lips.

"Don't stop," I whisper, my heart restless, but sure. "I don't ever want you to stop."

His eyes open, wide and glossy, and he bites my bottom lip

as his hand glides down my stomach. Seconds later, his fingers are inside me like they were yesterday. I feel high and lost but in the most amazing way. Like my mind finally left the dark place and I can grasp at the light again.

I want more. I need more, however I don't know how to ask for it.

My hips rock against his hand as he feels me from the inside, groaning against my mouth as I drag my teeth along his lip, nipping at it before releasing it. Pieces of his brown hair brush across my forehead as I move my body, needing more. His chest is heaving, as he slips his fingers out of me.

"Callie, where's the line?" he asks, returning his fingers to my wrist, holding me down beneath him, his eyes scanning mine. "I need to know where to stop."

I shake my head from side to side, looking him in the eye. "I don't want you to stop, Kayden. I said it and I mean it."

His pupils contract as he processes what I said. "Callie, I…"

My heart slows as the moment starts to dissolve. Images of my past catch up, but then they swiftly vanish as he lifts his hips up to unbutton his jeans and kick them off. Seconds later he's out of his clothes and has a condom on. He lies back on top of me, bare skin to bare skin, and he kisses me with passion, desire, everything, as he entangles our arms together above my head. My nerves mix with my anticipation and I feel every single aspect of the moment. The roughness of his skin on his palms, the smoothness of his chest as it touches mine, the wetness of his tongue inside my mouth, the tingling all over my body. Sweat beads my skin as my body heats with want and I open my legs up as his body forms with mine. When he inches into me, I feel the pain, but I also feel the invisible chains around my wrists break and shatter.

He sucks in a breath as my legs constrict around his hips and he gradually eases farther into me. He moves his lips away from my mouth and looks into my eyes while caressing his fingers across my cheek. Then, he pauses, before giving one last rock until he's completely inside me.

Every part of my body and mind open up as he kisses me. It burns at first as he moves back and forth, and I almost cry out for him to stop, but the pain subsides and my muscles unravel as my head falls back against the pillow.

It's a moment I'll remember forever, because it belongs to me.

Kayden

I have never been so fucking terrified in my life. Not when I was being yelled at, beaten, or even when I stood up to my dad. I've had sex before, plenty of times. It was all for fun, even with Daisy. There was nothing there; I thought it was supposed to be that way. As Callie looks up at me, trusting me, I'm lost. No one has ever looked at me like that before; no one has ever made me feel the way I feel at this moment. It's like every one of my scars has ruptured and the pain is real, but I can't stop.

I kiss her fiercely, moving her arms above her head as I thrust inside her. It feels so good and I never want it to stop.

Her eyes are glossed over and her pupils dilate as her lips part. Her neck arches as she gasps in pleasure and she bucks her hips against my movements. I let go of her arms and my palms scan downward to her breasts, feeling her skin as I suck on her neck. Her fingers sketch each scar, leaving a path of heat everywhere she touches and it nearly drives me crazy. Her back bows up as she cries out and moments later, I join her, knowing I can never go back from this. The way I feel is irreversible; overtaken, wanted, needed, connected. I'll never be able to let it go.

As we catch our breaths, I tell myself that it will be okay; that I can handle it and for an instant, it feels like I can.

I let out an uneven breath as I slip out of her and roll onto my back, tugging my hands through my hair. Rotating on her hip, her warm body follows mine. She rests her cheek against my chest, gliding her leg over my waist.

"Are you okay?" I finally dare ask her, fighting through my own racing thoughts.

She nods, sketching the lines of my stomach muscles with her pinkie. "I'm more than okay."

I shut my eyes and put my chin on top of her head. "Callie, there's something I need to tell you."

She lifts her face away from my chest and peers up at me. "What's wrong? Did I . . . did I do something wrong?"

I touch the tip of my finger to the bottom of her lip. "No, it's not you. It's me. There are things about me that you don't know and I think I need to tell you."

She sits up and my gaze drifts to her body, so fragile, just like her heart. "You're making me nervous."

"I'm sorry," I back out as feelings of shame rush over me. "I'm just stuck in my own head."

She frowns. "Kayden, you can tell me anything. There's no judgment here."

"I know that," I say with honesty as my hands grip her waist possessively. Lifting her up, I set her down on top of me, so one of her legs is on each side of my hip. "We'll talk about it, but a little bit later."

Wetting my lips with my tongue, I cup the back of her head and bring her mouth toward mine, as I slide my other hand up the front of her, gripping her breast, wanting to go back and relive the only peaceful moment I've had in my life.

Chapter Eighteen

**#33: Lay with Someone, Motionless,
Just Feeling Each Other.**

Callie

"I think I have to go inside," I say, checking the seventh message my mom has sent me. "Otherwise, she's going to come out here and see this."

"See what?" he questions innocently as he flips me over so he's above me and he takes my breast into his mouth, tracing circles over my nipple with the tip of his tongue.

I gasp as my thighs ache for him to be inside me again. "You're going to get me caught up again."

He leans away with a smile on his face, but his cheek is red and puffy. "So?"

I fake a stern look. "I'm not kidding. She'll come out here with her key and open the door to this."

He laughs, still not fully believing me, but frees me from

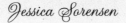

his arms. "Fine, you win. I'll let you go, but we're coming right back as soon as you deal with your mother."

I laugh softly as I wrap the sheet around me and pad over to my bag to take some clothes out. I feel a little shy even after what we did. I manage to put my clothes on before I let the sheet go. He doesn't question what I'm doing as he gets up and puts his jeans and shirt back on.

I glance out the window at the dark sky. Everything seems perfect, untouchable, like I'm holding my life in my own hands for once. "How late is it?"

He turns his arm and checks his watch. "Like seven thirty."

"No wonder she's freaking out. I missed dinner."

He laces his fingers through mine as I open the door. "So how bad is this going to be?"

I lead him down the steps behind me. "She's going to ask you a thousand questions and be super cheerful."

"What about your dad?"

"He'll yammer about football, I'm sure."

My phone beeps and I pause at the bottom of the steps to check the message.

"Is it another one from your mom?" he wonders and I shake my head.

Seth: Hey, darling. How's it going? Good I hope. Did you eat some delicious treats?

Me: Maybe . . . But what kind of treats r u talking about?

Seth: OMFG!!! Did u? Because I had this really weird
    feeling that you did.

Me: Did what?

Seth: U know what.

I glance up at Kayden, who laughs at me, his eyes crinkling at the corners. "It's from Seth."

He leans over to get a better look and I cover the screen with my hand. "Are you talking about me?"

I bite at my lip, feeling my cheeks warm. "No."

"You are," he says proudly. "Even after that, I can still make you blush. God, I'm good."

I lower my head, allowing my hair to veil my face. "I'm not blushing."

"You so are." He hooks a finger under my chin and tips my face up. "And I'm glad." He brushes his lips lightly across mine, giving me a soft kiss that I feel all the way to my toes.

I pull away, smiling, but pause when I catch sight of the extra car in the driveway. "Whose car is that?"

Kayden tracks my gaze and shrugs. "I'm not sure."

Confused, I push open the back door. Seconds later, it all leaves me; every breath, every heartbeat, every kiss, every moment of my own. Black spots pop across my vision as I take in my brother, Jackson, sitting at the table, wolfing a piece of pie straight out of the tin. Across from him sits his best friend Caleb Miller. He's flipping through a magazine, his dark hair scraggily and long, like he hasn't had a haircut in years. When he glances up my gaze instinctively shoots to the floor.

"Well, if it isn't little Miss Callie all grown up," Caleb says and I stare at the pencil on the table in front of him, envisioning what it would be like to stab him in the eye multiple times and inflict as much pain as possible.

"Mom thought you ran away," Jackson says, licking the whipped cream off the fork. "She texted you a thousand times."

"Good for her," I snap. I've always had this bitter hatred toward my brother for bringing that asshole around. I know he didn't know, but I can't turn it off. "Can you tell her that we stopped by and that I'm okay so she can stop texting?"

"No," Jackson says. "I'm not your messenger. She's just in the living room. Go tell her yourself."

"Why are you even here?" I ask and Kayden's finger grazes the inside of my wrist. I blink at him. I'd almost forgotten he was there.

Kayden shakes his head, and his emerald eyes convey something I don't like. He can see it—sense it—hidden deep beneath the surface of my skin.

Caleb rises up from the table and heads across the kitchen, his movements unhurried like he doesn't have a care in the world. "So how's college football?" he says to Kayden. "I've heard it's a lot more intense at that level."

Kayden doesn't take his eyes off me. "It's not that bad. You just have to be tough enough to make it."

Caleb eyes Kayden's inflamed cheek with a sadistic look

336

in his expression as he opens the cupboard. "Yeah, you look pretty tough. Nice shiner by the way."

Kayden gives him a cold, hard stare, his fingers wrapping inward into his palms. "Didn't you get kicked out of college for selling pot on campus?"

"Hey, I had to make a living," Caleb says, slamming the cupboard shut. "Not everyone has Daddy's money and a scholarship to live off of."

Kayden's jaw tenses and I jerk on his arm. "Can we go?"

He nods, backing toward the door with my hand in his and his eyes boring into Caleb, who's growing uneasy.

"No way," Jackson says to me. "You are not leaving me here to be smothered by Mom."

"Shouldn't you be in Florida or whatever?" I ask with rage and unsteadiness in my voice. "You weren't supposed to be here."

He messes with his hair as he gets up from the kitchen table with the pie tin in his hand. "We had a last minute change of heart."

"Didn't you have to work?" I ask derisively. "Or did you just quit another job?"

"I have a fucking job, Callie." He tosses the tin into the kitchen sink and glares at me. "So quit being a cunt. I don't know why you always have to talk to me like this."

"Hey." Kayden steps in on my behalf, moving in front of me. "Don't fucking call her names."

"I can call her whatever I want," Jackson retorts, folding

his arms over his chest. "You don't know the shit she put this family through. Her little issues or whatever they are have made my mom basically crazy."

Caleb watches me with interest, waiting for me to react. I can't look away from him. I want to, but he's overpowering me because he knows what my issues are—he put them there. I slowly start to die, wilt into pieces like I'm a night-blooming cereus, the flowers that bloom only once a year at night and die before sunrise, their lives and happiness short lived.

"Leave her alone." Caleb arches his eyebrows at me with a smile surfacing at his lips. "Maybe Callie has reasons for the way she acts."

Take me out of here. Take me out of here. Save me. Save me. Save me.

Suddenly, my legs are moving and I'm being dragged somewhere. The back door swings open and I'm hauled down the stairs into the center of the driveway.

Standing at the bottom of the stairs and in the light of the porch, Kayden observes me with uncertainty in his eyes, his hands on my shoulders. "What's wrong? You have this look in your eyes…"

I let out a strangled breath. "I don't like my brother very much."

The muscles in his neck move as he swallows hard. "Callie, I know what fear is. Trust me. I've seen it on my brothers' faces, felt it many times. You're afraid of him. I can see it in your eyes."

"Afraid of my brother?" I play dumb, praying to God he won't find out, fearing what will happen if he does.

"Don't do that," he says sternly, placing his hand on my cheek. "You're afraid of Caleb. He was... he was the one who did it to you?"

"Yes." I don't even mean to say it, it just falls out into the world. I stare at him, listening to my heart thump inside my chest, to the wind sing, to the sound of someone breaking somewhere in the world.

He forces a lump down in his throat. "Callie... I... you need to tell someone. You can't let him keep going around living his life."

"It doesn't matter. Too much time has gone by and even the cops can't do anything about it anymore."

"How do you know?"

I shrug, feeling detached from the world. "Because I looked into it once to see—to know that I no longer have any options. What's done is done."

He shakes his head, his jaw set tight. "This isn't fair."

"Neither is your life," I say, wanting my moment back. *I want it back. Please, God, give me it back.* "Nothing really is."

Silence builds and it all crumbles out as I collapse into his chest, tears spilling out as the secret I've carried with me breaks into lighter pieces. He scoops me up against my protests and cradles me against him as he carries me up the stairs and into the room as I sob out every tear I've been holding inside me.

He lies down on the bed with me and I bury my face into

his chest. Somehow, I stop crying and we lie, unmoving, feeling each other's pain. Eventually I fall asleep in his arms.

Kayden

After she falls asleep, I watch her breathe in and out, trying to make sense of the world. Rage washes through me like a fucking wave crashing against the shore. I want to kill Caleb. Beat him to death in the most painful ways.

When I hear her brother and Caleb leave the house, laughing as they get in the car and drive away, talking about going to a party, something snaps inside me. All the rage I've channeled ruptures and suddenly I know what I have to do.

Callie saved me that night from a fight that would have probably left me dead, but she also saved me from myself. Before her, I was dying inside; there was nothing in my heart, but an empty hole.

Gently slipping my arm out from beneath her head, I grab my phone and sneak out the door, looking at her one last time before I leave. Trotting down the steps, I text Luke to come pick me up, then I start walking down the sidewalk away from her house toward the unknown.

I walk a ways in a direction I've never been, letting the cold air consume me. About fifteen minutes later, Luke's truck pulls up to the curb. I hop in, rubbing my hands together as the heater blasts against my skin.

"Okay, what's up with the totally random fucking message?"

He adjusts his beanie lower on his head and cranks up the heater. "You do realize I was about to get lucky with Kelly Anallo?"

"Sorry," I mutter. "Where were you?"

"Down at the lake." He cranks the wheel to the right and drives down a side road. "There was a party going on."

"You didn't happen to see Callie's brother and Caleb Miller down there, did you?"

He halts at a stop sign, cranking up the defroster as the windshield fogs up. "Yeah, they pulled up right as I left to come get you."

"Then drive down there." I motion my hand for him to drive. "I have something I need to do."

We drive in silence as I bounce my knee and drum my fingers against the door. The truck bounces as we weave through the trees and surface out the other end. When we pull up, I spot Caleb by the bonfire near the shoreline, chatting it up with some blond chick wearing a baggy jacket over a tight pink dress.

"I need your help with something," I say as Luke shifts the car into park and starts to get out of the car.

He pauses with his leg outside. "What's up? You're acting kind of weird...it's freaking me out a little."

I don't take my eyes off Caleb. He's shorter than me by an inch or two, but I remember him picking a few fights at parties and he can definitely hold up his own. "I need you to have my back."

Luke gapes at me as he puts a cigarette in his mouth. "Are you planning on picking a fight?"

I nod unwaveringly. "I am."

"So you want me to make sure you don't get your dumb ass kicked?" He cups his hand around his mouth and flicks the top of the lighter.

"No, I want you to stop me before I kill him." I flip the handle and hop out.

"You what?" A puff of smoke rises in front of his face.

"Stop me before I kill him," I repeat and slam the door.

He meets me around the front, flicking the end of his cigarette, sending ashes to the ground. "What is this about, man? You know I don't do well in reckless situations."

I pause at the end of the line of cars. "If someone you... cared about a lot got hurt in the worst way possible by someone else, what would you do?"

He shrugs, staring at the fire. "It depends on what it is?"

"Something really bad," I say. "And it scarred them for life."

He takes a slow drag off his cigarette and then turns his head toward me. "All right, I got your back."

We hike over to the fire, the rage inside me burning as brightly as the flames. People are yelling, laughing, filling up beers from the kegger on a tailgate. There's music bumping from one of the car stereos and a lively game of beer pong is going on by the lake.

Daisy shows up in front of me with a huge grin on her face

and a plastic cup in her hand. "Hey, party boy, I knew you'd show up."

I shake my head with annoyance and step to the side. "Get out of my way."

She's taken back and presses her hand to her chest, like she's a wounded deer. "What is wrong with you?"

"He realized what a bitch you are," Luke chimes in gladly and blows smoke in her face.

"Oh my God. You're such an asshole," she says, fanning her hand in front of her face, looking at me expectantly to defend her.

I wave her off, dodge around her, and march straight for Caleb. Weaving through the people, I step out into the open near the fire. When Caleb's eyes meet mine, his expression falls, but he doesn't budge. He knows what's coming and he waits for it like he wants it.

I step toward him and a smile curls at his lips as he starts to lurk toward me. "What the fuck are you doing here?" he asks. "And where's pretty little Callie?"

I sucker punch him in the jaw, which is where I make my mistake, but I can't take it back. The crowd gasps and the girl in the pink dress drops her cup, spilling beer onto the dirt, and she skitters to the side.

Caleb crumbles to the ground clutching his cheek. "What the fuck?" He stumbles to his feet, wiping away the blood dripping from his nose. "Who do you think you are?"

I swing my fist at him again without an explanation, but this time he ducks and slams his fist into my side. My ribs pop, but it's nothing compared to what I'm used to, and I rebound, bringing my knee to his gut.

He coughs, hunching over as he spits blood on the ground. "You're so fucking dead."

I pop my knuckles, shuffling forward to hit him again, but he jumps up and charges at me. With his head down, he rams into my stomach, knocking the wind out of me, and our shoes scuff against the dirt as we struggle to stay upright. Someone screams from the crowd and it's followed by yells as we hit the dirt.

I smash my fist into his face over and over again, seeing red, only red, like it's been bottled up inside me for years. Someone tries to pull me off, but I shove them off repeatedly. I don't know how much time lapses as I continue hitting him. Finally someone is able to get me off of him.

I shake off their hand, thinking it's Luke, but the red and blue lights flashing against the still water bring me back to reality as a police officer slaps handcuffs onto my wrists.

"Don't move," a cop yells and I'm shoved forward, falling on my knees into the dirt.

With my bloodstained hands behind me, I take in what I've done. Caleb's still breathing, but his face is so engorged and bloody there are no features left. I'm not sure I care, though, because when it all comes down to it, Callie got her justice.

Being in jail seemed better than going home and I refused to call my dad. In the end, one of the officers calls him, because of his highly respected status in the town. My dad's always been big on the donations, which makes people automatically think he's a great guy.

Hours later, I'm in the kitchen of my house, sitting at the table. My mom went to pick up Tyler from the airport and had to take a cab, because neither of them will be sober enough to drive. It's just my dad and I in the house. Something's about to end, I just don't know what.

"This is fucking bullshit." My dad circles around the table and kicks the bottom of the counter with his boot, putting a hole in the wood. "I get a call in the middle of the God damn night to bail your ass out of jail, for beating the shit out of someone." He pauses, running his finger along a small cut below his eye that was caused by our fight. "You're really on a roll today, you little shit."

"I was taught by the best," I mutter, my ribs stinging, my arm throbbing, yet somehow, I feel more content than I ever have.

He picks up a chair and throws it across the room into a shelf, breaking a vase. I don't flinch. I just trace the cracks in the table with my thumb. "Where did I go wrong with you?" He stomps around the island that's in the middle of the kitchen. "You've been a fuckup since you were two."

I stare at the wall, picturing Callie's smile, the sound of her laugh, the softness of her skin.

"Are you listening to me?" he shouts. "God damn it, Kayden, quit ignoring me!"

I close my eyes, reliving how it felt to be inside her, touch her, kiss her all over her body, the smell of her hair.

My dad's hands slam down on the table and my eyes shoot open. "Get up."

I shove away from the table, knocking the chair to the floor. I'm ready for it. As he bends his elbow back over his shoulder, swinging his fist forward, I curve mine up and slam it into his jaw. The pain stuns us both as our fists connect with each other's faces. There's a pause, where he really looks at me, like he's seeing me for the first time, before he seizes me by the shoulders and throws me against the wall.

"Knock it off, you little shit!" He knees me in the side and I hammer my knuckles into his cheek in retaliation.

Again, he's shocked and it takes him a moment to recuperate. All I think about is how afraid he looks, the lack of confidence in his eyes, and the unsteadiness of his posture.

He grabs on to my shirt, desperate to gain control as he pushes his hand against my face, shoving me back against the cupboard. Digging my fingernails into the palms of my hands, I curve my fist upward and strike him in the side of the head, hard. He lets out a grunt as he shoves me back and I crash against the counter, banging my hip against the tile and knocking knives to the floor. I start to move forward, but he runs at me with his head down. I speed up, bending my knees to hop over the island, but he catches the bottom of my shirt and jerks me down to the floor. I fling my arm behind me, reaching for him, but he ducks down.

I feel numb. Completely dead inside as I spin around on my heels and shove my hands against his chest. He refuses to let go of me, even when he trips to the floor, and he yanks me down with him. I try to roll on top of him, but seconds later I feel something sharp pierce through my side and everything stops.

My dad rises to his feet, holding a blood-soaked knife. "Why can't you ever listen?" He drops the knife onto the floor beside my feet and it clanks against the tile. His face is as white as a ghost as he backs away. "You fucking..." He drags his fingers down his face, before he takes off for the front door, leaving it ajar behind him and cold air gusts in.

Every part of my body aches, like a thousand knives have been stabbed into me instead of one. Pivoting to the side, I crawl up, and lean against the counter, moving my hand away from my side. Blood coats my trembling fingers and leaks out of the hole in my shirt, filling the cracks in the tile floor below me. I shut my eyes as I fight to breathe, but the pain is winning.

I think about Callie, what she's doing, what she'll do when she hears about what happened. It hurts, even though it's not supposed to; the thought of me leaving her, of her leaving me, of never having her again. I can't hold it in.

Reaching to my side, I pick up a knife, my hand unsteady as I put the tip to my forearm. It's what I've done for ages to shut it off. It started when I was seven when I realized that cutting myself helped me breathe—helped me live through the hell of life. It's my fucked-up secret; the darkness that lives within me. With every incision into my skin, the pain begins to subside as blood covers the floor.

Callie

I wake up to an empty bed and panic erupts through my body. Where did he go? I grab my phone off the nightstand and text Kayden multiple times, but he doesn't answer. I slip my shoes on and run out the door to go look for him. I need to talk to him about last night and let him know that we need to just let it go because with him in my life, what happened with Caleb isn't as scary.

Morning is clipping over the mountains and the sky is a bright pink, but the beauty of it is very misleading compared to what's going on down below. The wind is raging, blowing in a storm and chilling the temperature.

My father is at the kitchen table when I walk inside. His brown hair is parted to the side and he's got his tie and slacks on, ready for Thanksgiving dinner this afternoon.

When he peers up from his food, his eyebrows furrow. "Are you okay? You look like you've been crying."

"I'm fine." I glance in the living room, before backtracking to the center of the kitchen. "Where's Mom? I need to ask her if I can borrow her car."

"She's taking a shower." He stands up from the chair and

348

drops the bowl into the sink, observing me. "You look like you've lost some weight. Make sure you eat a lot today. There's going to be a game after dinner and I want you to play this year."

"Okay, fine." I can hardly hear him as I browse through the messages on my phone, but there aren't any from Kayden. "Can I borrow your car for a little bit? I promise I won't be gone for too long."

He reaches for the keys in his pocket. "Are you sure you're okay? You look really upset."

"I'm fine," I assure him, unnerved because normally he doesn't notice these things. How bad do I look? "I just need to check up on a friend."

He tosses me the keys and I catch them effortlessly. "Would this friend be one of my old quarterbacks?"

I wrap my fingers around the keys, feeling the jagged sides cut into my palm. "Mom's been gossiping, hasn't she?"

He shrugs, stuffing his hands into the pockets of his slacks. "You know how she gets. She just wants you to be happy."

"I am happy." And at that moment it doesn't seem like a huge lie. "I just need to find someone." I turn for the door.

"Be back in an hour," he calls out. "You know she's going to want your help. Your brother never came home last night. He probably stayed out all night getting drunk, so he won't be any help."

"Okay." I step out into the cold, feeling something hit me in the chest, but I'm not sure what it is. My phone goes off in

my pocket and I'm surprised to see Luke's name flash on the screen.

"Hello," I answer as I run down the driveway and hop into my dad's car.

"Hey," he says in an anxious voice. "Have you talked to Kayden at all?"

"Not since last night." I slam the door and start the engine, not bothering to let the defroster warm up. "I don't know where he went. He just took off and I can't get a hold of him."

"Me neither." He wavers as I crane my neck and back the car onto the road, squinting to see through the frosted rear window. "Listen, Callie, last night he did something really bad."

I align the car onto the road and shove it into drive. "What happened?"

"I got this weird call from him," he says. "Asking me to pick him up. He had me take him out to the lake and he... he beat the shit out of Caleb Miller."

I press the gas pedal to the floor and the tires squeal. "Is he okay?"

"He's fine, I guess, but he got arrested and his dad had to bail him out."

My heart stops. "His dad?"

He pauses. "Yeah, his dad."

I wonder if Luke knows about Kayden's dad. "I'm heading over to his house right now to check up on him."

"Me too. Where are you?"

"Like a few blocks away...On Mason Road."

"Okay, I'll see you in a few," he says. "And Callie, be careful, his dad's..."

"I know." I hang up and grip the phone in my hand as I drive up the hill that leads to Kayden's house.

The two-story mansion looks huge in front of the hills, towering toward the sky. By the time I park beneath the tree, the wind has kicked up and brown leaves blow through the air, nearly shadowing the forest that surrounds the house. I hop out of the car with my heart thudding inside my chest, and sprint across the lawn and up the stairs, swinging my arms to get the leaves out of my face.

The front door is agape, swaying in the wind. When I step into the foyer, a nauseous feeling burns in my stomach. Something doesn't feel right. I glance in the living room and then call up the stairway, "Hello?"

The wind is my only answer, howling at the window, blowing leaves into the house, along the hardwood floor, and slamming the door against the wall. I walk into the kitchen and turn the corner. Nothing could ever prepare me for what I see.

Time stops—everything stops. A part of me dies.

Lying on the floor, in a pool of blood and a pile of knives is Kayden. His eyes are shut, his arms and legs slack, and there are fresh cuts tracking up his wrists. There's a hole in the side of his shirt, where something sharp has punctured through

351

it. There's so much blood, but I can't tell where it's coming from—it looks like everywhere.

My arms fall to my side as my knees give out and I crumple to the floor, landing on a knife. "No, no, no, no!" I pull at my hair, feeling the pain, and rip some of the strands out. "No!"

I shake my head a hundred times, hoping the scene will vanish, like I hoped my twelfth birthday would. But it stays. It always stays. Tears veil my vision as I press down on one of the cuts on his wrists to stop the bleeding. His skin is so cold, like ice, like death. I move my hand to his arm, his cheek, above his heart. With an unsteady finger, I dial 911 and sputter out the details.

"Does he have a pulse?" the operator asks when I tell her the situation.

My heart squeezes tightly in my chest as I press my fingers to his pulse and a faint murmur bumps against them. "Yes."

"Is he breathing?"

I stare at his chest, wishing for it to move—praying it will move. After a while, it slightly elevates and then falls down unsteadily.

"Yes, he is. He is. Oh my God." I press my quivering lips together, sobbing as I hang up and wait for the ambulance. The phone falls from my hand as I run my fingers through Kayden's hair, wondering if he can sense me.

"Kayden, wake up," I whisper, but he's still. "Please, God, wake up."

"Callie...what..." Luke steps up behind me.

I don't budge. I can't look away from Kayden. If I do, he might disappear.

"Callie, can you hear me?"

"Don't make a sound. It'll be over quickly. You'll barely feel a thing."

"Callie!" Luke practically screams and I blink up at him as hot tears stream down my cheeks. "Did you call an ambulance?"

I nod, feeling everything around me—in me—crumble. "I tried to save him…I-I did, but I couldn't…I couldn't…"

Luke kneels down beside me, looking at his friend on the floor, his face draining of color, his brown eyes huge and horrified. "It's not your fault. He's breathing. He can get through this…he can."

But it is my fault. All my fault. I wrap my arms around Kayden, breathing him in, never wanting to let him go. "Please, stay with me."

"This is all your fault," Caleb says. *"If you tell anyone, that's what they'll think."*

Sirens flood the air as leaves sweep through the kitchen, swirling around with no other purpose than to go wherever the wind carries them.

I should have done more. Said something. Stood up for him like he did for me.

I thought I'd saved Kayden that night at the pool house, but I was wrong. I just bought him time until the next windstorm swept through.

Their story continues . . .

The dark secret Kayden has kept for years is out.
But to save him, Callie must reveal a truth
that can tear them apart.

Please turn this page for a preview of

The Redemption of

Callie & Kayden.

Prologue

Callie

I want to breathe.

I want to feel alive again.

I don't want to feel the pain.

I want it all back, but it's gone.

I hear every sound, every laugh, every cry. People move around the room frantically, but I can't take my eyes off the sliding glass doors. There's a violent storm outside and rain is hammering against the concrete, dirt, and dry leaves. Sirens flash as ambulances drive up under the port and the glow lights up the rain on the ground, red, like blood. Like Kayden's blood. Like Kayden's blood all over the floor. So much blood.

My stomach is empty. My heart is hurting. I can't move.

"Callie," Seth says. "Callie, look at me."

I blink my gaze off the door and stare into his brown eyes filled with worry. "Huh?"

He takes my hand in his. His skin warm and comforting. "He's going to be okay."

I stare at him, forcing back tears, because I have to be strong. "Okay."

He lets out a sigh and pats my hand. "You know what, I'm going to go see if he can have visitors yet. It's been almost a damn week. You'd think they'd let him have visitors by now." He gets up from the chair and walks across the packed waiting room to the receptionist desk.

He'll be all right.

He has to be.

But in my heart, I know he won't be all right. Sure, his wounds and broken bones may heal on the outside. On the inside, though, the healing will take longer, and I wonder what Kayden will be like when I see him again. Who will he be?

Seth starts talking to the receptionist behind the counter. She barely gives him the time of day as she multitasks between phone calls and the computer. It doesn't matter, though. I know what she'll say—the same thing she's been saying. That he can't have visitors, except for family. His *family*, the people who hurt him. He doesn't need his family.

"Callie." Maci Owens's voice rips me out of my daze. I blink up at Kayden's mother with a frown on my face. She's dressed in a pinstripe pencil skirt, her nails are done, and her hair is curled up into a bun on the top of her head. "Why are you here?" she asks.

I almost ask her the same thing. "I came here to see Kayden." I sit up in the seat.

"Callie honey." She speaks like I'm a little kid, frowning as she stares down at me. "Kayden can't have visitors. I told you this a few days ago."

"But I have to go back to school soon," I say, gripping on to the handles of the chair. "I need to see him before I go."

She shakes her head and sits down in the chair next to me, crossing her legs. "That's not going to be possible."

"Why not?" My voice comes out sharper than it ever has.

She glances around, worried I'm causing a scene. "Please keep your voice down, honey."

"I'm sorry, but I need to know that he's okay," I say. There's so much anger inside me. I've never been this angry before and I don't like it. "And I need to know what happened."

"What happened is that Kayden's sick," she responds quietly and then starts to get up.

"Wait." I get up with her. "What do you mean he's sick?"

She slants her head to the side and gives me her best sad face, but all I can think about is how this is the woman who let Kayden get beaten by his father for all those years. "Honey, I don't know how to tell you this, but Kayden injured himself."

I shake my head as I back away from her. "No he didn't."

Her face grows sadder and she looks like a plastic doll with glassy eyes and a painted on smile. "Honey, Kayden's had a problem with cutting for a very long time and this...well, we thought he was getting better, but I guess we were wrong."

"No he doesn't!" I scream. Actually scream. I'm shocked. She's shocked. Everyone in the crowded waiting room is shocked. "And my name is Callie not honey."

Seth hurries up to me, his eyes wide and full of concern. "Callie, are you okay?"

I glance at him, then at the people around the room. It's gone quiet and they're staring at me. "I...I don't know what's wrong with me." I reel on my heels and run for the sliding-glass doors, bumping my elbows onto the trim when they don't open quickly enough. I keep running until I find a cluster of bushes around the back of the hospital, then I fall on my knees and throw up all over the mud. My shoulders shake, my stomach heaves, and tears sting at my eyes. When my stomach is empty, I fall back on my heels and sit down in the wet dirt.

There's no way Kayden could have done that to himself. But deep down in the center of my heart, I keep thinking about all the scars on his body and I can't help but wonder: what if he did?

Kayden

I open my eyes and the first thing I see is light. It burns my eyes and makes my surroundings distorted. I don't know where I am... *What happened?* Then I hear the deep voices, clanking, chaos. There's a machine beeping and it seems to match the beat of my heart as it hits my chest, but it sounds too slow and uneven. My body is cold—numb, like the inside of me.

"Kayden, can you hear me?" I hear my mom's voice but I can't see her through the bright light.

"Kayden Owens, open your eyes," she repeats herself until her voice becomes a gnawing hum inside my head.

I open and close my eyelids repeatedly and then roll my eyes back into my head. I blink again and the light turns into spots and eventually into faces of people I don't know, each of their expressions filled with fear. I search through them, looking for only one person, but I don't see her anywhere.

I unhitch my jaw and force my lips to move. "Callie."

My mom appears above me. Her eyes are colder than I expected and her lips are pursed. "Do you have any idea what you put this family through? What is wrong with you? Don't you value your life?"

I glance around at the doctors and nurses around my bed and realize it's not fear I'm seeing, but pity and annoyance. "What..." My throat is dry like sand and I force my throat muscles to move as I swallow several times. "What happened?" I start to remember: blood, violence, pain...wanting it to all end.

My mom puts her hands next to my head and leans over me. "I thought we were over this problem. I thought you stopped."

I tip my head to the side and glance down at my arm. My wrist is bandaged up and my skin is white and mapped with blue veins. There's an IV attached to the back of my hand and a clip on the end of my finger. I remember. *Everything.* I meet her eyes. "Where's Dad?"

Her eyes narrow and her voice lowers as she leans in even closer. "Gone on a business trip."

I gape at her unfathomably. She'd never done anything about the violence when I was growing up, but I guess I was kind of hoping that maybe this would have pushed her to the end of her secrecy and her need to always defend him. "He's on a business trip?" I say slowly.

A man in a white coat with a pen in his pocket, glasses, and salt-and-pepper hair says something to my mom and then he exits the room carrying a clipboard. A nurse walks over to a beeping machine in the corner beside my bed and starts writing down stuff in my chart.

My mother leans in closer, shadowing over me, and whispers in a low tone that conveys a lot of warning, "Your father's not going to have any part of this. The doctors know you cut your own wrists and the town knows you beat up Caleb. You're not in a good place right now and you're going to be in a worse place if you try to bring your father into this." She leans back a little and for the first time I realize how large her pupils are. There's barely any color left except for a small ring around the edge. She looks possessed, by the devil maybe, or my father—but they're kind of one and the same.

"You're going to be all right," she says. "All the injuries missed anything major. You lost a lot of blood, but they gave you a blood transfusion."

I press my hands to the bed, trying to sit up, but my body is heavy, and my limbs weak. "How long have I been out?"

"You've been in and out for a couple of days now. But the doctors say that's normal." She starts tucking the blanket in around me, like I'm suddenly her child. "What their more worried about is why you cut yourself."

I could have yelled it—screamed it to the world that it wasn't all me. That it was my dad, that he and I had both done the damage. But as I glance around the empty room, I realize there's no one here that really cares. I'm alone. I did cut myself. And for a brief second I kind of hoped it would be my end. That all the pain and hate and feelings of being worthless would *finally*, after nineteen years, be gone.

She pats my leg. "All right, I'll be back tomorrow."

I don't say anything. I just roll over and seal my eyes and mouth shut and let myself go back into the comfort of the darkness I'd just woken up from. Because right now, it's better than being in the light.

Chapter One

 # 62 Don't Break Apart.

Callie

I spend a lot of time writing in my notebook. It's like therapy for me almost. It's extremely late in the night and I'm wide awake, dreading going back to campus tomorrow morning and leaving Kayden behind. How am I supposed to just leave him, bail out, move on? Everyone keeps telling me that I have to, like it's as simple as picking out an outfit. I was never good at picking out outfits, though.

I'm in the room above the garage, alone, tucked away in the solitude with only my pen and notebook for company. I sigh as I stare at the moon and then let my hand move across the paper almost on its own accord.

I can't get the image out of my mind, no matter how hard I try. Every time I close my eyes, I see Kayden, lying on the floor. Blood covers his body, the floor, the cracks in the tile, and the knives that surround him. He's broken, bleeding, cracked to pieces. To some people he probably seems like he can't be repaired. But I can't think that.

I was once shattered to pieces, destroyed by the hand of another, but now I feel like I'm beginning to reconnect. Or at least I did feel that way. But when I found Kayden on the floor it felt like part of me splintered again. And more of me broke when his mother told me he did it to himself. He cut himself and has probably been doing it for years.

I don't believe it.

I can't believe it. Not when I know about his dad.

I just can't.

My hand stops and I wait for more to come. But that's all I seem to need to write. I lie down in the bed and stare at the moon, wondering how I'm supposed to move forward in life, when everything important to me is motionless.

❧

"Wipe that sad frown off your face, missy." Seth is holding my arm as we walk across the campus yard. It's cold, rain is drizzling from the gloomy clouds and the sidewalks are covered in murky puddles. There's practically a river running off the rooftops of the historical buildings that enclose the campus. The grass is sloshy beneath my sneakers and the icky weather matches my mood. People are running to and from class and I just want to yell, *Slow down and wait for the world to catch up!*

"I'm trying," I tell him, but my frown still remains. It's the

same frown that's been on my face since I found Kayden. The images hurt my mind and my heart like shards of glass. I know part of this is my fault. I'm the one who let Kayden find out about Caleb. I barely even tried to deny it when he'd asked me. Part of me had wanted him to find out and part of me was glad when Luke had told me Kayden had beat up Caleb.

He nudges me with his elbow and constricts his grip when I trip over my feet and stumble to the side. "Callie, you need to stop worrying all the time." He helps me get my balance. "I know it's hard, but being sad all the time isn't a good thing. I don't want you going back to the sad girl I first met."

I stop in my tracks and step right in a puddle. The cold water fills my shoes and soaks through my socks. "Seth, I'm not going back to that." I slip my arm out of his and wrap my jacket tightly around myself. "I just can't stop thinking about him...how he looked. It's stuck in my head." It's been a few weeks since it happened and it's always in my mind. I didn't want to leave Afton, but my mom threatened me, saying if I failed the semester she wasn't going to let me stay at the house for Christmas break. I'd have nowhere to go. "I just miss him and I feel bad for leaving him there with his family."

"It wouldn't have matter if you stayed. They still won't let you see him." Seth brushes his golden blond hair out of his honey-brown eyes and looks at me sympathetically as rain drips down on his head and face. "Callie, I know it's hard, especially when they said he did it to...when he did it to himself. But you can't break apart."

"I'm not breaking apart." The drizzle of rain suddenly shifts to a downpour and we sprint for the shelter of the trees, shielding our faces with our arms. I tuck damp strands of my brown hair out of my face and behind my ears. "I just can't stop thinking about him." I sigh, wiping away the rain from my face. "Besides, I don't believe that he did it to himself."

His shoulders slump as he pulls down the sleeves of his black button-down jacket. "Callie, I hate to say it but...but what if he did? I know it could have been his dad, but what if it wasn't? What if the doctors are right? I mean they did send him to that facility for a reason."

Raindrops bead down our faces and my eyelashes flutter against them. "Then he did," I say. "It doesn't change anything." Everyone has secrets, just like me. I'd be a hypocrite if I judge Kayden for self-infliction. "Besides, they didn't send him. The hospital transferred him their so he could be watched while he heals. That's all. He doesn't *have* to stay there."

Seth offers me a sympathetic smile, but there's pity in his eyes. He leans forward and gives me a quick kiss on the cheek. "I know and that's why you're you." He moves back from me, turns to his side, and aims his elbow at me. "Now come on, we're going to be late for class."

Sighing, I link elbows with him and we step out into the rain, taking our time as we head to class.

"Maybe we could do something fun," Seth suggests as he opens the door to the main building on campus. He guides me into the warmth and lets the door slam shut behind us.

He releases my arm and shakes the front of his jacket, sending raindrops everywhere. "Like we could go to a movie or something. You've been dying to see that one…" He snaps his fingers a few times. "I can't remember what it's called, but you kept talking about it before break."

I shrug, grabbing my ponytail and giving it a good wring so the water drips out of the end. "I can't remember either. And I don't really feel like seeing a movie."

He frowns. "You need to quit sulking."

"I'm not sulking," I say and massage my hand over my heart. "My heart just hurts all the time."

His shoulders lift and descend as he sighs. "Callie, I—"

I raise my hand and shake my head. "Seth, I know you always want to help me out and I love you for that, but sometimes hurting is just part of life, especially when someone I lo…care about is hurting too."

He arches his eyebrows because of my almost slip. "Okay then, let's go to class."

I nod and follow him up the hall. My clothes are wet from the rain and there's water in my shoes. Even though it's cold and the water sticks my clothes to my body, it reminds me of a beautiful time full of magical kisses and I need to hold on to that.

Because for now, it's all I've got.

∽

I've been staring at my English book for so long it feels like my eyes are bleeding and the words look identical. I rub my eyes with my fingertips, pretending like the room doesn't smell like pot and that Violet, my roommate, isn't passed out in the bed across from mine. She's been like that for the last ten hours. I'd be worried she was dead, but she keeps muttering incoherently in her sleep.

On top of studying for the English exam, I'm supposed to be writing an essay. I joined a creative writing club at the beginning of the year and at the end of it, I'm supposed to turn in three projects; a poem, a fiction story, and a nonfiction piece. As much as I love to write, I'm struggling with the idea of putting truth down on paper for other people to read. I'm afraid of what might come out if I really open up. Or maybe it's because it seems silly to write a paper about the truth of life when Kayden's in an institution living the truth. All I've typed so far is: *Where the Leaves Go by Callie Lawrence.* I'm uncertain of where I'll go with this.

The rain from earlier has frozen into fluffy snowflakes that sail from the sky and a silvery sheet of ice glistens across the campus yard. I tap my fingers on the top of my book, thinking about home and how there's probably three or four feet of snow and how my mom's car is probably stuck in the driveway. I can picture the snowplow roaming the town's streets, and my dad doing warm-ups inside the gym because it's too cold to be outside. And Kayden is still in the hospital under supervision because they think he tried to kill himself. It's been a few weeks since it happened. He was out of it for quite a while from all the blood transfusions and lacerations to his body. Then he woke up and no one could see him because he's considered "high risk" and "under surveillance"(Kayden's mother's words not mine).

My phone is sitting on my bed next to a pile of study sheets and an array of highlighters. I pick it up, dial Kayden's number, and wait for his voicemail to click on.

"Hey, this is Kayden, I'm way too busy to take your call right now, so please leave a message, and maybe you'll be lucky enough that I'll call you back." There's sarcasm in his voice like he thinks he's being funny and I smile, missing him so badly it pierces at my heart.

I listen to it over and over again until I can hear the underlying pain through his sarcasm; the one that carries his secrets. Eventually, I hang up and flop back on my bed, wishing I could travel back in time and not let Kayden find out that it was Caleb who raped me.

"God, what time is it?" Violet sits up in her bed and blinks her bloodshot eyes at the leather-banded watch on her wrist. She shakes her head and gathers her black and red streaked hair out of her face. She gazes out the window at the snow and then looks at me. "How long have I been out?"

I shrug, staring up at the ceiling. "I think like ten hours?"

She throws the blanket off her and climbs out of bed. "Fuck, I missed my Chemistry class."

"You take Chemistry?" I don't mean for it to sound so rude, but the shock of her taking Chemistry shows through my voice. Violet and I have shared a room for three months and from what I can tell, she likes to party and she likes guys.

She gives me a dirty look as she slips her arm through the sleeve of her leather jacket. "What? You don't think I can party *and* be smart?"

I shake my head. "No, that's not what I meant. I just—"

"I know what you meant—what you think of me, and everyone else." She snatches her bag from the desk, sniffs her shirt and shrugs. "But some advice. Maybe you shouldn't judge people by their looks."

"I don't," I tell her, feeling bad. "I'm sorry if you think I judged you."

She collects her phone from the desk and tosses it into her bag, then heads for the door. "Listen, if some guy named Jesse comes buy, can you pretend that you haven't seen me all day?"

"Why?" I ask, sitting up.

"Because I don't want him to know I've been here." She opens the door and glances back over her shoulder. "God, you've been a little snippy lately. When I first met you, I thought you were like a doormat. But lately, you've been kind of cranky."

"I know," I say quietly with my chin tucked downward. "And I'm sorry. I've just been having a rough few weeks."

She pauses in the doorway, eyeing me over. "Are you..." She shifts her weight, looking uncomfortable. Whatever she's trying to say seems to be hard for her. "Are you okay?"

I nod and something crosses over her face, maybe pain,

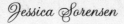

and for a second I wonder if Violet's okay. But then she shrugs and walks out, slamming the door behind her. I release a loud breath and lie back down on the bed. The feeling to shove my finger down my throat and free the heavy, foul feelings in my stomach, strangle me. Damn it. I need therapy. I reach for my phone without sitting up and dial my therapist's number, aka Seth, and my best friend in the whole world.

"I love you to death, Callie," Seth answers after three rings. "But I think I'm about to get lucky so this better be important."

I scrunch my nose as my cheeks heat. "It's not...I just wanted to see what was up. But if you're busy, I'll let you go."

He sighs. "I'm sorry, that came out a lot ruder than I planned. If you *really* need me, I can totally talk. You know you're my first priority."

"Are you with Greyson?" I ask.

"Of course," he replies with humor in his tone. "I'm not a man whore skank."

A giggle slips through my lips and I'm amazed how much better I feel just from talking to him. "I promise, I'm fine. I'm just bored and was looking for an escape from my English book." I shove the book off the bed and roll onto my stomach, propping up on my elbows. "I'll let you go."

"Are you really, really sure?"

"I'm one-hundred-percent sure. Now go have fun."

"Oh, trust me. I'm planning on it," he replies and I laugh, but it hurts my stomach. I start to hang up when he adds, "Callie, if you need to hang out with someone, you could call

Luke…you two are kind of going through the same thing. I mean, with missing Kayden and not really understanding."

I bite at my fingernails. I've spent time with Luke, but I'm still uncomfortable being alone with guys, except for Seth. Besides, things are weird between Luke and I because we haven't officially talked about what happened at Kayden's. It's the white elephant in the room; the massive, sad, heartbroken elephant. "I'll think about it."

"Good. And if you do, make sure to ask him about yesterday in Professor McGellon's class."

"Why? What happened?"

He giggles mischievously. "Just ask him."

"Okay…" I say, unsure if I really want to. If Seth thinks it's funny than there's a good chance that whatever happened might embarrass me. "Have fun with Greyson."

"You, too, baby girl," he says and hangs up.

I hit end and scroll through my contacts until I reach Luke's number. My finger hovers over the dial button for an eternity and then I chicken out and drop the phone down on the bed. I get up, slip on my Converses—the one's stained with the green paint because they remind me of a happy time in life. I zip up my jacket, put my phone into the pocket, and collect my keycard and journal before heading outside.

It's colder than a freezer, but I walk aimlessly through the vacant campus before finally taking a seat on one of the frosted benches. It's snowing but the tree branches create a canopy above my head. I open my journal, pull the top of my jacket over my nose, and begin to scribble down my thoughts, pouring out my heart and soul to blank sheets of paper because it's therapeutic.

I remember my sixteenth birthday like I remember how to add. It's there locked away in my head whenever I need it, although I don't use it often. It was the day I learned to drive. My mom had always been really weird about letting my brother and I anywhere near the wheel of a vehicle until we were old enough to drive. She said it was to protect us from ourselves and other drivers. I remember thinking how strange it was, her wanting to protect us, because there were so many things—huge, life-changing things—she'd never protected us from. Like the fact that my brother had been smoking pot since he was fourteen. Or the fact that Caleb raped me in my own room when I was twelve. Deep down, I knew it wasn't her fault, but the thought always crossed my mind: why hadn't she protected me?

So at sixteen, I finally got into the driver's seat for the very first time. I was terrified and my palms were sweating so badly I could barely hold on to the wheel. My dad also had a lifted truck and I could barely see over the dash.

"Can't we please just drive Mom's car?" I asked my dad as I turned the key in the ignition.

He buckled his seatbelt and shook his head. "It's better to learn on the big dog first, that way driving the car will be a piece of cake."

I buckled my own seatbelt and wiped my sweaty palms on the front of my jeans. "Yeah, but I can barely see over the wheel."

He smiled and gave me a pat on the shoulder. "Callie, I know *driving is scary, like life. But you're perfectly capable of handling this, otherwise I wouldn't let you."*

I almost broke down and told him what happened to me on my twelfth birthday. I almost told him that I couldn't handle it. That I couldn't handle anything. But fear owned me and I pressed on the gas and drove the truck forward.

I ended up running over the neighbor's mailbox and proving my dad wrong. I wasn't allowed to drive for the next few months and I was glad. Because to me driving meant growing up and I didn't want to grow up. I wanted to be a child. I wanted to be twelve years old and still have the excitement of life and boys and kisses and crushes ahead of me.

"Fuck, it's freezing out here."

My head snaps up at the sound of Luke's voice and I quickly shut my journal. He's standing a few feet away from me with his hands tucked in the pockets of his jeans and the hood of his dark blue jacket tugged over his head.

"What are you doing out here?" I ask, sliding my pen into the spiral of the notebook.

His shoulders rise and fall as he shrugs and then he sits down beside me. He stretches his legs out in front of him and crosses his ankles. "I got a random call from Seth telling me that I should come out here and check up on you. That you might need to be cheered up."

My gaze sweeps the campus yard. "Sometimes I wonder if he has spy cameras all over the place. He seems to know everything, you know."

Luke nods in agreement. "He does, doesn't he?"

I reciprocate his nod and then it grows quiet. Snowflakes drift down and our breaths lace in front of our faces. I wonder why he's really here. Did Seth tell him I needed to be watched?

"You want to go somewhere?" Luke uncrosses his ankles and sits up straight. "I don't know about you, but I could really use a break from this place."

"Yeah." I don't even hesitate, which surprises me. Does that mean I'm getting over my trust issues?

He smiles genuinely, but there's intensity in his eyes, something that's always there. I used to be intimidated by it, but now I know it's just him. Besides, I think he hides behind it; maybe fear, loneliness, or the pain of life.

I tuck my notebook underneath my arm and we get to our feet. We hike across the campus yard, heading toward the unknown, but I guess that's okay for now. I'll know where I'm going when I get there.

Chapter One

Two months later

Ella

Every night I have the same dream. Micha and I are standing on opposite ends of the bridge. Rain beats down violently from the dark sky and the wind kicks up debris between us.

Micha extends his hand and I walk toward him, but he slips away from me until he lands up on the railing of the bridge. He teeters in the wind and I want to save him, but my feet won't budge. A gust of wind slams into him and he falls backward, vanishing into the darkness. I wake up screaming and full of guilt.

My therapist has a theory that the nightmare signifies my fear of losing Micha, although that doesn't explain why I won't save him. When she mentioned it, my heart sped up and my palms began to sweat. I never looked far enough into the future to realize that maybe one day Micha and I may not be together.

A forever? Does such a thing exist?

With as much time as we spend together I wonder where our relationship is going. The last time we saw each other was at Grady's funeral. It was the second toughest day of my life; the first being my mother's funeral.

Micha and I had been out on the cliff that overlooked the lake, with a black jar containing Grady's ashes. The wind was blowing and all I could think about was how much death owned life. At any moment death could snatch up life and take it away, just like it had done with my mom and Grady.

"Are you ready for this?" Micha had asked, removing the lid from the jar.

Nodding, I extended my hand toward the jar. "I'm as ready as I'll ever be."

From behind us, the car was running and playing Grady's favorite song, "Simple Man" by Lynyrd Skynyrd, a song that fit Grady and his lifestyle perfectly.

He moved the jar toward me and we held onto it together. "What's that thing he used to say all the time?" Micha asked me. "About life?"

"It isn't as important to feel great about all the things we do," I say softly. "But how we feel toward the end when we look back at everything we've done."

Tears streamed from my eyes as we tipped the jar sideways and spilled the ashes off the cliff. As we watched them float down to the lake, Micha wrapped his arm around me and took a shot of tequila. He had offered me a sip, but I had declined.

My insides shook as pain rushed through me, but I quickly repressed it. Though sunlight sparkled down on us, there was a chill in the air as I observed the lake that seemed to hold everything. It was connected to so many deep, painful memories of my past with my mom and myself.

"Earth to Ella." Lila waves her hand in front of my face and I flinch. "You seriously space off more than anyone else I know. Class got out like five minutes ago... What the heck is that drawing of? It's creepy."

Drawn back to the present, my gaze sweeps across the empty desks in the classroom and then falls on the pen in my hand, the tip pressed to a sketch of my face, only my eyes are black and my skin looks like dry, cracked dirt.

"It's nothing." I stuff the drawing into my bag and grab my books. Sometimes I lose track of time and it's unsettling, because so did my mother. "It's just a doodle I was messing around with during Professor Mackman's boring lecture."

"What's the deal with you? You've been like super spaced out and super grumpy," Lila asks as we walk out of the classroom and push out the doors, stepping into the sunlight.

I adjust my bag on my shoulder and pull my sunglasses down over my eyes. "It's nothing. I'm just tired."

She stops abruptly in the middle of the sidewalk, narrows her blue eyes at me, and puts her hands on her hips. "Don't shut down on me now. We've been doing so well."

I sigh, because she's right. "It's just this dream I've been having."

"About Micha?"

"How'd you guess?"

She elevates her eyebrows. "How could I not guess? All of your thoughts are about him."

"Not all of my thoughts." I dwell in my thoughts about my dad, who's in rehab and how he won't talk to me.

We stroll down the sidewalk and she links arms with me. There's a skip to her walk, and her pink dress and blonde hair blow in the gentle fall breeze. About a year ago, Lila and I looked very similar, but then Micha cracked through my shell and I opted for a happy medium. I'm wearing a black Spill Canvas T-shirt and a pair of jeans, and my long auburn hair hangs loosely around my face.

"Where should we have lunch?" she asks as we reach the edge of the parking lot. "Because our fridge is empty."

"We need to go shopping." I scoot over as a group of football players walk by in their scarlet and gray uniforms. "But we also need a car to go anywhere, since you won't take the bus anymore."

"Only because of that creeper who licked my arm," she says, cringing. "It was disgusting."

"It was pretty gross," I agree, trying not to laugh.

"My dad's such a jerk," Lila mutters with a frown. "He should have at least warned me when he decided to tow my car back home. It makes no sense. He doesn't want me there, yet he takes my car away because I ran out during the summer."

"Dads tend to be jerks." At the end of the sidewalk, I veer to the left. "Mine won't talk to me."

"We should make a Dads Suck Club," she suggests sarcastically. "I'm sure a lot of people would join."

I strain a smile. I don't blame my dad for his negative feelings toward me. It was my choice to leave that night my mom died and now I have to deal with the consequences—it's part of moving on.

I stay under the shade of the trees as we head up the sidewalk toward the side section of the school. "Let's just eat at the cafeteria. It's the easiest place to get to."

Her nose scrunches. "Easy, in the sense that it's close. But other than that there is nothing easy about..." She trails off as her eyes stray to the side of the campus and a conniving smile expands across her face "Here's an idea. You could ask Blake to give us a ride somewhere."

I spot Blake walking across the campus yard toward his car. He is in my water base media class and talks to me a lot. Lila insists it's because he has a thing for me, but I disagree.

"I'm not going to just go up and ask him for a ride." I tug on her arm. "Let's just eat in the cafeteria—"

"Hey, Blake!" she hollers, waving her arms in the air, then giggles under her breath.

Blake's brown eyes scan the campus and a smile expands across his face as he struts across the lawn toward us.

"He knows I have a boyfriend," I tell Lila. "He's just nice."

"Guys are hardly ever just nice, and I'm using his little crush on you to get us a ride out of here," Lila whispers. "I'm so sick of being stuck here."

My lips part in protest, but Blake reaches us, and I cinch my jaw shut.

He has a beanie over his dark-brown hair and blue paint spots dot the front of his faded jeans and the bottom of his tan T-shirt.

"So what's up? His thumb is hooked on to the handle of the ratty backpack slung over his shoulder and he looks at me like I'm the one who called him over.

We're almost the same height and I can easily look him directly in the eyes. "It was nothing."

"We need a ride." Lila flutters her eyelashes at him as she coils a lock of her hair around her finger. "To get some lunch."

"You don't have to take us," I intervene. "Lila just really needs an off-campus fix."

"I'd love to take you anywhere you need to go," he offers with a genuine smile. "I'm headed back to my apartment first, though, so if you don't mind stopping you can just come with me now."

From inside my pocket, my phone starts ringing the tune "Behind Blue Eyes" by The Who and my lips curve into a grin.

Lila rolls her eyes. "Oh dear God. I thought you would have been over your giddiness by now. You two have been together for almost three months."

I answer the phone, loving the flutters in my stomach that are caused from just hearing the song play. It reminds me of how his hands feel against my skin and how he calls me by my nickname.

"Hello, beautiful," he says charmingly and the sound of

his voice sends a quiver through my body. "How's my favorite girl in the world?"

"Well, hello to you too." I amble toward a leafy tree in the center of the lawn. "I'm doing great. Are you having a good day?"

"I am now." He uses his player's voice on me. "I'll have an even better day if you'll tell me what you're wearing."

"Jeans and a ratty T-shirt." I press back a smile.

"Come on, pretty girl, it's been like a month." He laughs into the phone, a deep noise that makes my insides vibrate. "Tell me what you're wearing underneath it."

I roll my eyes, but tolerate him. "A red, lacy thong and matching bra."

"That's a really nice mental picture you painted there," he growls in a husky voice. "Now I'll have something to help take care of myself later."

"Just as long as you're taking care of it yourself," I say and there's a drawn-out pause. "Micha, are you there?"

"You know I'd never do that to you, right?" His tone carries heaviness. "I love you way too much."

"I was just joking." Kind of. Lately, it's been bothering me that he spends so much time with Naomi, especially because a lot of his stories involve her.

"Yeah, but you always joke about it every time we talk and I worry that deep down you believe it."

"I don't," I insist, although the thought has crossed my mind. He's a lead singer in a band. And gorgeous. And charming. "I know you love me."

"Good, because I have something to tell you." He pauses. "We got the gig."

My mouth instantly sinks. "The one in New York?"

"Yeah... Isn't that great?"

"It's awesome... I'm really happy for you."

Silence takes over. I want to say something, but the sadness has stolen my voice so I stare across the campus at a couple walking and holding hands, thinking about what it's like to have that.

"Ella May, tell me what's wrong," he demands. "Are you worried about my being gone? Because you know you're the only girl for me. Or is it... is it Grady? How are you doing with that? I never know since you won't talk to me."

"It's not Grady," I say quickly, wanting to get off that subject. "It's just that... it's so far and I barely get to see you as it is." I slump back against a tree trunk. "You're still coming up here this weekend, right?"

He lets out a gradual breath. "The thing is, to make it to New York in time, we have to leave tomorrow morning. And I'd drive over there tonight, just to see you, but we have a performance."

My insides wind into knots, but I stay calm on the outside. "How long are you going to be gone to New York?"

He takes a second to answer. "About a month."

My hand trembles with anger or fear... I'm not sure. "So I haven't seen you in almost a month and I'm not going to be able to see you for another month?"

"You could come visit me in New York," he proposes. "You could fly out for, like, a week or something."

"I have midterms." My voice is sullen. "And my brother's wedding's in, like, a month and all my extra money is to pay for that."

"Ella, come on!" Lila shouts and my eyes dart to her. She motions me to come over, while Blake stands beside her with his hands stuffed into the pockets of his jeans. "Blake's waiting on us."

"Who's Blake?" Micha wonders curiously.

"Just a guy from my class," I explain, leaving the tree and heading toward Blake and Lila. "Look, I got to go."

"Are you sure you're okay?"

"Yeah, Lila's just waiting on me."

"Okay… I'll call you after my performance then."

"Sounds good." I hang up the phone, realizing I forgot to say good-bye, but the word wouldn't have left my mouth anyway. It feels like we're slipping away from each other, and he was the one thing that brought me back out of my dark place. If he leaves me, I'm not sure I can hold onto the light.

Micha

"Fuck." I hang up the phone and kick the tire of the band's SUV, which is in the middle of a parking lot of a shitty-ass motel in the bad side of town where crackheads walk the streets and every building has graffiti. It makes Star Grove look classy.

The sadness in Ella's voice worries me. She's still struggling with her personal demons, Grady's death, her mom's death, and won't completely open up to me about everything. There's always a thought in the back of my mind that she might vanish again.

A car backfires as I walk back to the motel room. On the stairway, I weave around a man making out with a woman who's probably a hooker to get to my door.

This is what I'm choosing over Ella? Sometimes I wonder why.

"Wow, you look like you're in a pissy mood," Naomi remarks from the bed when I slam the door of the motel room. She's painting her toenails and the room stinks like paint thinner. "Did you have a bad day?"

Clearing my throat, I empty out the change from the pocket of my jeans and drop my wallet down on the nightstand. "What gave it away? The door slam?"

"You're so hilarious." She sits up and blows on her nails. "What did Ella say to you this time?"

"She didn't say anything." I unzip my duffel bag that's on a chair between the television and the table. "She never does."

"That's the problem." Naomi likes to put her two cents in on everything and sometimes it gets on my nerves. "That she doesn't tell you how she feels."

I grab a pair of clean jeans and a black, long-sleeved shirt from the bag. "I don't want to talk about this."

"But you do when you're drunk." She smirks. "In fact, I can't get you to shut up when you're wasted."

"I talked to you about stuff once." I walk backward toward the bathroom. "And I was having a really shitty day."

"Because you miss her." She clips bracelets around her wrists. "Here's a thought. Why don't you just bring her on the road with us?"

I pause in the doorway. "Why would you say that?"

"Dylan, Chase and I have been talking and we think maybe you'd be a little bit more..."—she hesitates—"pleasant to be around if she was here."

I cock an eyebrow. "Am I that bad?"

"Sometimes." She gets up and slips on her shoes. "It's like you're the same as when Ella disappeared for eight months, only sometimes it's worse. You're always so down and you hardly ever go out with us."

I rub my face with my hand, taking in what she said. "I'm sorry if I've been acting like a douche bag, but I can't ask Ella to come with us."

Naomi grabs the keycard from the dresser and puts it into the back pocket of her jeans. "Why not?"

"Because she's happy," I say, recalling the many times she chatted to me about her classes and life in an upbeat tone that made me smile. "And I can't ask her to give that up, even though I'd love to have her here."

Naomi shrugs and opens the door, letting in the sunlight and warm air that smells like cigarettes. "It's your decision. I was just giving you an outsider's point of view. Do you want to come out with us tonight? Drinks are on Dylan."

"Nah, I think I'll stay in tonight." I wave her off and she leaves, closing the door behind her.

I pile my clothes in the stained bathroom sink and turn on the shower. The pipes squeak as the water sprays out. Raking my hands through my hair, I let out a frustrated sigh. My fingers grip the counter and my head falls forward.

My mom told me once about how she met my father. He lived in the town over from Star Grove and one day when they were both cruising, they ran into each other. *Literally.* The front end of my dad's truck slammed into the back end of my mom's car. Her car was trashed, but they ended up talking for hours after the tow truck had come and gone and my dad had offered to drive my mom home.

She said it was instant love, or at least that's how she interpreted it in her hormonal teenaged brain. She was supposed to be leaving for college at the end of the summer, but she stayed behind and married my dad instead.

She said she regretted the decision, but I'm not sure if it's because my dad turned out to be a cheating dick, or if she was just sad over the loss of her future.

I push away from the counter, coming to the conclusion to let it go for now. Ella and I are tough enough to make it through a month.

We already made it through hell and back.